OUTCAST

Storm in the Kingdom

Enjoy the read

ALAN ROBERT LANCASTER

Alan RL

12/10/14

New Generation **Publishing**

'This year came the king back again to Aengla Land on Saint Nicholas' day; and the same day was burned the church of Christ at Cantuareburh... Cild Eadric and the Britons were unsettled this year, and fought with the castlemen at Hereford, and did them much harm'.

The Saxon Chronicle (E), 1067

Historical Background

The historical characters of this saga are known from numerous sources, including Snorri Sturlusson's Icelandic Sagas and the Saxon Chronicles.

King Harold is known to have had many Danes and Anglo-Danes amongst his household troops - or huscarls. His mother, Gytha, was aunt through marriage to King Svein and Jarl Osbeorn of Denmark through her brother Ulf. There had been many Danes living in England, some first generation, others whose families had lived in Danelaw Mercia since the 9th Century division by Aelfred. Their ancestry was celebrated in the bringing of the BEOWULF and HROLF KRAKI sagas to England in the ninth century.

After the Conquest many English nobles, churchmen and warriors left for Denmark and Flanders, raiding with the Danes on England's shores. Others roamed further afield, joining the Byzantine emperor Michael's Varangian Guard at Constantinople - known to the Norsemen as Miklagard (the Great Fortress City) = changing the composition of this elite body. Having originally been composed of Swedes (Rus), the make-up of the Varangian Guard changed over the years via West Norse to Anglo-Danish.

Harold Haroldson was born to King Harold's queen, Aeldgytha in early 1067 at Chester. Mother and son were spirited away to Dublin to keep them from possible harm from the Normans.

Nothing is recorded of them beyond that.

Eadgytha 'Svanneshals' (Swan neck) fled from Winchester with her youngest son Ulf and daughters Gunnhild and Gytha to Exeter together with Harold's mother Gytha. They were joined there by Harold's older sons by Eadgytha, Godwin, Eadmund and Magnus. Even as the Normans gained entry to the city the family went their separate ways, the womenfolk and children initially to Steepholm in the Bristol Channel, and then to Flanders once the hue and cry had died down.

Godwin, Eadmund and Magnus left for Dublin, where they were given men and ships by King Diarmuid. They raided in the West Country, on the Bristol Channel coast of Somerset where Godwin's lands were, and were beaten off by the local fyrd and Normans under the Breton Count Brian. Godwin and Eadmund are known to have survived, but Magnus is thought to have died of his wounds. There is also a story that Magnus did not die of his wounds but lived out his days in his native Sussex as a monk. His older brothers are said to have left for Denmark.

Ulf, Harold's youngest son by Eadgytha is thought to have been captured and imprisoned by William, later freed under an amnesty in 1087. He was befriended, along with Eadgar the Aetheling by Robert 'Curthose', William's eldest son, and is thought to have gone with them on Crusade in the early 12th Century. King Eadweard's widow, Eadgytha retired to the nunnery at Wilton Abbey along with Harold's daughter Gunnhild after surrendering Winchester to William. Wulfnoth, Harold's youngest brother, was brought back to England long after the Conquest and taken to Winchester, where he died an old and lonely, broken man.

Harold's elder daughter by Eadgytha, Gunnhild, is believed to have been abducted from the nunnery at Wilton by Alan 'Fergent', Lord of Richmond, who had received lands of her mother's. In fact she fled the nunnery to be with him. She later 'took up' with his kinsman Alan 'the Black', despite Archbishop Anselm's attempts to get her back to Wilton.

Harold's daughter Gytha began a dynasty when she married Prince Vladimir 'Monomakh' of Smolensk and later Kiev. Her eldest, a son called Mstislav – or Mistislav - Harold was born in Novgorod. From him stems King Valdemar of Denmark and later Queen Elizabeth II of England by way of Queen Margrethe of Denmark.

Historical Notes

To familiarise you with Anglo-Saxon terminology and place names used in the saga of Ivar:

Burhbot   work on burh (town/city) defences, alternative to *fyrdfaereld* when defensive work needed to be upgraded or replaced under threat of siege/invasion

*Brycgegeweorc*up   keep of bridges as part of defensive strategy under threat of siege/invasion

Butsecarl   seagoing *huscarl*/warrior

Ceorl   commoner, free peasant/freed man

Discthegn/Hraegle thegn   household steward/general steward

Ealdorman   Anglo-Saxon predecessor of Earl

Earl/Eorl   Anglo-Saxon equivalent of Norse *Jarl*

Earldoms   status given to former kingdoms of England from and including the time of Knut/Canute

Fyrd   regional militia or territorial forces were raised by the king to defend the realm for limited periods only, to repel invaders – not for aggressive purposes

Fyrdfaereld   territorial military duty, a form of national obligation for limited period from several weeks to a couple of months before being stood down

Hersir   West Norse landowners, latterly household warrior retainers, similar to *huscarls*

*Hundred*a   southern or south-western shire district, charged with upkeep of law and local defence (see also *Wapentake*)

Huscarl   household warrior, often landed, Danish origin, introduced by Knut into England

King's thegn   obligated to answer king's call to duty

Norns   three old crones, seers, *Skuld*: Being, *Urd*: Fate/ *Wyrd,* and *Verdandi*: Necessity

Shire reeve   later sheriff

Scramaseaxe   scramasaxe, the weapon associated with the Saxons, a curved blade on the top side with a concave split-edged blade on the other

Skalds   Norse hall poets, retained by kings and/or jarls to recite the heroic deeds of their paymasters

Skjaldborg   Norse, shieldwall, literally shield fortress, defensive/offensive formation of overlapping shields, used both in England and Scandinavia

Thegns   or thanes, commoners ennobled by the king, usually held '*book land*' from king or ecclesiastical establishment

*Thrijungar*or   'Thirdings' (Ridings), the divisions of Yorkshire and Lincolnshire, each with its own *thing* or parliament

*Wapentake/Vapnatak*district within 'Thirding' in regions of northern and eastern (Danelaw) England, similar to Wessex Hundreds, literally *weapon take*, or weapon store

Wyrd   fate, woven by *Urd*, one of the three *Norns* who sat at the roots of *Yggdrasil*, the World Ash Tree – decided the personal outlook of everyone born to man in *Midgard*, (Middle Earth)

I have attempted to maintain the early mediaeval geography in the saga with the use of the 11th Century communal and regional references or names. The spellings use modern-day characters, as some of the original ones were never translated into the Gutenberg alphabet when printing was introduced to England in the 15th Century by Caxton. The main place/regional references and names used are:

Aengla, Aengle, Aenglish   Anglia, English – people, English language and collective noun for people inhabiting Aengla Land: England

Andredesleag   Andreds Weald, the thickly wooded hills across southern Sussex and south western Kent

Beornica   Bernicia, northern half of *Northanhymbra* (Northumbria), ruled from *Baebbanburh* (Bamburgh)

Bretland   Brittany

Cantuareburh, -byrig   Canterbury, capital of Kent

Ceaster   Chester, capital of Mercia

Centland, Centish   Kent, Kentish

Danelaw   formerly Eastern Mercia, the lands east of Watling Street offered by King Aelfred to Guthrum and the other Danish lords as part of the Treaty of Wedmore

Deira   the southern half of the kingdom and later earldom of Northumbria, ruled from *Jorvik/Eoferwic* (York), in 10th Century ruled as separate Kingdom of York by Eirik 'Blood-axe'

Deoraby   Derby, one of 'Five Boroughs' of Danelaw, with Lincoln, Leicester, Nottingham and Stamford

Dyflin   Dublin, southern Ireland

East Seaxan, East Seaxe   East Saxon(s), Essex

Eoferwic and *Jorvik*   York, the first is the Anglian, and the latter is the Norse name from which the modern York stems

*Five Boroughs*are   the main towns of the *Danelaw,* Derby, Leicester, Lincoln Nottingham and Stamford (Lincs.)

Frankia   France

Laegerceaster   Leicester

Lindcylne   Lincoln

Lunden   London, there were other versions in the Saxon Chronicle, this version was used in the pre-Norman era

Lunden Brycg   London Bridge

Middil Seaxan, Middil Seaxe   Middle Saxon, Middlesex

Mierca   Mercia

Miklagard   Constantinople, 'great city/fortress'

*Norse*the   West Norse are the modern Norwegians and their colonists in the Atlantic islands, including the British Isles; the East Norse are the Danes, Goths and Swedes, historically also settlers in the *Danelaw* in England and Ireland; also Rus, an ethnic group largely absorbed by their Slavic neighbours, originally in northern and central western Russia/ Ukraine.

Northanhymbra   Northumbria, see *Beornica, Deira*

Northfolc   North folk/ Norfolk – a sub-group of *East Aengle*/East Angles - see also *Suthfolc*

Northmandige, Northman/Northmen   Normandy, Norman(s)

9

Norwic   Norwich

Seaxan, Seaxe   Saxon(s)

Snotingaham   Nottingham, one of the 'five boroughs

Staenford   Stamford, Lincolnshire, another of 'five boroughs of the Danelaw

Staenfordes Brycg   Stamford Bridge, East Yorks

Suthfolc   South folk/Suffolk, East Angles

Suth Seaxan, Suth Seaxe   South Saxon, Sussex

*Wealas, Wealsh*Wales,   Welsh – term was applied by the Saxons, meaning 'foreigner'

West Seaxan, West Seaxe   West Saxon, Wessex – abolished by the Normans as retribution for Harold's 'perfidy', he was regarded as a usurper, and traditionally he still held his lands in Wessex until his death

West Wealas   name given by the Saxons to Cornwall

Wintunceaster   Winchester, capital of Wessex

SOME OF THE CHIEF SETTLEMENTS IN LATE 11th CENTURY
BRITAIN

KIRKJUVAGR

LJODHUS

DINAS EIDIN/DUNEDIN
BERUWIC
BAEBBANBURH

CARDEOL   DUNHOLM

EOFERWIC

MAN

DYFLIN   CEASTER   LINDCYLNE
                MENAI   SNOTINGAHAM
                        DEORABY

HLIMREKR   NORWIC

VEIGSFJORDR   STAEFFORD
                        SCROBBESBYRIG
CORK   VEDRAFJORDR   RHOSGOCH   LEAGACEASTER
                        NORTHANHAMTUN
                        LUNDEN
                                CANTUAREBURH

                WINTUNCEASTER
EXANCEASTER
                    WIHT

ACKNOWLEDGEMENTS & DEDICATIONS

I have to thank my family, Kath my wife, my daughters Joanne and Suzy, my son Robert and son-in-law Ash for their patience, forbearance and untold assistance with producing this book and 'cleaning up' my laptop system. The assistance given by my offspring has been of a technical nature, whilst my wife's has been of a historical nature, furnishing some useful information about the old Roman roads that were still in use at the time of the Conquest, and about London in the years 1066 and after.

Thanks also go to Barrie Nichols, my former Geography and Maths teacher who has encouraged me to proceed with the saga, and shown interest in the project.

To some of my former colleagues at Mount Pleasant Sorting Office for their input and suggestions on the storyline and content whether used or not, thanks again.

HINDSIGHT

'Well done, fellow Aènglishmen. I am proud of you! The Northman Willelm was given a mauling here today. Let us do this to him whenever he comes again! We must be ready again soon now, as I do not think he will let us off so easily', Eadgar the Aetheling hailed his men for the rebuff they had fearlessly dealt the Northmen at Lunden Brycg.

He had won the following of his earls and Ansgar, his stallari, having showed them he was able to lead their stand against the Northmen's attack on his shieldwall. Whether he could wield any real might over his Witan, and sway them to hold together for him had yet to be seen. That the higher churchmen wanted Willelm to be king was well known, but the earls might yet hold firm for him.

However, it was not to be. Eadgar was passed over again by the Witan for the kingship, this time under threat from Willelm after he had cut Lunden from its granaries in the south and west. Fearful for their holdings and high standing, the whole Witan agreed to submit to the Northman duke because they believed him to be stronger than he really was. None felt ready to call his bluff.

Ivar swore to Eadgar that he would take his friends to the south coast to seek out Willelm's food and weapon stores.

He hoped Eadgar could send ships when winds allowed, and cut the duke's ties with his homeland. A run of narrow scrapes saw Ivar gambling with his wyrd, making new friends and losing older ones. He and his friends underwent hardships in their bid to stay free with Bishop Odo's men closing in on them in eastern Centland and Suth Seaxe.

A rescue bid to free friends in Hrofesceaster ended in the deaths of more dear friends. Theorvard was hit by crossbow bolts, dying in the escape. Oslac's young friend Sigegar and others also fell to the Northmen's terrifying new weapon.

On reaching Lunden Ivar left Theodolf at the 'Eel Trap' to have his wounds nursed and made his way to see his king, unaware that Eadgar had once again been abandoned by the Witan. Eadgar freed Ivar from his oath of loyalty to him, but a new threat reared its ugly head. A warrant was served on Eadgar by an eager young Northman noble for Ivar's arrest. With Thegn Osgod's help, Ivar fled to the 'Eel Trap' to

15

warn his friends that Gilbert de Warenne was in pursuit. At the inn he met Eadmund, one of Harold's sons who, with his ceorl Bondig was on his way to his father's hunting lodge at Leagatun. There he was to join his elder brother Godwin and the younger Magnus

De Warenne was left fuming at the locked Eald Gata Bar, whilst Ivar, Eadmund and the others slipped away on the Colneceaster road.

They hid behind dwellings as a mounted Northman patrol made its way to Lunden burh, and reached Leagatun later that night.

At Leagatun Godwin and Magnus greeted their kinsman warmly, but Magnus later risked offending him by asserting that all of their father's huscarls were all expected to die with him. For his part, Ivar wonders where they were, that they did not heed their father's call to arms against the Northmen.

A parting of the ways was not to be, however, through their blood ties. It dawned on the brothers, too, that their kinsman had the skills they needed to teach their fyrdmen to fight the outlanders. During the weeks leading up to Willelm's crowning, Ivar and his friends used their time in honing the fighting skills of the body of East Aenglan fyrdmen summoned by Godwin to join him and his brothers the following year on their way west to Exanceaster.

Shortly before the Yule Feast Ivar let Godwin know that he wished to attend Willelm's crowning on midwinter's day, alone and disguised as a monk. Harold's sons were unhappy that he might lead the Northmen back to them, but on assurance that he would give Lunden a wide berth they pressed him to taking three of his friends.

Cyneweard knew the way, so he went with Ivar, Saeward and Oslac, riding by way of Ansgar's hall north of Lunden. Cyneweard took word from Godwin to Ansgar, pressing for his loyalty.

Ivar parted company with Ansgar as friends, despite the shire reeve maintaining he must swear and abide by his oath to the new king.

In Eadweard's abbey church Ivar and Saeward joined the West Mynster monks at Willelm's crowning, Archbishop Ealdred conducting the rite with Stigand. The earls and thegns from around the kingdom witnessed Willelm being made king and swore oaths to uphold the Northman duke's right to the kingship.

Unbeknown to Willelm he had another witness. Watched by Ivar, the new king endured the rite that lasted most of the short midwinter's day. Before it was all over the nobles and churchmen shouted their salute to the new king,

'Vivat, Vivat, Vivat!'

Outside the Northman guards took it on themselves to set fire to the nearby buildings and kill the onlookers for what they thought was an attack on their lord within. A riot followed, men were killed but Willelm was unaware of it all until he left the church.

The Northman nobles entrusted with guarding the church tried to keep Ivar, Saeward and Abbot Eadwin's monks from leaving until the king had gone. However, Ivar and Saeward slipped away into the snow-covered marsh at the edge of Thorney. An inn was soon found to rest the night before riding on to Leagatun.

Wondrously the landlady of the inn turned out to be Braenda, still taking care of her lover. Count Eustace came to the inn, hoping to have his way with Braenda but was made to leave by her willpower. She and Ivar then enjoyed one another's company again. True to form Ivar found he was alone again the following morning, and in the cold. Braenda had gone, leaving the derelict old inn to its ghosts. Meeting with Thegn Hereward, Ivar learned that the inn had long since been abandoned. Hereward also enlightened Ivar about the lack of a following for his kinsmen outside West Seaxe and the southern shires and that they should look for men there.

Meeting with a ceorl on the edge of the heath above Hamstede led to Ivar and his friends resting the night in his home. In the morning Gilbert de Warenne roused them, and his men bound their hands for the ride to Bearrucing where King Willelm awaited Ivar.

In Lunden the young Northman noble sought more men from his lord, Rodberht de Bruis, to escort the prisoners out from Eald Gata along the Colneceaster road. A crowd gathered along the road through Stibenhede and a riot followed, during which Ivar and his friends were freed with help from Theodolf and the weaponsmith Thor. Ivar and his friends parted company with Thor and they fled the Northmans' wrath to Leagatun.

Racked with guilt, Ealdsige rode to seek out Ansgar, and on to Leagatun to warn of Ivar's likely fate at the hands of Willelm.

His greed having led to his ruin, Ealdsige was further troubled that the bag his was given his reward in had worn, the coins lost in the snow on the way. The only way out of his misery was for him to leave through a worsening snowfall.

Lastly, word came from Dean Wulfwin that Ivar's being at the West Mynster had led to Abbot Eadwin demanding Ivar attend the king for his sin in taking on the guise of a monk to spy on him.

1

'Do you mean to do what Abbot Eadwin wishes?' Eadmund asks me at table.

'Is there a way out without bringing the Northmen down around your ears?' I chew on the stubble on my lower lip, mulling over the likelihood of hearing an answer that might prove useful to me and turn toward Godwin. He too looks to be thinking hard about this new dilemma.

'You could go to Naesinga', Magnus offers, before his older brother can answer. This brings a smile from Godwin.

'Why did you not think of that?' Eadwin answers before Godwin even opens his mouth. 'Godwin can say that you went with your friends before any of us saw where you went'.

Godwin thumps on the doorpost, shaking it so that cobwebs fall from the walls onto his hand. He has doubtless thought of something that would never have dawned on me.

'How can we be sure that Willelm will not use *us* to coax him back to within his reach?' he asks, the corners of his mouth tighten with the pain of the knowledge that the king will do his utmost to draw me into his web. 'He will surely feel that we know his whereabouts. The only thing for it is for us *all* to take ourselves off to Naesinga'.

'What – do you mean just pack up and take everything up into the woods?' the corners of Magnus' mouth draw down to show his distaste. 'Who would *tell* Willelm about us being here?'

'There must be Aenglishmen who would know, second-guess us, who are ready to meet this Willelm's demands in return for favours. We cannot hand him over to the Northmen! How will that look to our fellow Aenglishmen, Magnus? Besides, he is our kinsman. No, we *all* go to Naesinga together. I will not give so much as a thought to letting that grasping Northman bastard get his hands on you', he looks at me now and grins wolfishly, 'when we have more need of you!'

Godwin looks around the room and beckons to his father's old discthegn to join him,

'Come here Burhwold, I want to talk about moving everyone to Naesinga! Have we any stores there?' Godwin puts an arm around Burhwold's shoulders and looks back at Eadmund. He laughs and shouts out, 'Did you ever think that one day we would be doing this, brother?'

'I cannot think it ever crossed my mind. We had best get on with it before this new king of ours pays us a visit!'

Godwin lays out his thoughts on the household's move out to Naesinga. In the thick of the woods, Harold's second lodge is nothing like as big as this one at Leagatun.

At Naesinga there are fewer rooms and outbuildings, so more of us will have to share. But I can see few other ways around this. Food stores are packed, clothes and weapons stowed on sleds, horses saddled, sleds brought from the outhouse.

I could have sworn we were on Sjaelland, to look at the carvings and paintwork on the sleds and harness-work! We are all drawn into the bustle. Theodolf lets Gerda get on with putting together hers and Brihtwin's few belongings whilst he helps with harnessing the horses.

All the while Godwin's huscarls under Healfdan are set to watching out for unwelcome visitors. They stand armed with spears and swords, shields slung over shoulders, cloaks drawn back.

They need to be able to take any errant Northmen to task. We are well guarded as we stow everything we cannot carry under the covers on the great sleds. Nothing is left to fate in Godwin's bid to keep me from falling into Willelm's clutches.

'You will be safe with us, Ivar, mark my words', Eadmund assures me with a wide grin, then adds the grim warning, should I have thought of going on any more jaunts to torment the Northman king, his brothers or his underlings, 'only take no more foolish risks like toying with our guests before we are ready to take them on, or Godwin may just hand you over himself!'

'Our guests-' I am nonplussed.

'He means the Northmen', Magnus grins sheepishly.

'Fear not, kinsman, I shall stay clear of Willelm's men for the time being', I nod at Eadmund with a wry smile and wave to Saeward to bring Braenda to me.

'I feel sad that we must leave our father's lodge here for a time', Magnus comes up behind us and turns around to gaze at the timber building that Harold was so proud of.

'We will be back here again, sooner than you think'. Eadmund smiles at his younger brother, 'By then Ulf will be old enough to join our hunting parties'.

This is the first time since seeing them again that I have heard any of them speak of their youngest brother. He will be with his mother and sisters in Winchester, out of harm's way for now. But he will be chafing, I should not wonder, eager for when he can join his older brothers chasing deer and boar, and fighting alongside them.

'How is Ulf these days?' I ask Godwin as he lifts himself into his saddle.

'*What* –? Oh, Ulf is well enough. The last I saw, he was with mother. Gytha and Gunnhild were teasing him about his pining to be with us', he leans on the back of his saddle to look at me.

'I think mother told him to think of the days to come when she could hold him back no longer. He was still unhappy when we rode for King Maelcolm's court, but that is the way of young lads'.

Godwin turns to see that all is well and signals Burhwold to get the horses moving. He follows the sleds and we - his brothers, my friends and I – ride behind him.

Healfdan keeps his eyes to the south as he takes the rear of our small column with Godwin's most trusted huscarls on either side of him. We skirt Leagatun-at-Stane, keeping the river on our left until we reach the heath.

From there we cross an open expanse of grazing land to the nearest woodland track west of Cingheford.

Wolves watch us as we make our way to Wealtham by way of Saewardstan, bypassing Saewardstanbyrig so that the sleds do not capsize on the steep bank.

Smoke is being blown westward under heavy, snow-bearing cloud as we pass along between the dwellings at Saewardstan. Cattle in the sheds low as our horses' hooves clatter on the stony road, dogs bark and one or two well-wishers wave to us.

Healfdan makes a halt to speak to one of Godwin's huscarls who is billeted here with some of the fyrdmen he and his fellows are teaching. As we pass him he looks from his men to the four of us, Oslac, Cyneweard, Saeward and me. The look on his face betrays nothing of his thoughts but I have an uneasy feeling about him in the pit of my stomach.

Magnus and Eadmund wave back at the children who flock to the roadside to watch us pass. I do not know if there is anyone here at the roadside who recalls either Theodolf or me, but one or two of the old men watch us riding by as if they know who we are. They ought to know who Harold's sons are, having seen them as often as not with him on his way to Wealtham.

'It is not so long since we passed through this way, eh, Ivar?' Theodolf calls back to me, leaning over the side of the sled he drives grinning broadly,

'I was telling Gerda about how my father nearly came to blows with Thegn Thorfinn up the hill there'.

He points back over his right shoulder to Saewardstanbyrig as we head uphill at the end of the line of dwellings and pass the inn. I turn in my saddle and look behind me and im Thorfinn standing outside his hall beaming up at us on our horses as I do so. The pain of losing a friend is still with me, so much so that it could never be drowned with tears. I turn to look ahead again and try to smother the memory of the friends I had before the Northmen came.

Yet, without their coming I would not have met many of them. I would not have come across Hrothulf again because I would not have crossed the Hvarfe when I did. Nor would I have met Theorvard, Ubbi or Karl. I shake my head as if doing so would put them from my thoughts, but I could have saved myself the effort.

I might have crossed paths with Thorfinn earlier than I did if Harold had given me lands in East Seaxe as he had offered, and with him Burhred, Aelfwin and Aelfwig would have been my friends sooner. Who knows which way our wyrds would have taken us.

Yet thankfully I have new friends now, whose company I hope to keep around me for longer. Saeward I already knew, and through Aelfwin and his brother Aelfwig I have come to know Wulfmaer. Through Theodolf I have also come to know Oslac.

There is a feeling of hope within me now. I feel the road ahead will lead to better things as we crest the rise on the leftward bend out of Saewardstan. Wealtham comes into sight, nestling in the deep snow on the eastern bank of the Leag. Naesinga is north-eastward beyond Wealtham, on the way to Hearlaue through the broad woods of Eoppinga. We should be safer there. Leagatun is so close to Lunden burh we would be beggared once Willelm was given to understand that Harold's sons were there.

He would not hear that from his own men in the winter time, unless they lost their way to Ansgar's hall, but it would likely be an Aenglishman who led them there, seeking some gain in betraying us.

I hear Magnus ask of Godwin,

'Where would the huscarls dwell at Naesinga?' Magnus' higher voice carries in the chill wind.

'They stay where they are in Saewardstan and Wealtham until summoned to teach the fyrdmen', Godwin answers calmly, as if Magnus should be able to read his thoughts. Eadmund looks past Godwin at his younger brother, shakes his head and smiles.

'Naesinga is as far from Saewardstan as is Leagatun', Eadmund reassures Magnus. 'There are more dwellings there, and at Wealtham for them to stay in. It will not be for long, fear not'.

'We do not need them to be under our noses'. Godwin finishes as Healfdan rejoins us and he turns to his huscarl to speak to him, 'Is everything well with Cuthwulf and Godgar? Do they have enough to eat without being a burden on the good folk of Saewardstan? I would not want them to think that the Northmen were the better of two evils'.

'No, my Lord, we are no burden on them', Healfdan bolsters Godwin and looks at me. He says with a slight sneer,

'Cuthwulf says that they kill deer for the pot and keep the wolves away from the stock pens. I doubt the Northmen would do that for them'.

Godwin turns back to Magnus and Healfdan gives me a look of scorn behind his lord's back. What have I done to earn that?

Dean Wulfwin is asked for when we reach Wealtham's abbey gates and ride into the yard. We dismount and do not have long to await him,

'Godwin I am delighted to see you. You are all well, I trust, Eadmund, Magnus and your good self?' Wulfwin greets them each in turn with a broad smile and walks up to me, still smiling, although for me his smile is strained. 'I would like to speak to you when you have some time to spare, young man'.

A nod from me tells him that I know this will be no friendly get-together. He turns away again and greets Oslac and Cyneweard. Saeward is given a frosty glare and Wulfwin tells him to join me soon in his quarters.

'Do you know how long it took me to calm Abbot Eadwin?' Wulfwin asks us both when we are alone with him. He expects no answer because he suspects that we know what it will be. He looks sternly at me.

I was the guiding hand and Saeward was sent along to make my self-awarded task easier, but that does not save him from rebuke. If anything, it makes Saeward look worse because he helped me to look like a man of the church.

My part in Abbot Eadwin's trouble was in setting the blade at his neck, so to speak. Saeward's was in leaning on the blade, adding to Abbot Eadwin's misery. Willelm was not happy with the abbot and made him squirm. He knew without asking that I must be behind the bid to belittle him.

Saeward, on the other hand, was the tool with which I belittled both church and king. Wulfwin's anger at Saeward can know no bounds. He was meant to dampen my desire to humble the Northmans. At least that is how Eadwin sees it, Wulfwin tells us. Yet there is a flaw in Wulfwin's thinking.

'Then why did you send the habits to Leagatun, my Lord Dean Wulfwin?' I ask. Hopefully the wind will be taken from his sails.

'Habits - *what* habits am I to have sent to Leagatun?' Wulfwin rounds angrily on me now. For some reason he stops and thinks on what I have asked him. Have I pushed him back into a corner?

'A couple of days before we rode to Thorney habits were brought to us. I thought we had your blessing'.

'Who handed you the habit that you wore', Wulfwin asks testily, 'into your *hands?* – Think on it'.

'Saeward handed it to me and I had thought you sent it with your blessing, my Lord, perhaps thinking why I wanted it was to pass unseen into Lunden. He told me that it had been left for me by someone unknown to him on their way to Bearrucing Abbey'.

Wulfwin stares at me, trying to fathom my story. He softens a little, shaking his head. He does not give much away when he has you in his grasp, so when he begins to smile I think he believes me,

'Ivar – Ivar why is it I think you a fool when you take me for one? What stories you tell me when you think you are cornered! I am as unlikely to give you away to the Northmen as Abbot Eadwin. You both took me for simple. I sent you no habit, thinking Saeward would talk you out of leaving for the West Mynster'.

'As for Saeward', Wulfwin turns to my friend and fixes him with an icy stare, 'he risks everlasting damnation if he goes on behaving the way he does! I might forgive killing, if you did that to save your life, as I might for lying or stealing. Lying and stealing to wheedle your way into Ivar's trust has to be the limit! Why did you do this, Saeward?'

Dean Wulfwin rests his hands on Saeward's shoulders and looks him in the eye,

'I do not wish to see you here unless you can behave yourself like a God-fearing Christian. Ivar I would ask you to see to it that Saeward no longer needs to lie to do you favours, but I know in my heart that that would be folly. Am I right?'

I nod half-heartedly and look sideways at Saeward before answering,

'My Lord Wulfwin we will be fighting the Northmen for some time to come, I hope not for too long. In order to stay free we may both need to lie to cover our tracks, and to steal. Killing has come to be a way of life for us these past few weeks. Saeward does not kill because he likes to. Indeed he has pangs of guilt. The weaponsmith Thor, who works with Asmund near Lunden Brycg told Saeward needed to keep his sword sharp and his aim sharper and God would forgive him his mortal sinning.

'I must pray for his fallen foe's soul afterward, so Thor said', Saeward tells the stunned Wulfwin.

'Thor is a devout man', Wulfwin raises his eyebrows and looks heavenward.

'Thor is a *Christian* priest, my Lord, who prays at the church of Saint Clement by the river Temese', Saeward adds.

'I do know, Saeward. I do know', Wulfwin assures him. 'There are other priests who answer to the names of the old gods! Now, Saeward, promise me you will curb your foolishness. It is not too late to come back to us here'.

'My Lord Dean Wulfwin I am more useful to the kingdom with my friends. I thank you for your offer to take me in again, nevertheless. One day I may take your offer –'

Wulfwin chides him with a threat,

'One day this Northman king may reach you before you can reach out for a guiding hand back to the Lord! Do not forget, I cannot keep you from harm out there'.

Saeward purses his lips, says no more and looks to me.

'You have at Godwin Haroldson's table, but you must earn it, Saeward', I tell my friend to nodding from Wulfwin. 'They will take none of your foolishness'.

'When you are on that path you are at the mercy of your wyrd. I hope you think about that in the days to come', Wulfwin tells my friend. He gives his blessing grudgingly, 'I hope your wyrd is kinder to you than you merit'.

Saeward listens to his erstwhile master, then turns to me,

'Our time is done here, Ivar. I think Lord Wulfwin has something he needs to talk over with one of the canons'.

We bow our heads to Wulfwin, who suddenly seems old and frail.

'Did Wulfwin share any thoughts on me?' Godwin winks as Saeward and I show again in the doorway in the failing daylight. Another heavy snowfall threatens before we reach Naesinga.

'Brother, you are too taken with yourself', Eadmund chides good-humouredly. Magnus looks from Godwin to Eadmund but keeps his own counsel. He does not share his brothers' wit. Magnus is more his mother's son, despite trying his best to level up to them. Still, he has escaped his mother's apron strings, unlike young Ulf.

Godwin stares haughtily at Eadmund and looks back to me with a knowing grin as I ease myself into Braenda's saddle.

'Is it true, you named her after your woman?'

Eadmund and Magnus grasp at this flimsy straw to add their own wit, much to my dismay.

'When you mount her, do you think of your woman's wide flanks and rich red mane?' Eadmund asks.

Magnus offers, to a chorus of laughter,

'He thinks of the firm silky skin of her thighs astride him'.

Healfdan is doubled up, but not with the wry humour shared by Harold's sons. His mirth is more the sort that tells you not to rest too easily beside him.

'Who told *you* I like having her on top?' I lean forward toward Magnus and try to stop myself from laughing. 'I tell you, if she caught you talking of her in this way, she would freeze your blood with a look, the way she dealt with Count Eustace. He was none too happy when he left in a blind hurry!'

Magnus is wide-eyed with awe when he asks me,

'Is it *true* she is a spay wife?'

'Aye well, if that were so you had best hope not to cross her'. I watch as the horror takes over from his youthful smile and add, 'Unless you can run fast enough, so she does not turn you to stone!'

Laughter echoes around the yard.

'You will grow out of this fear', Godwin playfully ruffles Magnus' hair in the way of an older brother who forgets his younger brother is no longer a child.

'Hwicce can be good, if it is on your side', Theodolf's deepening voice can be heard from behind Healfdan. 'She has saved our hides more than once, I can tell you'.

Everyone's gaze rests on my young friend as Godwin asks him to put in plain words how she has saved us, but he bows to me and answers that it is for me to tell them about Braenda's power,

'After all', he smiles meekly, 'she *is* Ivar's lover'.

All eyes are turned on me now.

'I have already told you some of what has happened', I savour the moment. Inwardly I taste the warmth of her lips on mine and smile. 'But one night, when the fire crackles in the hearth and the hobgoblins dance in the groves, I will tell you more'.

'That sounds promising', Godwin smiles.

Sitting on her horse beside Theodolf, Gerda holds her son tightly. She nibbles at his ears, making him giggle so that he does not feel the cold's bite on his small face. Behind her Ingigerd peers over her shoulder and catches my eye. A smile parts her lips. She looks sideways at Healfdan to see whether he has seen her smile.

Healfdan's eyes are elsewhere.

'Healfdan, see if my men here need anything before we leave for Naesinga', Godwin tells him and wheels his horse around.

'It is high time we left. The snow clouds are massing again and we ought to be indoors before the weather worsens'.

'Tomorrow we shall be well out of reach of Willelm's men, eh, Ivar?' Eadmund adds.

'Aye, kinsman, but always within reach of Braenda', I laugh. Magnus shudders but pretends not to have heard me.

Someone has gone on ahead of us to Harold's lodge at Naesinga. Thin wispy smoke rises from the roof of the lodge, to be beaten down by a crosswind from over the trees a little way to the east. There are no creatures to be seen on the snow-laden open grazing land ahead. All livestock has been taken in to feed on the fodder that the ceorls stored in their haylofts during the afteryear. The wolves will have to sate their hunger on the deer. From the north-east come the great grey clouds, heavy with snow.

We reach Naesinga in good time. Darkness will be on us very shortly. Even now I can see only the outline of the trees on the low hills beyond the buildings. Someone leaves the lodge holding high a flickering torch to see that we are Godwin's party and not unwelcome callers.

'*Guthorm*, you are well I hope!' Eadmund cheerily salutes the ceorl. One of Harold's men, Guthorm is too old to be of any use as a fyrdman any more.

Like Burhwold, a retainer of long standing, Guthorm no doubt recalls welcoming Godwin's grandfather. Now he ushers us into the yard.

The sleds are drawn into a small paddock, where they are unloaded and the horses unhitched. Burhwold and Winflaed are followed into the lodge by Gerda carrying a sleeping Brihtwin. Ingigerd casts a look over her right shoulder at a scowling Healfdan and vanishes into the dwelling next to the lodge, where the unmarried women of the household will live whilst we stay at Naesinga.

When we leave for the west they may stay here or Godwin may allow them to come with us. The Northmen might have thoughts of claiming them on their own with no menfolk to look after them. If they come here Burhwold will say that we all left to go westward, but there is a lot of land to cover should they begin a search.

Eadmund looks across the back of his horse and beams broadly,

'Once we have eaten, you can chill our bones by the hearth with the stories of your lover and her unearthly life'.

I think she will show herself sooner or later.

She may charm him as she does many men. What Braenda can do, if Eadmund is foolish enough to cross her, is she will chill his marrow. My wyrd is drawn with hers. The spirits of Elmete will guide her to me now I am out of Centland.

Eadmund smoothes the bristle under his nose the way Harold did when he was looking forward to seeing Eadgytha. He leans toward me,

'I am looking forward to meeting this woman of yours one day Ivar'.

'You should give her a wide berth, I think', Godwin digs him in the small of his back with his knuckles, making him squirm. 'From what I have heard, if she freezes your blood you will be of no use to me in the months to come'.

'She shows herself how you would wish to see her', I warn Eadmund. 'But she can also show herself in ways you would not wish'.

'Then she is a shape-shifter?' he asks, his eyes opening wide mockingly.

'Something like that', I nod, 'but not in the way of Loki'.

'Not altogether in the way of what?' A committed Christian like his father, Magnus shows his lack of knowledge of the old gods.

'Not like Loki, the old god of mischief. He could turn into an otter, a hawk or even a salmon to mislead or escape his fellow gods', Eadmund grins as he shows how much he knows.

'Magnus knows nothing, Ivar. His eyes and ears have been shut fast by the fool monk who taught him how to read and write. It just shows how useless some folk are!'

'Do you mean me or Father Cutha?' Magnus bridles, his right hand clenched threateningly in a fist.

'Well, both of you, if you like!' Eadmund laughs and ducks out of the way of Magnus' flailing fists.

'You bicker like a pair of silly old maids, both of you!' Godwin swears and pushes Magnus away from Eadmund.

'A pair of silly old maids, eh?' Eadmund sneers, 'like as if you are well-versed in the way silly old maids behave! Come on, I will fight you any day!' Eadmund dances about in a mock fight, imitating his younger brother, who stands there tight-lipped, saying nothing more.

'What I want you to do, Eadmund, is take some men out and find a couple of bucks for the table', Godwin tells him. 'Show them how to throw a spear, or loose off an arrow. Can you do that? Take Ivar; I should not think he has done much hunting for sport lately'.

I nod to Theodolf talking to Gerda by the door. He looks back askance as I say his name,

'We had Burhred and Theodolf to do our hunting when we rode down into Centland and Suth Seaxe'.

Before Healfdan can frown at being ordered about by Eadmund, Theodolf calls out,

'We need no horses if we know where to hunt', he tells Eadmund with a smile. 'The deer gather in the glades where they can strip the bark from the young trees and graze on the grass by the evergreen bushes'.

'Listen to that, Eadmund. Have you ever heard such wisdom from so young a fellow?' Godwin praises a blushing Theodolf, 'For God's sake, take the lad with you. Make use of him, and learn!'

Ingigerd ogles Theodolf, taking her cow-eyes off Healfdan. We will have to watch him, lest he deliver us into the hands of a grateful Willelm for the sake of his hurt feelings.

Eadmund has seen Healfdan cast dark looks at Theodolf and ushers us out into the darkness, out of harm's way.

'You know the glades and dells hereabouts?' Theodolf asks Eadmund once out in the darkness, going to our horses for our spears, he for his bow, 'I think we will have to watch out for boars, too'.

'We will not be hunting for boars', Eadmund looks askance at me.

'We may not be hunting for them, but they may come across us out there, if we get too close to their sows', I warn my young kinsman.

'Theodolf, he needs to know what a boar can do if you are not on your guard. Show him your wound'.

Eadmund understands when Theodolf draws his woollen shirt high enough to show him the gash he suffered from the boar's tusks in Centland. He nods and lets Theodolf pull the shirt down before the winter chill gets to him,

'I know now what you mean. I will watch out for any tuskers. Perhaps we should take another man with us?'

'Best bring Oslac', I offer to Eadmund's jerky nods.

Moments later not only Oslac appears in the stable, but also Saeward and Cyneweard.

'These woods will be crowded with all of us crashing about in the undergrowth!' I chortle as they gather their spears for the hunt in the dark. Saeward and Cyneweard grin broadly, and Theodolf begins to laugh,

'This will be like old times'. He can hardly speak for mirth.

Oslac puts in before we leave the garth,

'Ah, but it will be better, chasing deer instead of being chased by Northmen!'

'When we are ready, everyone - be still!' Eadmund looks bothered at the delay to his hunting.

We file out, ghostlike through the oaken gate and into the now windless, still cold of a midwinter's night. The storm clouds have passed to the west and the stars sparkle brightly in the deep dark blue heavens. Ahead of us as we leave the comfort of the lodge is the Pole Star, and the Great Bear to it left stands out amongst the tiny pinpricks of light.

'Left I think here', Eadmund points north-eastward and leads us away from the cluster of dwellings.

'Lead on, kinsman', I wave him away and the five of us stride purposefully into the woodland.

'Watch out for thickets where the tuskers may be. We do not want to have to carry you back, Theodolf', Saeward offers helpfully.

'Thank you', Theodolf answers Saeward's earnest worry with a finger to his mouth, 'but can you try not to talk too much. You might awaken them, and then where will we be?'

'With a boar's tusk up your arse, like as not!' Oslac quips under his breath and grins wickedly.

The six of us pick our way through dark woodland with care. One of us stands on a dead twig, which cracks dully under the thick covering of snow. We halt, making sure nothing else moves. On starting off again Theodolf waves us down and points to our right. I see nothing from where I am standing but Saeward nods.

'He has seen a boar', Saeward whispers and gives me a worried look.

We stand still for what seems to be forever. Theodolf watches the boar as it roots in the darkness, blissfully unaware of us. At last he motions us on and we creep slowly through a clearing.

Theodolf stops again and beckons to Oslac, who stealthily makes his way forward to join the lad. They ready their bows and take aim. There is a slight breeze now, which carries our smell away from where Cyneweard points.

Theodolf and Oslac are still teaching their bows on what must be the most handsome pair of bucks that I have seen for some time when the boar that we thought had gone away suddenly rushes from between bushes midway between Theodolf and the buck.

Oslac brings his bow down, aims at the charging boar and holds the arrow until it is close enough for us to smell its breath and looses off the arrow. At the same time Theodolf's arrow flits soundlessly, almost unseen by the naked eye. Both animals drop as if crushed by some unseen giant's hand. It is only when both of our bowmen have let fly their arrows that we see something else in the undergrowth at the western edge of the clearing.

'God, there are wolves about!' Cyneweard yelps like a startled pup and points to three of them slinking close to the snow-covered earth towards the felled animals.

The other buck bounds effortlessly across the clearing between the wolves and us; there are more wolves that way and the buck tries in vain to escape them by darting toward us. Oslac has another arrow across his bow and looses it off before I see that there are more wolves behind us.

'For God's sake, what do we do now?' Eadmund panics, whirling around as if demented.

'We make believe that they are Northmen!' Theodolf laughs and puts another arrow across his bow, ready for his next target. 'Best make sure we have the first buck and the boar to take back for the table. We can leave the other buck for the wolves. Oslac and I will make sure the wolves stay back whilst you carry them to the garth'.

'We will, by all means - we will!' Eadmund is taken aback.

He and I take the boar, its feet tied over a long staff, whilst Saeward and Cyneweard shoulder the buck between them. Together we take the track back to the safety of the lodge with some of the wolves following. Oslac aims at a careless wolf that comes too close and fells it with an arrow through its neck.

The rest of them hang back, unsure. Three young males seize on the dead wolf but the others shadow us back to Naesinga.

'Open the doors - *quickly!*' Eadmund calls out, sweating under the weight of the boar. We are both hot from running with the heavy beast. Saeward and Cyneweard are behind us, with Theodolf and Oslac aiming their bows at any wolf foolish enough to try to close in on us before the gate opens.

'We have a buck, oh - *and a boar for the table!*' Godwin whoops when he sees what we have brought back.

'Aye and we have brought company!' Eadmund nods at the wolves beyond the paddock walls. 'Oslac and Theodolf did well for us this evening. We will feast tonight, thanks to them!'

31

'I would not want to do this every night', Theodolf turns to come into the lodge as a single wolf strays into the paddock.

Horses within the stable whinny and stamp their hooves, frightened by the closeness of these wild hunters. A few wolves edge warily closer, hopeful of easy prey.

Oslac holds his arrow at the ready and looses it, cutting down another rash young male as he slinks toward the stable doors.

'Leave that one outside the wall for his fellows to tear up', Godwin has been watching from the doorway and stands aside for us as we enter the lodge.

We can still hear the growling and barking of the pack, fighting over the carcase. Eadmund gives a shiver and shakes his head,

'That is the last time I offer to find meat for the table in the dark! Ivar can take Healfdan and some others next time', he laughs off his ordeal and I cannot help seeing Healfdan look away in terror.

2

'*Ivar*, wake up!' Someone shakes me by the shoulders early the following morning. 'There is someone here to see you'.

I sit up on the cot bed and rub my eyes, and look around to see who it is has pulled me from a dream I would happily have stayed in. Braenda and I were bathing in a warm pool sprinkled with rose petals, Ingigerd washing my back with sweet-smelling oils.

My manhood has been aroused, feeling Braenda's soft hands caressing my chest - just as someone shook me!

'Ivar rise, make yourself fit to be seen! *What* have you been dreaming of?' Saeward stands close by the bed in the small closet. I look up at him as he points at my manhood. When I look down it shifts across the top of my thigh and I feel a shiver down my back.

I look up at him and ask an awkwardly blushing, squirming Saeward,

'Do you never have dreams where you are being spoilt by at least one good looking woman?' I ask him and he squirms uncomfortably, leading me to ask, 'What do *you* dream of?'

'I think all those years with the brothers have cast aside any dreams of women that I might once have had', Saeward shamefacedly admits. 'Even then I was only a spotty child and the only women I had anything to do with were my mother and sisters. I *have* had thoughts about the young woman that Healfdan is so keen on'.

'So have I, Saeward. But that is where they must stop, or Healfdan may step in and take you to task', I can warn him as much as I want, but by the look on his face, I think my warning may not be heeded. I talk Saeward's thoughts away from Ingigerd and ask, 'Who is my visitor?'

'It is Wulfwin', he answers, still yearning for Ingigerd.

'What does he want now?'

I may as well be talking to myself, for all the good it does asking him. Dressing quickly, I leave my sword belt, scabbard and sheathed knife on my bed and follow Saeward to the main room.

'Ah, Ivar, I am glad you are here', Eadmund greets me as I enter the room, Saeward coming in close behind. 'Dean Wulfwin wishes to speak to you about what you had aforethought for the rest of the winter'.

'I have nothing in mind as yet, other than helping to teach your fyrdmen their weapon skills', I answer Eadmund flatly and then look to where Wulfwin sits in Harold's high-backed chair close to the hearth.

'You will have to think about what you will do', Wulfwin joins in. 'I have word that Abbot Eadwin is to call on the king at Bearruging Abbey that the king has forced upon him. I would say the next stop for him would be Wealtham, and I would have to direct them here on pain of death. I am not a man of the church, merely a Dean, whose calling is to oversee the teaching of the sons of the nobles. Willelm might acknowledge my role as such, but I was given my role by Earl Harold. My standing at Wealtham is not as secure as Abbot Eadwin's is at the West Mynster'.

'We have to move *again?*' Eadmund groans and thumps the door frame, shaking cobwebs and dust onto the floor.

'I may be able to hold them, but for no more than a day. My canons could regale them, but Willelm is not known for his forbearance. He will be bound to want to hasten events to their grisly end. I do not know if Godwin listens to your counsel, Eadmund, but I would recommend you begin to put together an argument for when he returns from Leagatun', Wulfwin looks up at both of us in turn as he delivers his bad news.

'*Now* see what you have done, Ivar!' Eadmund chides me again for my foolishness. 'You ought to have seen the outcome of your prank. These Northmen are not well known for their wit, as we are. They take things much too earnestly for their own good!'

'He would have sought you out sooner or later, Eadmund', Wulfwin puts in and adds, 'as you are the sons of King Harold'.

'Yet who would have told him about us being at Leagatun?' Eadmund straightens and stares at Wulfwin, as if he himself might have let the Northmen know about them being there.

'Spies are everywhere', Wulfwin suddenly lowers his voice and looks at Gerda.

'No, not her of all those I know. She is trustworthy, I would vouch for her!' Eadmund seems to be unaware of changing loyalties in Willelm's new kingdom.

'No, I did not mean her, Eadmund. Even against their own kind, when they must pay to keep their holdings, some men may sell out their grandmothers! Ansgar, for one, has given his oath'. Wulfwin stands and saves the hardest for last, 'Have you not thought that he might see handing you on a plate to Willelm as the best way of keeping his standing as stallari and shire reeve of Middil Seaxe?'

Eadmund is dumbstruck. He is the only one of the brothers here who has any standing.

Magnus is still abed, it seems, but even so it is to Eadmund that we must look whilst Godwin is away.

'When will Godwin return to Naesinga?' I ask, unaware of why he has gone there.

'In the morning, most likely', Eadmund turns to give me my answer, and then looks back at Wulfwin, 'by which time Abbot Eadwin will be in Bearrucing, I trust?'

'If not by then he will be there at the latest before midweek. Yesterday he would have given his blessing at the West Mynster, and put his affairs in order before readying himself for the long ride', Wulfwin makes a knowledgeable guess at Abbot Eadwin's likely movements. 'He is not so old that he would be infirm'.

'Then we must be ready to move again by the time Godwin returns', Eadmund reasons.

'Why did he go to Leagatun?' I ask now, as it seems wyrd is pressing me into another corner that I have made for myself.

'There are deeds there that father did not take to Thorney'. Eadmund takes a deep breath before finishing, 'Should they be seized, we could not live either at Leagatun *or* here. King Eadweard gave the land to father when Earl of East Aengla. This Northman king would sooner give it as a gift to one of his underlings for killing father'.

'You would have to send them somewhere for safekeeping', Wulfwin offers.

'Perhaps if we sent them to the Holy Father, then our rights to these lands would be acknowledged', Eadmund answers Wulfwin, nods and folds his arms, resting his chin on one thumb.

'If we were talking of anyone else, I would agree with you, kinsman', I warn Eadmund. 'But this is Willelm, and he does not feel bound to abide by other men's laws He has underlings to reward for helping him to the crown, and he has two greedy brothers'.

'If he were not told the papers were being taken, he would not know to try to stop them, surely?' Eadmund looks hard at me as if I were telling him that he and his brothers could not keep their land, even with the blessing of the Holy Father. He has only once dealt with Willelm save when Willelm paid court to King Eadweard.

At that time Eadmund was not long into learning to handle his weapons, and the old king had asked him to show Willelm some of the tricks he had learned, which he was happy to do.

Never having met Eadweard's kinsman before, the young Eadmund had agreed to a bout of mock combat with Willelm. He was not as happy when he was forced down onto his knees with the cold, hard steel blade of a Northman's sword pressed onto his mailed chest.

However, Harold saw it as a good lesson for his second son and cheered whilst Willelm smirked. Still, Eadmund knows only Willelm's fighting kills, not his statecraft. He may yet learn about that side of the man, his narrowness of aim and the depth of his greed. Only when Eadmund and his brothers know what they have to stand against will they know how to win Godwin's right to the kingship.

'What do you think I should do, should I send a rider to bring him back whether he has the deeds or not?' Eadmund asks us both, Wulfwin and me.

Wulfwin shakes his head and I take my cue from him,

'By all means Eadmund', I counsel, 'let Godwin bring the deeds here. He can send men of the church with them to put his case to the Holy Father. With luck right may be brought to bear on Willelm to grant you these lands.

'Aye, send them by sea from one of the East Aenglan havens, not overland by way of Centland and Flanderen', Wulfwin agrees.

'Ivar is right, Eadmund', Magnus agrees behind me.

I do not know how long he has been there. He adds for good measure, watching Eadwin.

'The Northmen will be watching all the havens on the south coast between Dofnan and Pefense'.

'We could send the mission from Bosanham, where they will not have to pass the Northmen's ships on their way to the Middle Sea', Eadmund adds, nodding.

'Sound counsel indeed from such a young head!' Wulfwin nods his heartfelt agreement with Magnus. 'Let Godwin know what you think, and hopefully he will not take too closely after his father'.

'Why do you say that, my Lord Wulfwin?' Eadmund is taken aback by Wulfwin's judgment on his father.

'With respect, Eadmund, he would listen neither to Leofwin nor Gyrth when they pleaded with him not to rush to Haestingas. Ansgar had little enough skill with leading so many men, so he would not have been able to counsel Harold wisely. There is only one he would have listened to, but he was no longer alive to be asked, even were he in favour', Wulfwin rests a hand on Eadmund's shoulder to show that he was not to be blamed for his father's shortcomings.

'*Could* father have won?' Magnus asks me.

I agree with Wulfwin, thinking back on the haste with which Harold sought to deal with Willelm,

'There were a number of us who thought that his haste cost us the fight, aye'.

I have to look away as Magnus' bright blue eyes bore into me.

'However, Willelm forestalled your father's aim of holding the Northmen at Caldbec Beorg until more men came. Even when the light was failing and your father was dead, there were fyrdmen coming from as far afield as West Seaxe. Indeed we could have sent Willelm scurrying back to the south coast, and even Northmandige!'

'Aside from some of the Northmen having second thoughts before coming, he had to offer our land and our silver to tempt young landless nobles to his cause', Wulfwin adds. 'I hear they needed a lot of talking over to his way of thinking and came only because he told them that our Aenglish warriors were no match for them'.

'It is of little comfort to us now', Eadmund goes over to the crackling fire that Burhwold has replenished, 'that our men were held in such high esteem by Willelm's vassals'.

Magnus tells me behind his hand,

'We are to be given crumbs, like hearth hounds'.

'We are not hearth hounds, nor are we begging just yet!' Eadmund looks sharply at his younger brother as he tells him off. 'One day we will make them sorry that they ever set foot on our Aenglish earth!'

'Well said, my Lord Eadmund!' Bondig claps loudly. He has been standing at the doorway, waiting to speak to Eadmund and cheers heartily for his master.

'Bondig, you have word from Lord Ansgar?'

'Aye, my Lord, I have been told he has offered a score of his best men to swell our numbers. They are young men who have no kin to hold them back, he said. He also said Lord Godwin should keep the best, even after our struggle, to teach newcomers to fight'.

'I take it that the king does not know the numbers in Ansgar's household', Magnus does not seem to be taken aback that Ansgar has offered his men, almost as if it were something he took for granted.

This to me is a wholly new side of Ansgar, as bold a sign as he can give without bearing arms against the Northmen himself. He plainly thinks of the friends he lost to Willelm's men on Caldbec Beorg, men such as Thurkill and Godric.

'When did Godwin ask for these men?' Wulfwin scratches his beard and puts forward my unasked question.

'He asked for them before he knew Willelm was to be crowned', Eadmund folds his arms and answers baldly. Wulfwin arches his brows, taken wholly aback by Ansgar's show of boldness.

'Ansgar had sent word that he would let him have his answer within the week. The men should be on their way before the month is out'.

The shire reeve is playing a risky game.

If Willelm came to hear of Ansgar's gift of men for Godwin's cause now that he has taken his oath, he could have his head. I hope Ansgar has thought of this. I have nothing against the man; to be truthful I have a great liking for him since we fought side-by-side against Willelm. But this sounds to me as if he is sailing very close to the wind.

'Did Ansgar not swear an oath of loyalty to King Willelm?' Wulfwin shakes his head in deep thought.

'He said he had to', I speak for Eadmund because I was there at the West Mynster and saw him do so, along with the young earls and many of the thegns.

'Do you *trust* Ansgar?' Wulfwin asks Eadmund.

'Why, should I not? He is after all an Aenglishman!' Eadmund is riled by Wulfwin's searching.

Wulfwin answers Eadmund's rebuke with a warning,

'I would take care when dealing with a man who had given his oath to this king and still honours his word when he could be sternly dealt with'.

'What does *that* mean?!' Eadmund is truly annoyed now. 'He gave his word that we could have these men, and he has sent them, that is all'.

'I think Wulfwin *should* be listened to', I put in. He is not beholden to Godwin. Wulfwin was your father's *friend*, not a retainer'.

'Very well, then', Eadmund answers snappily, 'speak your mind, Dean Wulfwin'.

'Ansgar may not seek to betray you, unlike Abbot Eadwin, who clearly holds the Northmen dearer than his own kind, but at least one of these men coming here may be paid by the king. Keep an eye on them, *all* of them, but do not let them know they are being watched. A traitor will soon show himself', Wulfwin offers.

Eadmund shudders suddenly and smiles,

'As you must know better, I shall take your word. I feel a chill coming on. Does anyone want mulled ale?'

Godwin shows early the following morning, just as another heavy snowfall begins. He has with him a score of Ansgar's men, who must have joined him coming back through Wealtham.

These men must be hungry', Godwin calls out for Burhwold, 'thirsty too, no doubt!'

Gerda and Ingigerd bring beakers of ale to the newcomers who gather in the main room of the lodge as best they can. There is hardly room for so many. Healfdan eyes them hawkishly as Ingigerd moves amongst them, handing out full beakers.

One or two of Ansgar's men make eyes at her, until they are elbowed by Healfdan. One tall, well-built golden-bearded fellow glares up at Healfdan and Ingigerd in turn. Perhaps he figures that Healfdan has already laid claim to her. He grins sideways at Healfdan before Godwin begins his speech to the newcomers.

'You really ought not to see the woman as yours unless you are married to her. I will wrestle you for her!' the fellow beams at Healfdan.

'You will do no such thing!' Healfdan roars and tries to grab hold of the fellow's tunic.

'Are you going to wrestle me *now?*' the fellow laughs and heaves Healfdan over his shoulder, laying him low.

'Where is Healfdan?' Godwin asks.

'He is down here', I answer on Healfdan's behalf, 'on the floor, having made the mistake of showing his bad manners to one of your guests. Stand up Healfdan, be a good fellow. Your lord wishes to speak to you'.

With some effort and help from his assailant, Healfdan rises to his feet and answers Godwin,

'Lord Godwin, I was about to clear up a misunderstanding when this fellow floored me!'

'What was the misunderstanding, Healfdan?'

I think Godwin has an inkling of the matter in hand from the way he asks.

'I humbly seek your forgiveness, Lord Godwin. I thought the young woman was untaken. I offered to wrestle Healfdan for her, but it seems she is spoken for', the tall newcomer answers for Healfdan now, to gales of loud laughter from his men.

Godwin tries to hide a smile, bringing more laughter from Ansgar's men. He asks,

'Forgive me my friend. I do not know your name. To whom shall I offer this toast?'

'Offer the toast to Healfdan's woman, Lord. For a man to want to risk being floored by me, she must be some woman!'

Raucous laughter follows.

When his friends have been hushed by some loud coughing from him, he tells us his name,

'My name is Guthfrith, Lord', the fellow announces for all to hear, 'and I drive all the women wild with my good looks, my long hair and beard!'

'*A modest man, too, I see!*' Godwin sizes up the newcomer, to more loud laughter and cheering.

'Think on this, nevertheless, Ingigerd is Healfdan's woman. Let no man make that mistake again, even you Guthfrith! Drink to Ingigerd – oh, where has she gone?'

'She has fled the room to hide her blushing!' I call out, to more laughter.

It will be hard enough to find a turncoat amongst these men without ruffling feathers. There is not one of them I could not get to like. Troublemakers they are not, but they may trouble Willelm's men soon enough when asked. Guthfrith will be easy enough to handle as long as Godwin shows he has wit and guile.

Godwin plants his feet wide apart to show he is the master here, then folds his arms and asks Guthfrith,

'Ansgar fares well, I hope?'

'Aye, my Lord, he does', Guthfrith answers swiftly, 'but he ails for friends all the same since he gave his oath to this new king of ours, Willelm the Northman'.

'His friends have fallen away *for that?*' Godwin raises his eyebrows at Magnus and me. Eadmund walks around Ansgar's men, each giving him a friendly grin as he passes.

'Guthfrith answers curtly, nodding at Godwin,

'Aye, my Lord'.

'How do you see your lord's oath to the Northman king?' Godwin tries to wheedle an answer from the poor fellow, giving no hint of his own thoughts. 'Was it wise of him Guthfrith, do you think?'

'It is not for me to say, my Lord Godwin', Guthfrith answers, shrugging. He is loath to give away anything he might think about his paymaster. 'I am not the one who wishes to hold office from the new king'.

'All right then, would *you* have given your oath of loyalty to King Willelm had you been Ansgar?' Godwin watches Guthfrith, standing there, awkwardly shifting his weight from one foot to the other, as if walking slowly without moving forward.

Guthfrith gives Godwin a pained look and shakes his head, saying nothing.

'Your loyalty speaks well for you, Guthfrith. I would not have you think ill of your lord', Godwin smiles suddenly and gives Guthfrith his hand in friendship.

'Give me your best and I will reward you well. I may make you a thegn, with land wherever you wish. However, never lose faith with Ansgar'.

Godwin stops to allow his words to reach even those at the back. When he thinks he has the ear of every man here, he goes on,

'It is true he has his own welfare at heart, but he has also to think of the welfare of those under him, such as your good self. A Northman lord might not be as forthright toward his underlings as gutless toward his king. I have heard that Willelm is a demanding overlord. It would take a brave man to look at this king and tell him if he were giving way to greed or graft. *Ansgar* would do that!'

Guthfrith looks thankful to be let off the hook, but Godwin is not done with him yet,

'Did you *offer* to come to me, Guthfrith, or did Ansgar give you no other way out? Answer truthfully, but think of your answer before you give it'.

Guthfrith does not dither with his answer,

'We are hand-picked, my Lord. My Lord Ansgar sent for each of us by name, knowing us able keep our word to him, yet do the bidding of those he trusts with our wellbeing'.

'Then I trust he has not stinted in giving his best', Godwin looks around Guthfrith's fellows and gives them a welcoming smile. He takes Guthfrith's outstretched hand and lays his other hand on top. 'As such I welcome you all to my household. Eat, drink, fight well when the time comes and as I have already said, *you will all be rewarded well!'*

Guthfrith and his men cheer, but Healfdan looks unhappy.

Eadmund and Magnus greet the new men one-by-one after Godwin whilst Ingigerd busies herself bringing more beakers of ale, helped by Gerda and a hobbling Winflaed. Talk turns to boastful shouting, and with more ale the hubbub becomes louder. One fellow's boast rings out above all others,

'I shall twist every Northman off his saddle!'

'Shut up, *fool!*' Guthfrith shouts the man down.

'No, let him prove himself!' I call out to Guthfrith, 'In the morning we will have some time before saddling up –'

'*Saddle up, why?*' Godwin turns to me, alarmed.

'Wulfwin rode here yesterday, to tell us that Willelm might be on his way to catch me. Abbot Eadwin has been summoned to Bearrucing to account for himself and ride here with the king', I tell him. 'Has neither Eadmund nor Magnus told you?'

'They have told me, but I cannot see Willelm riding out *here* for you when he is on his way to Cantuareburh to swear in more thegns, and then on to Northmandige - with hostages, I might add, one of them being Eadgar'. Godwin grins broadly as he tells me to take cheer from his news, 'We are all off the hook for the time being, until the Bastard comes back next year with his queen'.

I take in a mouthful of dry, smoky air and breathe out.

'Thank God for that!' I swear, coughing and to laughter from Godwin and Eadmund I take a gulp of ale to wet my smoke-parched throat. They too are thankful that Willelm will not be bothering them for a time. I have a thought, and ask Godwin if he knows the names of those whom Willelm has left to watch over his new kingdom,

'I hope to God it is not Odo!' After spitting out onto the hearth to show my dislike for Willelm's half brother, I wipe my mouth with my sleeve.

'Lord Ansgar says the king has left a Willelm fitzOsbern as his sentinel on this side of the river', Guthfrith tells under his breath. 'Bishop Odo has the other. FitzOsbern will be giving Ansgar his remit until the king shows again'.

'Where will Willelm fitzOsbern have his quarters, in the east or at Thorney?' I ask. The last thing I want is another of Willelm's brood breathing down our necks here in East Seaxe.

Guthfrith only shrugs. I have asked him more than he knows, or more than he has been told to give out.

'No matter, my friend, I was just thinking aloud', I tell him. He nods again and gives me a slow smile, as if thinking I was asking after knowledge I was not meant to hear.

'As we have time to breathe, I shall put you all up nearby with a good thegn', Godwin takes Guthfrith's arm.

'You can stay with Thegn Aethelwin at Saewardstanbyrig'.

My ears prick at talk about of Saewardstanbyrig. I did not know a new thegn had been appointed there, and if so by whom?

'Who is this Thegn Aethelwin?' I ask Godwin.

'He is a man whose name was put forward by Ansgar when Willelm was looking for someone to take the over from the earlier thegn, a man named Thorfinn put there by father'. Godwin turns to me and asks bleakly, 'Why do you ask?'

42

'I fought alongside Thegn Thorfinn. He came with us to Northmandige', I answer. 'That was when your father was asked by King Eadweard to speak to Willelm. Thorfinn was struck down by a Northman horseman about to spear Ansgar'.

I think back to when I last saw my friend alive, grinning and pointing Ansgar's untried fyrdmen to where they should stand,

'He was the only man *I* knew who could speak the Northmen's Frankish tongue'.

'*You* knew him?' Eadmund asks, eyes wide open, 'He taught me how to fight with an axe'.

'That had to be after your humbling by Willelm', I bite my lip almost as soon as I raised the story. He still plainly feels the humiliation from the way he rounds on me.

'I *had* to let him win. Father *told* me to', Eadmund gripes. 'Besides, *he* said he would sooner fight with a sword'.

'It is the chosen weapon of kings', Godwin agrees.

Eadmund gives me a steely glare, as if to tell me not to bring up anything like that again for outsiders to hear. I smile ruefully and he nods acknowledgement before turning away to talk to his older brother. Godwin stares sidelong at me, as does Magnus, before coming back to me and taking me aside.

'That was uncalled for, Ivar', Godwin under his breath. 'I hope you will not broach that story with anyone else about. As it is Eadmund will have to show his fighting skills for them all to see he can fight his own corner. How would you set about making him look good?'

'You mean I am to allow myself to be humbled?' I cannot believe my kinsman would demand that of me.

'Aye - but so you do not think I want to make *you* look bad, make it look real for *him*. If you make it look too easy, he will still be undone! Think about it, kinsman. I know you meant no slight, but you cannot be allowed to get away with offending a king's brother'.

'No indeed', I understand that I must make him look a warrior leader, even if my own name is tarnished in so doing. I can always regain my good name when fighting Willelm's men.

It is now days since my dressing-down by Godwin. A day of teaching has been set at Wealtham, when at the height of the day he will ask for a one-to-one bout between us, and Eadmund must offer to take his brother's place. He will allow his younger brother to stand in for him.

'Are you looking forward to this?' Theodolf tries to disguise glee at my overdue humbling, as he puts it, 'You asked for it, making Eadmund look foolish in front of Ansgar's men! I mean you no harm,

Ivar, but sometimes you do not seem to help yourself by trampling in the cowshit! If Eadmund can humble you in front of everyone today, without you giving him the upper hand, so much the better. I think you will have your work cut out for you, though'.

'Is that a back-handed way of telling me that I am too good a warrior to lose to him?' I ask with a lopsided smile.

'You know what I mean', he answers and walks away.

Theodolf has Hrothulf's way with words, and he has made great strides in achieving this self-assuredness since leaving his woodland home in the afteryear. Put this way, it makes me think the demon is with him again. I peer closely at him, Cyneweard and Oslac giving me odd looks as I do so. I ask in an offhand manner,

'Is this *you* speaking, Theodolf?'

Theodolf is taken aback. He cannot recall the times he became Braenda's mouthpiece, when she felt she had been slighted by my womanising?

'*What was that?*' Theodolf looks me in the eye, unblinking.

I begin to feel Braenda had taken him over altogether.

'You took me to task before, once when we were on our way back from Centland, and again when we were in the 'Eel Trap''.

He looks haplessly at the other two, who were not with us then, and back again at me. They have no knowledge of what this is about, and go about readying their own weapons to begin teaching Godwin's fyrdmen.

Cyneweard takes a whetstone to an old seaxe that Godwin has seen fit to arm him with, and Oslac tends to his arrows, cutting goose feathers for the flights of new ones he has been making, sighting along their length for straightness.

I stand, stretching myself just as Saeward enters the shed we have been sharing as a weapons and limber store for the past week or so, and notes that there is enmity in the air,

'Has Theodolf had another of his turns?' he asks jovially, and sees he has spoken out of turn.

Oslac puts down the small knife he has been using and looks up at me,

'I have no inkling of what is being spoken of here, nor do I think it is anything to do with me. In the whole of my time fighting with the fyrd in the Danelaw or Centland, I have never met anyone like you', he pauses to sharpen the knife. 'Will the pair of you make friends again before Cyneweard and I ask Godwin for our release to leave for home? Saeward is as bad as the pair of you! Wulfmaer does not know how lucky he is at Wealtham, away from this ever-worsening cat-fighting!'

44

'I have already taken steps to make life easier for you', Theodolf looks away, at something that seems to be happening outside. 'Gerda and I are to be wed in the church at Wealtham on Sunday next. After that we will be on our way to Saewardstan, where a small dwelling awaits us on Thegn Aethelwin's land'.

'All I can say is, may the Lord bestow you with blessings!' Saeward almost shouts and takes Theodolf by the hand, as do Cyneweard and Oslac in turn.

I feel four pairs of eyes bore into me. Theodolf's eyes seem to burn with anger now he has told me, as if to say he is glad to be rid of my company. Finally my last link with Hrothulf will be broken, as if he seeks to punish me for his father's death.

The close-knit threesome I took with me to Caldbec Beorg has been torn apart by my wish for Hrothulf to fight alongside my kinsman.

Oslac snaps at me and stands, staring into nothingness,

'Wish the lad well, *for God's sake*, and let us get to it!' He is ready to go out into the weak sunlight to watch me fight.

'I wish you well, Theodolf, I really do', I hear myself say. 'Gerda will make a good wife for you. Treat her well, look after them both as Dunstan would hope you would. Your father would be proud of you, I am sure'.

Theodolf looks long and hard, taking me in, eyeing me as I step forward to offer my hand and wish them both well.

'There will be time for well-wishing, Ivar', he gives me a wan smile, 'but first we must see you take a fall, to make Lord Eadmund happy'.

Laughter and backslapping echoes within the small paddock as the others joke about Theodolf's forthcoming trials after his wedding night bliss,

'Wait until those babies start showing from her belly', Oslac warns, good-naturedly, 'then we will see you with hollow rings around your eyes!'

'God, he will be worn out working and keeping her busy with all the offspring!' Cyneweard laughs, 'Think of all the work he will have to do around the place, making cribs for babies, playthings for Brihtwin and more babies for Gerda!'

Saeward reminds him of the duties of a neighbour on the land,

'Think of all the help you will have to give to the ploughman in the fore year, when you are not helping the miller with his heavy bags of meal! Did no-one tell you about that? Your bowmanship and fyrd duties will fade into the background for most of the time'.

For the first time Theodolf looks worriedly at me and hurriedly leaves us.

'Did he think he would be swanning around, teaching men daily how to draw a bow?' Oslac shakes his head and laughs, at first soundlessly, and then throws his head back and makes what sounds like a moorland grouse, a loud guttural, gargling noise.

Cyneweard stands bemused as both Saeward and I join with Oslac, rocking back and forth. We all watch with renewed mirth as Oslac collapses backward, no longer able to overcome his laughter. It is not long before Ansgar's men who, neither knowing what it is we are laughing about nor wishing to seem aloof, join in with our laughter.

Finally Oslac draws himself to his full height and asks,

'Much as I think highly of these fellows', he shakes his head, as he shakes off the laughter, becoming earnest again. 'I wonder what goes through their heads. Have they nothing better to do than laugh for the sake of it?'

'Be careful, my friend. Much as I like *you*, I would have no trouble using you for a tent peg!' Guthfrith's frown fades and he laughs at Oslac's beetling brows as he adds, 'No, what *am* I saying? I should set you atop one wall of this lodge to scare off the crows. Well I would think you could scare off the mid-winter's evil spirits, but the New Year is well past. If we are still together at All Hallows' Eve I will use you then!'

'I should be fool enough to stand here and *let* you!' Oslac's brow beetles anew to fresh laughter.

'If we had all day to do nothing it would be fine, but Ivar and I must needs hone our skills in single combat', Godwin has come out into the open without them hearing. He stands briefly in the lee of the hunting lodge and watches as Guthfrith and his men clamber onto the paddock wall to watch the forthcoming show.

I follow him across the snow-laden grass paddock, unsheathe my sword and swipe the air with it.

'Axes, Ivar, we will fight with axes', Godwin calls out as he lifts his from the ground, a very handsome double-headed axe.

'If you will allow, Godwin, may I fight him instead? Do you mind Ivar?' Eadmund comes out into the open.

'By all means, Eadmund', I answer and he nods happily, grateful to prove himself in front of everyone.

None of these men has been told of my fight with Brand. They do not know what is afoot, either. I must lose for the sake of friendship between us. As Saeward brings my axe for me, the onlookers around the outside of the fence eye the craftsmanship. Guthfrith elbows one of his friends and points it out to him. He clicks his tongue as if looking at a handsome woman, and blows a long, low whistle when Saeward hands me my axe.

'That is a fine axe you have there, Ivar. Shall we trade weapons?' Eadmund asks, smiling broadly at me, and chides softly when I do not answer straight away, 'Come now, you cannot deny a kinsman the right to handle such a fine weapon'.

He cannot know of the curse. Is he playing with me? I take his axe and weigh it. The finely forged double head is heavier than my single blade, a real Viking axe. How has *he* come by it?

'Take it, Eadmund. Take my axe, but do you really trust me with such a fine two-headed axe?'

I hold the weapon as I would my own, then draw my hands further apart along the shaft until I feel at ease with it.

'Yours is a lot lighter than mine at the top, but the handle is longer - and heavier. I shall relish trying it out on you!' Eadmund takes a swing with my axe around his head.

I hear and feel the rush of air. Only Theodolf here knows about the curse on my axe, but says nothing. Eadmund and I pace, sideways, around one another.

'We do not *need* shields?' Eadmund asks out aloud with a sly grin and raises a laugh. He shouts, 'All the better to hold our axes, eh, two hands being better than one?'

I see Brand, trying to get me to look into the sun. The sun here is behind one of the outhouses, not yet fully risen, and can therefore blind neither of us. Eadmund goes around again and takes a swing, missing my head by inches. I duck from habit, bringing my axe upward around my shoulder. One of the blades of his axe shears away some of the links on the shoulder of his mailcoat. He looks at the damage inflicted on his mailcoat and smiles, seeming to say,

'I will get you back for that, fear not!'

He rushes at me and takes a swipe with my axe blade that proves to be a little short. I have no need to step back and he rushes again, tripping across my right foot that I lift to shin-height. He lands awkwardly but keeps my axe at arm's length so as not to fall on the blade.

I allow him time to find his footing and watch him move around in front of me, to my left. He lunges at me with the blade down and I think he will bring it up and around to my left as he nears. I read him wrongly and he suddenly brings the axe blade up, leaving open his midriff to a side swipe.

My young kinsman jerks to a stop before the blade shears his mailcoat front, across his chest, forcing a grin as he brings my axe down at my shoulder. I pull away and he clubs me with the back of the blade instead, causing me to drop stunned to my knees. He holds my axe as if ready to cleave my left shoulder to my waist and stops as if someone had hauled him back,

'What... are *you* doing here Gerda?' Eadmund looks down wide-eyed at me.

'Eh - what is going on?' Godwin ducks through a gap in the low wall and strides across the now dirtied snow to stand at Eadmund's right shoulder. 'What has Gerda to do with anything?'

Eadmund scowls and drops my axe at my feet,

'I suddenly saw her there in front of me!'

'You are not talking about Theodolf's bride-to-be, are you?' Godwin demands

'In God's name, why *would* I?' Eadmund howls loudly.

I am not sure I believe him. Nor, to judge by the dark look Theodolf throws him, does he. I would not want to be in Gerda's shoes. Only Godwin can berate his brother if he cannot bring himself to believe Eadmund's protested guiltlessness.

I know the truth, but I cannot betray the curse to my kinsman now. I share that knowledge only with the now dead Ubbi, until my wyrd leads me to my own grave. They would not believe me anyway and I would be dismissed as a foolish heathen to try and sway them. Christians are not meant to believe in dark otherworldly knowledge!

'Do you have faith in your woman, that she would not betray your trust?' Godwin asks Theodolf. Both men are now put to the test. Single combat between *them* would be out of the question. Theodolf is not on a par with my kinsman Eadmund, nor are his fighting skills with an axe.

Theodolf has no way out but to show faith with Gerda. He nods sadly and everyone keeps their own counsel. They may not believe Eadmund, but their doubts will stay unspoken either for fear of their own safety or because of his standing.

Theodolf must stand by her, keep her from further harm.

When they are wed they will be away from Harold's sons. One day Theodolf will take her with him to Aethel's home. Eadmund will be a shadowy memory, out of reach.

Nor would he be within reach of Morkere. Maerleswein would be Theodolf's lord there.

'We must have words, Eadmund. You can perhaps enlighten me, but beyond that we must hope to forget your misdeeds'. Turning away from

Eadmund Godwin tells me under his breath, 'I only hope Theodolf can find it within himself to believe in his woman for Brihtwin's sake'.

With this Godwin turns and strides back to the lodge, trailing Eadmund behind him like a father leading an errant child. Eadmund can look no-one in the eye for now. Time alone will cure that. Everyone here has one task only and hard-won skills will help push what happened today from their thoughts, or at least to the back of them. Winter will soon be over and we can be on our way to the west. Meanwhile my blood-chilling tales of Braenda's flightings will sharpen them by night. On that thought I look forward to our next meeting.

3

Eadmund corners me one morning when we are readying ourselves for Theodolf's wedding to Gerda. Theodolf is willing to overlook his woman's error and has offered Godwin and both his brothers a welcome to their wedding.

He crooks a finger at me,

'Ivar, I should like to speak to you'. Eadmund has on his best breeks and boots, and a fine tunic of blue dyed wool. The women, young and older, have been eyeing him with awe since he showed for the morning meal.

'Whenever it suits you', I assure him. 'I will listen to your every word'.

'Now, I think, will be the best time', he steers me by my elbow to a corner of the main room of the lodge, 'You *did* believe me when I said I was never with Theodolf's woman?'

'Does it matter that much to you whether I believe you or not?' I look into his eyes, deep dark pits in the meagre light cast by flickering torches.

'*Of course* it matters to me. I did *not* bed her! I heard about your axe that brings about seeing things. When Guthfrith handled your axe on the morning I fought with you, would he not have been plagued by the same sights?'

'Guthfrith handled my axe, aye. So did Saeward, but do you think he had visions? No it has nothing to do with that'. I despair of keeping my secret from my kinsmen.

'It has nothing to do with what?' Eadmund demands.

I press him to hear me out before answering. He nods.

'I will tell you but you must keep it to yourself. Swear that what I tell you will go no further'.

'It will go no further', Eadmund half-heartedly agrees to speed me on. 'Not even Godwin?'

'Not even Godwin', I answer, staring into his eyes, 'nor Magnus'.

When I have finished telling him about the curse, the fight with Brand, and the Northman on Caldbec Beorg who thought he had me beaten he looks lost. At length he turns to me and asks,

'So the curse cannot lie?'

'How do you mean?' I ask by return.

'When I saw Gerda there was no way that the axe I held could have shown me anyone else but the woman I bedded last', he looks away from me again and then adds. 'Theodolf knows I bedded her, so why does he not try to come after me?'

'Perhaps he *would* come after you, were you both men of the same standing. He may be biding his time. I *know* he would come after me, even though as you are I am of noble birth but something else comes into play between us'. I think my answer puzzles him more than it answers his fears. He screws his eyes up at me and shakes his head, as though he has given up trying to understand.

'We are due a cup of ale'. With this Eadmund sheds his fears and I follow him into the lodge, looking to shed my own.

We mount and join everyone else outside Wealtham's church. My friends match Ansgar's men in their finery. All are well turned out, still sober. That will no doubt change once the church rites are behind us. Men will forget their manners, and there will be fighting.

Theodolf has a pair of Magnus' own fleece-lined calf-skin boots, a blue woollen tunic given by Eadmund as a sign of friendship – you could say out of guilt. He looks like a thegn with all this finery he proudly wears, and with the dark-tanned leather breeks I saw Hrothulf pack away when we came south; his own must have been too well worn for this day of all days. Godwin has given him a purse of silver coins to pay for a room at the inn for the night, and Brihtwin will be looked after by a maid.

Before we all enter the church Godwin has us all stand in line and issues a stark warning to every man here – and I am not to be left out - that fighting will be punished. However, we can get ourselves as drunk as we wish later, as long as we can make our own way back, wolves or no!

'...This warning must be heeded', he finishes and marches into the church with us all following on behind.

Theodolf is there at the altar, awaiting his bride with Cyneweard as his best man. The priest has not shown with his choir, so we have a wait ahead of us. My young friend is on edge, as is Cyneweard. Neither of them has ever been to a wedding. I think I would be edgy in his boots, and wonder if Braenda could have anything like this aforethought for me.

But then why *would* she? Having outlived one husband, Sigurd, what would she gain from being seen parading herself for me like a maiden? After all there was always someone likely to attack her for it.

Theodolf's bride enters, flanked by Ingigerd on her left and Braenda on her right with long, braided red hair. *Is* it Braenda or can it be only I see her, not another woman like her? The woman sees me staring and looks away, and when they are closer I see she is not Braenda after all, but a much younger woman.

Gerda looks like an aetheling's bride dressed in white with silver fox fur lining around her scooped neck. Theodolf is not the only red-blooded male here who stares, unable to believe his eyes. The other women jealously frown at Gerda for so brazenly daring to draw the men's eyes with her rare comeliness, and that she is no longer a maiden.

Theodolf can still not believe his luck, I can see. Yet fleetingly his look of awe turns to a scowl as his eyes take in Eadmund in front of me. He smiles again as Gerda joins him in front of the waiting priest. Other than the scowl at Eadmund, everything goes off well. Even the feasting and drunkenness passes good-naturedly. Everyone forgets his worries in numberless cups of ale or mead. I steal a fleeting look at the woman I thought to be Braenda, now with one of Ansgar's huscarls.

She can not therefore be my woman. Once, when I look her way I swear she smiles back at me, but then she looks away again at her man lest he be watching her. My loins begin to ache for Braenda.

Later, having drunk too much and feeling sorry for myself, I head back to Naesinga in the dark with some of Guthfrith's men.

The woods are still, the trees bare of leaves, yet still foreboding. The howl of a wolf adds to the eeriness. One of the men is chewing a leg of lamb as he rides along in front of me, and throws the bared bone into the bushes, scaring a young doe.

'What would I give for some meat from *her*, eh?' he laughs.

'Do you want me to bring her down for you?' one of the others asks, pulls out a bow and is about to turn his horse after the frightened animal when he hears rustling in the bushes nearby. 'There must be more of them'.

He dismounts and we halt whilst he stalks this unseen creature.

'I would not be so sure it is another deer, if I were you', I warn him, 'there could be a boar rooting about in there – or a bear'.

He looks back over his shoulder and grins, telling me bravely,

'Good, then we will have boar – or bear. I would sooner have boar meat than deer or bear, nevertheless. It is juicier, like meat from hogs only richer'. He turns, takes a few more strides and holds his bow at the ready.

The rooting goes on and our hunter slows, becoming more wary yet still moving forward. The rooting stops, so does he. We stay seated in our saddles, searching the murky undergrowth with our eyes, wondering what can be in there. The hunter closes on the bushes and one of his friends calls out a warning,

'Stay clear of the bushes, Godric. *For God's sake*, stay away from the damned bushes!'

Godric half turns and looks at his friend as the bushes shake and the huge dark shape of a boar comes crashing out onto the track. Our horses shy and Godric is knocked off his feet. The animal he was stalking has come out at him!

'Good Lord Jesu - *Christ in his heaven.* What *now?*'

The animal is on him and one of the others has his bow in his hand, ready with an arrow.

'Careful, you could kill Godric', Guthfrith warns.

'Let the boar kill him instead?' The fellow roars and looses off the arrow.

The arrow finds its mark in Godric's right arm and the boar turns tail in fright.

'Jesus, help me!' Godric whines wretchedly as three of his friends dismount hastily and rush to him, leaving one with the reins of the others' horses. The boar turns back at the nearest of Godric's friends, who yelps at the threat of the tusks nearing him. Before he can flee the boar butts him and his horse rears up, knocking him forward onto the boar. I leap from my saddle and hurl myself across the track, brandishing my dagger.

As I close on the boar an arrow thuds into his right ear, flooring him. I fight to stop myself from falling onto the dead boar and stand awkwardly with the dagger in my right hand. We each look toward the dark figure that shows from behind the trunk of a beech tree.

'*Mine*, I think', Oslac prods the dead boar and laughs hoarsely. 'There is enough of meat on him that should do us *all* for tomorrow night at least!'

One man laughs,

'There is plenty of meat on Hemming too'.

'Perhaps that was why the beast took a liking to him!' one of the others joins in the laughter. '*He thought he had a mate!*'

Helping him to his feet, one of Hemming's friends asks him,

'Hemming, are you well enough to ride?'

'Never mind asking *him* if he is well enough to ride! What about me with this *arrow* in my arm?' Godric demands angrily, pointing to the offending shaft. The point has lodged in the soft flesh of the upper arm, not into muscle or a blood vessel.

'You will not be doing any fighting for a time', Hemming notes sourly to Godric, 'but how am I to sit on a saddle long enough to get anywhere? I will have to *walk* back to Naesinga!'

'Better run, it will do you good', Godric sneers, 'you need to shed some weight, damned *pig* butcher. No wonder the boar sought you out!'

'Stand in your stirrups', I offer.

'Stand in the stirrups, *all the way back to Naesinga?*' Hemming whines churlishly at the thought of bouncing up and down in his stirrups all the way back to the lodge on this rough woodland track.

'Crouch forward in your saddle, then', Oslac laughs, 'as if you were riding in a horse race. Although God only knows what you would be like then!'

Godric frowns and shouts loudly enough for everyone to hear all the way back to Wealtham,

'Will one of you pull this damned arrow from my arm?'

'Leave it and we will ride back to Wealtham so that one of the brothers can tend to it', I offer. 'You might otherwise suffer from loss of blood. Saeward will do it for you'.

Godric groans as his two unwounded friends help him into his saddle. Hemming slowly eases himself back onto his saddle, his mouth twisted with the pain. Oslac walks back with us to his horse.

'I thought you had gone back to Naesinga', Saeward gives me a look of shock when our horses enter Wulfwin's yard again.

'We have two wounded men. One has an arrow in his arm that one of his friends foolishly loosed off, and the other has been butted in the backside by the boar his friend tried to save Godric from', I shake my head and laugh at the memory. 'God help us if the rest of Guthfrith's men are like these!'

'What was that about Guthfrith's men?' Eadmund has come out into the darkness to see what the fuss is about that causes so much mirth amongst his men.

'A boar will provide meat for the table at Naesinga, and two of your men will need beds in the infirmary here', I answer, pointing a thumb at Godric and Hemming.

'Who killed the boar?' Eadmund stands open-mouthed.

'I did', Oslac steps forward.

'*Did you put the arrow into Godric's arm?*' Eadmund snaps at Oslac.

'No, that was *Wilferd!*' Godric rasps and coughs, a cloud of hot breath shooting from his mouth, to the delight of everyone standing around.

'At least Ivar was not attacked due to your dimwittedness!'

I grin and wink at Godric,

'Perhaps it is as well I can look after myself, Guthfrith'. After this, by the time I get back to my bed I will not want for any woman to help me to sleep.

For some months now we have seen neither hide nor hair of Willelm fitzOsbern, or his men. Bishop Odo has not put himself out to find me, if he still thinks that I am alive. The king has not yet left for Northmandige, but seems he is in no haste to learn of our whereabouts. No-one has yet stirred to see what is happening on this side of Lunden, to see the king's laws are being obeyed.

We have been in the grip of a hard winter, and our new masters are not yet used to our weather.

Word has reached us from the west, of unrest in Hereford shire. A thegn, Eadric, is said to have withheld his oath to King Willelm. Trying hard to keep his earldom, Willelm fitzOsbern has been pressing him both to yield and to pay the king's fee to hold on to his book land.

'If fitzOsbern is that much in need of something to keep himself busy, then we should aid him', Godwin licks his lips at the thought of honing his men's war skills.

'The fyrdmen must be put to good use sooner or later', Eadmund agrees and turns to me. 'How many days were you on the road to Eoferwic in the after-year, Ivar? Was it five days, or six?'

After some head-scratching I offer,

'It must have been six days before we reached the Hvarfe. We were there in less than a week. Wealas has to be a lot closer, but we would have needs skirt Gleawanceaster'.

'Why *skirt* Gleawanceaster?' Eadmund asks sharply.

'If the Northmen are in Hereford, they must also be there', I turn from Eadmund to Godwin. He has land in north Sumorsaete and sees a need somehow to claim the land around the Seoferna's mouth.

'They would be cut off in Hereford if they lost the land this side of the mouth of the Seoferna', Godwin agrees.

'Our strength in the west has been in keeping the Wealsh from passing Gleawanceaster, so father used to say. Having fought them as often as he did, he ought to know'.

'Do we skirt Oxnaford as well?' Eadmund asks me now.

'We could ride through Chedelingtun', I answer, nodding, 'that is fairly close to the road west without giving ourselves away'.

Magnus has been sitting, nursing a cup of ale in his lap since we began talking. He looks worriedly from me to Godwin and back to Eadmund, and offers his outlook,

'Surely Chedelingtun is just outside the burh itself?'

My answer has Godwin smiling wryly at his younger brother,

'The Northmen would hardly know we were there if we rode by night, through the woods. They would not think so many men could ride past almost under their noses'.

'You may be right', Godwin agrees. He cranes his neck to look over his shoulder at his younger brother. 'Ivar has done this sort of thing before with father, I have no doubt'.

'Not with your *father* - with Tostig against Gruffyd', I correct him.

Magnus looks sourly at me, talking of his uncle but Godwin nods for me to go on.

'We needed to go around a Wealsh encampment on the River Deag by night, to reach Gruffyd's lands at the same time as your father landed along the coast the other side of Menai. As we had to pass between their lookout posts without them being aware of us, Tostig told us to tie cloth around our horses' hooves to smother the sound of our passing on the harder ground'.

'No doubt the Wealsh were taken off guard when you reached Gwynedd without alerting them', Eadmund smiles and strokes his beard.

'Father will have missed him at his side when he met Willelm in battle', Godwin muses, drawing a look of loathing from Magnus.

'Tostig was a good leader', I agree with Godwin. 'But they knew soon after, of our being there'.

'He kept close counsel and knew when to strike. Once we were well into Wealas we burnt their crops and homes to make Gruffyd show his hand. His underlings showed theirs first, though, cutting off his head and handing it to Harold in a blood-soaked bag, which he dropped onto Eadweard's table when the old king was regaling guests at his Gleawanceaster hunting lodge'.

Eadmund and Godwin burst into wild laughter. Magnus looks sourly at them, but grins foolishly and breaks into gales of laughter with them, setting one another off again until Godwin tells me wryly,

'King Eadweard would have no doubt been happy at that! I can see the old king eying the blood-soaked bag dumped in front of him as he takes his meal with his guests!'

'*God*, I think that would have got me up onto *my* feet!' Eadmund laughs again, 'Were you there, Ivar?'

I shake my head and tell them,

'Tostig led us back to Eoferwic. There was no encampment by the Deag when we crossed the river going back'. I think of Tostig as he was then, still the best of friends with his brother, their father. We feasted for a night and a day afterward. Harold came to Jorvik in the summer and asked me to join him as one of his huscarls.

'When did you *first* come to Naesinga?' Magnus asks, although it is not plain to me why.

'We stopped here on our way back from Eoferwic. I had been given leave by Tostig to join your father's household', I lift my cup of ale and take a mouthful. 'Before then I had only ever seen the lodge at Leagatun'.

Without looking at her, Godwin holds out his cup for Ingigerd to fill, and asks me,

'Did Tostig not begrudge father taking you from his household?'

'You knew Tostig as well as I did. He was not one to show his feelings, and it is likely he did think your father over-reached himself. But I had been one of Tostig's huscarls for a few years by then. Perhaps he felt it was just a short parting of our ways'.

I hold out my cup as Ingigerd passes and she slops some of the ale over my hand. She takes hold of her apron and dabs my hand with it, throwing me a look that tells me that she has had enough of Healfdan. I grin back and watch as she leaves the room for another pitcher of ale, and go on,

'I was *raised* with them. When King Eadweard gave Tostig the earldom of Northanhymbra, your aunt Eadgytha offered I should follow him north', I call to mind. 'That was the saving of me! When Tostig called on King Eadweard a little over a year ago his huscarls still in the Earlsburh were killed to a man'.

'You were thankful for that, then', Godwin nods and picks up his cup from the table to toast the memory of their father. 'In father's name, I offer a toast to thank him for our kinsman's life!'

I smile broadly and answer the toast with another,

'I offer this ale to you, Godwin Haroldson, that you may be king by the next Yulefeast!' I hold up my full cup to those of my kinsmen in thanks for their friendship and forbearing, 'To Eadmund and Magnus, his earls, long may they rule together!'

'To come back to this matter of our joining Thegn Eadric, when do we go?' Eadmund brings us back down to earth.

'Not before the snow has gone, otherwise we leave a clear trail to follow', Godwin warns.

'That could be Easter at the earliest!' Magnus spits into the fire and the dying embers hiss.

'Then *let* it be Easter!' Eadmund choruses with me.

Magnus protests loudly,

'What if Willelm fitzOsbern seeks us out *before* then?'

His words are overheard by some of the men awaiting their duties for the day in the fore house.

'Would you not think they would have to ask their way of folk around here?' I elbow him.

'Do you think they will tell the fools the right way to reach us here in Naesinga? They have no way of finding us without help. Who do you think will betray you here?'

Magnus looks across his right shoulder at me, trying to think of an answer and can only offer,

'There is always the one who thinks only of his purse'.

'You think there will be another Ealdsige?' Eadmund jokes.

Godwin looks askance at his brother.

'Too many know that tale by now. No, brother, few around here want to end their days being shunned by their own kind. Believe me, Magnus, no-one will hand us over'.

'Aye, and the Bastard's brother has squeezed his tenants dry in that part of East Centland around Hrofesceaster', Godwin tells him sourly. 'If those poor souls could thwart his tithe gatherers, they would dearly *love* to do it, and relish the laughter of seeing his fox-hair bristling with anger!'

'When Willelm shows back at Bearrucing –'Magnus begins.

Eadmund covers his brother's mouth with a well-ringed hand.

'What is the matter with you today, Magnus? He cannot sail back before the winds blow fair for him!' Godwin assures Magnus with a pat on the back and a friendly shove toward the door, 'Whatever happens, leave be and let *me* worry about that'.

With Magnus looking sourly at him, Godwin goes on,

'You should go out and make sure our men learn their war-craft skills in the way I want them to. I am told we should not see King Willelm much before All Hallows at the earliest, *if* then'.

'FitzOsbern may seek to buy someone's tongue', a smirking Eadmund ducks when an ale cup flies over his head at me.

It hits me on my chin, spilling ale everywhere.

'God, Ivar, I am sorry you have to listen to this again! Give that fool brother of mine a thump from me and give him one for yourself',

Godwin stands, staring angrily at Magnus as I nurse my bruised chin, 'by the time the greedy fool knows his tithe books show he is out of pocket, we shall be on our way west. Trust me!'

'I trust to your better knowledge, brother. Tell me something I would sooner hear, about how our men in Wealtham are coping with their weapon skills', Magnus sniffs, picks up his ale cup and drains it without taking his eyes off Godwin.

Godwin stares back at Magnus, awaiting the worst news,

'Have you heard something I would rather not?'

Folding his arms, the younger brother answers,

'Wulfmaer told Oslac what to do with his bow and stumped off back to his mill to ask for work. Cyneweard followed him back to Saewardstan and almost strangled him with his bare hands at the answer he was given', Magnus looks at me as he answers.

'What *was* he told?' Godwin looks from him to me, but when I shrug, looks back at Eadmund for the answer.

'Not before Ivar shows he is able to swing a sword rather than sit quaffing ale with lazy, good-for-naught nobles!'

'Go and bring him back here, now!' Godwin demands from me as if I were to blame for Wulfmaer's deeds.

'Do we need him that much?' I ask, perhaps proving Wulfmaer's point for him.

'We need *him* as much as we need you. At this time perhaps we may need him *more!*' Godwin snaps back. 'He might be right about you'.

I stand, throw my cup across the room and yell loudly,

'Show me a Northman and I will show you how he can be killed, whether on horseback or on foot!'

Godwin snarls at me, wiping dripping ale from his tunic,

'Begin by begging forgiveness for your cheek!' When you have done that, get yourself out there and bring Wulfmaer back without harming him. I want him back, willing to teach my men his craft'.

'*I* can teach them *my* craft! Wulfmaer knows nothing he did not learn during his fyrdfaereld from the *huscarls!*' I pull out my dagger from its sheath and bring it down onto the table before Godwin has time to blink.

Healfdan heads toward me, sword drawn at arm's length. I bring my left hand down onto his sword arm and he drops the weapon, his mouth twisted in agony.

'I cannot think who has been teaching *your* huscarls their skills, Godwin, because they have no hope of making a stand in a shieldwall against Willelm's horsemen. How do you think they could teach anyone *else?* True Wulfmaer is a good fyrdman, but you need men like

59

Oslac and Saeward to teach your men to fight Willelm's men! They have stood the test. Wulfmaer has been with us, but let him fester in his mill. Watch him crawl back, begging you to take him in. His skills are no better than are young Cyneweard's, believe me, I know'. Godwin glares at me as I finish telling him what he needs to hear and no-one had yet dared to tell him, 'Cyneweard is eager to learn. *That* is what we need. Most of your men as they are now would run!'

My fighting skills are useful to him but to look at him now he plainly wishes he could do without me. Standing slowly he walks around the table toward me. He draws my dagger effortlessly from the table and hands it to me, hilt first, and lays into me with his tongue,

'If you want to help with teaching the men your skills then do so! No-one has told you not to, have they? Or are you trying to tell me I am wrong in how I am going about this? *First*, Ivar, learn manners. I will not have you behaving like a spoilt child, however much older you are than I am! Teach my men how to fight - like Northmen, *if you must!*

'We *could* teach the Northmen to fight like Aenglishmen!'

Sheathing my dagger to laughter from everyone in the room I tell them,

'It took Willelm all day to break our shield wall. He had to draw the poorly-taught Suth Seaxan fyrdmen from the crest of the hill to break through our line. The Northmen and their allies could make no headway until very late in the day, almost in darkness'.

'*Then teach my men to stand their ground!*' Godwin shouts, and then tells me in a forced whisper, 'Do it soon and we can try them out on our way west'.

Eadmund looks worriedly at me and tries to reason with Godwin,

'To try out our shield wall, we first have to draw *them*. No, we should best attack them in quick raids and fall back quickly. A standing line is only of use when we have them cornered and there is little else they can do other than to try to push through us'.

'Aye Godwin, surely we should learn to fight like the Wealsh', Magnus joins in the argument, 'where we melt into the woodlands, hills or fens and leave them to fret over where we might strike next!'

'Whichever way your men learn their war craft, you and your brothers must learn *alongside* them', I prod the table to make the point. 'Show your men you are willing to fight alongside them'.

Godwin chews his upper lip in mulling this over. Eadmund and Magnus both nod when he looks to them. Seeing sense he agrees,

'Very well then, so be it'.

'Moreover your teachers will have to know that they can shout at you, to put you right when you fail to rise to their challenges', I add to further laughter.

Godwin again looks to his brothers, who nod again, less eagerly than before. Magnus frowns and lifts his full cup from the table to drink.

'Is there any more?' Godwin asks, fearing the worst. To his relief I shake my head as I walk across the room and pick up my cup from the floor. Ingigerd comes with a cloth to wipe up the ale and keeps her eyes down at the floor, even when rising to walk back to the kitchen.

'We begin *now*', I tell them. Magnus flinches.

'*Must* we?' Godwin groans, sighs and puts down his cup that he has just picked up with a thump that splashes what little ale he had left in it.

'I did not mean you to leave your ale, Godwin. Do you think I am such an ogre?' I laugh and pour out another drink for him from the pitcher that Ingigerd left on the table, asking Eadmund and Magnus,

'Does either of you want more ale before we go outside? You may need it'.

Eadmund grins foolishly and holds out his cup. Magnus looks stony-faced at me and shakes his head solemnly. When Godwin and Eadmund have downed their drinks they follow me, Magnus trailing us into the bright light of day. Young Magnus shields his eyes as the low sun strikes them. Healfdan, standing beside me, sneers when he sees his young lord flinch.

'Healfdan, you might show us all how you hold that Dane axe of yours when standing before an attack', I look at him to see how he takes my order.

He looks to Godwin, who nods. Seeing there is no other way for him, he steps slowly to the middle of the roped-off green that we use as a teaching ground. When he stops he takes the handle easily in his right hand and cradles the blade with his left; everyone outside the ring watching to see what comes next.

'Healfdan, if I come for you with my spear how do you ward me off?' I ask.

He steps forward, right hand gripping the weapon tightly, ready to bring it into play. With his left he brings up his shield. I stride across the green toward him, holding the spear easily, right hand uppermost.

When I am a few steps away from him I change my grip on the spear shaft, ready to thrust. He stands his ground, watching me like a hawk. When I bring my arm up Healfdan raises his shield higher so all I see is the top half of his head. Instead of throwing the spear I lunge with it at his feet, under the shield, and take him unawares. Luckily for

61

him he recovers quickly, and brings the shield down to push the spearpoint onto the earth. When it breaks from the shaft he grins at foiling my attack. Everyone around yells and one of the onlookers calls out to cheer him on,

'Healfdan, go into the attack!'

Before he can bring his axe up against me I heft mine from my waistband and weigh it in both hands, the blade in my left.

Healfdan copies me, eyeing me warily as I edge sideways around him. I put myself in front of the sun, making me harder to see against its golden glow.

'Eadmund watch', I call out to my young kinsman. 'You may find this to be a useful lesson. What is he doing wrong?'

Healfdan looks from me to Eadmund without turning his head fully away from me, keeping his eyes on me. He has the worried look of a man fearful of erring. Eadmund stands, arms crossed, and watches Healfdan closely.

We move around one another warily. I keep the sun to my left and make a feint toward his left.

Healfdan steps back and raises his axe, still gripping the axe shaft tightly enough for his knuckles to whiten. I move to my right and bring my axe one-handed around his left, where he parries with his axe shaft. The blade of my axe chips some of the wood from his axe shaft but he overlooks this and withdraws one step.

'He seems to be gripping his axe very tightly', Eadmund notes, his words whipped away from Healfdan's hearing by a sudden gust of wind from the east.

Healfdan looks uneasy, unsure of what he should do next because he cannot have heard all the warning. He comes at me and swings the axe sideways at my chest. It is my turn to step back, and in so doing bring down my axe blade on his axe shaft. Healfdan watches in shock as the shaft of his axe snaps and the blade digs itself into the snow-covered earth. Loud cheering follows from the men who came with us from Leagatun.

Godwin and Magnus look on in bewilderment. Eadmund giggles like a maiden and calls out to me,

'He should by rights have been cut in half!' he strides across the paddock and slaps me on my back, 'Everyone here is awestruck! How did you learn to fight like that?'

'I learned from watching your grandfather, Godwin's namesake', I smile at my kinsman and laugh loudly. 'He was the only man I knew beyond the lands of the Danes who could wield a war axe as well as a

Norseman! Did he not marry the most comely Dane at the court of Svein Forkbeard, my aunt?'

Healfdan shakes his head at me in disbelief and tells me,

'I had you for an ale-swilling noble dandy!' he laughs feebly, still shaking.

'Never knowingly undervalue your foe, Healfdan! This was just me *teaching* you, but the Northmen also have axe-bearing warriors. Lighten your grip, friend. The worst that can happen is that your axe falls to the floor when your foe's axe comes down on yours like that. I saw some of the wood chipped away on the shaft of your axe and aimed for that, otherwise you could have come back at me and it might have been me shown up to be the fool!'

Godwin roars at his men to take up their weapons again and grins back at me, glad I have shown them a skill level to aim for,

'Get back to learning, everyone! The time is over for standing and gaping. Show your teachers your skills and learn from your mistakes! Now it is my turn to learn at the hands of the master'.

The rest of the day is spent showing how to best their opponents.

Our breath hangs on the thin mid-winter air throughout the rest of the short day like small clouds. The sweat pours from my back like a waterfall, and I am sure this is the hardest day Godwin and his brothers have had since they met me again! They will be cursing me well into the night over their back pains.

'You earned your meat today, kinsmen!' I tell them later, in the feasting room with my cup of ale held high in salute.

'Aye Ivar, you made *sure* of that!' Eadmund laughs into his ale, blows the froth onto the table and collapses back into the back of his chair, laughing, 'I shall sleep so well tonight, Ivar, that the women will wonder what is wrong with me!'

What little I saw of him during the afternoon when I had time to catch my breath, I know he will be much the better for it. Having called a halt to the teaching, I ride to Wulfmaer, to speak to him, asking him to think over his gripe with me and to talk him into coming back with me to watch as everyone strives to learn.

The following day he is well pleased with what he sees and rides back to Wealtham with spirits raised, good food and drink under his belt. No doubt also he will be the wiser for having thought badly about me.

'Many will make good warriors in time, and I hope, live to tell their grandsons how they learned to fight alongside their king', Wulfmaer shares his thoughts with me before he leaves with three of Ansgar's men should Wulfmaer be beset by wolves. 'He shouts back to me as he leaves Naesinga between his escorts. 'When we are ready they will ride with us into the night and fall on our Northman foe in the dawn of the new day. Willelm will be hard-pressed if we have many hundreds more like these!'

I lie awake long into the night thinking of Wulfmaer's parting words. My thoughts turn to Braenda, and stray to Ingigerd. I have seen her in her loose shift, showing the tops of her firm young breasts. In recalling the way I saw her earlier in the evening, I think to myself that she was light on her feet, as a good-looking young woman should be. She passed between us at the table like a young doe, often leaning against me as she reached over me from behind. It was as if she wanted me. I may be wasting my time thinking about her, but she is wasted on Healfdan. As I rest my weary bones that night, lying on my back on the narrow cot bed, the door to my bed-closet creaks lightly. I take it to be the wind buffeting against the eastern end of the lodge.

Something stirs in the darkness beside me. Unable to see in the pitch blackness, I feel a small, warm hand pass over my naked waist and grasp the hand, squeezing tightly. When I hear a young woman's sob of pain I know then Ingigerd is with me.

In that first breath many things enter my thoughts. One is the likelihood of Healfdan going berserk at the thought of his woman being bedded by me of all men. The last thing I want is him breaking into my bed closet in a blind rage as Ingigerd thrashes about in the heightened throes of joy.

'Does Healfdan not know you have left his bed?' When I pull her to me she presses herself hard against me, telling me,

'There is no need to worry, Ivar. I am already with child by Healfdan. He will never know', she reassures me.

If it is her wish to be have my seed in her as well her man's, then so be it. Why should I fret needlessly? It is only when we are coupled that I know it is not Ingigerd I have in my bed.

I hear Braenda ask,

'Would you have liked Ingigerd's furrow around your seed-bearer?' She pumps me harder. Giving a throaty laugh she quips, 'This is welcome, not having to do all the work. I want you, Ivar. I have been aching for you these last weeks!'

When she is spent she throws herself onto her back and breathes hard and fast. When her breathing has steadied she rolls over, back onto me and begins to stroke my chest with her tongue.

'Give me time, Braenda. You are working me like an ox!'

I laugh and bring my right arm around her back to stroke it. As I stroke her I feel a long weal on her skin, as if her skin had healed from being beaten or whipped.

'That was the fat son of a sow, Sigurd! I could not stand the thought of him coming back to the Earlsburh and beating me again, so I had him killed by Morkere's thegn, Eadwy'. She breathes steadily, tracing with her finger around the hairs on my chest and down to my navel. She goes on, 'The poor young fellow had lost his family to the Norsemen and needed to settle the score. As Sigurd had Norse blood ties, I thought Eadwy might wish to wreak his anger on him. Everyone thought it was Harald Sigurdsson's younger stallari, Styrkar – or even Copsig - who killed Sigurd, is that not right?'

'I know *I* did', I answer, trying not to laugh with her tickling my loins. 'They were both still around. Styrkar lay low when the Northanhymbrans came close enough to harm him. He should have died with his king, as his standing would demand. I also thought it might have been Copsig'.

I nearly bite off my tongue, not because I feel guilty at being alive when my king and kinsman is dead, but because Braenda has slipped my manhood into her. Her soft, silken thighs enwrap me as she rocks herself backward and forward. Seeing nothing in the pitch blackness I lose myself in the thrill of feeling her pressed against me.

'She could never give you this much of herself at her age'. Braenda means Ingigerd. 'Own up, Ivar - you thought you would profit from her being with child, did you not?'

'The thought had entered my head', I answer, smiling to myself.

'I think that is highly likely. Still, what is more *I* had you. *I had you!*' she hisses into my right ear and bites it.

'I can muster no more strength to fulfil your lust', I warn her.

'What makes you think I *want* more?' I can sense her mischievous grin in the dark. She thumps me playfully on my chest and I groan for her 'Go to sleep, and think yourself damned lucky it was I who came to you!'

Hearing no more from her I join her in sleep.

4

I am shocked into wakefulness by loud banging on the door of my bed closet. I try to prise open my eyes and grope around for my breeks in the half-darkness of a numbingly cold early morning.

'Wake up, Ivar. *Wake up!*' I hear Magnus' anguished cry. 'Wake up, Healfdan has gone berserk! He has killed Ingigerd and is threatening to gut Guthfrith!'

'What has that to do with *me?*' I am half asleep and cannot think straight. But things are coming back to me now.

'Healfdan will not listen to Godwin or Eadmund. He is bawling that unless you come, he will feed Guthfrith to the wolves!' Magnus breathes heavily from running.

'Of all men, why is it *me* he wants?' I cannot think what Healfdan's anger with Guthfrith has to do with me.

'He says he saw Ingigerd enter your bed closet last night!' Magnus snarls at me, wolf-like.

'Then why in God's name is he threatening to kill *Guthfrith?*' Has Magnus lost his reason along with Healfdan? Why is Ansgar's huscarl in danger and not I?

'Guthfrith said that if you had not raked her garden, *he* would have done it *himself!*' Magnus suddenly makes sense. I was not to hand, so the first man to cross Healfdan's path who utters something stupid has to be Guthfrith.

'I will pull on my clothes and come. Where is everyone?' I gather my clothes and hurriedly pull them on as Magnus nods towards the yard.

'Make haste before Healfdan loses his wits and Guthfrith his life!' Magnus makes towards the door and looks back at me, 'Why in God's name - *why* did you have to go and wreck everything when we were so close to reaching our goal?'

He slams the door to behind him and thumps away on the wooden floor to the stairway. The sound of his footfalls is lost in my haste to make ready. When my sword belt is buckled and I have rammed my feet into my boots, I follow my young kinsman outside.

'*There he is!*' someone shouts to Godwin, who turns and stares dully at me as I near him and Eadmund.

'Why do you have to be such a fool with women?' Godwin asks me loudly, trying to shame me.

'Healfdan has killed his woman and now threatens to finish off one of Ansgar's huscarls!'

'So I heard', I stare at the crazed Healfdan, still holding Guthfrith by the craw against one of the tall posts the men hung targets from to test their bowmanship.

'There is no need to be so calm about it, this is *your* doing!' Eadmund chides.

'*What* is my doing? Healfdan was unsteady on his feet last I saw him. He was mistaken about seeing Ingigerd enter my bed closet. It *was* a woman he saw, but not his. As for Guthfrith, saying something stupid about raking her garden would not make the fool Healfdan feel any better. Healfdan, leave him be!' I call across to the fellow and stride across the yard toward them.

'You want me to kill *you* instead of Guthfrith?' Healfdan rasps, sneering, without taking his eyes from Guthfrith, who tries to pull away. Ansgar's man is rammed back against the post. 'I am not finished with *you* yet!' Healfdan bellows at the chalk-white Guthfrith and thumps him in the chest.

'I will teach you about raking when I have dealt with Ivar!'

'You mean to kill Guthfrith *after all?*' I ask, biding my time. 'Why did you kill your woman, you fool? Why did you not just call me out in the morning?'

Healfdan purses his lips like a child, almost bursting into tears. I stand, hands either side of my hips, head cocked, waiting to hear his plea. On hearing none I go on,

'*We* could have fought it out, man to man, like the warriors we are supposed to be. Killing Ingigerd served no-one's ends. What will you do now when you are lonely in the night?'

'I will get another woman, *what else!*' Healfdan's upper lip curls in the sort of sneer I have come to dislike on him.

'Somewhere *else* you might, but not here. These women are afraid of you now. They might however think more of you if you take me on in single combat. Just think, in beating me you may become a hero now you have put it about that I bedded your woman. Think on that and let him go, you can always take him on when you have finished me off'.

I look across the yard at Godwin, who scowls when I wink at him. Eadmund also turns away when I look at him. He too wanted Ingigerd but will not admit to it. Come to think of it, at least half the men must have had their eyes and hearts set on her.

No-one speaks for what seems an age.

The stillness is broken only by the mocking of the crows, filling the crisp morning air with their harsh calls.

'Well, Healfdan, *what is it to be?*' I have to berate him, goad him into doing something very soon. Guthfrith must be freed to go about his daily tasks, and learn to keep his thoughts to himself.

'Is it only *women* you can kill, because they have no strength to fight you off?'

Healfdan's eyes bore into me. His baleful stare offers an end to this stalemate, so I goad him further until he can take no more,

'You want your men to think you pick on those who cannot stand up for themselves? Either way you cannot lose, eh?'

Healfdan snarls like a cornered beast and presses his knife blade harder at Guthfrith's neck, prompting Ansgar's huscarl to snap at him,

'*Christ*, you fool - you want to get it all over with *now?*' Guthfrith wrenches himself free of his captor and puts his hand over his neck to stem the flow of blood from the wound.

Healfdan stands brandishing his knife with childish relish, daring me to take him on, screeching with glee at my willingness to take him on,

'Very well, then. As you have offered yourself, *come* for me!'

He cannot wait for it to begin now, adding,

'Lay down your sword and we can give these good folk such a show of knifemanship to tell their offspring of in years to come!'

I smile thinly at Healfdan, firstly to show him I am happy he has made up his mind to put an end to his foolishness, and secondly because I will be able to show my mettle in the eyes of the onlookers. My kinsmen can take pride in sharing a blood tie with me. I shrink from *no* trial or ordeal, whatever the weapon chosen, and stride to meet Healfdan on an equal footing as I did with Brand.

'*Get ready to meet your maker!*' Healfdan tells me, grinning wolfishly.

To loud laughter from all around I answer,

'When you meet yours, you can tell him Ivar Ulfsson sent you. You can greet mine whilst you are there!'

My wit is answered by a note of scorn when he snaps back,

'When you stop talking we can get on with this!'

68

His jibe brings guffaws from some of his cronies, and tells me he is rattled. If he wants to finish the fight before he has begun, is he as sure of his skill with a knife as he makes out to be?

I will see if I can further unsettle him with more talk. So far he has only walked crab-like in front of everyone.

I see some are becoming tetchy with his lack of keenness to come to grips with me. Perhaps if I goad him more,

'We can get on with it when you stop shuffling crab-like in front of everyone instead of tackling me, man to man!'

His cronies begin to shout for Healfdan, who snorts his scorn, coming at me, slashing at thin air with his knife. In over-reaching he stumbles on a tussock of grass but rights himself quickly, and changes his grip on the knife. Taking the knife from his right with his left hand, he rubs the sweat from his right hand on his woollen shirt and snatches the knife back into his right hand without looking away, fearful of me going for him if he takes his eyes off me.

Again he comes at me, scything widely. I sidestep to his left and he changes his grip again, jerks his hand outward to catch me with the blade and lashes out as he comes at me. Each time he rushes he has to turn quickly to look. If I can edge him back to the tussock of grass that he stumbled over, I might gain the upper hand.

With a shorter reach than his, being half a head taller than I there is no hope for an easy win, I must outwit him. Healfdan comes scything again, the knife still in his left hand.

When he is close enough to scrape me I duck under his outstretched arm and come around his right. As I pass below his reach I thump him in the ribs with the back of my fist.

He spins drunkenly and tries to grip his knife, for all the pain shows through his scowl. As the shouting and cheering goes on, more mockery is heaped on Healfdan now than before. By not having ripped open his side as I could have done when I passed, I feel I have belittled him in front of his friends.

'Healfdan, you fool, cut him to shreds!' someone yells out from behind the closest onlookers.

Another takes up the shout from further away,

'Slice him like a hog's belly, Healfdan!'

These two earn themselves vexed looks from the others. But Healfdan is clearly shaken by my foray under his reach. He glares at me, sweating heavily, although the morning air is still crisp. Late snow drifts down from an otherwise clear sky.

He comes again, switches the knife from left to right hand and scythes madly, closer to the tussock he stumbled on just a short time ago. He has let himself become riled, loses his footing and stumbles. With a loud groan Healfdan goes down, knife hand over my left knee. I raise my knee and bring my left hand down in a fist onto his, the hilt of my knife on his knuckles. His knife drops to the scuffed snowless patch of paddock grass and he drops heavily onto his elbows. His friends groan loudly when I bend down and take Healfdan's head by his ears, shaking him like a hearth hound, demanding an answer,

'Have you had enough?' I ask him.

He reaches for his knife, cannot grasp it for the pain I have inflicted on his hand and whines bitterly, loudly for all to hear,

'Why will you not kill me?'

'I want to hear you have had enough, Healfdan. Your lord will punish you for the killing of Ingigerd!' I keep my grip on his ears for all his fierce head-shaking to get away from me.

'You are hurting my ears!' Healfdan sobs to the howls of mirth from the onlookers, even his cronies cannot hold in their scorn.

'If you pull his ears long enough he will look the ass that he is!' one wag yells out. 'Best you put him out of his misery now, if it is what he wants!'

I look toward Godwin, who shakes his head dolefully, turns slowly and walks back to the lodge. Eadmund and Magnus follow him without looking at me, and Guthfrith walks across the grass to me.

'You should have killed him, Ivar!' Guthfrith growls angrily and looks down on the wretched Healfdan, 'You might as well have done, as he will be worth nothing any more. If he is punished by Godwin for slaying the maid, it will be no more he has coming to him now'.

'We have to keep him tethered up somewhere until we are ready to ride west', I hear Saeward say behind me.

'Aye, otherwise he will go straight to the Northmen and tell *them* of Lord Godwin's whereabouts', Guthfrith adds and, nodding his agreement with Saeward, lifts Healfdan to his feet. 'Someone take this wretched creature and tie him to a post in the store room!'

Another of Ansgar's men offers,

'We could chain him. There is a smith here who could make a chain strong enough to hold Healfdan'.

'Until we *have* a chain, bind his hands, Wulfgar', Guthfrith snaps. To another standing close by he says, 'Sigeferth, you go and tell the smith we need a chain strong enough to hold a bear'.

'Are you hurt?' Saeward asks me.

'No, the blade missed me each time', I assure him. Guthfrith leads me with one hand on my elbow back to the lodge. In shaking myself free of his grip I let him know I can walk without help,

'I have just told Saeward that I am unhurt', I smile.

'We need to follow Lord Godwin inside and learn from him what we should do with Healfdan, to tell him what we think and see if he agrees. Put away your knife first', he urges me onward. I thought he had my welfare at heart!

I sheathe my knife and follow him into the warmth of the lodge with Saeward following. My stomach rumbles with a pressing hunger, but I do not know how long it will be before I eat before Godwin has finished.

He may chide me, although he would broadly agree with my not killing his huscarl. It should be for him to say what happens to his underlings, not me. I only agreed to the knife fight to free Guthfrith.

'*Did* Ingigerd sleep with you last night?' Eadmund grabs me by my upper arm before I walk into the main for a belated morning meal.

'Healfdan was mistaken if he saw her enter my bed-closet. He had too much to drink at the wedding. Like any red-blooded man here I thought Ingigerd would be a catch, but she was not for me. It was the drink talking in him', I answer without offering anything further, such as Braenda coming to me.

'Did you have *anyone* with you, who can speak for you - like a hall maid perhaps?' Eadmund questions me closely.

What is this in aid of? As if *I* had killed someone?

'Do you mean *Braenda*, by any twist of fate?' I ask in turn. He looks, pained, from me to Godwin, as though handing me to his older brother for further soul-searching.

'I think it is safe to say Eadmund *does* mean your spay wife', Godwin's eyes narrow. Perhaps he is trying to weigh his standing as a Christian lord with mine as the earthly spouse of a hwicce woman, a shape changer perhaps. He is trying hard to be on my side, but there is a priest in the room with us now, Father Cutha.

'*What* is this Lord Godwin asks, about a spay wife who enters your bed-closet?' Father Cutha stares disbelievingly at me, 'How do you come to know this woman? Does she ride on the wind?'

'I have not heard that they ride on the wind, Father. To the best of my knowledge I have never seen her being carried by the wind. I only know that after she visits me in the night, she is gone by the morning'.

Cutha stares at me, bemused. I smile and add, trying to make myself understood,

'She has always done that, ever since I first met her in Wealas when we rode there to fight Gruffyd', I let Father Cutha know how long I have known Braenda.

'You have known her from before Earl Harold's kingship?' Father Cutha's eyes open wide. 'Are *you* hwicce? I mean why would she bed *you* if you had no power over her?'

'When I first met her I had no inkling of her background. She was - *is*, a good-looking woman. It was she who first spoke to me'.

'Braenda was a housekeeper for Gruffyd's widow, now *Harold's* widow Aeldgytha', Godwin tells him.

'When did you first learn she was a spay wife?' Father Cutha searches more closely, turning slowly back from Godwin to me. I feel he is trying to brand me an outcast in the eyes of my God-fearing kinsmen.

'I was first made mindful of her being *linked* with hwicce in the woodlands near a friend's home in the north. When I stayed at his home, and when we rode south to join King Harold against the Northmen she watched over me- I am not allowed to finish.'

'I have been told of the spell put on your axe by a Wendish weaponsmith. You seem drawn to otherworldly beliefs', Father Cutha smiles craftily, as if I had been led into some kind of word-trap, 'Lord Godwin should be careful, if he wishes to be a Christian king, about those he keeps company with. Godwin Haroldson, I would counsel you sever your links with your heathen kinsman. Men who have dealings with spay wives have no right to be with us of the Christian kinship!'

Godwin closes his eyes as in pain, and looks pityingly at me before speaking,

'He is right, Ivar. You are kin, but when I am king I must have men who truly believe in God's good works, as did my father'.

I break in, grinning, perhaps taking for granted my kinship with him,

'It did not seem to bother your father'.

'Did father know about your woman being a spay wife? I do not think so. Had he known, he would have told you to break with her', Godwin fumes. 'If you cannot, leave and go your own way!'

'She is the one who cannot break with me', I stand square to Godwin. 'But even if it were the other way around, I do not think I should keep the company of a man narrow-minded enough to be led by the nose by a priest!'

'Ivar, do you know what you are saying?!' Eadmund blusters, but I wave him aside.

Magnus breaks in from behind and I turn to look at him, a wry grin twisting his mouth as he asks,

'Does our kinsman hold his spay wife dearer than he does us?'

I smile at him, answering,

'You might say that, in the light of what your brother said just now'.

'What hold does she have over you?' Magnus asks further, still grinning.

'You have never had her in bed with you, or you would not ask so foolishly', I outstare my kinsman and his grin fades.

He turns to his eldest brother who, no longer scowling, tells me in friendlier manner,

'Take what you need, Ivar. I am sorry it has come to this', Godwin breaks off, breathes in and finishes. '*I* hold no grudge against you, skilful fighter and warm-hearted kinsman that you are. I will not take up arms against you stay one last night and share the table with us in the morning. We may see you one day soon, and I will gladly fight alongside you in the shield wall', Godwin says the last under his breath so Father Cutha cannot hear him, and pauses, trying to summon a smile.

His awkwardness is shared by Eadmund and Magnus. I can see the church ruling this land, as it does now with Willelm. Father Cutha smiles drily at me, inwardly gloating over his hold on Godwin.

'Ask your friends if they wish to leave with you', Godwin begins again, 'I will not throw them out, as I would not willingly throw you out if you denied her. Your friends are welcome to stay. Theodolf has settled here with Gerda and her young son'.

'Saeward is still a God-fearing fellow, as is Wulfmaer I know. Cyneweard and Oslac strike me as being Christian in their bearing'.

'We were all at Theodolf's wedding', Oslac says for me. 'Ivar stood witness to it'.

'Aye, Ivar *was* there, too', Cyneweard agrees, 'so why is Ivar being shown the door, just because this woman seeks him out?'

Father Cutha sighs and looks heavenward, looking for help from his maker, and then looks down at the floor. Have words failed him?

'Your *woman* did not come to the church though, did she?' Godwin sets the seal on Father Cutha's work. 'Ivar, I wish you the best of luck in your undertakings. My door is open to you when you feel you can do without her and need us. We shall share bread now, as in the morning before you leave. Eat, drink, feel welcome under my roof and perhaps by morning you will have had second thoughts about the outcome of your soulless life with Braenda'.

'I thank you', I take Godwin's right hand in mine and rest my left on top, 'but I am set in my ways and do not need the fellowship of a priest to keep me warm at night'.

Godwin winces and looks away, as if I had said he needed the company of men. I tell him,

'Tomorrow I shall set out for the west to seek Thegn Eadric. We will see one another again. I do not bear grudges. Follow your own path if you want it blessed to gain a greater following'.

Looking at Father Cutha I warn,

'As long as Father Cutha does not go spreading tales of me riding the wind with Braenda, our friendship will not be threatened by doubts about your leadership. Now *can* we sit to eat? I feel as if I had not eaten for days!'

In the morning I gather up my weapons, my sword belt and knife sheath. I have on my longer mailcoat, the one I took from the Northman rider in the south, as it is much like our own mailcoats that many of Harold's huscarls wore. I also still have the key that I found in the folds of Earnald's habit, which I hand to Saeward, together with a small silver cross,

'You may find a use for this. A smith may even be able to make a lock to fit it into'.

He looks crestfallen at my leaving because he has at last found a bolthole. Fearing he would be made homeless, he was hopeful of fitting in with my kinsmen. He would have felt at home at Thorney, a king's huscarl if Eadgar had been crowned.

But that was not to be. Instead he is here at Naesinga, teaching Godwin's fyrdmen to become masters of the axe and sword. One day he will become a king's huscarl when Godwin ousts the Northmen.

Cyneweard and Oslac are to come with me. I have heard nothing from Theodolf, but it is not likely I shall. A family man now, he teaches men to draw the war bow when he is not out in the field behind oxen and plough, if not in the mill. It may be in his blood, or his wyrd.

Watched by Godwin's men, the three of us amble out to the stables with our war gear over our shoulders. Guthfrith is nowhere to be seen. Nor for that matter are Godwin and his brothers. Burhwold stands sadly at the stable door, at his feet a bulging bag which he tries hard to lift when we are a few strides away.

'Hey old man, *leave that bag to me!*' Oslac puts a hand on Burhwold's shoulder, urging him to leave the bag on the ground.

Burhwold looks up at me and smiles weakly as Oslac hefts the bag onto a packhorse given by Godwin to bear our food and drink,

'I am sorry to see you go, Lord Ivar', he reaches for my right hand to bid me farewell and gives me a small purse, 'Lord Godwin asked me to give you this'.

'We will meet again one day, Burhwold', I assure the old man and press his hand in friendship.

'Ours is the path to pastures new', Cyneweard is the next to bid him farewell, 'for we must ride to help our fellows in the west against their Northman overlords!'

Oslac hugs Harold's old discthegn as if he were bidding farewell to his own father,

'Burhwold, before you know we will be greeting one another once again!'

'I hope so, Oslac. I really hope so!' Burhwold's eyes are brimming. 'Winflaed and I are well down the road you follow, and although you will never catch up with us in our lifetime, we may well cross paths in the life hereafter'.

Oslac nods sagely. Burhwold feels he will not see us again in his own lifetime, and he may be right but I hope to prove him wrong. He follows us to where our horses have already been fed, watered and saddled by Godwin's thralls,

'Aye, we *shall* cross paths again', Oslac gives Burhwold words of comfort with a few pats on his back before he mounts, 'and sooner, rather than later, *I know it!*'

'Well what *else?*' I laugh and settle my axe into the saddle pouch I had made for it during our days at Leagatun. Once I have hoisted my belongings onto the back of the saddle I ease myself up onto Braenda and reach down to Burhwold for a last farewell.

He takes my hand, looks up into my eyes, and summons up a bright smile as we lead out our horses into the morning sunlight. His voice cracks as he waves to us,

'*Farewell, my friends!*'

'*Farewell, Burhwold!*' I call out for the three of us and loosen Braenda's reins for her to break into a slow trot out of the lodge yard to the whiteness of a new fall of snow.

Some of Godwin's men also wave to us as we set off on the road westward to Wara on the first leg of our long ride. Unbowed by Cutha's stern looks and furrowed brow, women and children flock to the gateway waving before the gates are slowly pulled to behind us.

'What happened to Guthfrith and his men? They were not here to see us off', Cyneweard sounds hurt by what he takes as a snub to our short friendship with them.

'Godwin must be glad to see the back of us, too!'

'Do not see him too harshly', Oslac turns in his saddle to look at the lodge before we take a turn in the woods and it is partly hidden from view by the still snow-laden trees. 'You heard Father Cutha. He is the one who made Godwin aware of his standing as a Christian leader. He must show himself to be a stalwart of the church, as his father was before him, and he cannot do that if his kinsman beds a spay wife, can he?'

Oslac laughs and turns to look along the track. Only the birds chatter loudly on this late winter's morning. The fore year will soon be upon us and the smaller creatures of the woods will begin searching for food again after their long sleep. The deer will need to fatten up again after the lean pickings of winter, and the wolves will make sure they do not fatten up too much! Thankfully the bears will not awaken first.

As we ride I see someone stir amongst the starkly bare trees ahead on the wending track.

'Someone awaits us! It could be an ambush', Oslac warns.

'Aye, I have seen', I assure him and allow Braenda free rein.

'Robbers, do you think?' Cyneweard sounds fearful.

I have to laugh at the fearful look he gives me,

'I hardly think they would show now if they were going to rob us!' I slap his back. I can see them better now. One lone rider stands out to the right of them. 'No, they are sitting waiting for us to draw near', I can see them better now, and one fine figure of a man stands out amongst them as a lone pine would on a hillside, 'that is where Guthfrith has been hiding!'

'Godwin thinks we are out hunting. He bade us good luck and went on talking to his brothers about what to do with Healfdan'.

He laughs as he thinks back on it,

'I would have slowly strangled him and left him for the wolves!'

'Healfdan has followers amongst Godwin's men', I warn. 'When he is sober he is a good leader, even if he shows little skill with weapons. Godwin cannot ride roughshod over those men he knows best for fear of losing them. The fyrdmen have not finished learning yet, so Healfdan will still be needed for some time to come!'

'Perhaps so, Ivar, but you are too even-handed. Healfdan has something more than luck on his side, I say', Guthfrith chews on his lower lip and looks disgustedly back toward Naesinga. 'We have been told by Lord Ansgar to do Godwin's bidding. We will ride west with them to join with Eadric in Hereford shire, whatever we ourselves might think of their undertaking. If the Northmen heard of Ansgar's dealings with Godwin, he could be in trouble!'

'Who would tell him?' I ask.

'Would you believe me wary of Healfdan on that score?' Guthfrith snarls. 'I have this feeling about it in my bones. He is up to no good but Lord Godwin trusts him, even though he will have to pay Wergild to Ingigerd's kin on Healfdan's behalf for her killing'.

76

'Perhaps Godwin will *not* help him out for much longer, if he has to put Healfdan on trial as a murderer', I know she has kin.

I recollect seeing a mother clucking after her daughter, chiding for not pushing Healfdan toward a wedding. No doubt she has a father, too. He will not stand by and allow his daughter's killer to be treated lightly for Godwin's sake.

'Hopefully there *will* be an end to that before we ride west', Guthfrith looks me in the eye. 'If only you were not so keen on the spay wife!'

I chew on my answer before giving it, making sure of my words before I utter them. Although Guthfrith is unlikely to go around at Naesinga passing on my warning, I am wary of some of his men. Aside from Godric and Hemming, they are unknown to me. I lean closer to him. Whatever I say aloud may carry in the still air,

'It is not so much that I will not deny *her*, but she seeks me out wherever I may be. She also watches over me, and for that she takes my lovemaking as her reward. Godwin is the loser, not I'.

Having looked around before I finish, I add in hushed tones, 'As for Father Cutha, there is something I do not trust about him. I would lay silver on *him* being fitzOsbern's man, not Healfdan'.

'I would not say too much about Father Cutha if I were you, Ivar. He has a greater following in these parts than you might think. Even Dean Wulfwin is wary of him', Guthfrith tells me in little more than a hoarse whisper.

'Saying he is in the Northman's pay may make things worse for you with Godwin'

When the sky darkens with the threat of more snow we look for somewhere to stay the night. We are a little way to the north-west of Hamelamstede, in miles almost a score-and-a-half from Naesinga - still easily within reach of Willelm fitzOsbern.

'I am looking out for an inn', I tell Oslac. We are each of us raking the skyline with our eyes. 'Do you see any lights?'

'Do you want to put your head down only a stone's throw from the nearest burh?' he asks me in turn, scanning the woodland ahead of us.

'You may be right', I answer, taken aback my own lack of foresight.

'We should ride some way on. We covered more miles than this each day riding from Lunden to Jorvik. Let us press on'.

'There was no deep snow then', Oslac allows for the weather we have suffered since this morning.

Cyneweard picks up on my use of the Norse name Jorvik,

'You mean Eoferwic, surely? I hope the two you are not going to start elbowing me out by using Danelaw names for Aenglish burhs'.

'I am sorry, Cyneweard', I laugh to cover my foolishness, forgetting Cyneweard might not like my use of Norse names, 'We will use the Aenglish names from now on'.

Oslac grins at Cyneweard. He has been with the young Seaxan for longer than I have. For all many of our friends at Naesinga were part Danish, such as Guthfrith and Hemming, there were nevertheless many Seaxans amongst Godwin's huscarls and fyrdmen. The banter crossed our different tongues and left one side or the other non-plussed from time to time.

As I press Braenda into a canter Oslac draws level with me. He leans forward in his saddle to call to me,

'Do you feel we are being followed?'

I look around and shake my head, a little tired from the long hours of riding. I fear my wits have been dulled by the pain in my backside from the saddle.

'In the woods, back there to our right, Ivar', Oslac points to where he thinks someone may be shadowing us.

I was looking in the wrong quarter.

When I look over my right shoulder I see a rider – no, two – following a short way behind.

'Is it just the two of them?' I ask Oslac.

'As far as I can tell, there are only two, aye', he calls back, having overtaken me in looking for any others who might be behind us.

Are they Northmen?' Cyneweard is fearful. 'We should try to lose them, do you not think?'

'Northmen ride in greater numbers; there would be at least six or seven', I assure him.

'These are our kind', Oslac nods.

'Then they might be robbers', Cyneweard looks worried now. 'Could there be others about?'

'There *could* be', I answer, grinning at Oslac. He shakes his head in disbelief at Cyneweard's fears. Sometimes Cyneweard shows himself to be timid, perhaps from having a mother like Aelfthryth, shielding him beyond childhood. Little wonder then his father despaired of him.

Pulling on Braenda's reins to slow her to a trot I look back again, but our 'shadows' have halted out of sight. Oslac is sure only two are following us, not scouts for a band of outlaws or Northmen.

'It *is* just the pair of them', Oslac belays my doubts with a wide grin, 'so we can ride on without fear of being robbed. I think I know who they are. When they are nearer we should let them show themselves and catch up with us'.

'How so - what makes you think we *should* know them?' I look back at Oslac and somehow I know who he means, 'Saeward and Theodolf?'

'I would not swear to it but we will soon find out', Oslac spurs his horse into a canter.

Cyneweard and I press our horses to keep up with Oslac, and when I look back our shadows have put on a burst of speed too. But why would *Theodolf* want to come with us when he has a woman to keep his bed warm, and a child to feed? And Saeward seemed to be happy to stay at Naesinga with Godwin. Still, we shall know before long whether it *is* them. The light is fading now and if they want to join us, they will have to do so before they lose us in the darkness.

'I see lights ahead', Oslac halts to let us draw level with him and points northward off the road we want to follow. If there is an inn here, this will be the only offer of a bed for the night for miles around. We still have our shadows behind us,

'I would say there is an inn ahead. Someone is leading horses to a building at the back', Oslac tells me.

I follow his finger and see the old fellow he means, and ponder aloud,

'*Three* horses being led to stabling?' Whose horses can they be? I ask Oslac, 'Are there any others?'

'Another fellow follows behind him with more', he shows me. 'Four, I think'. I count with Oslac whilst Cyneweard looks around for our shadows.

'Seven mounts altogether. They must be Northmen'. Oslac adds, looking my way. He waits until I look back at him before asking, 'What shall we do - go in after them or follow the road for longer, to look for another inn?'

I follow the two men with my eyes, chewing my upper lip. Running a finger across the bristle under my nose, I answer with a shrug and a sigh,

'We enter. *If* it is Saeward and Theodolf following, we look as though we do not know them. Should there be a fight they will help us. The odds of seven to five are better than seven to three'.

As we near the inn we see the fellows who had taken the horses from the Northmen, if they are indeed Northmen. The elderly fellow, with long, wispy grey hair, shambles toward us to take our horses. The other one, heavy, dark and oafish-looking, tramps back to the inn by the front door.

79

When the elderly fellow asks for the reins of our horses I ask him in turn who the horses belonged to that they had led to the stable when we rode up.

'They are from the Northman stronghold of Oxnaford', he tells me, 'sent out into the land around to oversee the gathering of tithes, and to keep from harm the king's men whose task it is to weigh each landholder's payment. They are here to see it is as much as they think it should be. Woe betide any landholder who wavers'.

'Did *they* tell you that?' I look askance at him.

'The thegn told me', he stares at me. '*I* cannot understand what the Northmen say'.

'That would tally with the seven horses', Oslac nods, looking at me.

'Who are *you?*' the fellow stares from me to Oslac, wary of us. From our manner we are as outlandish to him as the Northmen. Is he likely to warn the thegn and the Northmen within?

'We are traders, riding to Oxnaford to seek a buyer for goods we have from Flanderen', I lie, 'but if you are worried about our weapons, these are hard times, what with freebooters from the northlands and Friesland robbing honest traders of their cargoes. We need to be well-armed to take them on. What is your name, fellow, that I know to whom I should turn for counsel?'

'I am Aelfnoth. I look after the horses for the innkeeper, Bruning. He was the one who you saw going back inside after he took the other horses to the stable. I have a helper at the back of the inn who sees to brushing down the horses. Garwulf will take care of yours'. Aelfnoth brightens a little now, believing us to be harmless, and reaches for Braenda's reins, 'You are the *third* party to come since dusk'.

'The days are lengthening little by little, but the ride is still hard', Oslac smiles. 'No doubt others feel the aches from long hours of riding as darkness grips the land'.

'No doubt they do', Aelfnoth nods and eyes Oslac's bow warily as he leaves us to take our horses to the stable, leaving us to head for the door at the front of the inn. Aelfnoth calls out to us,

'Not *that* door - use the one at the other end'.

'Why should we use the side door -?' Cyneweard blurts. Oslac puts a great hand over his mouth to stem the flow of further words.

'I do not see why *we* should use the side door when the thegn and his Northman friends can use the front one. Is our silver not as good?' I too am angered by this unseemly fawning on the Northmen.

'Bruning wants it that way', is all Aelfnoth offers by way of answer. He throws up his hands in despair and looks glumly at us to show that he does not agree with his master.

'*Bruning wants it that way*', Cyneweard mocks Aelfnoth's reedy griping to laughter from Oslac and me. I look back and see Aelfnoth looking hurt after us as we make for the main door.

'Best keep the peace and use the end door as he says, Ivar', Oslac sniffs, grappling with his bow and saddle packs pulled from his horse.

I nod unwillingly and lead on past the offending door, throwing my own saddle pack over my shoulders and swaying with their weight for half the length of the inn. Cyneweard has little to carry and offers to take one of my bags, but I turn down the offer,

'They even each other out, weight for weight', I smile thinly back at him and stride on to the door.

As we turn the corner our shadows show themselves unhurriedly and behave as though they have not yet seen us.One of them does look like Theodolf, ungainly and raw-boned. Working the land must have suited him, but why is he *here* and is the fellow with him Saeward after all, as Oslac thinks?

The inn is warm and welcoming within. The overweight Bruning stands talking by a huge vat with a tall, wan young fellow who must be the thegn. They seem to know one another well enough for Bruning to laugh and joke with him. The Northmen have taken off their helms and unbuttoned their neckguards.

They are settling down with their welcoming drinks as we come to a halt just inside the doorway and drop our gear to the floor. Bruning's laughter stops when he sees us. He straightens up, stares dully at us and presses to know who we are,

'You look as if you might be outlaws'.

He casts a long look at our belongings on the wooden floor and asks my name. On being told he turns back to his guest, as if to say he thinks nothing of me,

'I have never heard of you', he sneers. 'Ivar, is that not a *Danish* name?'

'I am a trader who wishes to reach Oxnaford to find a named buyer for my wares. We have come a long way from Lunden haven and beds for the three of us would come in handy', I answer smartly, lying about the first part. Nevertheless my aching bones bear out a need for something softer than a leather saddle to put my head on for the night.

Bruning's sharp eyes take in my gear and light on my axe. He chortles and asks,

'What need have you of these weapons if you are a *trader?* Have you no men to fight for you? Is that axe for sale? The thing might take off someone's head in an argument. It might fetch a pretty penny if you are selling'.

'As I told your man Aelfnoth, we sailed here from Flanderen and the weapons are needed to see off Friesian and Norse freebooters. We are all Aenglish, Oslac and I from the Danelaw and Cyneweard is from Middil Seaxe, so why the unfriendliness?'

'You cannot be too careful these days'. Bruning no longer distrusts us or sneers. He bearing becomes easy-going, 'So many things happen at once. We get older, our taste for new things fades and our land is ruled by outlanders'.

'Oh, how so - what things have happened? We have been at sea since the summer, all the way from Ladoga near the Eastern Sea to Brugge', I fold my arms and wait to hear what he has to say. When he adds nothing further I add that we came back around the Danish isles and along the coast to Flanderen with fur pelts caught by the Finns and Rus fur trappers.

It goes against the grain to have to pretend to know nothing of what has happened in the past months. This is merely to lull Bruning and his thegn into believing I am indeed a sea-going man who has only lately reached these shores.

'You know nothing at all of what happened lately? The usurper Harold was slain and the rightful king, Willelm was crowned at the West Mynster. He is away in Northmandige, seeing to his affairs there. Willelm fitzOsbern is his steward here', Bruning tells me.

He is unmistakably their man, but at least knows what we would need to know were we newly landed. So fitzOsbern is the king's stallari northwest of the River Temese. I have to know more from Bruning, as he seems to be a wellspring of knowledge about the way the kingdom is ruled under the Northmen.

'Is this Earl Willelm the king's stallari over the whole land?' I ask, making him think I am in awe of the man's might.

'Bishop Odo holds the king's warrant south of the Temese from Hamtun shire eastward', the thegn answers for Bruning, 'and he seems at last to have mastered the Centishmen under his lordship'.

Oslac gives a snort. A gut feeling rises in me that his temper may get the better of him, but he claims he has been dozing off listening to us,

'I am sorry, Ivar, what was that about Centland?'

'We need to sit down before he falls down, Bruning', I smile, keeping up the sham.

The innkeeper takes his leave from the thegn's company and leads us to another door,

'Forgive me, friend. I will take you to a room with three bed closets and warm, soft beds. You will be well looked after, as three of Lord Gilbert's men will be in the next room'.

Bruning lights a new candle and in his rolling gait strides ahead, up steep, narrow stairs and waits as we struggle manfully with our 'wares', up creaking treads and await our host as he lumbers up past us and fishes out a huge key from his apron. Cyneweard with my second bag finds it heavy going behind me and breathes heavily under the weight,

'Ivar, what have you got packed away in this bag?' he cackles when he finally lets the bag drop onto the floor outside my room.

'All our silver from Ghent and Hammaburg is in there', I lie.

What I do have folded away in there is a Northman hauberk. What Bruning would make of that in my bag needs no deep insight. He would warn his Northman masters before we had time to make our way back to the door.

'I thought you said you traded in Brugge? No matter, Ivar', Bruning checks himself with Cyneweard's talk of silver, 'You must be rich!'

Oslac looks sternly at Bruning, and at me, and asks,

'Ivar, why put it about that we have riches in our bags?'

Have I given us away to a man with a wit much sharper than his looks let us think? The innkeeper ogles the bag, plainly wondering how much silver could be in there that could be so heavy.

'What did you say you were you selling there?' Oslac asks me, still making out he was asleep.

'We had furs from the east and sold them in Brugge', I repeat what I said earlier, looking at the bag, 'And that in Ghent we bought goods that I knew my buyer in Oxnaford would like. I cannot tell you too much about it because he would want to be first to set eyes on them. You know how it is with customers you wish to keep'.

'You need say nothing more'.

Bruning winks and pushes open a groaning door for us. 'Let me know if you need anything. Lord Gilbert should be here soon, I must be downstairs to greet him as befits a man of his standing'.

'Be assured', I remark, 'that we will test your hospitality to the utmost, and tell our friends far and wide'.

'That is as much as I would hope from you, friend', Bruning grins, showing blackened stumps. He hands me the flickering candle and makes his way back downstairs, whistling tunelessly.

5

When we drop our bags and weapons on a short table I look around in the dancing candlelight at the sparsely furnished room. Save for the three bed closets, one that takes up the width of the room and two side-on opposite, there is only the table, a straight-backed chair and a couple of benches.

'By the look of you, when Bruning spoke of this Lord Gilbert, you knew the fellow', Oslac suddenly speaks up.

'Be still, there may be someone listening at the door!' I warn him before he says any more, although I may have said enough already myself.

Cyneweard goes to the door, opens it noiselessly, and looks around in the gangway. He closes the door, shaking his head,

'Surely we would have heard creaking from beyond the door'.

Before I speak further I stride to the door, look up and down along the gangway and close the door as quietly as I can,

'How many Lord Gilberts can there be amongst the Northmen?' I ask, adding, 'Not that I think either of you knows the answer to that, but I have had dealings a Gilbert de Warenne twice now. I do not doubt if we meet again I shall not be so lucky a third time'.

'Are we to stay in this room all night, then?' Oslac makes no show of liking our room.

'By no means do you need to stay in this room, Oslac. You and Cyneweard can go downstairs. Eat, drink, let them think you are merry', I give him some silver, enough to buy more than they need, 'and learn from the thegn what he knows. Ply him with ale'.

Looking up at me Cyneweard thumbs his dagger and asks,

'Do we *need* to know the name of this thegn?'

I look at my young friend and nod gravely,

'Aye, it would be useful to know who it is we may one day have dealings with again. If he so easily binds his oath to this Northman king of ours, I wonder, can Godwin trust him?'

'I should ask how soon this thegn thinks he will see his Northman master', Oslac yawns. 'It may not be this evening. We shall be gone anyway. I will send Cyneweard to let you know'.

'That would be kind of you. We should not trust Bruning too much', I steer them both to the door. 'His greed has been awakened by my story of wares from overseas for a buyer in Oxnaford. He may try to sneak into our room to see for himself when he thinks we are not looking. Best tell him I need to rest, and if he hopes to take me unawares he will be deeply distraught at finding my blade at his throat'.

'What about the pair we think are Theodolf and Saeward?' Cyneweard asks before they leave the room.

'*Should* Saeward and Theodolf show, send them to our room when you think no-one is watching. Bruning and the thegn can be lulled into thinking there are only three of us. I should like to ask Theodolf what he is doing here, and if it *is* Saeward with him they can show together around the door'.

I close the door behind them and walk to the table to ready my food. My stomach feels squeezed. Nevertheless as I take my bags to the bed-closet I hear rapping on the door.

I call out loud enough only to be heard through the door,

'*Who is there?*'

'Open the door and find out', Theodolf answers testily. I do not need this from him.

'Come in, the door is on the latch, not bolted. Tell me, why you think you need to follow us. You have a wife and Dunstan's child to take care of', I laugh and throw my bags into my bed. When I turn again Theodolf stands at the door grinning sheepishly. '*Well,* what have you got to say for yourself?'

I find it hard to keep the scowl. Breaking into a wide smile I have to ask him,

'Have you taken leave of your senses, following *me?* You have a woman to keep your bed warm for you!'

'She will keep. She might even miss me whilst I am gone, unless your kinsman finds his way to her bed again!' Theodolf's grin turns to a look of sadness.

'Why would he do that?' I lose my smile too. When I think of the new-found joy Theodolf showed when he first set eyes on Gerda, I too, feel a deep sadness for him.

'You believe the worst in your new bride?'

85

'Remember what he said when he had your axe in his hand. Does it lie, or can you deny what your *own* eyes and ears told you?'

Theodolf feels he has been betrayed by Gerda.

'Did he mean *your* Gerda?' I try to comfort Theodolf, but he will hear no plea for her good name.

'How many women are there at Naesinga named *Gerda?*' he throws his head back and cups his face. 'Why *else* would he wear that pained look whenever he looks my way?'

'We do not know who he bedded before we met him in Lunden burh. How many women with the name Gerda do you think live in Lunden burh or in the southern half of the kingdom? There must be a fair number of women with the same name!'

Theodolf stands looking at me through his fingers without saying a word, rocking backward and forward. He brings his hands down to his side and tries to smile, leaving me to guess at what can come next. Yet when I think he is about to take a softer line on Gerda he tells me simply,

'I have brought Saeward with me'.

'I thought so. Bring him in here', I answer. 'I want to know why he has come with you'.

Theodolf opens the door and looks to the left.

He whistles softly, as if summoning a hall hound and Saeward shows moon-like from the darkness, smiling.

'Your room is as bare as ours!' Saeward looks around from the safety of the doorway, thinking perhaps to be rebuffed harshly by me.

'It is likely the Northmen's rooms are stuffed with all the trappings of comfort', is all I can bring myself to say. 'We have a chair and a couple of benches, and a small table to eat at. What more should we need?'

'Is this the Ivar we know and love?' Saeward laughs, 'Where is that hatred of the Northmen that we have come to know you for? We could finish off these sots downstairs in the twinkling of an eye. Just give us leave to send them to their makers!'

I put a hand over his mouth to calm him down and tell him under my breath,

'We will let them go their own way, along with that tithe-gathering thegn. No-one is to know where we are headed. When we are west of the Seoferna we will need to ask about the whereabouts of Eadric, and there will be Northmen everywhere there, too. Eadric will take them wholly unawares when he does strike. Their lords will be at a loss what to do. For now I am a trader'.

Saeward hangs his head in mock shame and grins sideways at Theodolf. They seem to have grown closer in these last weeks, since Godwin entrusted them with teaching his fyrdmen their war crafts.

'You will have time enough to slake your thirst for Northman blood', I feel I have to chide Saeward for his blood-lust.

Theodolf chortles, drawing my eyes to him.

'You would never have known Saeward had misgivings about using his weapons Thor and Asmund made for him', Theodolf gives me food for thought.

'We must pay our respects to them when we are in Lunden burh again', I feel as if I had shunned them since I passing their workshop on my way to see Eadgar, but there was no time to look in on them before having to flee Willelm's clutches.

There is a knock on the door and Cyneweard enters. He stands behind Saeward and Theodolf. The three of them greet one another eagerly before Cyneweard scratches his head to think about why he has come upstairs to see me, and tells me after a short, awkward stillness,

'The thegn is Aethelhelm. He does not think he will see Lord Gilbert before they begin their ride back to Oxnaford'.

The lad adds, by way of a warning,

'Thegn Aethelhelm wishes to speak to you of this fellow of whom you spoke to Bruning. He said to join him in a drink with Oslac'.

'Are you going down?' Theodolf asks of Saeward.

'No, I feel drowsy. Ivar, speak to this thegn Aethelhelm and I will watch over our things', Saeward tells me, looking sleepy.

'You already *look* half asleep', Theodolf stands over Cyneweard, thumps him awake and turns to me, 'I will stay with the fellow and keep watch on your things, Ivar. Bring me a flask of ale back with you'.

I take his right arm by the elbow as I pass him on my way to the door and grin as I warn,

'Of course I will bring back some ale for you, just as long as you stay awake to drink it Bruning strikes me as a sly sort of fellow. I would not put it past him to try to meddle with my ale and glean knowledge would otherwise not part with'.

'Wise words, Ivar, I would not put my trust in that toadying Seaxan either', Oslac joins me as we pass through the door. He stops suddenly and groans, 'I *am* sorry Saeward, Cyneweard. I did not mean the pair of you'.

When I show in the main room Aethelhelm stands, shows me to the bench on the other side of a short table, and pushes a beaker across the table toward me.

'Ah, Ivar, come join us and tell me about the world beyond these shores! Ale for our friend here', he waves at a handsome young woman to pour for me.

Oslac and Cyneweard sit close by, and thank the alewife when she fills their cups after mine.

Once seated I turn to the young thegn, giving him a friendly smile before asking him,

'Which of the lands beyond our sea would you like to hear about, Thegn Aethelhelm?'

Eyes wide on my using his given name, he licks his lips quickly and looks from me to his Northman friends.

'Can you begin by telling me who is the lucky fellow in Oxnaford, for whom you brought the wares Bruning speaks of?' Aethelhelm wastes no time in demanding knowledge I was loath to give the innkeeper.

'You should really not press me. His name has been withheld on his own wish. When I speak to him I shall ask if he has anything against your knowing what it is I have for him. It is enough for me to say he is a Miercan of good name, and may be known to you', I feel like a hunted buck at bay, keen hounds snapping at my heels.

'Tell me, then, is Count Baldwin well?' Aethelhelm tests me again.

'Which Count Baldwin do you mean? The old one died, and his son sits in his court in Brugge. I would say he is well -', I begin to answer, but I am cut short by one of the Northmen, who asks,

'Did you meet Tostig Godwinson's widow, Judith?'

'I do rightly know her', I lie, and stare him down. 'Nor do I know the count to speak to but by name. I am trader. For me knowledge of nobles and their kin is of use only if they buy goods from me. I may recall their names for when I see them next'.

'Aye', Oslac adds from where he sits by the hearth, warming his hands on the crackling open fire, 'it meant little to us who bought the amber sold to us by an eastern merchant. Nor did it mean much who sold us the ermine that we sold on to the Frankish nobles when we docked in Saint Valery. With our bulging purses we can buy a new sail or pay to have the bottom of our ship scraped –'

As I lift my cup to my mouth, the Northman who asked me about Judith finishes his ale and bangs the cup down onto the table before demanding of me,

'I think you *do* know of whom I speak!' He bangs the cup on the table twice to summon the alewife.

Before he can ask me any more the innkeeper cuts in,

'*Where is Saint Valery?*' Bruning asks. He has been standing listening to Oslac and his curiosity suddenly has the better of him.

'Saint Valery is on the coast near Le Havre ', I enlighten him.

Bruning seems to be happy with my answer, as does Thegn Aethelhelm. I daresay neither of them has ever been beyond Dofnan.

Had I told them Hammaburg was near Koenungagard they would be none the wiser. One of Aethelhelm's Northman friends listens more keenly than the others. I wonder how much he understands, or whether it is because I spoke of somewhere he knows of.When I look his way, he raises his eyebrows and turns to speak to a comrade in his own tongue. They laugh loudly, one of them casting a look of pity at Aethelhelm as he sits there, raptly listening to me telling of our sailing the Eastern Sea.

Aethelhelm and Bruning are happy for now. Neither of them bothers me again during my story-telling, which suits me. I down my ale, hold up the beaker for it to be filled again and go on telling yarns. It is not long before I begin to feel drowsy. Yawning and stretching, my back aches with a longing for sleep and I have to ask the thegn's forgiveness on leaving him,

'We have a long day ahead, Thegn Aethelhelm'.

I stand and plant my legs stiffly on the hard-packed, straw-bedecked earth of the inn floor, stretch again and make my way to the stairway. My head begins to spin and a deep blackness engulfs me. The ale was tampered with! Beyond that I know nothing more of what happens. My knees buckle and I hear Cyneweard yelling out to me from somewhere far away,

'Ivar, what is the matter with me?!'

I awaken trussed on the inn floor next to Oslac, my head still spinning. Looking around the main room of the inn tells me nothing, but I hear talking from beyond a door behind me. Aethelhelm can be heard over his friends, speaking the Northmen's Frankish tongue.

Oslac stirs beside me. He looks over one shoulder at me, groans loudly and lowers his head once more onto the brackish-smelling earth floor. He mumbles,

'Bruning put something in the ale, and it was not his piss!'

'I would say that, aye. What can we do about our being trussed like fowl here on this stinking dirt floor?' I answer, craning my head around to see him.

'I would not know. A knife would be handy, though. What is happening through there?' Oslac jerks his head toward the door behind, as helpless as I, on his back looking up at the beams. He must wonder how we could have been taken in by the callow Aethelhelm. The thegn has outsmarted us and now has us at the behest of his Northman lord, wherever he may be.

'Do you think Cyneweard has a knife?' I ask.

Oslac groans before answering,

'I hardly think he is awake to ask'.

I turn myself over onto my stomach to see where Cyneweard is and see him flat on the floor near where I had been sitting.

'How do we get away from *this?*' I hear Oslac ask.

I cannot begin to think, but sense someone else close by.

'Do not think you can escape this time', I hear someone say behind me, someone I know from elsewhere. With some effort I turn my head to look toward the stairway.

I see a tall fellow in the gloom, half-lit by the open door. He stands on the bottom step, leaning forward with one hand flat against the beam over the stair bottom. In the other hand he holds a half-eaten apple. With my head aching from Bruning's foul ale, and my hands and legs trussed like a fowl ready for the slaughter I can do little. Thinking is still painful, but something is coming back to me.

This fellow has crossed paths with me before, more than once from what he tells me. Through the grey fog that still veils my sight I look at him and try to think. With no little effort something takes shape... It dawns on me that the Lord Gilbert Aethelhelm spoke of is Gilbert de Warenne.

'You led us on a merry dance around Lunden, Ivar Ulfsson', his mouth twists. My hunter has caught up with me again!

'You outfoxed me twice, and fled our grasp the third time with your friends here', he nods toward Cyneweard and Oslac. 'Now I have you again, and you can rot in Lord Willem fitzOsbern's dungeon for all I care. The king will demand you be handed to him when he comes back from Rouen. You will be out of my hands soon, in the new stronghold at Northwic where you will await the king's pleasure', de Warenne smiles thinly but says no more.

He must have been told not to harm me, else he would have done me some mischief with his spurs by now. After all, I have made him look foolish before his masters more than once. I can not have harmed his outlook too badly, or else he would not have been made lord over Oxnaford.

'You have not done badly by your new king', I offer by way of filling time.

De Warenne sneers at the way I make light of my plight, but cannot hold back from gloating,

'He saw something in me, as he did with my elder brother Willelm. Whether or not I have bettered myself, your prospects look dismally bad. Your friends will fare no better', de Warenne takes his hand from the beam and lets his left foot drop to the inn floor. He stands idling in a sudden shaft of sunlight when Bruning stamps through the door.

'From where I lie here I might agree with you', I think to myself, 'for now'. It seems to me that many of the highest of this king's lords share his name, but young Gilbert here might not share their name, nor does he share my insight. Now I have other things to think of, such as the whereabouts of Saeward and Theodolf? They cannot be asleep still, surely. I know Saeward is dead to the world until his eyes open with the cock's first crow, but dawn came some hours ago. And what of Theodolf, did he sense something was amiss since we did not go back up to our room last night?

Whether Bruning went up to look in my saddle bags is a moot point, too. My guess is that when Oslac, Cyneweard and I fell asleep, he was kept busy with Aethelhelm's demands to bind us and forgot about looking for my wares. Cobwebs drop onto me from above, loosened from the rafters by someone in my room. Neither de Warenne nor the young thegn saw the cobwebs fall, or hear the faint creak of floorboards.

Neither of them sees the cobwebs draped across my nose and forehead that I feel whenever I blink. Aethelhelm and Bruning leave the room and go outside.

'Will we be allowed to ride our horses?' I ask, trying to blow away the cobwebs.

De Warenne answers drily without looking at me,

'I shall not make the same mistake again'. He strides to the door to talk to the thegn and Bruning outside before turning back to me. 'No, you will be bound over your saddles like bags of grain until we reach Lord Willelm fitzOsbern's stronghold at Hereford. I shall ask him for your horse as my just reward for catching you. She is a beautiful animal, *too* good for the likes of *you!*'

He strides around the room, humming and helping himself to Bruning's best ale. There is smugness about him that may come useful later. I am sure Saeward is upstairs somewhere, wondering what has become of us. Gilbert de Warenne goes to the door and calls Aethelhelm to him,

'Thegn, have these three taken to their horses', he barks loudly. 'Let them be tied over their saddles. They will not escape me again!'

There is still no word of the other two; are they even in the inn? Aethelhelm barks something to his Northman bodyguards and the doorway darkens once more. Cyneweard, Oslac and I are man-handled out to the stable, where Aelfnoth, downcast at the fate which has befallen us, has saddled our mounts. Only three horses are led out.

'Were there not two others?' Aethelhelm asks Aelfnoth, 'I am sure two others came to the inn with them late last evening'.

'I forget, my Lord', Aelfnoth answers meekly.

He looks down at the earth by Aethelhelm's feet, hoping not to be asked anything further lest he gives away anything that could endanger our friends. He would not need to deny ever having seen them, as a denial would only bring swift rebuke, perhaps a whipping. So he leads the thegn to believe that an old man's memory is failing him.

Aelfnoth must have seen them away already if their horses are no longer in the stable. He knows where they are, I am sure, but says nothing to us for fear of de Warenne or Thegn Aethelhelm overhearing and prising knowledge from him.

'Where you are going, you will not need your swords and axes', Aethelhelm smiles wanly at me and goes on, 'I have told Bruning he will get a good price for your weapons. That axe looks as though it could be worth a lot of silver'.

De Warenne signals his men on when he thinks they are ready, and the three of us jiggle about over our saddles as we pass over the rough ground eastward toward Hamelamstede. Having spent some time on my half-brother's ship across the sea from Roskilde Fjord eastward as well as westward, I do not fell the bumping about as easily as does young Cyneweard. From the look of him, my young friend must wish he had stayed in Saewardstan.

Oslac may show wear before we make our first stop.

We pass through woodland going westward, the going good over crisp snow. Saeward and Theodolf leave my thoughts as I listen to the birdsong on this sharp, sunny morning. When we round a bend on the road I hear an arrow hiss through the air. Our rearmost guard is struck through his windpipe and he slides, mute from his saddle to the road. His horse trots on. Neither de Warenne nor Aethelhelm know what is happening behind them as one by one each of our closer guards drops to the road, the last with both hands clutching at the goose-feathered arrow in his chest, eyes wide in still-born horror. Only two Northmen behind Aethelhelm are spared, because they are ahead of us, too close behind their leaders to see anything untoward.

Saeward on his mare comes quietly up to Braenda from behind and takes the trailing reins. Theodolf holds his bow at the ready, following the Northmen until Saeward signals him with a songbird call. They rein in without a sound and cut our bonds.

Aethelhelm and de Warenne ride on, too far ahead to know what is happening, thankfully deeply gripped with their talking to know that we are about to leave them. We are not too far west from the inn that we cannot out-ride them and take our weapons from Bruning, before sending the young lord on his way with a flea in his ear.

Before de Warenne rounds the next bend he looks back beyond his few remaining men and his jaw drops.

He yells at what few men he has left to ride after us, pointing his sword at me and screaming in his own tongue, but too late to stop us. The five of us ride like the wind through the trees, cutting across the bend in the road, risking life and limb over the branch-strewn woodland floor. Theodolf and Saeward take up our rear should any of de Warenne's men threaten to catch us whilst we are still unarmed.

A hidden dip could spell ruin for us. The Northmen's horses thunder on after ours, scaring birds and small animals as they crash through dead bracken, dead tree trunks and undergrowth, ducking under low overhanging branches. They know they must try to cut us off and catch us before we get to our weapons.

The ground rushes up us as we duck beneath the last of the lower branches before we come back to the road we followed last evening. Once back on firmer ground, our horses quicken and we see the inn through the trees. Theodolf reins in and turns his horse, hoping to bring down another Northman, or even Aethelhelm, to put them off chasing us.

I yell back at him as Braenda thunders toward the inn,

'Hold them back - just long enough!'

Bruning is shocked to see us stride up to the main door and backs away into the darkness of the inn. I snap at him when he tries to bar my way in,

'Where are our weapons?!'

'*What weapons?*' he cowers behind the half open door, snivelling, then pushes the door to in a bid to slow me down.

I kick the door in on him and grab him by his fat neck as he tries to fend me off,

'*Where are our weapons?*' I demand again, 'Bring them – *now!*'

Theodolf has caught up with us now and stands outside, to one side of the door with his bow at the ready again. I do not know if he has brought any others down. Saeward stands with his axe at the ready at the other side of the door.

'*Where are our weapons?!*' Oslac threatens the ashen Bruning, his right fist on the innkeeper's chest, pushing him back onto the wall beside the door.

'In there – *you will find them in there!*' Bruning prods the air, panic-stricken, to his right. He yelps as Oslac begins to rain blows on his fat stomach and whimpers, his jowl low over his right shoulder, '*Have pity!*'

Cyneweard elbows open the door of a side room, frightening the young maid on her knees on a cot-bed. She points fearfully to a corner of the room and tries to hide behind her bedsheet.

If he were not pressed to get our weapons, I think Cyneweard would take her here and now without a second thought.

Theodolf, back at the inn, looses off a couple of arrows and brings down another of Aethelhelm's Northmen. We now have an ashen-faced Gilbert de Warenne and his tithe gathering thegn Aethelhelm at our mercy with only one man left from their bodyguard.

In no hurry to meet his maker, Aethelhelm's nerve leaves him and he turns his horse to flee, but de Warenne grabs his shoulder belt before he can leave and brings him crashing to the ground.

'*Run,* will you, craven Seaxan?' the Northman kicks his underling and pulls his one remaining man back before *he* can make for safety. But holding back two faint-hearted men proves too much for him and he too feels the urge to flee.

Rubbing his bruised shoulders Aethelhelm scrambles back onto his mount and rides for dear life after his Northman master. The three of them make a sorry sight, their horses pounding headlong over new snow back to Oxnaford, followed by our jeers.

Having found our war gear we help ourselves to Bruning's best ale from the vat kept for Aethelhelm's men. Aelfnoth joins us and offers a toast,

'I drink to your lord who will turn back the Northman tide!' he licks his lips mischievously.

'Aye, and who might that be?' Oslac asks as he tightens his sword belt and takes up his bow from an array of stolen belongings.

'Why, the lord *you* fight for!' Aelfnoth answers, his eyes wide open. He looks taken aback by Oslac's seeming lack of understanding.

'We have no lord', Cyneweard answers as he and Oslac gather our things. There are many other men's swords, daggers and axes in the wall cupboard behind the maid's bed. I wonder how many others he has drugged and handed over to his Northman masters.

I cough for Bruning's stable man to look up at me and tell him,

'What Cyneweard means, Aelfnoth, is that we seek Thegn Eadric in Hereford shire', I put my sword hand on his shoulder.

'He is with the Wealsh aethelings', Aelfnoth chatters. 'Something is afoot in the Wealsh foothills to the west of Hereford. In the aetheling

Rhiwallon's stronghold he and his brother Bleddyn have joined Thegn Eadric and the Northman lords are afraid of attacks on their new wooden strongholds. That is why they need the tithes, to pay for new weapons'.

Oslac beetles his brow threateningly at Aelfnoth, and then beams broadly,

'For an ostler you know a lot!' Oslac regales the old man with a loud burst of laughter, and slaps him on his shoulders. Aelfnoth finishes the ale I poured into a beaker for him and is about to help himself to more when Bruning shows behind him and pulls the beaker from his hands.

'*You leave that ale alone, idle wretch!*' Bruning snaps, slapping Aelfnoth over the head with the flat of his fat hand. The old man's matted grey hair flies into his eyes as he tries to duck his master's spite and he cowers on the earth floor next to the vat.

'Bruning, you fat turd!' Saeward yells, giving us a rare insight into his otherwise good-natured soul and balls a fist under Bruning's nose, pushing him against the wall behind.

'Why not finish him off now?' Cyneweard pulls out his dagger and stares balefully at Bruning, scaring the fellow out of his wits, 'After what he did to us, I think killing him would be a kindness when you think what *else* we could do. Come here, Bruning while I cut the hairs on your backside with my dagger!'

'Whatever you have aforethought for him, Cyneweard, it will have to bide another day. We must be away beyond Oxnaford before we can think of stopping again'. I warn my friend of the long ride ahead, 'We must reach the Wealsh hills soon, if we are to find Eadric before he takes on Willelm fitzOsbern in Hereford'.

All eyes are on me now, and then my friends' gazes alight on Bruning. I have been careless enough to outline my aims in front of him and he may just warn his friends.

A very frightened Bruning tries to hide from Cyneweard under a table before we let him loose with his dagger. Oslac looks under the table and glowers at the innkeeper, who jerks his head back into the darkness and bangs his head on the table leg behind him. He begins to shake and whimper in sheer terror. Aelfnoth is there first, amazingly quickly for an old man, and draws Theodolf's dagger from its sheath before my young friend can stop him.

Bruning's end is bloody. His last breath leaves his mouth in a gurgle of red froth as he flops over onto one side with a long cut to his windpipe. Aelfnoth's revenge must have been long in coming, but was blindingly swift.

'Do any other Northmen know this inn beside Lord Gilbert?' I ask the old man, wondering whether he might be missed. It will look odd to them if the ostler suddenly seems to be running the inn.

He shakes his head, looks down at his erstwhile master and then looks me steadily in the eye,

'Sometimes the Northmen stop by on their way to Hamelamstede. I could say Bruning is away visiting his sister'.

'He has a sister?' I try to think of a woman perhaps as ugly as he and put away the thought. A cold shiver runs down my back at the thought that someone else in this world might look as ugly as him. Aelfnoth weighs his words before answering,

'He does indeed – or *did*, as he is now dead. You would never believe brother and sister were like chalk and cheese. She was here once, when Lord Gilbert first came and he took a shine to her. He was moonstruck, poor fellow'. Aelfnoth looks down again at the dead Bruning and scowls. 'Aye, she looks altogether unlike him. I think perhaps her mother must have gone with another man!'

'Why, what does she look like?' Saeward asks now, as if we had time to ponder just how un-alike they could be.

'What does it matter what she looks like? We must be away. Lord Gilbert will be out after our blood!' Oslac curses Aelfnoth for bringing up the matter and stalks outside to mount his horse.

'You may as well answer him now', I nod to Aelfnoth, press Saeward's right shoulder and joke with him, 'as he seems to be looking for a woman – *any* woman'.

I follow Oslac and leave Theodolf and Cyneweard with Saeward, calling out to them on my way out through the door,

'Be out soon, friends. Time presses and my friend Gilbert de Warenne will be back, if he is not on his way already!'

When Theodolf leaves the inn ahead of Saeward and Cyneweard, he gives me a sly grin and tells me coyly,

'You should have stayed to hear Aelfnoth out, Ivar'.

'What does *that* mean?' I lean over and fix him with a keen eye, looking closely into his as he answers.

From behind Theodolf Saeward booms,

'It means Bruning's sister has red hair and her name is Braendeswitha'.

'How many red-haired Aenglish women do you think there are with the name Braendeswitha?' I laugh, 'There must be *hundreds!*'

'Aye you are right - *hundreds!*' Theodolf echoes my words and swings himself into his saddle. He looks pained and rubs his behind where the boar butted him.

'I felt that too', I pity him with that wound. Fighting the Northmen after being wounded twice in such a short time, even months ago, will not be easy. He needs a longer rest. We will see how long it takes before he begins to miss his Gerda's warmth and caring ways, and we have to tell him to make his way back to her.

Setting aside thoughts of Bruning's sister being my hwicce lover I turn her namesake onto the road west,

'We should give Oxnaford a wide berth and ride northward before going west', I offer, waving farewell to Aelfnoth and the maid

Cyneweard snorts,

'How long before they share a bed?'

'I would say not as long as it would take her to share your bed!' Oslac taps him open-handed across his cheeks with both hands, 'Come, Cyneweard, if we make Hereford tonight I will pay for a woman to bed you!'

'You think you would have to *pay* for one? Am I not handsome enough?' Cyneweard mocks himself and sets us all off laughing. We are still laughing when we see polished metal glinting in the winter sunlight through the trees of a copse on high ground.

'Do you think Lord Gilbert is already back?' Saeward asks. We slow to a trot and I look up across the sunlit clearing.

'Whoever it is, I hardly think Gilbert de Warenne has ridden so fast from here to Oxnaford and back', I answer, holding up both hands to shield my eyes to look around for any others and shrug, 'There are no others to be seen, *anywhere*'.

'So who can it be - Northman or Aenglish?' Oslac asks.

'Without asking them, I cannot say. Keep riding west and see what happens', I answer, watching to see if they turn our way.

Much as I would like to know, without going out of our way to see, they would have to show themselves before I rightly knew. If they are Northmen, I would like better odds. If Gilbert went back to Oxnaford, where did Aethelhelm go? Would he not be with him, on pain of punishment? His lands would be made forfeit by our kind-hearted king, as others –living or dead - have been robbed of theirs.

'Whoever it is, they might not even be looking our way', Theodolf offers more in hope than wise counsel.

'They will be looking our way', I have allow, pressing Braenda into a canter, 'but we can only hope they will be slower than us, their horses not being as fresh as ours. Come, let us put on a burst of speed and see what happens'.

We spur on our mounts and I keep an eye out for whatever these unknowns do. If they are watching us to see which way we leave, they will make for us. As it is we have not ridden far before the riders break from the copse and make for the road.

'Now we will see how fast they can ride!' Oslac spurs his mount into a gallop and we follow his lead.

When I look back I count at least a half-score of men in full chain mail with long shields. Their war gear will slow them enough to give us a good start.

One of them waves his long shield over his head as if signalling – to *us* or *others?* A of scan the wide dale shows me there is no-one he could be signalling to. Is he be trying to warn us? We will give them a run and see how friendly or otherwise they are before we stop to ask questions.

'Is he trying to signal to us?' Saeward yells, echoing my thoughts. 'That looks like a Northman's shield he is waving'.

'Keep riding', I yell back. 'Just keep *riding!'*

He spurs his mount to ride three horse girths to my right. Oslac is already ahead, Cyneweard and Theodolf behind us.

The five of us are riding furiously westward before I call out loudly, 'Head off - *to the right!'*

Oslac looks back at me and I point northward. He nods and pulls his reins to bring his mount about. It takes him a little time to catch up with us, riding toward the brow of a low hill with a stiff breeze blowing across our path. When we come to a rise I see there are more riders coming toward us from the north-west.

'God, who are *they?* We will be caught in the middle if we cannot out-ride them all!' Saeward calls out to me, trying to be heard over the gusting wind.

On looking back I see the same fellow waving his shield again and another has begun waving his above his head, a *round* shield.

'They must mean us to stop!' Saeward yells above the pounding of hooves from my right, having looked over his shoulder more than once to see who they are. Cyneweard shouts from behind,

'The ones behind are not Northmen, those ahead *are!* They have lances, not spears!' he points ahead at the riders who carry pennons on their lances and brightly painted kite-shaped shields.

I rein in hard, turning Braenda's head sharply to the right and hope I have not hurt her. A little thought is in order here and those riders ahead are fast closing on us. Oslac is furthest ahead and I have to shout him back. He can not have heard as he rides on, but suddenly draws on his horse's reins when he is hazardously close to the leading Northman riders. When I think Oslac is looking my way I point back. He nods and we four turn about. The nearest of our pursuers from behind is only a short gallop away now and beams as he nears us. He takes off his helm to show who he is.

'Osgod, what are *you* doing here?' I yell against the wind as he rides up to me, half-hidden by the shield he took from a dead Northman at Lunden Brycg. 'Listen we must make a bold show. There are a score of Northmen behind the brow of the hill there!'

'They are close behind you already, Ivar, faltering', Osgod laughs, pointing at the Northmen who have drawn up sharply and mill around less than a quarter of a mile behind us.

They must have thought Osgod's men were their own and that the five of us would put up no fight.

'I think perhaps more than a show of boldness will be needed. Harding, take some men with you and chase away these hungry-looking wretches!'

A tall, heavy-boned fellow with a fiery mane that sticks out from around the rim of his helm, Harding looks too big for a horse. A bushy red beard hides his neck from sight. With him are a number of Osgod's men I recall seeing at Lunden Brycg, one of whom was almost thrown off the bridge for cheeking me when we came out of Centland.

If he can fight I may forgive him, but I am not sure Oslac would, even if the fellow single-handedly fought all Gilbert de Warenne's men.

We watch as Harding and his half dozen Northanhymbrans give the Northmen something to worry about. They beat a hasty retreat back over the hill, out of sight, as we laugh and jeer.

Osgod roars above the din of cheering,

'Blow your horn, Aelfhelm. We would not want Harding to over-reach himself and chase them back to Oxnaford!'

More cheering welcomes Harding and his heroes from behind the brow of the hill.

'We thought you were about to chase them all the way back to Oxnaford, Harding!' Osgod laughs and thumps his friend on the shoulder. 'Here is the best man I can think of for chasing stags, Ivar. He looks as big as a damned stag himself!'

Harding reaches over to greet me and his hand almost dwarfs mine. He grins toothlessly at me and looks back to Osgod,

'Now we are rid of them, what to do?'

'We are to ride west with Ivar and his men, Harding. Lord Maerleswein has told us to annoy the Northmen without letting anyone know who sent us!'

By way of an opening Osgod tells me,

'Harding has a freeholding by the River Leofen at Rudby with a hundred and fifty sheep to his name –'

'They *were* one hundred and fifty before the Scots drove half of them off. Tostig was in Rome with Earl Harold, which is why King Maelcolm thought he could raid', Harding curses, and then smiles disarmingly, adding – as much to tell Osgod as me,

'Luckily I have made up most of the numbers since then. Do you have land Ivar?'

'I have no land, friend. That is why I am fighting for Lord Godwin, to wrest the crown from Willelm for him and hopefully be given a thegn's land somewhere', I answer ruefully.

'You are fighting for Godwin, you say?' Harding stares, 'Is that Godwin Haroldson?'

'Ivar is a kinsman of theirs', Osgod warns him.

'I thought Eadgar wanted to be king, as was his grandfather and those before him', Harding sniffs. 'Are the Godwinsons chasing the crown for themselves?'

'I offered my sword to Eadgar, and for a few weeks I and my men were his huscarls but the earls and churchmen sold out to Willelm for fear of losing their land and rights. Foremost amongst them were Eadwin and Morkere. Some were even ready to pay for what belonged to them!' I brace myself for whatever else Harding might have to say against Harold's sons or kinsmen.

'They sold him out to *Willelm?!*' Harding barks, taken aback as though this is the first he has heard of it, and stares at Osgod, 'Is this true. *Did* Morkere and Eadwin sell out to the Northman bastard?'

Osgod nods unwillingly.

'You knew about that?' Harding almost knocks Osgod from his saddle as he pushes him.

Osgod nods again and throws me a look as if to say, 'Why did you have to tell him?'

'Where were Harold's *sons* all this time?' Harding stares at me as he asks.

'They say they were with King Maelcolm, and knew of the loss of their father only when they rode south into Beornica', I answer, altering Godwin's words a little to make him look better, although I cannot see why. I owe him no loyalty since he let Father Cutha turf me out of Naesinga and a warm bed. It would not look well in these men's eyes if I were to tell them that my spay-wife's fixation on me led to my being cast out by Godwin's priest.

'Is Godwin coming west?' Osgod asks, glad of being let off the hook. He is still Morkere's man when all is said and done.

Not knowing what else Godwin's are I answer,

'He hopes soon to ride with Eadric and Rhiwallon. For the time being his men are learning their fighting skills near Wealtham in East Seaxe. They are short of good men and we were teaching them the finer points of the shield wall'.

'Sticking spears up their arses to keep them in line and their eyes ahead?' Harding snorts at his own wit.

'They are good men', Saeward's gruff tone sobers Harding. 'Many are mere ceorls or freed men, their thegns having died with King Harold. The last time they were attacked they saw off Tostig's raiders in East Aengla'.

Harding looks bemused and raises his eyebrows at Saeward. Osgod is glad Harding can be dumbstruck by the feats of others and claps his hands to show his liking.

'Tostig ranged far and wide along the southern and eastern coasts before he set sail northward to meet Harald Sigurdsson, making several landfalls. He was beaten back with greater losses each time', Osgod allows and nods, rightfully stirred. He asks Oslac about his fighting skills, 'Did you also fight Tostig's men, Oslac? I saw you with Theodolf here when we threw back the Northmen at Lunden Brycg'.

'Aye, but Tostig's Flemings were mostly rabble, at least those that landed in Centland. Tostig kept his best men aboard. There were quite a few who landed but they were no bother. We sent them packing, back to their ships. By then they numbered a score or so less. No stomach for the shieldwall', Oslac, jabs like a man fighting off an attacker.

He grins at the now open-mouthed Harding, who must have thought everyone in the south to be soft and untried in fighting.

'They were given a taste of my arrows in their arses!' Oslac laughs out louder now in rasping union with us all.

'I hope they were well aimed – *where it hurt most!*' Harding guffaws, his deep laughter sets off the rest of us again into painful fits of laughter.

We are ready now for any Northmen who may challenge us now on our way west to join Eadric.

6

Low snow clouds scud westward across low hills behind us as we enter Hereford shire. Crossing the River Leagadun we skirt Lithbyrig from the hills around Maelferna. This is a part of the kingdom I have never before set foot in, nor do I think have any of the others with me. We need to be careful here if we are to stay out of sight of Willelm fitzOsbern's men. The less anyone knows about our being here, the better it will be for Eadric. When we hit them we shall send them running back to their masters.

We stay away from the burh with its welcoming inns, warm fires, hot food and good ale... and its Northman guards.

We still need to find ale, food and an innkeeper with a short tongue. The food is easy enough to find. It is all around, on four legs or with wings, growing in the earth or in trees and bushes. The ale we cannot brew, being out on the road, and alewives like to be indoors at this time of the year... as does anyone in their right mind!

Osgod calls out to me, echoing my thoughts as we ford a small river that feeds into the Leagadun, downriver from Lithbyrig,

'We should look out for somewhere to stop for the night, to ease our saddle-sore backsides'.

I answer, to laughter from the nearest riders,

'My stomach was telling me the very same thing'.

'*Moreover*, we need ale to quench our thirsts', Harding echoes my afterthought, 'and soft womanly flesh in our beds'.

'Too true - we all want some of *that,* and whatever else comes with it', Osgod coughs into his hand to more laughter.

'There is smoke rising from behind the trees over there', Saeward calls out. He is above all this chatter about women and draws a few knowing glances. 'Shall I ride on and see if there is an inn there?'

'Aye, and we shall take our time catching up', I draw in the reins to slow Braenda to a walk. Osgod and his men do likewise.

'Why are we slowing down?' I hear Oslac ask. He has brought his horse alongside me together with Theodolf and Cyneweard.

'Saeward has gone on ahead to see if the smoke behind the trees there comes from the hearth of an inn', I tell him and waffle a finger after the vanishing Saeward, who has now entered the woods. 'We are taking our time to catch up with him. If there is somewhere to stay he will signal from the trees over there'.

'Good! My tongue is turning to parchment', Cyneweard agrees.

Before anyone has time to talk further about the worth of a halt at an inn, Saeward shows again between the trees and waves with both arms high over his head. He is too far away to call to, so we urge our horses into a canter. When we are close enough I call out to him,

'Is it a big inn?'

'As big as the one we stayed in last night, although I could not tell you if the innkeeper is friendly.

'Somewhere out-of-the-way like this is bound to be friendly', I assure him.

'Why worry over whether he is friendly or not?' Harding snorts. 'He will soon open his doors wide when he sees our number!'

'We do not want to upset anyone here and turn them against us', Osgod reminds his friend. 'We are only fighting the Northmen and not the whole of West Seaxe or Mierca'.

'*God forbid!*' Harding answers, tongue-in-cheek. His broad grin tells me I should not put it past him to start a riot anywhere in this part of the kingdom.

'*I mean what I said*, Harding!' Osgod rebukes him sternly. Although they are both thegns, Maerleswein has given Osgod command.

'We are far enough away from Northanhymbra, with almost all of Mierca between us and Eoferwic that we do not want to have to ride back with our tails between our legs! Lord Maerleswein said not to behave churlishly toward these folk'.

'Do you *honestly* think I might be heavy-handed with these good folk?' Harding sniffs and takes on the air of a man affronted.

'I *know* you!' Osgod has the last word and Harding throws up his hands with a wry smile at me.

As we ride on with the late birds calling and flying homeward across the darkening greyness, The daylight is fast dying in the east beyond the hills.

The bare topmost branches of the taller trees in the west show like dark, beckoning fingers against the pale red of a sunset fast clouding over. It takes little time to reach the inn, riding at a fast trot uphill. As we near the building I see a homestead close by. Other dwellings stand ringing a thwait, a broad green ringed by tall trees on which children gather to watch as we dismount. They are joined by some of their elders.

'Who owns the land here?' I ask the nearest of the youngsters, a lad of perhaps twelve summers, who does not flinch when I dismount and walk toward him.

'My father holds these acres around us', the lad answers, 'from our lord –'

'His name is Willelm fitzOsbern', a tall, rangy fellow with a mop of dark hair comes from behind his son and draws him aside with both hands on the lad's shoulders.

'You are the landowner?' I must sound taken aback because he stares at me with ice-fire coloured eyes.

'No, as the lad said, I am the land*holder*. The man who should *owns* the land is in Wealas right now. His name is Eadric. Who are you?' the fellow squares up to me.

'I am Ivar Ulfsson', I answer, and put a hand on Osgod's shoulder. 'My friend here is Osgod, a thegn from Eoferwic'.

'He is a long way from his lands', the fellow is sparing with his words, 'and you are even farther from home, Dane'.

'We are on our way west', I bear him out, hoping not to give anything away, and wondering how he knows me to be a Dane. Having lived long with Harold and his kin, I pride myself in speaking the tongue like an Aenglishman.

'You are on your way to join Thegn Eadric', he tells, rather than asks me after looking our men up and down. I do not deny it, but smile briefly and say nothing.

'I wish I were free to join you. My new Northman lord is a grasping fool. Having crossed Eadric with his growing demands for tithes, and a foolish demand for Eadric to swear another oath of fealty to that bastard king, he leans on *us* all to make up the shortfall in his coffers!'

'What holds you back?' Harding plants one ham-sized hand on a fence-post and puts his weight on it.

'I have to keep the inn since the innkeeper fled to Wealas, his son killed by the Northmen for slighting fitzOsbern! If we do not till this land it will go to wrack and ruin. The woods have a way of growing back over clearings, and I have worked too hard to let this land fall back to what it was before – dense wilderness!'

I nod gravely by way of an answer.

In the fight against the wildwood the struggle is never-ending, and I would not be happy to see the trees and undergrowth take back my land if I were he.

'You have not told us your name, friend', I remind him.

He looks me up and down, takes in Osgod and, pointing at Harding, he counters with,

'He has not told me *his* name yet!'

Harding bristles and says nothing until he feels Osgod's stare,

'I am Harding, of Rudby in Deira', he proclaims stoutly.

'Well, Harding of Rudby, as you are plainly proud of your birthright, I am Osferth of Poteslethe'.

Osferth steps forward and greets us with a bright, toothy smile that seems to break up the darkness of his heavily bearded face, 'and this is my eldest son, also called Osferth'.

'There must be some laughter in your hamlet when your wife tells off your son for misbehaving!' Harding treats us all to his grating laughter.

Osferth loses his wide smile and looks solemnly at Harding before answering,

'She can no longer tell off either of us, friend. She was killed when the Northmen rode into our hamlet and killed Wulfric'.

'What can I say - how ashamed I feel at my foolishness? Can you ever forgive me?' the Northanhymbran clasps his hands together in front of him and casts his eyes down, abashed at his own shortcomings.

'You were not to know. None of you has ever been here before', Osferth calms him and makes toward the inn door. 'Come into the inn and we shall drink to her. I see her daily when I look at my three sons. Young Osferth has her eyes and skin. I have my sons to cheer me when I feel at odds with myself'.

He nods at two other young lads who follow us into the inn, neither of whom can have lived more than six or seven summers. The others of the hamlet go about their tasks as though we had never set foot in their hamlet. Our being here will add little light to their lives once we are gone again.

'There is enough food, but if you wish to stay overnight there are not enough rooms', Osferth tells me. 'Some may sleep in my barn'.

Osgod is first to ask,

'How many rooms do you have, Osferth, and how many beds?'

'I have four rooms, one with three bed closets and the others each with two', Osferth and watches closely we try think on who should bed down in them.

'Draw lots', Harding offers.

'Osgod and I can share the room with two bed closets', I tell Osferth, adding, 'Harding and two others can share another and that leaves two rooms with two beds each for everyone else to draw lots for'.

'I have a better way', Cyneweard looks Harding up and down and then says, 'we *all* draw lots'.

Osgod looks from Cyneweard to me and a smile slowly spreads across his mouth,

'How do you stand for this Ivar?' he asks, taken back by the ease with which Cyneweard speaks to me. 'Do you always do things this way, with your men overstepping the mark?'

Osgod is a thegn, and his word is final with his men. He has been given the leadership of these men, given to him by Maerleswein. I, on the other hand, will have to rely on my friends again in times to come for fellowship when Osgod and I are apart again. I cannot afford to upset them. My nod signals to Cyneweard that I am ready to draw lots with the others but Osgod will still have none of it. He tells his men what they will do, and they follow him.

'Do what you feel is right for you, Ivar. I will share a room with Harding and the other rooms can be shared out by lot, as you wish'.

Cyneweard looks at me and nods, acknowledging that I have given way. He will look back on this one day, when we are in a tight corner, and hopefully do something for me. He looks sideways at Osgod, who pointedly ignores him and begins to talk with Harding. Cyneweard asks Osferth for reeds to cut for the lots and is shown to the back of the inn,

'There are reeds outside, left from when we mended the thatch on the inn. There may be some that are useful for you', Osferth watches after Cyneweard as he vanishes into the darkness.

He then asks me, pointing to Saeward, Oslac and Theodolf,

'Are you their friend or their leader?'

A stiff westerly wind blows at us when we leave early in the morning, taking the edge off the coldness of the hills. Having readied us all for the day ahead with hot porridge, bread, cheeses and ale, Osferth shows us the road to follow,

'Take the left fork when you reach a church in the settlement of Hope and bear west. Soon you cross the River Wye as it courses southward to Rossa and the River Seoferna', he pauses to let us grasp what he already told, then goes on.

'At Ewyas your way leads northwest along the Black Mountains. Someone will take you from there to Rhiwallon's stronghold in the western foothills. I hope you have warm clothing, because you will climb up over the high tops!'

'There is no way through?' Osgod looks worriedly at Osferth, then at me and turns to Harding, 'Did you bring your thick woollen shirts and fleece robes?'

He grins hugely at me, as if it were all a great joke, and claps his hands together,

'Then let us to it, friends!'

My own thoughts are that the cold can be no worse than on the tops of the moors above Hviteby, so why is Osgod so fearful about scaling these Black Mountains?

'These mountains cannot be any higher than those between Sciptun and Kirkeby Ireleth', Harding laughs, hauls himself into his saddle and pulls hard on the reins to turn his horse into the wind. The beast is skittish and prances, unwilling to head into this blustery wind. The big fellow swears and fights to regain mastery of his horse.

'What has got into her?' Osgod turns to mount his own horse, but she dances sideways away from him, bumping into Braenda, 'Come on, horse - behave!'

Osgod still has hold of his horse's reins but she will not let him anywhere near her until Osferth walks up to her and strokes her neck slowly. He waves Osgod to mount as he does so and she stands stock still, her eyes rolling back. She then eases and is ready to ride.

'*Your* mount knows how to behave', Osferth looks up at me and looks Braenda over with the eye of one who knows horses. 'She is Wealsh?'

'Aye, from the north, from Gwynedd', I answer, patting the side of her neck.

Saeward takes it upon himself to tell Osferth,

'She was bought by Earl Harold at Ivar's behest'.

'*You* told Earl Harold to buy horses in Gwynedd?' Osferth asks me wide-eyed.

'He was going to buy Wealsh ponies anyway, as he had heard they might be good mounts for hunting boar', I make it plain that my kinsman was in no way beholden to me for counsel in buying horses. 'A well-known swine breeder had several of these fine animals to sell–'

'You bought the horses from Ifor of Menai?' Osferth breaks into a broad smile and pats Braenda gently on her neck.

It is my turn to be taken aback,

'That was his name. You know of him?'

'He is my brother-in-law', Osferth laughs. 'He offered to look after my sons when he heard of his sister's death but they stayed with me because they know nothing of the Gallic tongue. Many of our Wealsh kinsmen speak no Aenglish'.

'How did you meet your woman?' I ask Osferth, 'What was her name?'

'I was with Earl Aelfgar when he first joined with Gruffyd', Osferth eyes me warily. He knows somehow that I was with Harold. He goes on, 'Raiding far into West Seaxe. Her name was Rowena, and she was a handsome woman'.

'And she had a handsome name', I agree and turn to see Saeward cross himself.

Osferth smiles at this and adds - to be of help to me – why he thinks my friend is so fearful,

'He is crossing himself because of the myth. Rowena was the name of one of Vortigern's queens. She was hwicce, a spay wife'. He points at Saeward, still smiling, and asks, 'How does he know of the legend, and why does he cross himself after all this time? That was *long* before the Seaxans first came to this green island the Celts called Britain'.

'It would take too long to tell you the whole story, but in short I have a woman who shows from nowhere from time to time. Her name is Braenda', I make clear the link, 'the same as my horse'.

I am about to loosen the reins for my horse to walk on when Osferth asks,

'Is she a Miercan woman with flame-red hair, who was the housekeeper of Gruffyd's widow Aeldgytha?'

He smiles when he sees me troubled at his insight.

'Aye, she was', I nod. 'She is now Harold's widow.

This is too eerie to be true. Is there no-one or nothing Osferth does not know?

'I know her, too', Osferth confirms my worst fears, 'but not in that way. She was my wife's friend'.

'It is time to ride before the weather closes in over the mountains', Osgod is bored with our talk of spay wives and hwicce.

To me it is all too uncanny, and from the corner of my eye I catch sight of Saeward crossing himself again. I call back to Osferth as we leave the inn yard,

'She was in Eoferwic when I next saw her, given in wedlock to an oaf called Sigurd. He was killed by an outlaw near Richale'.

'*She* had him killed', Osferth answers, 'and Thegn Eadwy was *her* tool'.

Osgod's head seems to have been almost wrenched around and he blenches with disbelief. He looks at Osferth as if the fellow had grown another head. Next he looks at me and asks, almost choking the words,

'Did he say that Thegn *Eadwy* killed Sigurd?'

'He did', I bear out what Osferth told me.

'How does *he* know that?' Osgod looks around for Osferth, 'Where is he now?'

'Likely he has gone indoors. God, it is cold suddenly', I put my head down against the sudden chill. The wind gusts down from the hills and I look over my right shoulder one last time. No-one seems to be around now. It is as if everyone had suddenly gone in to their hearths... as if they had gone from this earth.

'Come, let us put this hamlet behind us', Harding shudders quickly and spurs his horse into a canter. We all follow into the wind, keeping our heads down against a sudden squall. The cold rain hits my helm and runs over it down onto my collar.

'Did you see there was no church here?' Saeward crosses himself again.

Jiggling his knees against his horse's withers to hasten her, he has heard enough of spay wives and the departed. His Christian beliefs have been sorely tested this morning since we parted company with Osferth. I have an uncanny feeling that this is not the last we have heard of Osferth and his ilk. The hairs on the back of my neck feel strangely tight, stiff.

Throughout the afternoon we have been climbing steadily since leaving the banks of the River Monnow. There is a settlement below us to our right that must be Ewyas, but our road climbs further yet. Entering the settlement could be foolish, firstly because we would find it harder to regain the higher ground.

Secondly I see there are Northmen swarming between the ceorls' scattered wattle and daub dwellings.

'Do you think that is Ewyas?' Osgod asks me, pointing downhill at the dwellings.

'It must be. This is the road Osferth sent us on. We can call a halt whilst Cyneweard rides into the settlement –'

'Why would he do that, when there are Northmen down there?' Oslac breaks in, thinking I have not yet seen them.

'There are, I know - *how many?*' I ask, craning my neck. Oslac beckons me on, where I can see between the homesteads.

Osgod follows and peers down at them. Ant-like, they are doing what Northmen seem best at, looking busy for their lords.

'What are they doing?' he asks.

'I would say they are measuring the land', Harding tells him, 'to build a stronghold'.

'How can you be so sure?' Osgod looks from Harding to the Northmen, and at me, 'What have you seen that I have not?'

'They have marked out the side of the hill with red and white wooden pegs', Harding watches them, busying themselves with sighting.

From what we can see he is right. The site is one *I* would pick for a stronghold. Harold had likewise marked it out for himself when he was earl. Near to the road, it sits above the dwellings, overlooking the dale both ways, south and east. Unless the good folk of Ewyas leave soon, they will be pressed into building the Northmen's stronghold for them. Not wishing the Northmen to know we are here, we will not ride into Ewyas.

'There are only ten I can see', Harding licks his lips, keen to take them on, sizing up for a fight the few armed men they have with them.

'What would we do with their corpses?' I ask in turn. 'They will be missed. Besides, these are only the ones we can see from *here*. They might have others close by. Leave them be and we will seek out an inn for the night somewhere higher. Turn left and follow that track', I show Osgod where I mean to ride for and draw left on Braenda's reins.

Osgod, Harding and the others follow. The track drops behind a screen of trees and bushes, allowing us to bypass the site where the Northmen are taking stock of the dale below them. A short way ahead the track rejoins the stony road and Cyneweard watches the surveyors for any sign that they might have seen us until we are clear. He rejoins us not long after, urging his mount over stony ground to my side and soberly shakes his head when I look at him. We have not been seen for now.

Darkness creeps across the dale below as a low cloud follows us slowly uphill, until the only light we can see is from between the hills far to the west. Where we are the rain has begun to fall steadily. Through breaks in the hard-chased clouds above us pinpricks of light show brightly and all too briefly, like prized stones against the hillside.

In the blackness of the night I see light smoke trails pushed by the wind that comes as thrown by giants on the bleak, bare, threatening mountains around us. Where Wealas is from here I do not know. I have to guess that we are close, and that our road leads west by north from here.

My thoughts go back to when we were riding with Tostig, burning as we rode along the north coast of Clwyd, beyond the River Deag. Earl Edwin's men had sullenly watched us ride past Ceaster behind Tostig's boar standard.

Aelfgar their father had once raided Earl Harold's lands with Gruffyd but they had done nothing to help their western neighbours. It was for the Northanhymbrans to ride across northern Mierca to deal with Gruffyd in his Gwynedd stronghold.

Now Harold is in his grave, Tostig exiled in Flanderen and we ride to help an Aenglishman and his Wealsh allies against a Northman invader. Times are odd indeed.

To our left a beck gurgles downhill toward the Monnow. Sheeting rain is driven across the land when we finally find a hamlet we think to be far enough away from Ewyas not to be infested with Northmen.

We leave the looming mountains and follow a well-trodden track into the dale below us.

Sighs of relief come from Osgod's men as we near the settlement. Passing what looks like an old burial mound, we drop down between the homesteads and smaller dwellings. A river rolls steadily by, a short way to our right as we pick our way in the dark. We are looking for an inn or a barn. Any building will suit our needs, to get away from the sheeting, cold rain.

Someone leaves the shelter of his home to ask if we are looking for someone,

'Who is it you seek?' he peers up at Osgod, who nods toward me. I offer some small talk after telling him,

'We seek shelter from this grim weather'.

'This *is* a foul night to be out in, aye', he agrees with me. 'There are no inns here. The nearest is at Middil Wudu'.

'How far is *that?*' Osgod betrays his lack of neighbourhood knowledge.

'I would say now that is too far from here to ride through this night. How far have you come?' the fellow asks.

'We left Poteslethe this morning', I begin to answer, but stop because he throws his hands up into the air as if to ward us off. He blenches and crosses himself, as Saeward did this morning on taking our farewell from Osferth.

It is as if we had been straying amongst the damned.

'There is no-one left *alive* there, not since the outlanders stopped and paid their respects to Thegn Eadric!'

Saeward crosses himself, again and again and stares back at the fellow, who backs away from us, wailing,

'You cannot stay here, you are accursed!'

'I *knew* there was something wrong there!' Saeward curses and turns to me. 'Now we have to ride further into the night. I for one am too tired to ride any further! Can we not find somewhere nearer the river, up there – a barn perhaps?'

'You must *leave* here!' the fellow presses, slapping Braenda. I feel as if my horse was being pushed by strong hands and look down at the wild-eyed fellow over my shoulder.

Harding snaps angrily,

'What are you talking about? We stayed at the *inn*, where Osferth fed us and put some of us up in his barn. I am going no further this evening. Show us where we can at least get out of this driving rain until the morning!'

'*Spirits*, they are - *not* real folk, the Northmen killed them all for holding to Eadric', he fearfully recounts as I stare disbelieving back at him.

'Osferth said it was his *wife* who was killed, trampled under by their horses. He and his neighbours seemed real enough to *us*. What do you say, Osgod?'

I am tired, hungry and testy. The hold-up is needless, a barrier to our finding somewhere to rest the night. If he upsets our men with his wild tales of spirits I fear I may strike him down before we go on our way.

'They *were* all killed', another joins us, holding a torch at shoulder height. '*Believe* me, friend, the corpses were left out for the ravens and wild beasts to feast on. But you need to get out of this cold wetness. I can see Saegar is annoying you. How many of you are there?'

'There are a score or so of us', I answer for everyone, 'and we will pay for food. This foolish talk of demons does none of us any good!' I cast a withering look at Saegar and he scurries back to the warmth of his home.

'Follow me', the fellow tells me, 'I am Wulfric. Mine is the last house along the road', he goes on. 'We were once not so inward-looking, but since Eadric crossed the Northman lord we have been paying five-fold tithes, *and* working all day to make ends meet. You say you can pay your way. I will be grateful if in the morning you leave everything as you found it'.

He limps along beside Braenda, holding onto her saddle,

'I will not ask what your aim is in these parts, as to be party to your plans will only put at risk the wellbeing of my neighbours, such as they are. Life in these parts is bad enough these days without our being fraught by the bastard Northman duke's underlings'.

Osgod shudders with the cold and offers thanks for our host Wulfric's hospitality,

'If you can stable our horses, and sell us hay to feed them we will be beholden to you'.

'I have stabling enough for most your horses. Any others will have to be kept in the barn. It is not safe to keep them out of doors at this time of year. Wolves and bears abound here, and the smell of horses would bring them down from the hills miles away', Wulfric points at the thickly wooded hills beyond and then tells us, 'Behold my garth!'

Wulfric's home is pallisaded. Logs, nearly twice the height of a man on horseback, have been driven into the earth and sharpened at the tops to keep out wolves. A wood-built barn stands to our right – I would have thought big enough to hold a score of any lord's mounts. Ahead is a long, low wooden building which must be stabling. To our left as we enter through a gateway is a stone-built hall big enough to be the hall of a thegn.

'Eanwulf', Wulfric calls out as we near the hall, 'come out of your warm corner and help stable these men's horses!'

A bent, wizened old man shows from a side door and fusses over our horses, taking the reins from Osgod's men and drawing their mounts behind him to the barn. Another fellow, much younger, closes the gates behind us and brings down a long bar across iron brackets to make them safe against the world beyond.

'Eanwulf has been with me a long time, as you can see', Wulfric tells me as he leads my friends' horses after his old hraeglethegn, 'and he asks no awkward questions. His only need nowadays is for a warm corner to sleep in. Randwulf is the younger man. He and Wulfgifu, his woman, live at the back of the hall. The best of my men are out in the hills to the west somewhere with Eadric and Rhiwallon'.

Osgod and I lead our mounts into the dry barn.

'Are you a thegn?' Osgod asks when our horses are taken from us by Eanwulf, helped by Randwulf. We follow Wulfric back to his hall as he tells how fitzOsbern seized authority from him after Eadric and he refused to offer their loyalty to the new king.

'Like Eadric, I am a thegn who first withheld my oath from the Northman king. I had to bethink myself. Now King Harold is no longer with us, we have no Seaxan lord to keep us from harm'.

Wulfric lights one of the torches in the hall from the one he has been carrying. He goes on to tell us of what has happened lately and re-kindles the other wall-mounted torches until the hall is lit well enough to see one another well enough to know who was who.

'Unlike Eadric I have not been hounded from my home', Wulfric tells us as he light the last one. 'There, I think that is all of them. Now I will call my wife, Aelfflaed to see what we can do to make you feel at home. I gather you *are* looking for Eadric?'

'We *are* looking for him, aye', I relish the thought of putting something warm into my belly after a long ride without rest, and rub my sore backside. 'With luck Lord Godwin will come soon with his brothers and huscarls'.

'Lord Godwin – *Haroldson?* And by his *brothers* you mean Eadmund and Magnus?' Wulfric peers closely at me and shudders. 'I know what it must feel like to ride all this way up here from Poteslethe without a rest. I have only walked into our hamlet and back and yet I feel chilled to the bone! You were saying that Godwin Haroldson has men - *to fight the Northmen, you mean?*'

A handsome woman enters the hall and walks slowly toward us with her hands clasped together on her apron front. She asks,

'Are we giving these men food and shelter for the night, Thegn Wulfric?'

'Wulfgifu, do we have enough to feed a score of hungry young fellows?' Wulfric puts a hand on a slender shoulder.

'I *think* we have... I *hope* we have, Thegn Wulfric', Wulfgifu looks overcome at the sudden demand on her skills at furnishing so many outsiders with food at this late hour, yet she nods and curtseys for her master before leaving us to go out through another door.

'Good. The food we were keeping for our men will come of use', Wulfric calls after her. He turns back to me,

'You must tell me your names, first you'.

'I am Ivar Ulfsson –'I begin.

'You were a huscarl with Tostig Godwinson, then with Earl, er, King Harold', Wulfric breaks in. 'Of course, I knew I had seen you before. You passed by Ceaster on your way west to deal with Gruffyd. I rode there to pay my good wishes to Earl Eadwin's father, Earl Aelfgar, with a plea for pity on behalf of one of my tenants. I am sorry, *go on'.*

Wulfric stands by me as I tell him who my friends are. Finally, when I show Harding to him, he opens his eyes wide and grips Harding by both hands,

'Kinsman, how long has it been since I last saw you?!'

'You are kin to Harding?' Osgod is non-plussed as am I.

'He is my sister Aethelgifu's eldest!' Wulfric laughs at seeing Harding and looks him up and down in wonder. 'The last time I saw you, Harding, you were still learning how to *hold* a sword, let alone know what you were meant to *do* with it! Have you mastered it, yet?'

'I would like to think so', Harding laughs and hugs his uncle tightly, as if wishing not to let go of him after not seeing him for so long, 'I *hope* so, anyway, otherwise I will be no help to this thegn, Eadric!'

'You are far too humble', Osgod slaps his friend on the back. 'I would say Harding *has* mastered the sword, *and* the axe - and *bow* even. His holdings are as overrun with wolves and bears in winter as yours are, Wulfric, so he needs to look after the deer in his woods and the kine in his fields'.

'Osgod, do I not know your father and brothers in Staefford?'

'You take me for another, I think', Osgod answers. 'I was a huscarl of Morkere's until he had me made up to thegn by Eadgar. I only hope *my* lands are not taken from me by these self-seeking Northmen!'

'You would not be the first', Wulfric smiles warmly and leads us to a covered vat at the back of the hall.

'Nor would you be the last, by any means. My age should speak for my standing in the kingdom, but I am no longer thought of as highly as I once was - not by the Northmen anyway. You will all join me in a cup of ale, I hope'.

None of us is likely to turn down an offer like that and we all await our turn as Wulfric ladles ale into our cups until. Finally we stand, cup at the ready to drink to the health of our host.

'*Ale wassail!*' Wulfric roars when he has filled his own cup to the brim.

'*Ale wassail!*' we chorus Wulfric's salute and slake our thirsts with his ably brewed nectar.

Saeward finishes his drink first and belches loudly, bringing gales of laughter from us.

'Your manners leave a lot to be desired!' Oslac chides with a wry smile.

'He plainly enjoyed my ale', Wulfric beams and laughs warmly. 'Being a man of learning, he has given his second opinion!'

More ale, Saeward - Is my ale better than Wulfwin's?'

Saeward is stunned at Wulfric's knowledge and asks how he knows about his background,

'Ivar did not point out my having been at Wealtham'.

'I was once a guest of Earl Harold, together with Earl Aelfgar, when he was first made Earl of East Aengla. He suffered the hospitality, not admitting that he enjoyed it because of his mistrust of all things to do with Earl Godwin's kin', Wulfric recalls fondly. 'When Harold was Earl of West Seaxe, Aelfgar paid his respects to him again at Wealtham with little more zeal', Wulfric claps a dish-like hand on Saeward's shoulder, 'and you, my friend, you were but a lad serving at the table with your brother'.

Saeward looks crestfallen. Beorhtwulf must have been in his thoughts all this time, somehow and he has borne himself well these past months, despite the loss of his brother to Garwulf.

'Have I said something untoward?' Wulfric asks, looking from me to Saeward.

'His brother Beorhtwulf was killed by a brawling fool at the Earlsburh in Eoferwic', I tell him, but not that Osgod had to take Saeward back there for the revenge murder of a drunken fool, unworthy of the name Eadric. Some memories are best left unspoken of.

Wulfric does not ask what the brothers were doing in Jorvik, and comforts Saeward with another cup of ale,

'You can never hope to *forget*, but you can ease the pain of sorrow with good ale, Saeward. Drink to your brother – what was his name?'

'His name was – is Beorhtwulf', Saeward mutters.

'Beorhtwulf *should* live on, aye. We shall all drink to Beorhtwulf!' Wulfric lifts his cup, 'A toast to Beorhtwulf!'

'To Beorhtwulf, *all hail!*' Osgod takes up the call and we chorus his salute to Saeward's good brother.

Wulfgifu makes her way through between us to her master and tells him something, I cannot hear what for the loud talking taking place between Saeward and Harding about the merits of our host's ale. Wulfric bangs his empty cup on the table twice and calls out to us,

'I am told our fare is simple this evening, my friends. We slaughtered a young bull in honour of a young couple who wed yesterday. Tonight we have broth and cold cuts from the meat and bones, with bread or dumplings and turnips. We have the last of the windfall apples, too!'

Wulfric beams at the cheer this news brings from our number and takes Osgod aside to talk to him. We meanwhile make our way to the table, I earnestly talking something over with Osgod. He and his men seat themselves at either side of the table on benches that have been drawn there by two of Wulfric's household.

Wulfgifu comes back, a board laden with bowls and a pot in her hands,

'Eanwulf brings more', she assures Wulfric, who, listening to what Osgod has to say, merely nods his acknowledgement to her. 'Everyone will have enough'.

The first of Wulfgifu's broth is greeted with slurping and lip-smacking before Eanwulf shows with another board laden with the second pot. Those of us who have allowed the others to begin eating sit back and he fills our bowls with good, wholesome hot broth from his pot.

Another, plainer-looking woman brings boiled turnips and dumplings that are quickly wolfed down.

'Aelfflaed sit down. You are my wife, talk to my guests and leave the fetching and carrying to Wulfgifu, Randwulf and Eanwulf', Wulfric grips her hand when she nears him, '*Sit*, woman!'

116

When Wulfgifu shows next she has a basket of apples, which she sets down in the middle of the groaning table. Talk is loud, sounds of eating and belching drown out her wishing us all a 'Good night'.

Those few who have heard her nod and raise their cups in thanks to her for a well-earned square meal. The rest laugh and joke between mouthfuls of ale, washing down the last of the food.

On looking up from talking with Osgod, Wulfric sees Wulfgifu leave for the kitchen once more and tells me,

'Ivar, would you be so good and go after her, thank her for me? I did not hear what she said just now and only know now that she was wishing us a good night. Thank you, Ivar', Wulfric looks back to Osgod and takes up where he left off.

I follow Wulfgifu out to the kitchen.

'Wulfric has asked me to thank you for your good work', I tell her when I catch up with her.

Wulfgifu answers coyly without looking at me. Her manner is not offhand because she is busy doing something on a work table,

'My lord, Wulfric is an open-handed master'.

I stand there, watching her as she cleans a knife.

'Have you also had a long day?' I ask her. A foolish waste of my time answered with a mere nod. She still does not look at me and I quickly lose interest in her and go back to the main room to take my seat again.

7

Wulfric rises from his seat at the top of the table and walks slowly toward Osgod, sitting beside me and chewing on a morsel of meat from the broth. Stopping behind me he looks over my shoulder and asks my Northanhymbran friend,

'Do you think Wulfgifu likes him?' he asks about me.

'I have a feeling she might', Osgod laughs, looks at me and winks.

'Do you think Ivar should seek her out in her bed?' Wulfric presses Osgod further, hoping perhaps to stir me into pursuing her.

'Does she not have a man?' Osgod asks Wulfric in turn.

'Aye, she has a man. He stands behind you', Wulfric answers, pointing at a sullen Randwulf and bursts into laughter before adding, 'and he is a *watchful* man!'

I am sure Wulfric had been drinking before we came and has had too much. Is that also the reason for him taking us in?Osgod's men stare in disbelief at Wulfric. My friends know there is more to come. It is in the air and they are not let down.

'Would you say you are a better weapon master than I am, Ivar?' Wulfric stands behind me and puts his hands on my shoulders. He demands that everyone listens.

'I would say that when you are sober you might strive to beat me in a fair fight, Wulfric. Why do you ask?' I answer, looking across the table at Theodolf because he seems to mirror Wulfric's wit. His eyes meet mine, and then roll upward. When he looks back to me again he nods.

'Turn to look at me, Ivar, when you speak to me in my own hall!' All warmth has left him. No longer the open-handed host he was, he fills the hall with an air of threat. There is something else afoot here. A spirit who would wish me harm has taken over him.

I turn on the bench to look up at him and he takes a step back, an old man who has overreached himself in his cups.

When his eyes meet mine I see the burning fire of far-off youth. No sound comes from anyone in the hall. We eye one another, as if I had dared him fight me.

'In the morning you will be keener', Harding tries to calm Wulfric, 'more able to match Ivar's cunning'.

'Why wait until morning? We can clear the hall of tables and benches and have this out here and now', Wulfric does not sound as afraid as he should.

Not wanting to back down from a useless, foolish dare that he has built himself up to, Wulfric fears he must follow it through, I see that in his eyes. Was this why he sought us out? Or did he happen to be out there when we came into his hamlet, mulling over days to come without any real standing in his own settlement?

He wants to die on his feet, sword in hand in the manner of his Seaxan forebears.

'I would say rest for the night and think this through. We are here to seek out Eadric, and join with him in fighting the fool Willelm fitzOsbern. If you wish to join us do so, but seeking a fight for the sake of an ill thought-out challenge is foolish. I have no quarrel with you, Wulfric. You are an open-handed host and a good man. Wulfgifu is a fair woman, I must agree with you, but I see no reason to cut you down because you think I wish to bed her'.

'You think *you* are such a good fighter?' Wulfric glares down at me and I turn back to the table to savour his good - perhaps calm myself. He yells, almost screams, pulls at my right shoulder for me to look up at him again, 'Do not turn your back on *me!*'

His cheeks are flushed and his whole body shakes as if in a fever.

'I will not take up a challenge from you, my host', I look up at him and try to stay calm, 'because for one thing a man does not fight with his host, and secondly it must end in grief for you. Go to bed and rest. In the morning when you awaken you will wonder whether you dreamed this. I shall not hold it against –'

Wulfric flails at me but Osgod seizes his hand, and hisses a warning,

'Wulfric do as Ivar says, *for your own sake!* We will take our leave from you in the morning. No more will be said'.

A deathly hush comes over us in the hall. No-one stirs, not even to quench a thirst. Each man's throat must be dry, but the cups stay on the table. I can even hear Harding's breathing, although he is some way down the table, where he went to speak to one of his men before Wulfric took a turn.

'Wulfric, *do* as he says', Aelfflaed tries to hush him, trying her best not to rouse him to anger again.

He turns to look at her and tears well in his old grey-blue eyes. He drops to his knees and sobs, hands clasped as if in prayer for forgiveness. His shoulders heave as he doubles up and holds himself from the straw-covered floor, hands spread flat down in un-swept dirt. We all watch, hushed, as Aelfflaed walks slowly up to him. Hands tenderly cupping his elbows, she helps him carefully to his feet and leads him to a door at the back of the hall.

Before they leave the hall Aelfflaed turns and tells us all,

'Eanwulf will show you to your beds. Thank you, Ivar for your understanding. I will see you in the morning before you leave. I bid you farewell on Wulfric's behalf. He is ill and must rest'.

Osgod and I acknowledge her plea and stand waiting until they have left the room.

'Poor fellow', Osgod is the first to speak.

Eanwulf goes about the room like a ghost, picking up bowls, knives, spoons and platters. He looks at the closed door that Aelfflaed led Wulfric through to his bed and tells us,

'He was a good thegn until Lord Willelm came and took away his livelihood. It has been as if he were dead these past months. Your coming has stirred him from a living nightmare, and he has taken too much ale for his own good in such a short time'.

'When the ale takes hold of a man he needs to summon up his strength and wits and fight the need', I tell the loyal Eanwulf. 'Briefly this evening he was a young man again. When Wulfric is about again wish him well for me'.

He nods and leaves the room for the kitchen, soon to show again, to take a torch from the wall and beckon us to follow,

'Friends, if you will follow me I will take you to where you sleep tonight. Randwulf has already taken your weapons to your bed closets. He and Wulfgifu bid you good night through me'.

I stifle a yawn as Eanwulf leads, taking candles for us.

'Wulfric will still be abed when you leave', he tells me to nodding from the others. 'Your horses will be ready for you. I will tell you which way to take to reach Lord Rhiwallon'.

Dawn comes, grey, the earth damp still from overnight drizzle.

'Good weather for staying clear of fitzOsbern's men', Eanwulf stands in the yard and sniffs up at the air.

We have is a stiff climb ahead into the mountains that hide Wealas from us, and have stuffed ourselves with as much food as Wulfric can spare for our morning meals to fight the cold. Aelfflaed silently sees us out of her husband's hall and waves us off before going about her tasks.

Randwulf pushes open the gates and Eanwulf stops Osgod before he rides out after me. I am called back before I have gone too far,

'Wait, Ivar. Eanwulf has something to tell me'.

Eanwulf follows Osgod up to me and the old fellow shows us the way,

'Ride for Dodingtun and stay on that track until you come to the end, about an hour's ride. It may be a little more but it is downhill'. The old man breaks off, unsure for a moment, thinking. He draws lines with his finger through the air. When he thinks he has it, he looks up at me as if he has seen the second coming and finishes,

'Turning left there after a half hour's trot brings you to a crossroad, where you turn right. That track takes you into Wealas. Rhosgoch is a good few miles' steady climb further. You could be there before dark, unless more snow has fallen since yesterday. Even then it would only add a little more to your time on the track. Lord Rhiwallon's men will be watching out for newcomers'.

'I thank you for your help, Eanwulf', Osgod speaks for us all, with a nod from me.

'Were I half my age now I would come with you', Eanwulf tells us as he stretches out his hand to bid farewell, first to Osgod, then to Harding and me.

'That is understandable', Harding muses. '*Many* will feel that way. Mark my words, the Northmen will be gone before the summer's end. Then perhaps we can all live our lives again. I look forward to seeing my young son grow free into manhood'

'*Amen* to that!' I add, nodding again and nudge Braenda into a walk.

'Let us seek out our new Wealsh allies', Osgod laughs and turns in his saddle to bid a last farewell to Eanwulf, 'I am looking forward to meeting this Eadric, are you?'

I answer, scanning the track ahead of us,

'It has to be why we are here'.

Every bush, every tree can hide a foe. Still, we are now more than a score, well-armed and skilled with our weapons. Even if the Northman Earl Willelm gets word of what Eadric has in store for him and sends out bigger patrols we will be able to deal with them, should we have no other way around them!

Needless to say, the likelihood of any Northmen being out here is scant. They will be either down dale at Ewyas, or east of here in Hereford, unaware of what is happening up here.

Driving rain turns into sleet as we climb. Beards are caked in ice, capes glisten. Thankfully our gear is well wrapped and greased against the wet. This is a challenge like no other and hopefully Godwin will not be long in coming with his men, newly skilled and eager to hem in the Northmen in these wild hills.

'How many miles did Eanwulf say we have to cover before we are in Wealas?' Osgod asks me.

'He gave no inkling of how many miles as such, but no more than a day's ride', I half turn in the saddle, glad to turn away from the sleet even for a fleeting moment.

'Will there be any Northmen in these parts, do you think?' Osgod thinks out aloud.

Harding points out the sparseness of the trees and undergrowth around us and answers,

'The likelihood of Northmen being here, attacking us, is even slimmer now. There are few trees here big enough to hide behind. They would need more than two score or more of them to overcome us here.

Oslac looks around and agrees with Harding, shaking his head at Osgod for being so wary,

'Aye, they would not come this far from Ewyas for nothing', he sneezes suddenly, the whole dale head echoing. He wipes his nose on his cape and adds, 'We heard from Wulfric that men here have grounds enough to want to throw fitzOsbern and his ilk back into the sea, any sea. The killings and sullying of West Seaxan fellowship are grounds enough for hating them. It would be easy enough to throw them into disarray, hiding behind boundary walls and jumping onto them'.

Yet we are fighting men, the settling of scores not for us to act out on the Northmen once they are beaten. That can be left to the folk around here. When they see their tormentors beaten, trying to leave after we have shaken them, they will fall on them from all around.

'You have given it some thought', Osgod turns to my friend riding alongside me, 'have you done it before?'

'We have, aye, many times in Centland', Oslac recalls, although there were many more trees there, and it was as easy for them to ambush *us*. Up here it would be all to our good', Oslac answers, not taking his eyes from the track ahead.

I can see Osgod is thinking, looking at me as he rides.

'Was that with Ivar?' he asks Oslac, glad of the talk. It must take his thoughts from the driving sleet which makes the going slower now.

'It was mostly with my *Centish* friends, Thegn Osgod', Oslac tells him, relishing the memory but suddenly thoughtful at the loss of his young friend. 'Many good men are dead now, but we freed Ivar from the Northmen on Watling Straet by hiding behind the trees and bushes in wait for them. We loosed off our arrows at their leader and the two who rode close to Ivar and his friend Theorvard. Sigegar's arrows cut through the necks of the leader and one of his underlings'.

'Where is Sigegar now?' Osgod keeps the talk going.

'He was killed by a Northman's crossbow bolt', Oslac answers, betraying sadness at the loss of a valued friend, as was also Ivar's friend Theorvard and another two of my Centish friends'.

We have been following the track downhill toward a crossroad this side of a river, nearing a small, stone-built barn-like building. Osgod is still talking to Oslac about his time in Centland,

'You yourself are not a Centishman?' Osgod asks further.

'My father took us to Centland because my mother was homesick. We lived in the flatlands of Acsanholm and she pined for the green hills and dales of southern Centland'.

Still looking ahead, Oslac suddenly reins in.

'Acsanholm - is that not in the north of Lindisse, in Lindcylne shire? – 'Osgod does not know that my friend has seen something and is cut short here.

'There is someone hiding behind that stone barn', Oslac hisses to me, pulls out his bow from its sailcloth bag and feels for an arrow. 'Show, friend!' he shouts into the wind and is rewarded for his watchfulness when a tousle-haired fellow shows, clad overall in a dark woollen cloak.

'Nothing gets past you, does it Aenglishman? Mind you, that arrow would have been swept back at one of your own men by the wind. *Then* where would you be?' The man plays with the tangled hairs of his thick, dark beard before speaking again, 'Welcome Aenglishmen, to Cymru!'

'*What* did he say?' Harding asks me, non-plussed by a name he can never have heard before.

'He said 'Welcome to Wealas', I answer for him.

'What was the *last* word he said?' Harding squints at the Wealshman as though by himself he poses a threat to over a score of well-armed Aenglishmen.

'The word was *Cymru,* their name for their own land –'I am cut off by the Wealshman, bemused by my knowledge.

'You know that?'

'I have been in this land before, when our last king was still Earl of West Seaxe', I answer truthfully.

'You were hunting down the fool Gruffyd, no doubt! He had it coming, allying himself with the outlawed Earl Aelfgar. My lord is Bleddyn, the brother of Rhiwallon and now Lord of Gwynedd. He shares my outlook on Gruffyd', the Wealshman recalls. 'My name is

Bryn, brother of the innkeeper where Ivar here was robbed of his silver by the red-haired wench, Braenda!'

I like the sharp wit of this fellow, Bryn, and so do my comrades. Gales of laughter drown out the groan of the wind over the top of the mountain pass. As the laughter dies down Bryn milks more laughter from them,

'She did not spend his silver in Menai, mind, but waited until she was back in Ceaster before anyone saw a penny of her ill-won gains'.

'How many know *that* tale?!' I have to laugh with them when they begin laughing again.

'I think it must be part of folklore. Half of Gwynedd knows about it', Bryn raises more laughter, 'all the way to the River Deag!'

'Is that why we saw no Wealsh guards before we passed Ceaster, because they were too sick laughing about it to stop us leaving?' One of Osgod's men yells out from behind me above the laughter.

'Someone *else* with us was there!' Osgod can hardly say the words for laughing.

'It would be no small miracle if half of Northanhymbra did not know about it too', Oslac quips to me.

'I did not know about it', Harding admits.

'*You* were no doubt knee-deep in sheep droppings at the time!' Osgod laughs.

'In your part of Deira no-one goes much further than Gearum, do they?' someone else chides good-naturedly.

'How come you know about it?' I ask.

'I was there, with you and Hrothulf. You would not know me. I was a fresh young lad then. But I have been in too many fights since, and was in the Earlsburh when your other friend was killed by Garwulf, the sot. You did not know me well *then*, however. I am Asgeir. When Tostig was in Lunden last year I was with him. Otherwise I would have been killed by the good folk of Jorvik. Now do you know -?'

'I do not want to break up your get-together, Aenglishmen, but we have more riding yet and it will be dark soon', Bryn calls out to us. 'Hard-going when you cannot see your hand in front of your eyes! Best we ride like the wind now and you can finish looking back on your past when we are drinking in Rhosgoch'.

'How do we ride like the wind with this blowing at us?' Oslac demands.

'Head down, that is how. Not far from here we start climbing again, steeper to the top of the hill we call Clyro. The way levels off somewhat after a short way, and then it will be downhill to Rhosgoch. You will be able to breathe out again then'.

With a curt nod from Osgod Bryn leads away and we follow on without another word. My eyes are on the western skyline as I ride alongside Saeward. What I see fills me with foreboding - a low grey cloud drags across the hilltops, leaving a trail of white.

There is yet more snow on the way and we have a long way to go. It is hard to know what time of the day we are in without being able to see where the sun is.

'Do you think we will be in Rhosgoch before dark?' Osgod asks the Wealshman as we thunder across a small wooden bridge over the river Wye. Bryn says nothing, and Osgod shrugs.

With the snow thickening on beginning the climb up the western side of the dale, Bryn turns to Osgod,

'It will be some time after dark before we even see the fires of Rhosgoch', he sounds as if we hold the Wealsh weather against him. At least he has answered our worst fears.

When we near Rhosgoch's gates the earth is blanketed in thick snow. Caped men with spears and shields stand guard on the walls of the stronghold. Eyes bore into us from the walkways above when Bryn leads through the creaking gates of the walled burh, along narrow streets to Rhiwallon's hall.

Harding stares in awe at the dwellings, warehouses and shops to either side of us,

'This is a handsome burh you have here, Bryn. I would say it is much like Jorvik'.

'Is that good, Aenglishman?' Bryn turns, asking Osgod. 'At least it keeps the wolves from tearing our horses apart'.

'You have never been to Eoferwic, as we Aengle call the burh?' Osgod leans forward and dismounts behind Bryn.

'I have only ever been to Wintunceaster with Thegn Eadric', Bryn answers. 'This Eoferwic – is it a great burh?'

Osgod nods to our guide,

'Eoferwic is the greatest burh in Northanhymbra, begun in the old days before the Aengla came to these islands. The Earlsburh is built around a much older garth and is the home of Earl Morkere, when he is at home'.

'Eadwin's brother is away?' Bryn wonders aloud.

'They are both away until the new king brings them back from Northmandige, along with the aetheling Eadgar and Earl Waltheof', Osgod waits until we have all dismounted.

Bryn draws himself to his full height before leading us through the hall doors to Rhiwallon and Eadric. Two of the guards stand aside for us and we march ahead into a hall lit by wall-mounted torches and a great fire in the hearth midway along toward Rhiwallon's high seat.

'Who have you come to see?' asks a tall fellow, who does not look as though he belongs here. He does not sound like a Wealshman either.

'These fellows have come to see Thegn Eadric and Rhiwallon', Bryn tells him.

'Who are you?' the Aenglishman asks, looking at the first man behind Bryn.

'I am Thegn Harding, of Rudby in Deira', he answers.

Harding will have to do this many times before they know him to be a friend.

'And you?' the Aenglishman looks at me. Osgod stands behind me, looking up into the darkness at shapes carved into the pillars.

'I am Ivar Ulfsson', I allow a smile, albeit a wary one.

'Ivar Ulfsson – now where have I heard *that* name before?' He scratches a short, well trimmed beard and gives me a knowing grin, 'Were you in Menai not ten years ago? I can see from your bearing that you are of noble birth. Welcome Ivar... and you are?'

He looks at Osgod now. The young thegn has been looking around at the men around us, watching us pass by in idle wonder. Awed by the size of the hall he answers, straightening,

'I am thegn Osgod of Eoferwic'. The Aenglishman towers over him yet. Osgod goes on, 'I have been sent by my shire reeve, Maerleswein, to bother the Northmen with a score of Morkere's men. We have come to speak with Thegn Eadric and the aetheling Rhiwallon'.

'Maerleswein owns land in the south west of the kingdom, not in Hereford shire. Why has he sent you *here?*' The fellow breaks off, counting heads. 'There are more than a score here with you. Who are the others?'

'I have friends with me, Oslac, Cyneweard, Saeward and Theodolf', I point I give their names.

'Friends - not *underlings?*' out each of them as he answers curtly. Oslac bridles at the slight but says nothing and the fellow goes on. 'They fought against the Northmen?'

'They did, and *well*. I have been blessed, I think, with my friends who have afforded me counsel and company, as well as help in the fight against the outlander. However, only one who fought alongside me at Caldbec Beorg is with me now'.

'You fought *beside* King Harold?' His eyes widen. 'Who *else* outlived the king other than you?'

'Theodolf - he is the tall young fellow beside Harding', I beckon him forward, 'who stood near King Harold with his father, Hrothulf.

Two better bowmen you could not wish for. Now there is only him. Soon after that Theodolf and Oslac, together with a score or so other skilled bowmen at Lunden Brycg showed Willelm and his men were only flesh and blood after all!'

'Well said, Ivar!' Osgod slaps me on the back. The Aenglishman stares at him first, but a broad smile creases his mouth as he stands grinning at me.

'As you can vouch for your men, both of you, I will tell you my name. I am Thegn Eadric'. The smile soon goes as he adds,

'Nevertheless, I must make you aware that not everything you hear about me is true. Word is that I foreswore to give my oath to King Willelm. That is untrue, but there is also a tale going around that I have refused my tithes to Willelm fitzOsbern, and that *is* true. He has hounded me from my lands and laid waste settlements whose folk were my friends. For that he must pay with his life, if needs be. I also have something to tell you Ivar. At Bearrucing I saw Copsig'.

When my brow knits in anger at Copsig's name, he adds,

'Copsig spoke your name in passing to the king. They both seem to hold your welfare dear. Willelm swore you would be brought to book for your deeds in the south against Odo. He bade us offer you up to the Northmen if we saw you. Copsig later told me he himself has a score to settle with you'.

Looking from me to Osgod and back again, Eadric has given me news that takes my breath away and angers Osgod.

'Copsig was made earl of all the land north of the River Tese. Now there are three lords who rule over Northanhymbra. Morkere only has any standing in Deira and to the sea in the west. Maerleswein has the Danelaw and Copsig is to rule where *his* foes are thickest on the ground. I do not know what Gospatric and Osulf will make of it. Gospatric was made to buy the land he already owned. Willelm reigns in a way none of the Cerdicingas would have dared'.

He plays one against another, setting his underlings on us like hounds!' Eadric adds.

'I should let Gospatric know before Copsig sets foot on his soil!' I feel awkward, having come all this way to fight alongside Eadric and telling him I need to be elsewhere in the kingdom. 'Eadric, when do you mean to begin your attack?'

'There is time yet before we march on Hereford. Rhiwallon and Bleddyn must gather their men from across Gwynedd', he muses. 'We must sharpen their fighting skills, test them hard! There are weapons to be made and tried out. Men have flocked to me from all over Mierca, so they must be taught together. It is almost as if we are speaking some outlandish tongue when we talk to the Miercans! More used to raiding, our Wealsh neighbours are in *and* out before you even know they have been there –'Eadric stops short to allow a rider to pass word to him.

Bryn puts the man's words to Eadric in Aenglish and thanks his fellow countryman.

'You know yourself how they fight, Ivar. It is *we* should learn from *them*. Willelm fitzOsbern does not know how to deal with them. Aelfgar quickly learned of their skill at striking hard and moving on before anyone knew what was afoot. We need them more than they need us!' Eadric looks at the rooves to his right, and back at me.

'If you feel you must warn Gospatric and Osulf do so by all means. Bryn can find you a guide who will be able to lead you past the Northmen to Ceaster. Stay as long as you feel you need to. You and your friends have earned yourself a rest after coming all that way from East Seaxe, and Osgod is welcome to stay, to teach my men their war craft whilst you ride north'.

My thoughts are on how I might do that in late winter,

'From what Copsig tells me, neither would welcome seeing you. You have my blessing', Eadric slaps my left shoulder with the flat of his hand and walks on.

I hear myself telling Eadric as if I am bodily not there, but gloating over everyone,

'I would think he left out a lot in the telling. Copsig has sinned in many ways, and covering his back was his way even if it meant lying to others, so he must pay his dues. I think I know why he gave his oath to this Northman king. He has helped himself to Northanhymbran tithes before, now he wishes to line his coffers with their silver in the name of another king'.

'Are you taking any of your friends with you?' Eadric asks suddenly, wrongfooting me. Having heard of the prowess of three of them with the bow, he may wish to keep them here to show his men the finer points.

'I will have to ask them. If you mean to attack the Northmen at Eastertide I should be back by then', I take his hand, thankful he has granted me this.

'What has Gospatric done for you that you should warn him of Copsig's posting to Northanhymbra?' Osgod asks when we have been shown to our sleeping quarters. 'Osulf would not have thought twice of killing you along with all the other Danish huscarls still in the Earlsburh'.

128

'As a man of Deira, would you sooner have to stand against the Northmen on your own, or have Beornica on your side and crush the Northmen between you?' I ask him in turn.

'You think it would make any odds to Gospatric or Osulf if a Dane warns them? Think on this, Ivar, many of Tostig's huscarls were Danes, and they helped Copsig in his graft. They would want to know what you stand to gain from warning them. Only one of your friends is from Northanhymbra, and he is the son of one of Tostig's huscarls, so they could not help you turn Gospatric to your side. You might all be killed together and Copsig would be killed anyway as soon as his posting was made known. *I* think you should stay here, and when tidings of Eadric's raids reach them in Beornica, they will hear of your deeds in Hereford shire. Copsig will be dead anyway, and Gospatric can be won over. His loyalty is to the man he thinks is the rightful king. If he knows you have given your oath to Eadgar-'.

'If I tell Gospatric and Osulf that I have fought alongside Eadgar against Willelm at Lunden Brycg, then he must trust me!' I do not let Osgod finish. If Eadgar is the lynch-pin of our fight against Willelm, then I am home and dry.

'Barring Saeward, who has helped us since, we have fought against Willelm under Eadgar and Ansgar, *and* won. If they wish to come with me we may ride tomorrow, a Dane, a Danelaw man, a Northanhymbran, and two Seaxans', I tell him. 'In warning them of Willelm's appointed earl being Tostig's tithe gatherer, we make ourselves their allies!'

Osgod fixes me with a steady gaze, almost as if he felt he was dealing with a wilful child. Neither of us speaks for what seems to me to be an age. When he does finally speak, it is as if he were repeating a father's warning to an errant son,

'Do you *really* not understand, or are you blocking out my warning? You were *Tostig's* kinsman and huscarl, and then you were his brother's huscarl and somehow outlived the king, your kinsman. Now, when we are about to fight against the Northmen you want to ride almost the length of the kingdom to warn a man who would just as soon kill *you* as Copsig!'

I have angered Osgod without wishing to. He may well think, rightly, I am being stubborn.

However I feel I must be there when Copsig is finally humbled, to see him when he sees his killer just as he thinks his luck is with him. He could have taken another path, to fight a common foe. Being made earl by Willelm has sent him within reach of those who bear ill feeling toward him and his master will be unable to keep them from him.

There will also be those around Jorvik in Deira who feel he has done *them* harm by dragging their good name through the mud for his own gain. They will also wish to set right the wrongs carried out in Tostig's name.

'We will be back to raid Willelm fitzOsbern's strongholds, first to render his new one at Ewyas!' I assure Osgod.

He looks at me in a pitying way and chews his lower lip before answering,

'I would be happy to see you back alive. Although Gospatric is a kinsman of Eadgar's through the old king, and as such might be a friend to you, he is tricky. As for Osulf, he trusts few men from even south of the Tese, let alone from over the sea. If you think you can make them trust you, by all means go, but I cannot see why you should *need* to. Do you see what I am driving at? Harding does not know yet that you mean to do this, but he would tell you the same. He has kin over the Tese, in Ulnaby. He could act as a go-between'.

'He would trust me?' I ask, although I do not know why.

'He would trust you because I do. Do not misuse that trust or you will find him a steel-hard foe'.

'You will speak to him about what I am about to undertake?' I wonder at his willingness to do this for me when he has known me for so little time.

'I will speak to him. Say nothing about any of it to anyone before I have had time to talk it over with him', Osgod assures me. 'For now, shall we taste Rhiwallon's ale?'

'Who will come with me to Northanhymbra?' I ask of my friends in the morning. We are all seated together, Osgod and Harding, their men and us. A few of Eadric's men look over at me from the neighbouring table, wondering what is astir.

'Why is it we have to uproot ourselves to go all that way?' Oslac demands without looking up at me, stirring his porridge painstakingly as though the wish to eat had gone.

'Aye, Ivar, it would take us days just to reach Deira', Theodolf seems to be talking to his food.

His wish to be back at Aethel's steading has left him, it seems, but suddenly he sits up and asks mischievously,

'Your woman would not happen to be there, would she?'

Eadric takes his cue from Theodolf and grins hugely at me,

'You have a woman in Northanhymbra? No wonder you want to get away up there'. This draws laughter from those of his men who are within hearing, 'but why dress up your interest in this woman as a need to warn Gospatric of Copsig's coming?'

'I *have* a woman, aye, but she could be anywhere at this time, until she makes herself known to me', I tell Eadric.

'Aye', Bryn calls out, laughing hoarsely for everyone to hear, 'This is the woman Braenda, I take it? Braenda the hwicce woman, who vanishes at will and sets herself down on God's earth on a whim'.

'I would not counsel taking her name in vain - 'I begin.

'Aye, by God, she might turn me into a toad, eh?' Bryn bursts into with another challenge to her, 'She might even come and turn me to stone!'

laughter and everyone in the room joins in the merriment. He draws raucous laughter

'Worse things could happen, Bryn', one of Eadric's men calmly tells him when the noise dies down.

Bryn bursts into laughter again,

'Like what, Aenglishman? You will be telling me next that you believe in elves'. The boom of his mirth drowns out another voice.

'Like being burnt alive within your own skin', one of Eadric's men tells Bryn.

'Like *what?*' Bryn sounds annoyed now. He plainly thinks he has heard wrongly.

'Like being burnt alive in your own skin. None can see what is happening to you', the Aenglishman enlightens Bryn. 'It is as if you had been put in a pot of boiling water and you feel your eyes begin to pop, but to everyone else you look fit to go to sleep'.

'What kind of nonsense *is* that?' Eadric demands.

'*I* have heard of it. A man was making jokes about a hwicce woman and he suddenly stopped. This was at a feast, not in the daytime, mind', another enlightens us when he sees some staring blankly. 'All others in the hall wondered why he had stopped short. They thought the drink had overcome him because he looked to be dozing. Later, during the day after one of his friends asked him if he recalled going to sleep during the telling of a joke. He answered that his blood was on fire and that he feared dying because no-one knew his eyes were inwardly popping with the heat'.

All is silent now... as the grave. The second man finishes,

'He made no more jests about hwicce matters and has not suffered since'.

Bryn fixes the Aenglishman with one eye closed, his brow beetling.

'You say this happened one evening, at a feast, with everyone around?' he tests the fellow.

'Aye, this *was* in the evening. No-one holds feasts at *this* time of day, surely, not even here in Wealas?'

One of Osgod's men quips,

'They do some odd things here in Wealas'. He is stared down by several of Bryn's fellow countrymen.

'This is Cymru, Aenglishman!' Bryn spits out, 'No Aenglish hwicce women work their magic here because our Druid spirits shield us against *all* outsiders!'

'I thought you were *all* Christians in this land? No? Still I hope you are right, for your sake', the Aenglishman answers, 'I hope so!'

'When the mood takes me, I ask my forebears for help', Bryn stares icily at him and turns to look at when I clear my throat.

'Well, I was not thinking of seeing Braenda', I tell them. 'I merely wish to see how Gospatric finally humbles Copsig'.

'I am telling you not to bother. We will hear of his downfall one way or another. If you *must* go, Harding will ride with you', Osgod turns to look me in the eye. 'When he tells you it is best not to follow your path, *listen*. He will counsel you well'.

Harding nods by way of an answer. He knowsOsgod has deep misgivings about what I am about to embark on,

'Why you want to see Gospatric, I do not know', Harding growls. 'Both he and Osulf bear deep ill will to any and all Danes since Tostig's time, and their forefathers since long before that even. They see you as grasping good-for-noughts, only after silver to fill your coffers. If you can show them you are not like that, by all means do so'.

He shrugs before going back to his food. Before he takes another mouthful, he sits with the full spoon, blowing at it, fixing me.

'Do not mistake my meaning, Ivar. My *own* forefathers were Danes. I know they are the same at heart as the Aengle. There is good and bad in us all. I was born in northern Deira, and I am within reach of Gospatric and Osulf at Rudby. So whilst I call myself Aenglish they will not harm me. What would you do if they pull their swords from their scabbards when they hear you are another Dane?'

'I will stand my ground!' I will be neither bowed nor beholden to any man, 'Gospatric will understand that'.

'Let us only hope so, but my guess is that someone will test your gut with cold steel at his behest before he gives you a second hearing!' Harding shakes his head in disbelief at my doggedness and takes a mouthful of the steaming porridge.

'Who else is going with you?' Osgod asks, looking from one to another of my friends around me.

'I will go', Saeward makes to stand. Is he the *only* one?

One by one they stand, slowly, after Saeward. Cyneweard rises, then Theodolf. Oslac is the last to stand.

'Aye, we will go with you', Oslac smiles forbearingly, looking sideways at Harding, searching for another answer.

'As long as we are back in time to help Eadric, otherwise we might as well have gone straight to Northanhymbra'.

Snow flurries hide the far side of the dale when we are atop Clyro again. Aengla Land is on the far side, unseen through the whiteness. Our Wealsh guide presses his mount downhill and looks back at me,

'We must skirt Hereford and ride on to Scrobbesbyrig, where there are not yet as many Northmen. Willelm fitzOsbern has not yet deemed fit to build another stronghold to face Cymru. He has an underling, Willelm fitzScrob, to watch the hilltops to the west in Scrobbe shire. It will make attacking Hereford easier for Rhiwallon and Bleddyn'.

'How is that?' Harding challenges our guide.

'Your fellow countryman Eadric trusts you, Ivar', the fellow ignores the note of doubt in Harding's words and asks me. 'Are you sure you will be coming back?'

'I shall be back, fear not. What is your name, Wealshman?'

'Do you know 'Wealshman' is the Seaxan word for 'outlander', Dane? *You* are the outlander. I am of Cymru, do not forget that! My name, Ifor, is a bit like yours, eh?' He fixes me with a stare before going on,

'It means 'Lord', so be careful how you speak to me from now on until we part company', Ifor laughs affably, 'What does your name mean?'

'To be honest, Ifor, I have never asked. Do you know the meaning of your name, Saeward?' I ask the Seaxan.

'I heard Saeward is a wolf of the gods', he answers.

'Why do you ask?'

'Our friend Ifor asked me the meaning of my name. He tells me his name means something like a lord or god', I tell him. As I have never had a wish to be worshipped, I am missing nothing.

'I have never spent time thinking about my name', Saeward muses, 'although I do recall Beorhtwulf telling me the meaning of names. I think he said his name had something to do with strength'.

'He had an inner strength', I agree. A lump rises to my throat as I think back on Beorhtwulf's death.

Not knowing who we are talking about, Ifor merely nods. He leads us over high ground, and points out to houses ahead,

'Yonder is a small burh, Radnor. We ride along the bottom of Hergest Ridge and stop at an inn to water the horses. As we are in no great haste we can eat there. If we reach Leintweorden in the north-western corner of Hereford Shire around sunset we will be doing well. We have a snow cloud following behind us'.

He jabs heavenward with a finger over his right shoulder and we in turn look back at the threatening mass of grey looming over the mountain tops.

'We need not fear. It will pass on its way over Leofmynster. It may catch us as sleet and not settle on the track'.

'There are no Northmen in that part of Hereford shire?' Harding asks. 'We are not *worried* about them coming across us. If we have to we will kill them, but we wish to stay unseen until we are beyond their northern limit, in Scrobbe shire'.

We all look to Ifor, to hear his answer.

'Eadric told me not to go near any of the Northmen. *He* wishes us to stay unseen until we all attack their stronghold together at Hereford', Ifor answers, nodding slowly at Harding.

Harding mumbles something about it not being his wish to be seen, either, and lets Ifor add,

'It would call for a longer ride back into the hills behind Clun, adding hours to his ride and risking the safety of both himself and his horse on boggy ground, where snow would cover the sparse tracks and hide the bogs.

Close behind me are Harding, Saeward, Oslac, Theodolf and Cyneweard. Cyneweard and Oslac are a short way behind us, talking earnestly about something that has nothing to do with the rest of us. Theodolf rides ahead with Ifor and Saeward is alongside me, unable to think of anything to say. As I do not wish to talk either, his awkward stillness suits me as I scan the high ground to our right. Hergest Ridge could be used by Willelm fitzOsbern's men to look into Wealas, even if only to watch the sheep grazing.

I need not fear our being seen. The heavens are leaden, a blanket of sleet driven at us by iron-cold gusts of wind. No man would be foolish enough to stay up there for long.

As we ride into Radnor smoke rises from the rooves of small dwellings around an inn that stands square to the track we are following. Not a soul can be seen out of doors, but hounds bark and cattle low fearfully within wattle barns. As we come closer to an inn someone opens a door to a stable and stands, watching us nearing him. Ifor speaks to the fellow in his own tongue, telling him most likely that our horses need feeding and watering. On our dismounting a woman shows in another doorway. She tells Ifor something I cannot understand and cackles as she holds the inn door open for us.

'Take seats my friends', she tells us in Aenglish. 'I will be with you soon'.

The woman leaves the room with Ifor. An older woman busies herself at the back of the room, doing whatever she needs to make ready for cooking or whatever. A child enters the room from the back and stands looking at us. She turns on her heels and leaves shouting something loudly by the same way. The older woman yells after her and all is still again.

Ifor laughs and winks,

'It is as well Blodwen does not know your tongue'.

'How is that so?' Harding demands.

'Then you would know she was singing insults about Aenglish folk', Ifor laughs. 'You need not be offended, Ivar, she has high regard for Danes, markedly Dyflin Danes'.

'I would not be offended, even if I *were* Aenglish. It is a fool who lets himself be slighted by children', I answer for myself.

Ifor casts an askance look at me as he makes to leave the room again. He looks for an easier answer from my friends and, hearing none, vanishes into the darkness. Not long later he comes back into the room with a young monk in tow.

8

'Ivar, I have found a guide to take you on! This is Brother Aldo from Scrobbesbyrig. He is on his way home from here', Ifor tells me gleefully, as though he had unearthed King Cutha's treasure hoard from the hillside. 'He says he would be happy to show you the way'.

'Aldo', I greet the fellow and ask, 'is that not a Frankish name, brought by the Northmen to these lands in the days of King Eadweard?'

'It *is,* my son', he coughs, smiling, 'I am sorry, but I know you must be a lot older than I. We are told we speak to folk that way, even if they *are* older than us. Although I am Aenglish born, my father was Frankish warrior who came with Earl Ralf to these parts'.

'Was -?' I look closely at him.

'The fellow is dead – from a Wealsh arrow'.

Aldo makes a half-turn to see if Ifor says anything. The Wealshman keeps his own counsel and Aldo turns back to me, '*His* name was Drogo. Yet he was not much of a father to me. Having sired me on my mother he went his own way again, so his death is not so much of a loss'.

Ifor watches me, unaware that Aldo is looking at him again.

'I said his death is not much of a loss', the monk smiles, at Ifor. 'Anyway I was taken in by a kindly abbot, Wulfwig, who showed me a lot more kindness than my own father ever did'.

'A relief for your mother, then', I observe drily.

'She was no longer alive by then, either. A Wealshman took her life when he had finished with her', Aldo stares hard again at the unflinching Ifor, then catches me giving the Wealshman dark looks.

'No, it has nothing to do with him. It was one of Gruffyd's men, with Earl Aelfgar, who did the killing. She had already given me to a ceorl in Hereford Shire for a small sum. No doubt he thought I would work for him when I was old enough to understand what he wanted.

When we are at Scrobbesbyrig I will tell you the way to Ceaster from there'.

My friends nod their thanks as one.

'I thank you, Aldo. That will be welcome, Oslac answers for them'.

'Are there many Northmen at Scrobbesbyrig?' Harding asks Aldo, 'I came another way with my friend Thegn Osgod and our men, by way of Deoraby and Laegerceaster'.

Aldo frowns, thinking, and answers slowly, as if to a simpleton,

'There are *some*, but not as many as at Hereford'.

'I would take it kindly if you did not speak to me as if I were a halfwit, Brother. I am a thegn!' Harding grunts, taking Aldo's answer amiss.

I feel I have to speak up for the Brother,

'I would say Aldo was thinking his answer over. He did not mean to offend, Harding. In him we have a friendly guide'.

I grin at Ifor, who merely nods back at me and sits down to some food, brought in by young Blodwen who sits across the table from him, babbling to the Wealshman until he thumps the table with his fist. Clearly the girl has offended him. Although alarmed, she babbles on. Again Ifor bangs his fist on the table and yells at her,

'Blodwen shut up!' He shouts in Aenglish for us to understand, but then begins cursing in his own guttural tongue.

When she runs screaming from the room he turns back to us, laughing,

'She went on about how Aenglish folk live on their pride and do not need feeding!'

'I wish that were true!' Saeward sighs, rubbing his stomach at the sight of Ifor's broth.

Ifor merely snorts in anger at the girl's foolish talk,

'Whatever. I told her to ask Gwyneth to make more for you. There *are* some here who are simple. They believe whatever any fool will tell them'.

'*We* have *them* as well', Oslac laughs it off, 'I used to think we had enough for the whole land where I come from!'

'Where might that be?'

Although Aldo does not really want to know, he feels he should ask.

'I come from Acsanholm in Lindisse', Oslac answers brightly.

'Is that far from Lunden?' Aldo bravely offers.

Oslac sniffs at Aldo's lack of knowledge of the kingdom.

'It is as far from Lunden as we are now, I would think'.

Oslac's own knowledge is far-reaching, I grant him, but many a man goes little further beyond his own doorway than he could trip. I would think Aldo has not roamed far from where he began life.

'It is not far from the Great North Road, I would hazard a guess, eh Oslac?' Saeward turns to look at his friend.

'Aye, and less than a day's ride from Gagnesburh', Oslac agrees, grinning at Aldo's blank stare.

A look of mischief then spreads across Theodolf's lightly-bearded face as he joins in what he thinks is a harmless game,

'Or you could say it is as far from Gaegnesburh as Staenfordes Brycg is from Eoferwic!'

'Enough of this, you three', I chide, grinning, and make them aware that they rely on Aldo's goodwill to get them as far as Scrobbesbyrig. 'He could lose us anywhere if he had a mind to! How would you get us out of *these* hills, Oslac?'

'They are talking about Deira and Lindcylne shire', Saeward enlightens Aldo, who is plainly annoyed about the ribbing Oslac and Theodolf have given him.

Aldo's nose wrinkles and he begins to laugh good-heartedly,

'I had a feeling they were boasting their local knowledge'.

He takes a cup of ale from Ifor and asks,

'What if I were to babble about going from Rudelan to Ceaster, or from Scrobbesbyrig to Clun?'

He has a wit, this monk. I like him.

'You are right, Brother', Oslac admits his foolishness. 'Forgive us our sins'.

'I have a name, Aldo... Brother Aldo', the young fellow addresses Oslac sternly, as if he might be berating an errant novice.

'You are right, Brother Aldo', Oslac cannot help laughing. We all join in and are still shaking with laughter when Gwyneth brings in a board loaded with bowls, bread and a pot of broth.

Ifor says something to her and smacks her backside as she saunters away to the door, swaying her hips, shouting back at him in her own tongue.

'Women, eh, what could you do without them?' Ifor laughs after her.

As Oslac hands out the bowls, Harding ladles the broth, Saeward and Theodolf munch on the bread loaves. I burn my tongue on the first spoonful that I try to swallow.

'You will have to wait for it to cool down a little'.

Aldo scolds us as if talking to children. He may be right, 'Do you never say your prayers before you eat?'

'Ivar is a heathen Dane', Saeward tells him, smirking sidelong at me as I draw back with the sudden rush of pain from taking hot broth on my tongue. 'But for me the rest are heathen Aenglishmen'.

I try to grin at Saeward's prodding, but still feel the stinging on my tongue and it is all I can do to muster an 'Amen' with my scalded tongue when Aldo finishes. Theodolf shakes his head, trying not to laugh at me as the others break their bread and start dipping. Loud slurping from Harding brings a scowl from Aldo, but the thegn will not be put off getting the best from this good broth.

The sun greets us as we leave the inn to take the road along the dale of the River Lugg. Leofmynster is in the east, and from there the way north lies through Ludeford on the River Teme. Only a short way east of Radnor Aldo takes a left turn, northward.

'Where are you taking us, Aldo?' I shout against the wind as the monk smacks his small horse up onto a hilly track.

He yells back, jabbing the air northward,

'I am taking you to Scrobbesbyrig as I said I would!'

'But we should be following the road to Leofmynster, surely!' Harding roars from further away, trying to be heard above the groan of the wind.

'*Who says* that is the way?' Aldo looks open-mouthed back at Harding, hands outstretched, palms upward.

'Ifor said that is the way we would ride', Oslac butts in.

'*I* am your guide now, and Leofmynster is out of the way', Aldo protests, '*miles* out of the way!'

'But –', Harding throws up his hands and tries to turn his horse to ride across the wind, following Theodolf, Saeward and Oslac.

'Ifor may have been trying to get you caught by Willelm fitzOsbern? Perhaps *he* is in the Northman's pockets', Aldo over-rules Harding's gripe. 'Whatever - this track takes you *away* from any of their patrols'.

'Best not argue, Harding', Oslac shrugs before the thegn opens his mouth again.

Harding turns in his saddle to seek my whereabouts, asking,

'I was going to ask why Ifor would send us into the hands of the Northmen'.

'He *must* know. I would have thought. Having already come this way he might have skirted them himself', I answer Harding's fear and ask the monk,

'You are not hiding from Earl Willelm, are you Aldo?'

'My abbot has withheld this month's tithes, and has counselled that I use this track. I came to look in on an old friend of his, to bring him cheeses and to pass on words of comfort to the poor ailing fellow', Aldo gives us his reason for not wishing to meet any Northmen on his ride. 'He is a leper'.

'You spend time at a *leper's hovel?*' Theodolf steers his horse away from the monk. Where he has been keeping Aldo close company, now it seems he can not get far enough away from him and draws the reins hard to the left.

'I speak to him through a barred doorway', Aldo laughs, 'and pass the gifts to him between in iron bars. You only catch leprosy through handling their clothing or holding onto them where they are diseased'.

'You hope so', Harding grunts, guiding his horse away from Aldo's with a deft flick of his right wrist.

'I *know* so', the monk tells him earnestly. 'Believe me'.

'Aye, there are folk who take them food every day and stay to talk to them, and they do not catch it', Saeward tries to allay Harding's and Theodolf's fears. 'I know a leper hamlet near Waltham, where the only way to keep them from guests is a grille in a barred wooden door'.

'Have *you* been there?' Oslac asks, casting worried glances at Saeward.

'I have not, but my brother Beorhtwulf went there a few times weekly', Saeward smiles when he sees Oslac pull away from him, 'and if he ever caught it, his nose and lips would have rotted before the fool Garwulf killed him'.

Harding suddenly reins in his horse,

'Garwulf, *Osbald's* son killed him? Garwulf killed *your* brother?'

'You know him?' I ask. 'He hit Saeward's brother with his bare fist and Beorhtwulf's head struck a stone in the yard of the Earlsburh'.

'I know his father. He and his uncle have land at Ulnaby by the River Tese', Harding nods sagely. Somehow his horse trots along close to Aldo's, but now he does not try to turn her away again.

He has taken the monk's word that he is free of leprosy.

Our ride has been wet and cold since we left Radnor, with Aldo riding ahead, followed closely by Theodolf and Harding. Braenda bears this cold Wealsh wetness with due good spirit, having been well fed and watered along with my friends' horses by one of Gwyneth's thralls. At least we are now well below the snow line and heading for the banks of the River Teme.

'I know a ford ahead', Aldo assures us with a smile when he sees Theodolf looking warily at the swirling waters.

'This is going to be a canny crossing, even at a ford!' Harding thinks out aloud, 'Are you sure we can cross safely?'

'The river bends some way further downriver and we shall cross at Watredene', Aldo points eastward at the unseen bend of the river, where our horses are to wade through what is likely to be numbingly cold water. Our legs will be in it at least up to our knees. Theodolf casts a worried look at me, thinking the same thing, no doubt.

At last, where Aldo turns his horse toward the iron grey waters of the Teme, we see a steep bank on our side of the river, across from which is a pebble strand on the outside of the bend. Our horses pick their way carefully to the water's edge over greasy rocks in the riverbed.

Oslac remarks to anyone who happens to be listening,

'Take care, the rocks on this side are tricky'.

'The other side is a lot easier', Aldo points to a sandy track which winds upward from the wide strand to a lush meadow, covered by a light dusting of new snow, 'and there is an inn at the far side of the settlement where we can refresh ourselves for the rest of the ride ahead'.

A cluster of dwellings behind a fairly low palisade looks empty of life. No smoke rises from the rooves, where we would expect to see it. I have a feeling of foreboding. Can there be Northmen awaiting us behind the palisade, ready to bind us like hogs for slaughter and take us to Earl Willelm?

'Does no-one live there any more?' Saeward has also noted the lack of smoke from the homes.

'They will be in the fields', Aldo answers off-handedly.

'What fools do you take us for?' Harding growls.

'No-one in his right senses would be out in the fields in this!' Harding growls. He looks around at the trees and tells us, 'Have your weapons ready!'

Aldo kicks at his horse in an un-Christian manner and tries to make for the far side of the river before the rest of us.

'Catch that rat with an arrow!' Harding barks at Theodolf,He spurs his horse through freezing, foaming water with Theodolf close behind him, shouting at Aldo, 'Rein in, man – *rein in,* now!'

At the strand, heading for the track, Aldo bends low over the neck of his small horse. I would say that in ducking the arrow he knows one will be aimed at him. His horse flounders in the deep mud by the other bank and, as it bucks to free itself from quicksand he is thrown clear.

Oslac is first to clear the ford and grabs Aldo by his flapping hood as he hastily tries to clamber up to the meadowland. He roars as an arrow misses him and strikes at Aldo's throat,

'He has been struck by one of his own!'

The monk flops, sideways onto the pebbles by his now tired, panting horse.

Saeward shouts, alarmed,

'Where did that come from?'

More arrows fly at us from elsewhere amongst the bank-side greenery.

'*Get back here!*' Harding bellows at Oslac, who wrenches at his reins to turn his horse quickly. 'We cannot help you over there!'

Theodolf looses off some of his arrows at Northmen, who have rashly left the cover of the bushes to get a better aim on Oslac. Two fall lifelessly into the tangled undergrowth on the riverbank. Another howls with the pain as one of Theodolf's arrows lodges in his right arm.

'The bastard was going to dish us up to them!' Oslac pants when we clear the southern bank of the Teme at last. 'Now the Northmen know we are here, we have to get back to warn Eadric. Just think of it, we could have been led away to Hereford by them and that turd, Aldo would have been happily counting his reward!'

'I do not think he did it for the reward', I shake my head and look over my shoulder at Saeward, who seems to have been grazed by one of their arrows. 'Saeward, have you been wounded?'

'It is only a graze. I shall dress it when we next stop. We will not be crossing the river here?'

'Not today, we will not', I agree. 'Not here', I chew at my lower lip, trying to think of another way forward,

'But do we go *back*? Do they expect us to go back and show them where we have come from?' Oslac asks as he takes cover behind a tree from the Northmen's arrows. Luckily they have no crossbows with them.

'Who *says* to go back?' Harding demands, snarling, '*I* will slit his throat now for leading the Northmen to Eadric and Rhiwallon!'

'Ivar is right', Oslac puffs, trying to guide his horse through the shallows. 'We must find another way across. There was talk, was there not, of somewhere called Leofmynster - *east* of here?'

Saeward grumbles to me and mutters when he sees Harding stare at him,

'Without a guide, surely we do not know which way to go! Would it not be better to go back down the track even only a short way?'

'No, Saeward, Harding is right. Eadric would have to withdraw to higher ground, further away into Wealas from Hereford'.

I rest a hand on his shoulder. 'We will be like land-bound Vikings – *best foot forward!*'

'How do *they* go about it?' Theodolf asks, chuckling. 'What *are* land-bound Vikings, anyway?'

'Ivar means there is no going back, like Harding'. Oslac tells him, grinning, about putting ships on rollers, overland between the river-heads, 'That is how we reached Miklagard without crossing swords with the Caliph in the Middle Sea'.

'We will tell you one day', I smile at Theodolf's blank look, 'when we have time'.

'There is time *now*, surely?' Theodolf purses his lips like a child.

I look at Oslac, who gives a tired shrug,

'Until we find another ford over this God-forsaken river', he laughs, 'why not? There is all the time in the world!'

It takes the rest of the day to find another ford on the Teme, at Waeleford. We are some ten miles further east of where Aldo met his death at the hands of his so-called friends. A well-hidden, spreading hamlet nestles in the lee of a high hill, which blocks out the setting sun as the day yields to another early evening. To the right of us I hear water rushing past the back of the settlement, whilst on our left the Teme seems to pass calmly by.

'Would you know if we can find a track that leads north to Clunbyrig?' I ask a young, fair-haired woman. She is playing with a small child behind a dwelling in what is left of the day.

'There is a ford ahead, if you take that road to your left – there'. She smiles bewitchingly and points us to where an inn stands across the road from a clutch of small dwellings and outhouses.

My eyelids feel suddenly heavy, weary merely at the sight of the inn. I want to rest, as does Harding I am sure. My friends would feel the better for it by the pleading looks they give me,

'Is the inn open for trade?' I ask her.

She picks up the child and cradles it in her arms as she answers,

'The inn is open, but the outlander earl's men are already there. I might be right in thinking you would as soon not have to put up with their brashness as we have to. There is another inn over the river where you are going, five miles north, in Clunbyrig'.

I offer silver, a token of thanks but she shakes her head,

'With silver in my pocket, my husband the innkeeper would ask how I came by it. He is uncommonly friendly toward the outlanders with their silver. Keep yours and thank me in words. I am happy to help a handsome noble Aenglishman such as you'.

I thank her again, and ask

'You have been more than helpful - *what is your name?*'

'I am Ecgfritha, my Lord', she answers and is about to smile sweetly at me when someone shouts from the inn.

'Ecgfritha, *where are you?* God she is never about when she should make herself useful!'

'My husband wants me', she bobs quickly, clutches her child tightly to her bosom and hurries away'. 'I had best be off, and so should you be before the outlanders hear of you –'

'Ecgfritha, get yourself here now!' someone else yells, a woman, perhaps her mother-in-law, 'The time for playing is past and there are men's cups to be filled!'

'I *am* coming!' Ecgfritha yells back as she gathers her skirts to hurry back to the inn.

'And we are *going!*' I turn Braenda and we press our horses to ride past the inn. When we have passed and are set to wade through the icy Teme once more, I look back over my shoulder past Saeward. Several armed men have showed on the roadway and one points toward us. He stands, shaking a fist in anger. Before any of them has time to mount, we have cleared the ford, wet again, but safe thanks to a thoughtful innkeeper's wife.

I call out to Harding behind me,

'Clunbyrig has an inn, five miles or so north, she said'.

'Fair enough – but we shall be in *sore* need of a rest by then', he draws a hand across his brow to show how tired he is, 'and I for one surely could not ride any further!'

'Nor I', Theodolf calls from my left and the others chorus their agreement.

For some way all we hear is the drumming of our horses' hooves where the track is tightly-packed. Elsewhere the going is muddy where we pass between trees. The heavens are pitch black but for the few stars to the north. The Great Bear, and below it the North Star twinkle brightly ahead of us. We used these for sailing from Roskilde to Skagen when the ice allowed in late spring, and now we are using them on land to guide us north through southern Scrobbe shire.

No-one speaks until the first pin-pricks of light can be seen some way off. Is that Clunbyrig, or are we still short? As we close on the hamlet there is no sign of light. Our mounts trot along quietly between the few hovels. There is no sign of an inn here anyway, so we press our horses a little faster. With the dark mass of a hill on our left, our way climbs a little and we leave this God-forsaken settlement behind us.

'There are buildings ahead'. Saeward's sighting gives us some feeling of relief after more miles of darkness. This must be Clunbyrig.

'I see smoke from a hall, or an inn down the track - *there*', Theodolf points with his bow for me. I can barely make him out as a great bank of cloud passes over us, blotting out what little moonlight there is from the quarter moon to our left.

'It must be an inn', Harding reasons. He reins in to see better,

'There are what look to be stables or outhouses behind, away from the road. Take a closer look', he asks me. 'Should there be any of Willelm fitzOsbern's men down there, we will have to bypass Clunbyrig'.

'I can ride down there and see if there is anyone there that we would not want to meet', Theodolf offers, 'and wave you on if all is clear'.

'You could look into the stables or outhouses', I agree. 'Count any saddles you see that look like theirs'.

'What are you thinking of, Ivar? Do you want a fight at this time, when any sane man would be thinking of resting?' Oslac is wide-eyed, wondering if I have lost my reason. He thinks he can read me now, but I am thinking of something else.

Theodolf raises a hand and laughs,

'This might sound too simple, but what if one of us runs in and shouts that someone has attacked their comrades at the Waeleford inn?'

'That sounds good', Oslac laughs with Theodolf, 'what do you think, Ivar?'

'First we have to find out if there are any Northmen in there', I humour him.

'Then I ought to take a look', Theodolf nods to me, presses his knees into his horse's flanks and sets off alone into Clunbyrig. We can hardly see him when he has ridden past the first dwelling until the moon shows through a halo amid a broad blanket of thinner cloud.

The wind has picked up and whips at standing water by the trackside and pushes our cloaks and jerkins against our backs. I feel the sweat running down inside my woollen shirt, against my back, and shiver. The waiting makes me feel no better.

'What is that?' Saeward points downhill and we see someone waving a windblown torch.

'He said he would wave back at us', Harding answers Saeward gruffly. 'But it is a signal, what else?'

'Very well then - ride', I agree and knee Braenda into a canter.

Theodolf stands outside the inn door and waits until we are around him before he tells us,

'There are two Northman nobles in there, the innkeeper tells me, and they have Seaxan women with them. He also tells me that another four are in the thegn's dwelling over there', Theodolf points at a hall, set away from the rest of the settlement.

I think he has kept the best for last,

'One man is asleep in the main room of the inn', Theodolf grins, 'meant to be on guard'.

'We go in and fettle the so-called guard', Harding snorts at Oslac and me. 'If he calls out, we take on the other two in here'.

'What do we do with the women?' Saeward asks nervously.

'We send them packing!' Harding tells him. '*You* can have them if you want, not that you would know what to do with them'.

'Aye, it is not for us to deal with them', Oslac eases Saeward's anger at Harding and points with his thumb over his shoulder at a small gathering of Clunbyrig's dwellers.

'*We* will know what to do with the whores!' one man leers, brandishing a cudgel.

'I can believe that', I cannot help but smile, even though he sickens me with his show of rotten teeth, and warts on his chin and nose.

'Just deal with the outlanders and leave the women to *us!*' the cudgel-bearer snaps back at me.

The five of us creep across the earth floor of the inn and stand around the snoring Northman, ready to still his cry of alarm and stop him fleeing to warn his friends across the road. His bare head rests on his right arm at the table's edge, nose half-buried in the sleeve of a grubby jerkin.

I can hear grunts from upstairs, where one of the Seaxan women is being pleasured. Nothing stirs anywhere else. Oslac stands by the table, thinking how to deal with the Northman. He takes a step forward and places a finger on the guard's nose. Unable to breathe, the Northman raises his head and looks up at Oslac. Before he can cry out, Harding draws a piece of rope around his neck and pulls tightly.

All we hear is hoarse gurgling and the man slumps, his head thumping loudly onto the table.

'Innkeeper, bring ale - tell me what is there to eat?'

I turn to find him standing behind me, trying to look over my shoulder at the dead man.

'We can make a good broth, and there is hare on the back wall of the kitchen. Aside from that the usual greens, fruit – not a lot, really', the innkeeper grumbles. '*They* ate most of what we had'.

He kicks at the dead man, and then looks upstairs,

'Their whores gobbled a lot, fat mares that they are! The women were brought from elsewhere –'

'Stop gabbling man, bring the ale, cook the broth and leave the hare on the back wall –'

Harding breaks into the innkeeper's grumbling, only to be stopped in turn by Saeward.

'*I* would like hare. I am fed up with broth everywhere we go! Cook the hare, man, and be quick about it. I could eat a horse!'

Harding looks from Saeward to me, open-mouthed. I shrug and grin. Saeward at least has a warrior's hunger.

'What do you say, Oslac, Theodolf? Do you want hare?' I ask them both.

'I *would* like hare', Oslac beams and nods eagerly, '*and* broth – I am not bothered *what* I eat!'

'So, too, would I', Theodolf nods, aloof.

'In that case, you and I could share one, Ivar'.

Harding turns back to the innkeeper and smiles before asking of him,

'I hope you have enough for us all?'

'I will have a look', the innkeeper shrugs, not showing much hope', but first I shall bring you ale. Are you going to eat with that corpse sitting there beside you?'

'I had forgotten all about him', Oslac sniffs. Saeward and Theodolf carry him out between them and are back with us before the ale cups are thumped down in front of us.

The candles on our table are gutting by the time we finish our meal. The two Northmen have still not shown and at least Oslac and Harding show tiredness. The others may already be past caring and I am finding it hard to stifle my yawns when Theodolf shakes me into wakefulness.

'I heard someone moving around upstairs!' he hisses.

I sit up, cock my right ear but hear nothing.

'Is it the hare you have eaten that is playing tricks on you?' Saeward chortles, but then Harding puts a hand over the East Seaxan's mouth.

'There, you see? Someone *is* stirring!' Theodolf is proved right. Harding's hearing is plainly better than mine. 'If one of them is coming down we had best make ourselves scarce and take them off their stride when they are least ready for us'.

'And if it is one of the women?' I ask, 'How do we deal with her, ask for her understanding?'

'I think we should send her back upstairs to waken the other one', Saeward puts to me, 'then send them both outside, out of harm's way'.

'You mean out of sight. Sending them out there is more likely to put them *in* harm's way', I upbraid my friend. Saeward's upper lip curls back but he says nothing.

'Who *cares* what happens to them?' Harding is with Saeward here. I would guess so, too are Theodolf and Oslac.

Harding and my friends try to brow-beat me into agreeing with them to send the women out. Not knowing how the women came to be with the Northman lords, I have to give in,

'Well, whatever... I cannot think why I feel sorry for them. They are whores, their time paid by whoever cares to buy it'.

'All right, let them stay in here', Harding yields. 'But when we go in the morning they will be turfed out by the innkeeper anyway'.

'When we are out of sight it will be a free-for all', Oslac sides with Harding.

'He means your feeling for fairness gets in the way of duty toward us', Theodolf notes drily.

'What is my duty to *you*, my friends? You are my friends, and I will do my utmost to stop you being killed. These whores are no threat to any of us', are they?' I answer, to a show of wrinkled noses. Have I missed his point? I hear a sharp intake of breath from Harding. He tells me what he thinks they mean,

'He means your duty to the kingdom. These whores are tainted, they have taken the Northmen's silver. Either these good folk outside will kick the door in to get at them, or the innkeeper will turf them out after taking his due. Waste no feelings on them, Ivar. Think of all our mothers, wives, sisters and daughters'.

'If it were not for the whores the Northmen *would* take your womenfolk. *That* is what I am trying to tell you!' Sometimes I wonder why I waste my breath.

'Better *they* let themselves be used than your womenfolk asking why we let these whores be killed in some mistaken zeal. We can give the women the Northmen's horses to ride away on —'I am stopped by Theodolf when one of the whores appears at the doorway.

'I did not know there were more men here', she saunters, smiling, into the flickering light of a wall-mounted torch.

Theodolf does not pull back when she nears him,'

'You are a good-looking young fellow. Are you given?'

'Is he as good-looking as the Northman who bedded you?' Saeward smirks at her.

148

'That one upstairs – have you *seen* him?' she throws her head back and cackles. 'He will pay *well* for my time. Otherwise I should not have given him a second look! He must be as old as *you*'.

She looks at me as she says this. Not having seen him yet, I do not take this as an slight and answer,

'When I see this fellow you speak of, I shall see whether or not I should feel offended'.

'At least I can understand you better than him', she jerks her head upward. 'Where are you from?'

'I thank you for the back-handed tribute. My name is Ivar Ulfsson, and I am a Dane', I scratch my growing beard.

'I have been in this kingdom since the time of Knut 'the Great'. I should hope you *can* understand me, but I am not sure you understand how bad things are for you. I stand between the folk out there tearing you to pieces and my friends here who want to hand you and your friend over to them'.

Her haughty smile turns into a look of loathing,

'What, are you telling me you want my time with you for nothing - do you take me for foolish or forlorn?' She smiles haughtily and looks from me to the others, 'I would sooner have *him*'.

'No doubt you *would* have me', Theodolf laughs, 'but after that Northman bastard upstairs has had you, I would not touch you with the best will in the world!'

'Go back upstairs, wake your friend and bring her down', Harding tells her.

'What do you mean to do with us?' She may now believe what I have told her, about what will happen to them.

'If you do as we ask, nothing - otherwise we will hand you over to them without waiting for the innkeeper to turf you out in the morning', I nod to the door, meaning the folk outside. 'I offer you life. The Northmen's horses are yours, ride where you want and begin life anew with their silver'.

She nods acknowledgement of a way out and makes her way back up the creaking stairs. Not long after she shows again with her friend.

'Why would you do this for us?' her friend asks me.

'You and your kind keep the other women from being defiled', is all I tell her. Her level gaze tells me that I have erred in my understanding of why she is here.

'I am Sigrid, wife of the king's thegn from Waeleford. Aelfflaed here is my maid. The Northmen offered *no* other way out, since my husband died fighting with King Harold Godwinson. We could starve, or eat, and I have a young son'.

She stops talking of her own woes and looks toward the door. 'The rest are in the thegn's hall over the road, despoiling Thegn Saewold's widow and her maids', she pauses to watch how her words are taken.

'Their comrades are in the inn at Waeleford. Mark my words, there will be anger and tears in the morning', she finishes.

'My Lady –'Harding begins.

'*You* took me for a whore. Did the innkeeper tell you that in his wisdom?' the Lady Sigrid berates him, 'If you wish, *you* can have me too and then I can go down to the river and drown myself!'

As Sigrid begins to sob, Aelfflaed tries to comfort her.

'*None* of us wants you to kill you. If you have a child, you are needed. Go back to wherever the child is to take him away, the pair of you. Take him to a burh, where you can take care of him', I offer as she is being comforted. 'We will deal with these two upstairs when they awaken'.

'Why wait that long?' Oslac grins mischievously, feeling the edge of his dagger with his thumb. 'I need to know if this needs sharpening'.

'Aye, why let them cause uproar and bring the others onto us?' Saeward draws his sword.

'Very well then, let us take care of their needs', Harding winks at me and signals me to follow.

'If we all go up, we *will* awaken them and then there will be mayhem', I sigh.

Harding chides,

'Are you afraid of a wretched pair of Northmen shouting? Come, Ivar, slake your thirst for Northman blood. They killed your kinsman Harold and his brothers at Caldbec Beorg, did they not?'

'He would sooner be with these women when their customers bathe in their own blood!' Oslac laughs.

'Hush, man - do you want to wake them up?' Harding thumps Oslac on his barrel chest and hisses at him, 'Get behind me. The more there are of us, the less likelihood there is of them getting by us!'

'They are both sound asleep and as naked as the day they were born', Sigrid calls in a low voice after us.

Harding kicks the first bed.

Oslac waits at the head for the Northman to open his eyes. Before he can yell out a warning to his friend in the next closet, Oslac stuffs a rag into his gaping mouth. He is taken from the cot, bound hand and foot and led, half naked down the narrow stairs. We go to the next cot and this time I stand at the head. Saeward kicks the cot and the fellow wakes with a start. As he opens his mouth to yell I push a head bolster onto his face, push him back and wait until I think he is limp. When I pull it away he opens his mouth to yell again, so I push my mailed fist into the yawning cavern of tongue and teeth. Saeward tears off a piece of bedding and hands it to me.

'When I take my hand out, stuff it into his mouth', I tell Saeward, who duly does my bidding and now both Northmen have been hushed.

'What do we *do* with them?' Theodolf asks awkwardly.

'Are you asking me or Harding?' I ask by return.

'Well, I was asking whichever of you has an answer', he eyes us both and turns to Oslac. 'What do you say, Oslac, should we keep them alive or kill them?'

'If it were up to me-'Oslac gets no further before Sigrid comes in.

She looks at the overweight bareness of one and tells us,

'The older man, the first one you bound up, is the earl, Willelm, the king's right hand man as he kept telling me'.

Harding and I look at one another.

What she has told us has put everything in a new light. Do we kill him, or ransom him for silver, or even gold? Rights could be demanded for our fellows. However, rights are not always granted, not by this king's underlings. Odo would brook no demands from Aenglishmen under threat. He would let us kill Willelm and put a younger hopeful in his earldom, one who would be beholden to him. We would then be back where we began.

'How much silver do you think he is *worth?*' Harding asks me, 'How many silver marks should we demand?'

'Ask for as much as he weighs and see if they stump up the sum we thought of', I laugh and ask Sigrid, 'Who is this other one?'

She breaks off and stares balefully at the younger one,

'He is Earl Ricard fitzScrob, another of their king's cronies. He has been given land in Scrobbe shire, as I understand.

He is manhandled, naked above the waist, past her to the doorway.

'Is *he* going to be useful?' Oslac asks me.

'Perhaps', I scratch the itching new beard again. 'We could always kill them if their underlings threaten us'.

'It will cost us no more to keep them both alive', Harding adds wearily, hinting I might wish to do so. 'It will cost us even less to kill them both - *now*'.

My nod is met with a grunt.

'I thought as much', he grins, 'do we take them as they are?'

'How would we do that? We would have to let them dress themselves, and then they would surely try to escape', I scratch my jaw in deep thought.

We all stand waiting for one or the other of us to think of something before Theodolf jabs a finger into the air,

'What if - one or two of these folk outside takes word to Eadric, that we hold these two earls captive? There must be at least a couple of them able to ride', Theodolf offers helpfully.

'Ask the innkeeper if he knows of any of them who can ride', I tell Theodolf with a wary nod. I do not know if I can rely on any of them to evade capture by the Northmen, who will be swarming around these hills before too long.

Theodolf leads down the stairs, followed closely by Harding. I look around to see if any of their belongings might be of use, think better of it and take the stairs after them.

9

Two men are found, thought by the innkeeper to be trustworthy, to tell Eadric and Rhiwallon of our 'finds'. Their leaving awakens the Northmen from their drunken slumbers in the hall across the way.

Two of them dash out onto the road, still buckling on their sword belts, a third trips on the side of the road, crashing down nose first onto the still wet road. A fourth shows through the door, and is met by one of Theodolf's arrows in his bared neck.

'The fool should have pulled up his neckguard!' I chide, before thinking on whose side I am meant to be and shrug, 'It is just as well he did not'.

'Aye, and now there are only two of them!' Harding points at the second man, lying in the road.

'Perhaps the other two will cut their losses and ride back wherever they came. Then again, we would not be able to stay until anyone comes back for these two in here'.

'We had best make sure they cannot free themselves!' I curse our ill luck and look for the two surviving Northmen, who have been swallowed by the darkness.

I wave Oslac and Theodolf to either side of the dwelling they came out from. Saeward and Harding come with me straight across the road. A crossbow bolt hisses past my right ear and I know there must be another outlander in the blackness that we did not know of.

'The innkeeper said there were only four of them!' Harding's yell is rewarded by a crossbow bolt in his sword arm and he drops the sword, snarling, bleeding badly.

We are in the lee of the building now, pressing against the road-side wall. As I stare at the doorway in the darkness, I can make out the crest of a helm bobbing up and down. The owner may be searching for one of us, or he may be looking out because he is afraid. Fearful men err foolishly. We will wait a little longer until he shows, unsure of where we are. I put a finger to my mouth for Harding and Saeward to keep still and hold myself close to the doorway until the head vanishes. Keeping to the shadow of the wall I edge forward.

Luckily no-one looks out again until I am ready with my axe. The head shows again and I bring the axe down onto the helm with enough strength to crack the crown and draw blood from a gash in the man's skull. He drops flat in the doorway, felled like an ox. Kicking his body out of the way, I bring my axe up into another man's groin. Fleetingly I see Brand before me, but then I blink and look down at an open-mouthed Northman.

Another crossbow bolt sings past my left ear, and catches Oslac in the throat.

'Good God, *Oslac!*' I almost scream in my anguish at losing another of my friends to the Northmen.

The moon shows again, betraying the crossbowman in the back of the room, setting his next bolt onto the stock. In the way he looks up at me he knows he has been seen. He freezes long enough for Theodolf to loose off an arrow that bites into his open mouth, pinning him to the wattle of the back wall. The crossbow drops to the earth floor, its bolt still somehow held in the groove.

'I shall take this with me to think on Oslac', I tell Harding as I pick up the weapon. 'There must be more of these arrows in his pouch'.

Pointing to a bag held by a leather strap across the man's chest, he wrenches it over the Northman's head to hand it to me,

'If you learn to use this crossbow as you call it, as well as you use that axe, you will be a deadly foe indeed!'

'Are they *all* dead?' I ask only.

'There are two in here, another in the doorway', Harding reckons on his fingers, 'one out on this side of the road face down, the other outside the inn on his back, how many should there be?'

'The innkeeper thinks four, but I would say five. The other two left the roadside for the darkness – is there another door to this hovel?' I look around.

'Aye, there is - here', Saeward opens it and looks out to a small yard at the back.

'Two killed on the road, two seek shelter and a crossbow bolt loosed off', Theodolf growls, sickened at the Northman's treachery.

'There is another one - *where?*' Harding stares at me, chastened by Oslac's sudden death by a crossbow bolt. He does not want to follow my friend. We do not need more of them falling on us when we can do without fighting.

We are four now, and we must needs find a priest to bury Oslac, to give him his due worth.

'There will be more before we hand over the two earls'.

I look heavenward in sadness, knowing now we will have to use these noblemen as bargaining tokens to leave here, and be no better off for our pains. The Northmen will vent their fury on these folk, and I am not sure a single dwelling will be left standing when they have been driven off in chains or – worse still – killed where they stand, man, woman or child alike.

'We should kill them, surely?' When Harding sees me shake my head he shrugs and resigns himself to his fate. Reading my thoughts he adds, 'Well, whatever. We should leave here, soonest'.

'Aye, we take them with us', I tell him. 'Should we find ourselves unable to break through, we can *use* them'.

Theodolf stares down at the ashen Oslac lying by the doorway the way he fell, torn from us by the Northmen's crossbows, as were Theorvard and Sigegar.

'What about Oslac?' Saeward asks me.

Still looking at Theodolf I answer,

'We have to find a priest'.

The lad's mouth twists with anger at the sight of his friend with the crossbow bolt still lodged in his throat.

'I will take care of him', Saeward kneels to put his hand over Oslac's eyes and draws down the lids to hide his staring eyes.

Another crossbow bolt thuds into the doorway, splintering the wood above Saeward's head.

'I *saw* where that came from!' Theodolf draws his bow with an arrow ready to be loosed off. He makes his way warily, crouching, across the way to the inn and stares into the darkness along the road.

Again, when the cloud breaks, the moon shows the fifth Northman plainly. He is well within Theodolf's reach when the lad leans against the wall by its yard gateway. Unaware Theodolf is aiming at him the Northman sets his next bolt on the shaft, and pulls the cord behind the stop ready to let loose the bolt. Theodolf lets fly his arrow into the man's crop, the way Oslac died. For what seems an age the Northman stands with his hands trying in vain to pull the arrow free. By the time Theodolf reaches him he has dropped to his knees on the wet, muddy road, striving to rid himself of Theodolf's slender ash arrow with its barbed tip.

'I work these heads just for the Northmen', Theodolf had told me at Naesinga, 'after the smith has made the rough head and socket'.

Theodolf stands over the young fellow, little older than himself. When the Northman cranes his head up to look at him, Theodolf rests a foot on his shoulder and wrenches the arrow free.

The body falls back into a patch of mud and cow dung, cold, stiff and arched backward. My young friend would have us believe he killed to avenge Oslac's death. But I would say, from having been with him these past months that he savoured the killing of this Northman in much the same way as he savoured his own marksmanship in bringing down the wolf pack leader at Leagatun. I understand the deep-seated feeling against the Northmen for the killing of his father. He checks his arrowhead in the same way I check my axe or sword after a fight, saying nothing.

'Do you want the other one?' Saeward asks Theodolf.

Theodolf is looking the other way and misses what has been asked of him. When he thinks the young Northanhymbran is looking at him, Saeward points with his axe at the dwelling where Theodolf's other prey lies. When Theodolf nods mutely, Saeward enters the darkness and comes back out onto the road again with the bloodied arrow. With a smile, Theodolf takes the arrow from Saeward's outstretched hand and searches the gore-covered head for flaws,

'I thank you, my friend', Theodolf takes in Saeward. 'You must have pulled this arrow in the same way I did, else it would have snapped'.

'I watched a master at his craft', Saeward grins.

'You should let me look at that wound', he adds.

'It is fine, thank you Saeward', Theodolf pulls away when Saeward tries to look.

'Let me have a look', Saeward pleads, 'it will not take long'.

'No *really*, Saeward, I am *fine*', Theodolf begins to cough.

'*Let* him look, Theodolf', Harding counsels sternly. But Theodolf is having none of it. He pulls away again and turns to go away. It is then I see blood on his back.

'Let Saeward see your wound, Theodolf!' I order and Harding catches the lad by the arm as he brushes against him trying to draw away from Saeward.

'Theodolf, for God's sake, *do as Ivar says!*' Harding turns Theodolf toward Saeward and he, too can see the blood now.

'You *know* Saeward can help!' I add.

'Can he?' Theodolf asks, as if knowing there is nothing Saeward can do for him.

Saeward holds Theodolf's shoulders firmly and undoes his jerkin. When he pulls up the lad's woollen shirt he gasps,

'Ivar, look at this!'

Saeward holds the shirt to show a dark brown stain on his chest. A matted core of grey shows where he was wounded by the boar's tusk. Fine fingers of green have spread around the wound.

'*How* in God's name did you draw that bow?' I ask, staring into Theodolf's eyes. 'Do you *want* to die?'

I cannot think of the words I would need for Aethel if, or should I say *when* we lose him? She will demand to know how he could have been allowed to suffer like this - and for how long, she would ask.

'I was a little harder of late', he answers, trying to smile.

'Do you want to be a dead hero, or do you want me to heal you, if I can?' Saeward shakes his head.

Theodolf grins weakly,

'*Can* you?' he asks again, as if doubting Saeward's healing skills.

The last arrow he loosed off must have been the hardest, and to have wrenched it from the Northman's chest would have been the hardest trial of strength for him, with this old wound plaguing him.

'I shall have to keep you here', Saeward warns him, and looks to us for help in getting Theodolf to submit to staying.

I nod, agreeing with Saeward,

'We will have to weave a lie for the innkeeper and the Lady Sigrid to tell the Northmen when they come'.

Harding and I cobble together a tale that must be believable to the Northmen if he is caught. They must be told that Oslac and Theodolf were craftsmen who came and were caught in the sudden outbreak of fighting between us and the Northmen this evening. Theodolf will be tended by Saeward and the Lady Sigrid. She and her maid should be clad in the way of ceorls' wives, in plain woven cloth.

With everything agreed, I leave silver with the innkeeper for Oslac's burial. Having bound the pair of them we lead them away from Clunbyrig with grey streaks edging the clouds to our right as we leave.

Willelm fitzOsbern's big grey mare drags at her rope and I pull sharply to get her in line behind me. Harding follows with Earl Ricard trailing him on his chestnut stallion. We have a long ride to leave this south-west corner of Scrobbe Shire and out of range of Willelm's men.

We should find hospitality beyond the bounds of Scrobbe shire. In reaching the Danelaw we will be amongst friendlier folk.

'I shall know better where we are when we pass Lindleshealh on track for Steadford', Harding tells me.

Looking over my left shoulder at him, I ask,

'Have you thought about what we are to do with these two?' I catch sight of Willelm scowling from the corner of one eye.

'Hah, I wondered if you had something in store for us!' he bellows with mirth and almost lurches sideways off his mount when she stops suddenly.

I rein in and push him back onto his saddle lest I have to lift him bodily and risk him trying to attack me. Braenda snorts, shaking her head at me for bringing her to a halt so soon after getting into her stride. Still we have put many miles behind us, riding north-eastward, crossing two rivers since leaving Clunbyrig. A ridge guides us to the north-eastern corner of Scrobbe shire, to Lindleshealh. Where another, smaller river wends its way northward into the hills to our left, we leave our path to ride eastward.

A spring that bubbles up from the hilly ground to our left broadens and bends below our track. When we come to where this smaller river empties into the River Seoferna below the Wrekin, we are blocked by floodwaters. FitzOsbern grins smugly on seeing the deep frown on Harding's hairy brow, thinking we will have to free them both in order to cross.

Harding sees the smug grin when he turns to look upriver, cuffs the Northman and curses as if punishing a wayward son,

'Fool Northman, I should make you wade *naked* through it!' He turns to me and sucks his teeth before letting me into his thoughts, 'There is nothing for it but to ride north into Scrobbesbyrig, to cross the river by the bridge there. What do you think, Ivar? Is it worth a toss of the dice or will they be too many?'

'You know this land better than I. Are there not Northmen in Scrobbesbyrig?' Young Ricard fitzScrob asks Harding, eyeing him warily from where his horse has stopped to crop the deep grass by the riverbank.

'Your guess is as good as mine –'Harding begins. He stops, stares at me, turns back to fitzScrob and asks me over one shoulder,

'Very well then, we cannot cross even the smaller river here. Thinking back, we passed a ford where the river bends sharply'. So saying, he wheels about and throws Earl Willelm his best baleful glare to try to frighten him. The earl laughs and I give his mare a smack on her rump. She is in Braenda's way anyway. The big grey mare gives a start and pulls hard on the rope that I tied to her bridle. I tug hard on the rope to bring her around behind me again and we set off south-westward, back into the wind.

'There it is, the ford, such as it is', Harding gives me a sheepish grin when we see the strength of the flow even here.

We shall have a lively crossing with the water up to our horses' withers, if not around their necks! If it is bad news for us, our hostages will be even less happy. Their horses may shy at the slippery stones below the water and throw their riders. They are due for a ducking as much as we are. Although Earl Willelm's mount is taller than his friend's, she may be less sure-footed and he will have further to fall. I think back to when I was riding across the Deorewent, with Arngrim behind me on the old nag that Thegn Eadwy had given him. I would not want the earl breathing down my neck with a score of his men behind him.

'Watch their smiles fade when we begin to wade through the Hvarfe at Tadceaster!' I call out to Harding in front of me.

'We do not need to go that way', he shouts back at me. 'We can cross the Treonta at Deoraby, and ride northward through the dales to cross the Hvarfe upriver at Otheleag'.

'I was hoping to look in on Aethel's steading –'I begin.

'Should we have time, on our way back, we can rest the horses there', he answers dully.

'You know about Aethel's home?' I ask.

'Theodolf told me about the steading where he grew up. Do you think I might have known his father?'

'You may well have, aye. We were with Tostig's household and he rode with Copsig gathering tithes', I answer foolishly.

'*That murdering shit!* Your *friend* rode with Copsig?' Harding croaks, spluttering his bile with all the hatred he can muster. 'How does any man have a friend who could have ridden with *him*? What did this Hrothulf look like? Was he tall and fair, or short and dark?'

We are across the ford now without any mishaps but Harding – wet to his hips - looks fit to throw someone into the swirling waters. Hopefully it is not me. When I draw Hrothulf in words for him he calms down and tells me he does not recall seeing him,

'From what you tell me I *should* have known him but no, I do not know him from when Copsig brought some of Tostig's thugs – er, huscarls'. Harding cranes his head around to look at me, 'You, Ivar, you may be different but in the main Tostig's huscarls were greedy for silver. He rewarded them well, and the king was grateful to him for filling his coffers, but you can well guess *where* that silver came from!'

'Did everyone hate them so?' I ask, 'Was that *all* Tostig's huscarls, or just the Danes amongst them who had a bad name?'

'They were all tainted when Tostig was stripped of his earldom. You did right by leaving for Earl Harold's household'.

Glaring at the hapless earl when his horse pulls away, he goes on,

'Perhaps he knew better than you about what was to come', Harding smacks Ricard's horse again when he stops in front of Braenda. 'That year, when Earl Tostig helped his brother rid us of Gruffyd was his best. I mean it was his best for tithes. We had a good harvest that year. The old king was happy with him, but it was Copsig who stuffed his own coffers'.

Harding looks at the drip-nosed, wretched Ricard behind him. He swings himself around in his saddle and barks hoarsely,

'We will rest soon, Northman! You are *not* the only one here who suffered at the ford. We will let you have some water soon, all right?' He turns back to look at me, 'Ah, well, he will know what I mean before long. There must be some among them who understand Aenglish. Where was I? Our animals were doing well – sheep, cattle and hogs –'

'*I* understand what you say', Earl Willelm breaks into Harding's flow, riding almost alongside him. 'Well, *most* of what you say I understand'.

'*Do you*, indeed? *Most* is as much as you need', Harding throws me a crafty smile and looks across to the Northman, tapping the side of his broad nose,

'Perhaps we should talk about what to do with *you*? I shall know you understand by the looks you throw at me. I was talking to my friend - be a good lad and think on staying upright in your saddle'.

Earl Willelm nods, looks away and then turns back to Harding,

'What *do* you mean to do with us?'

'*In good time*, Northman – I will tell you everything in good time. Now mind your own', Harding snaps back at him.

'*Ride on*, keep your own counsel'.

Harding looks sideways at me, 'What have *you* got to laugh about, Ivar?' When I nod, still grinning, at the earl Harding looks around at him.

'Keep my own counsel – *what does that mean?*' Willelm breaks in again and I laugh out aloud.

'*It means shut your mouth!*' Harding barks at the Northman noble, grits his teeth and shakes his head in disbelief.

'*What - ?*' I ask, trying to stop laughing, although even I do not know what it was about the earl's words I found worthy of laughter.

'Laughing does not help, Ivar. This bastard will eavesdrop on everything we say now. What do you make of *that?*'

'I could think of something gruesome to do with him to stop his ears flapping. Or we could speak in Northanhymbran Danish', I offer. 'There is *no* way he would understand us then'.

Harding nods with a grin on his face,

'Even if he understood Danish, he could never understand *that,* enwrapped as it is with Aenglish words'.

'Shall we try it?' I ask, and begin to speak in dialect. Willelm cocks his ear to listen and soon gives up trying to follow us.

Harding laughs and speaks up in plain Aenglish for Willelm's sake,

'At least we can keep a *few* things from him!'

Even the earl smiles at that. He turns away, looking sidelong at Harding, to speak to his friend Ricard in *his* own tongue. They share a joke, teasing Harding. The younger fellow laughs out aloud and slaps his thigh.

'Two can play at *that* game, Aenglishman', he says for us and gives a hollow laugh, to show he has a wit of his own.

Harding grins broadly at Ricard, who thinks he has some common ground with us after this show of understanding.

After a few more miles Harding calls over one shoulder,

'We can rest here', he lifts his left leg clear of his saddle and slides down to the damp, partly snow-covered grassy trackside. 'I think we should wait until the light weakens before riding on. Scrobbesbyrig must be close. The Seoferna bends to the north-east here before winding westward through this broad dale. We will follow the track that way'.

Harding stirs the air with one finger at the narrowing track ahead of us, beyond a dark mass of woodland. Somewhere along here must be a bridge or ford, but for now we must rest. He knows the land here, so until we reach the Danelaw lands beyond the high ground in Deoraby shire we shall take the tracks or roads he shows me to.

I drop to the track beside Braenda and lead her to the waterside. Earl Willelm's horse follows and both animals take their fill from a small, clear riverside pool.

Whilst Harding takes stock of the food bags, I take his horse with Ricard's still roped to his saddle. They both drink long deeply from the same pool. Ricard's horse stamps and muddies the water, so I lead them closer to the riverbank.

'What is there to eat?' I ask Harding, who has the bag so near his eyes he looks like a horse with a nosebag.

'Bread, cheese, apples – the usual, and there is ale in a skin', Harding pulls his face from the bag and throws me an apple.

'Are there enough apples to give the horses?' I ask, crunching the late harvested fruit.

'Give our meagre stores to these beasts?' Harding is taken aback.

'Our *own* horses, not theirs', I tell him, taking another bite before sliding the rest between Braenda's teeth for her to crunch.

Harding digs into the bag again, tosses me another apple and gives me an odd look. I pay no heed to him and give Braenda the whole apple.

She takes a bite, half the apple. Her long teeth work the white flesh, up and down. When she has finished the mouthful she nuzzles me for the rest.

'Do I get that drink you spoke of?' Willelm recalls Harding's words.

'Shall I let him down?' I turn sideways to Harding, keeping an eye on the Northman. I have lost one hostage, thanks to my own foolishness. Losing this earl would be unforgivable.

'Do so at your own risk', Harding warns. 'If his hands are tied, he cannot get up to any mischief, but he can still try to run'.

'*Run* – where? Look around you. How do I ford the river with my hands tied?' the earl chides.

'Nor could I hope to find rocks on this riverbank sharp enough to fray these bindings on my hands'.

I hold my water flask for him to drink from. When I pull it away he looks sourly at me.

'It is not good to drink the water so quickly, even if you are thirsty'. I pull the flask away. He needs to know how far he can take my goodwill.

'You are my keeper now?' Willelm laughs. 'Give me some more water and let me worry about my own health'.

'If you wish', I hold up the flask for him and he comes toward me. As he nears me he begins to run. I turn aside and stretch out my left leg. He trips and falls, chest down onto the grass.

'What did I tell you Ivar?' Harding shakes his head wearily at me. He stands, having rested on his haunches, an apple in his hand. Closing on the Northman earl, he drops his apple and punches him in the stomach. Willelm doubles up and Harding next brings his knee up and brings both hands down onto the fellow's head.

'Did you have to do that?' I ask, looking at Willelm writhing on the ground.

'They are no friendlier toward our kind, either', Harding grunts, turning to look at me.

He wags a finger almost under my nose.

'Treat *them* as they would us, be kind to them and they see it as a weakness. You have a lot to learn, Ivar. He may be a noble, but how far back does the bloodline go? Not far, I would hazard a guess'.

Both Ricard and Willelm watch me from behind Harding as he tells me what I already know,

'His father may have been some lickspittle to that murdering duke Rodberht–'

'My father was no lickspittle!' Willelm snaps, having struggled to his feet, and is rewarded with a thump for his pains. He stumbles and drops to his knees.

'I do not care for your sort, shut your damned mouth or I shall pay my dues to you again!' Harding snarls down at the earl. He looks at me next, 'Well, *what?* Surely you do not feel *sorry* for him?'

'I have said nothing', I shrug.

'Your look says everything', Harding mutters.

'Would you do that were I free to use both hands to defend myself with?' Willelm dares him.

'*Oh*, what a fine try! Do you think I would let you smooth your ruffled Northman's cock-feathers at cost to me?'

Harding bends down and stares into the Northman's eyes,

'It beggars belief. You thought I would be so stupid. *Well I never –!*' Harding stops suddenly and snorts. He then breaks into a laugh, 'You *did* think I would free you for your own ends!'

Willelm follows up with a dare,

'What would be so wrong in *that?*'

Harding turns on him, fists at the ready. He stops as quickly as he turns and smiles as he takes the bait,

'Well, *why ever not?* I should show you the way we fight in Deira. You might tell your friends when back amongst your own again.'

'You fool', I tell him under my breath when he passes close in front of me, although I feel my stomach knotting because I know what must follow. We have the upper hand and Harding will throw that away showing off.

'Untie him, and we will see who the fool is here!' Harding tells me. Has he altogether lost his wits?

'What happens if he beats *you?*' I try to reason with him.

'*If* he beats me, he and the other one can go free – now', Harding foolishly tells me. 'Mark my words, Ivar, he will *not* beat me! Have you no faith in my fighting skills?'

'I have never seen you fight bare-fisted', I have to allow, and nod at Earl Willelm. 'But how do I know he is no better than you at fighting with his hands? He may have had nothing else to do *but* to learn how to fight, with whatever means he has to hand -'.

'I like a man with wit! Watch - and *learn!*'

Harding pulls off his coat, his jerkin and pushes up his tunic sleeves. He watches as I loosen Willelm's bindings and step back.

'Unbind my friend', the Northman demands.

'Not until *we* are done', Harding tells him flatly, handing his sword belt and scabbard to me for safekeeping, thumping fist into palm as he does so.

They stalk one another warily, Harding to the left, the earl turning to keep him in sight. Time passes them by as they clench and unclench their fists, grimacing, trying to gain the upper hand. Ricard fitzScrob says something to his friend, who answers with a wide grin.

Whilst these two make fools of themselves I watch the younger Northman. Although he is still bound, he seems to slowly press his mount closer to Harding's side. I walk wide around the two would-be fighters and take hold of the bridle of Ricard's horse,

'You can watch from further away'. I steer his horse away from the still circling pair, and call out to Harding,

'I thought you were going to show him how to fight, not to dance about like a woman!'

My jeering spurs them both and I forget about the young Ricard behind me on his horse. He has not forgotten about me, however, and brings his fists down onto the back of my head, hard enough to jar me. He rides his horse at Harding's back and bumps him off his feet. I shake my head and muster the strength to stand. I launch myself at the chestnut stallion as his rider seeks to push me aside.

Willelm fitzOsbern forgets about fighting Harding. He runs at and throws himself onto his grey mare as she closes on him, and the two Northmen kick their horses into a canter, northward away to Scrobbesbyrig.

'Christ Almighty, *stop them!*' Harding bellows at me. 'They will be back all too soon in Scrobbesbyrig to raise the hue and cry!

It is beneath me to turn his thoughts to having taken the earl's bait. When we are both mounted we press our horses to chase the fleeing Northmen. I say 'sorry' to Braenda under my breath and try to get more speed from her, but try as we might, the earls vanish into the dank mist that has crept across the track from the great River Seoferna.

'*God forgive me!*'

Harding reins in his horse to halt beside mine and buries his head in his hands. Although I say nothing he throws me a hurt look, shaking his head slowly.

'*Should* we be riding northward, toward Scrobbesbyrig?' I ask Harding. As the Northmen think we are heading that way, we may well be heading for trouble if we ride on. 'Is there somewhere we can cross the river before then?'

'You see the way the river flows. How do we cross it other than by a bridge?'

'There are no horse ferries here?' I ask.

'Not on *this* river, I would say. Did you see how wide it is here?' Harding groans, staring at the icy river that hurtles on in torrents from the hills to the north.

'I would have thought it must be shallower before Scrobbesbyrig, where it bends?' I offer.

No matter how long he stares, however, a crossing will not show itself to us. We have to look for it.

'I hope you are right', Harding lightens.

We shall never recover our hostages and the silver we might have earned by them. He adds a belated plea for forgiveness, 'I am sorry for yelling at you Ivar'.

'All I shall ask of you is not to make a habit of it. Hopefully someone has ridden from Rhosgoch and Theodolf is safe'.

The Northmen can be pitiless, like wolves, when they want to be, toward those unable to fight back. After all, where they hail from most are the same when it comes to grasping for the prize. I gear I have softened since I came to this kingdom. Sigrid and Saeward will look after Theodolf but they need the likes of Eadric and Rhiwallon or Bleddyn to protect them.

Now that Willelm is free with his young friend, we cannot hope to ride to Staefford through Scrobbesbyrig. I would have liked to know Sigrid better, but we are on our way north now, on an errand of my own choosing. We are only two, and therefore do not want to cross swords with the Northmen in strength. Even being seen by them will lengthen the odds on our return to fight alongside Eadric.

I sound out Harding,

'Would Gospatric give us men to ride back to Rhosgoch?'

'Why *would* he?' Harding's mouth twists downward. He laughs, 'Osgod told you they would just as soon see *you* killed, as a kinsman of Tostig's. Your friend Saeward staying behind with Theodolf means that you will be alone on your way back, as I may not be with you'.

I ask Harding, wondering if I am safe with him,

'What would you do if Gospatric threatened to kill me?'

'I would have to yield to his will, as would you', he shows worn teeth and smiles crookedly, adding calmly, 'However, as a thegn with land on the north bank of the Tese I am likely just to be scoffed at for taking you there'.

'I cannot, then, trust to your help', I search his eyes for a glimmer of friendship.

He does not answer. His loyalty is to Osgod and to his neighbouring thegns. The best that awaits me is Gospatric seeing in my warning a show of friendship. From what Harding tells me, will he allow me to ride free from threat back to Rhosgoch? He could see in my unwillingness to turn back as a lack of loyalty toward my own kind. A mark, as if it were cut into my forehead, that I cannot be trusted. I will take what my wyrd has in store for me. To shrink back from my errand now would be to show a lack of faith in it. He would gain from the tidings he takes but where would I go? In his eyes I could not go back to Rhosgoch, as Eadric and Osgod would question my wisdom in leaving to no good end.

'You are still going through with it?' Harding looks taken aback. My nod is met with a shrug. We must ride on and look out for a horse ferry to take us across the river.

The Seoferna seems to offer no crossings for some way.

Having forded a smaller river on our side, another enters some way beyond between the opposite banks of the main river. Sandbanks in mid-river litter the Seoferna where it follows a wide double bend. On nearing the inside bend Harding calls out in wonder,

'There *is* a horse ferry ahead!' He spurs his mount to a canter and I press Braenda to keep up with him. We reach the riverbank as the small floating stage nears us with a horse and rider aboard. A burly, greying fellow looks up at us as he pulls steadily on the rope that brings them both toward us, and then down at his thick rope.

He looks up again when he reaches the riverbank, his hair cut short over his forehead flattened by sweat and heavy mist. A matted beard hides much of his jaw, but his smile is unmistakable.

'I shall be with you very shortly', he calls up to us and waves us to the sandy track that leads from the bottom of the river bank.

We make our way to the head of the bank and let the lone rider pass before leading our mounts down to the river.

'It will be a fine afternoon', he greets us as he comes level with us and touches his forelock as he kicks his mount into a trot for the hills behind us.

'He is right, lords', the ferryman waves us to board.

'The morning will offer a sunny day to follow. Behind you the wooded hills will soon be bathed in a wonderful golden glow. This fore-year will be warmer than the last, I think'.

The ferryman smiles again, offering hope for our climb into the spine of the kingdom as he feeds the coins he has been given into a leather pouch on his belt.

'Good', Harding grunts as he leads his horse down onto the small floating platform. Harding's mare shies before clattering across the narrow landing and grunts like her rider as he pulls and the ferryman

166

pushes. Finally she is on. They await me now. I dismount and lead Braenda onto the platform.

The ferryman admires Braenda, but knows as little about horses as I do,

'He is a fine mount'.

'*She* is indeed a fine mount', I put him right.

'Ah, well', he raises his eyebrows. 'I only pull on this rope all day long until darkness stops me. I know little of the animals that I ferry back and forth', he gives me a toothless wide grin.'

'Have you been busy today?' I ask the fellow as he draws on the thick wet rope.

'I thought the mist would end my working day'.

'So you are lucky, both of you', he points back to the western bank, over one shoulder, '– and him'.

Sinewy arms draw steadily on the thick rope with the river water burbling past to our right, below us. Harding stands looking eastward at the dark woodland ahead. I turn to my left and my gaze follows the river upstream. Something stirs further along the bank we left and I draw Harding's thoughts away from the nearing shore,

'Do you see horsemen coming along past the bushes behind us?' I point upriver but by the time he looks that way the riders are hidden again by the trees.

'Where – did you say?' he jerks his head around and tries to follow my outstretched hand.

'There', I see the pennons on their lances more easily now. Harding looks to my fingertip, cupping his eyes.

'*God*, we were lucky!' Harding's dry wit gives me cause for a broad grin. 'Well, we *were* lucky!'

'We are here!' the ferryman breaks into my thoughts about how we would have fared, had we been threatened by those lances on the same side of the river.

'How many would you say there are?' Harding asks me, ignoring the ferryman.

'I would say a score or so', I look back and see them closer to where the horse ferry crossed from.

'Why do you say there are that many?' Harding stares at me and looks up to watch as the Northmen close on the landing we left behind. One of the leading riders struggles to hold his mount back from tipping him into the river.

'They ride in sixes. To be sure of catching us, they would bring four times that many. And then there are the two earls', I tell Harding, watching the Northman riders with him.

'You think it is *them?*' He screws his eyes, pays the ferryman and asks, 'Do you have to bring them over?'

'Do you think they would be so foolish as to come across two at a time?' the ferryman laughs. 'No, my friend, they have lost you. They must ride to Scrobbesbyrig and back over the bridges'.

Harding looks sidelong at him, but he is not finished yet.

'By you would be gone from here – *well gone, eh?*'

'You are no friend to the Northmen?' I turn to look at our ferryman.

'I hardly think so!' he scowls. 'I was once a thegn myself until that bastard earl gave my lands to one of his younger friends. His name was Ricard fitzScrob –'

'*Him* – we *had* them both, by Christ! We were going to ransom them!' Harding turns his horse to take one last look across the river, at the riders who have halted at the bank, 'It *is* them!'

10

'Do you want another rider with you?' the ferryman asks.

'Are you offering to come with us?' I ask. 'We have not asked your name'.

'You are right, my friend, you have *not* asked my name. As fellow thegns we should be more open with one another. I am Eirik Asgeirsson, thegn of Actun, a little way to the west below the hills'.

'Harding is the thegn here', I take one last look at Willelm fitzOsbern and Ricard fitzScrob and turn to take a good look at Eirik.

'*You* are not?' he asks me.

'I am not, no. I *was* to be made up to thegn by King Harold before we fought the man who is now king. Unluckily, King Willelm does not share kinship with me', I tell him.

'You were kin to King Harold?' Eirik looks me up and down and asks Harding, 'Did you know this?'

'No, I did not know. King Harold's kin did not cut much ice with us', Harding seethes, wanting to be away, but answers.

'We held our lands from the old king, from Earl Siward, the Church or from Gospatric, not from the Godwin clan. This fool rides with me to tell Gospatric Copsig is on his way to take the earldom given him by King Willelm.'

Eirik sees in this a way of leaving his hum-drum work.

'What could you do for us?' Harding tests him.

'I am good with sword *and* axe. You will see soon enough if we meet any of their comrades'.

'Aye, I would be glad of the company. I think Harding has other thoughts about you, but we can talk along the way. Eirik is not a Miercan name'.

'True', he answers, 'but there were no thegns in the Danelaw about to die when King Harold gave me my lands. Earl Eadwin was not happy about King Harold picking me, as he had it in mind for one of his own huscarls to be a king's thegn in that part of Scrobbe shire'.

'So you took what was thrown at you because you thought that if you turned it down, you would not be offered another?' Harding sneers.

Eirik overlooks or misses the cloaked insult, telling us instead,

'King Harold told me there may be better, but I wanted to show my father-in-law I was not as finicky as he thought'. He asks, 'How were you thinking of getting there from here?'

'I had thought of taking the road to Lindleshealh. From there I want to ride to Staefford', Harding answers without looking at Eirik, as though he might have something to hide.

'And from Staefford where do wish to you ride – north or east?'

Eirik is being friendly, helpful, but Harding will have none of it. He looks as though his temper is being tested by our new riding companion,

'Did you say you *want* to come with us?' he demands gruffly.

'I do', Eirik looks from Harding to me, as if to say, 'How do you put up with him?' However he keeps it to himself, and follows us on foot for a short way.

He climbs into the saddle of a chestnut cob hidden from sight in dense undergrowth and short trees, telling us,

'I leave her here daily. She crops the grass and knows to keep quiet', he strokes her neck and rides along beside me before speaking to Harding again.

'Why I asked about which way you are taking, is because Willelm fitzOsbern may already have patrols out that way from Scrobbesbyrig'.

Before Eirik repeats his warning, Harding asks,

'Is it safe to use the road east to Lindleshealh?'

'The Northmen are not masters of the roads beyond that', Eirik assures us. 'They might wish to stop you from leaving Scrobbe shire for that reason alone. Once you are into Staefford shire you are free – for the time being'.

Eirik urges his horse to ride alongside Harding and I press Braenda to keep pace with them. I want to know which way we should go, too.

'So which road would *you* take?' Harding sounds now as though he might be willing to put his safety in Eirik's hands.

'I would strike north, eastward past Scrobbesbyrig, toward Weme and then on for Ceaster shire before heading east'.

He stops to look at Harding, who nods wearily at him to go on, and adds,

'In the north-east corner of the shire we can cross into Deira by way of Ceadde. It would be easier from there on to Jorvik I think - through the lower hills'.

Eirik's way north is the way we crossed back into Deira with Tostig after beating Gruffyd. He sees me scratching under my by now scruffy chin and guesses I have something to say. He cocks an ear to listen to what I have to say. All I can think of is,

'You would go *that* way?'

Harding plainly thinks otherwise, and tells Eirik bluntly why he thinks we are going the wrong way.

'There are deep snowdrifts that way. We were set to come across the hills that way but had to use the roads and tracks along the Danelaw side until we rode into Oxnaford shire. That was where we crossed paths with Ivar and his friends'.

Eirik sees the smug look that tells him he is wrong, and pushes his luck in pressing Harding further,

'How many weeks ago is that?' Eirik will not let go.

'Not enough to warrant being stopped by snow-blocked roads. I would still head for Lindleshealh'.

Harding sets his teeth and Eirik can see now the older thegn will brook no more of his searching.

'Very well, we go to Lindleshealh', Eirik shrugs and turns his horse eastward. A brisk, cold easterly wind has set in and we will be riding into it up into the higher dales. Ahead are warnings that all may not be well. Harding's way north may as bleak as Eirik's sounds.

Nevertheless, at Staefford we can cross the river by a bridge built by the brycgegeweorc, the bridge building gang under one of the ablest thegns in Mierca. When they built the new bridge Earl Eadwin took on a fellow by the name of Ordwulf from Ceaster. He was as good as his word when he claimed Eadwin would have the best stone bridge an earl could want to ride over.

Whether they would allow it to fall into the hands of the Northmen is another matter. If Ordwulf were asked, he would only unwillingly allow them to use it.

At Saelt, in the next dale, where the still young River Treonta is crossed by a short wooden bridge, we make our way toward the lower hills. From Deoraby Harding's chosen way north will test our mettle.

First, however, we must keep an eye open over our shoulders for any Northmen who may be coming from Scrobbesbyrig.

Snow blown down from the hills at us cuts our line of sight by more than half. If we cannot see Willelm's men, nor can they see us in the dark, but whilst this works *for* us, it can also work against us. *If* they have riders out they will be upon us before we can see them to ward them off. We can only hope they will be so keen to be out of the cold, back in their quarters that they will miss us.

'There are bushes at the side of the road we can hide behind', Eirik offers and points to our right.

We turn our horses and make for their shelter. When I I see a horse's head jerking upward close by I call out to Eirik and Harding.

'*Not that way!*' I wave toward the trees. 'There are horses in there!'

They rein in as four of the riders break cover.

'God, have they seen us?' Harding breathes hard and stares back at them.

'Best to head into the blizzard, that way we may lose them!' Eirik warns. His horse almost keels over as he wrenches the animal's head around and I hear shouting from behind the bushes.

Are we to be caught *now?* I would stay free if I could. Their horses carry more weight than ours, and may already be tired from a long day of riding around the Staefford *hundred.* If we press our mounts into the coming whiteness we can hope to be blanketed from sight. They will give up, not wanting to follow us into the white wall of icy, cutting snow. I can still hear their shouts as we clatter along the stony road away from them.

'Get off this road onto the grass!' Eirik yells. The muffled thud of hooves as we hurtle over the soft earth beside the road will be lost to our pursuers with all the thundering of their own horses' hooves over the stones.

'They can still hear us, surely?' Harding sounds panicked.

'Shut up and keep riding into the snow. Try not to look back or you will slow down your horse!' Eirik barks back at him.

The shouting behind us fades. They may surely think they have lost us, but Eirik pushes his horse hard and we do likewise to keep up with him. We must be near Lindleshealh but we will not be able to overnight there. We have to find somewhere further afield ro stay ahead of the earl's men.

'How far away *is* Lindleshealh now?' Harding asks as we pull back on the reins to slow down.

'We are too close to stop there for the night. The Northmen will think it we are resting there and will knock on every door in the settlement. It is better we ride on to Stochetun. Tucked away as it is behind the next hill in a small dale, they will not guess it is even there', Eirik pants and digs his knees into the cob's flanks.

The snow is still being blown at us when we drop down from a low ridge onto the small hamlet. No hearth fires burn to show anyone to be still awake. There are no welcoming, friendly smiles.

'What was it that fellow said when he left you on the western bank of the Seoferna?' Harding asks in a way that tells me he knows well enough.

'About the afternoon being fine?' Eirik recalls too and laughs heartily, 'It will be where he is going. This snow will break by the morning, but he will be in Clun by then. It may well have been fine there. This snow is being driven toward Scrobbesbyrig by a wind that even I cannot fathom'.

'Why do you say that?' I ask.

'Well, because the wind was coming from the south-west when we left the River Seoferna. It only changed when we were nearing Lindleshealh'. Eirik scratches his forehead and looks upward, drawing a line across the heavens with one finger, 'and now it has died down again. See, the heavens are at peace, the stars are out'.

He looks upward and we follow his eyes.

'God's truth, *what is happening?*' Harding curses.

Eirik throws up his hands and looks at me, as if I might be wiser. I may well be, but how do you tell an outsider you have a spay-wife watching over you?

Harding leans toward Eirik and winks, nodding at me,

'*He* knows. For all I know he is a drinking friend to the old ones'.

'*What* old ones -?' Eirik asks, startled. He is plainly steeped in the Christian beliefs of his peers. He looks to me for an answer.

'He means the old gods, although which ones I would not know. Do you mean the old gods of Elmet or ours, Harding?' I am teasing Eirik but I still cannot think how I tell them about Braenda.

'How would *I* know?' Harding sounds annoyed with me again now. He breaks off suddenly, asking, 'What was that?'

'What was *what* - what is he talking about?' Eirik stops his horse. He sounds worried and sits up in his saddle, looks about and then back at me.

It is pitch black, with only the stars to show the way east. Clouds allowing, we will find our way by the North Star on our left.

'There is a light down there!' Harding stands in his stirrups and jabs the cold air with one finger.

'We must be close to Stochetun', Eirik mulls.

'That light may be an inn?' I ask.

'I do not recall seeing an inn here', Eirik answers, scratching behind one ear.

There are no other lights to show how near we are to a hamlet, but there could be more lights hidden by trees in the thinning woodland beside his easy downhill track. More woodland lies beyond the building from which the light shines. As we near a dip in the road the moon comes out of hiding from behind a string of cloud, allowing us to see how the way lies. A far-off twinkle shows through the woods as we round a bend on the downward winding track. Stochetun has to be close at hand, beyond what looks to be an inn.

'Do we go in, or wait until we are in the hamlet?' Harding asks Eirik.

'*I* think we should stop here', I tell them both. 'If there are any Northmen here in the morning they will punish the folk of Stochetun if they think we are about'.

'What would stop them from calling at this inn first, to see if we are there?' Harding demands testily.

'This is not the way into Stochetun that they would take', Eirik shows another way. 'The road from Scrobbesbyrig follows around the hill, from the north side',

'Then let us break our ride here', I dismount, already tasting the ale.

We lead our mounts around the building into a yard ringed by a palisade the height of a very tall, helmed man on horseback, high enough to keep out wolves that would seek out our mounts. Having looked for a stable lad and found none, we see to our own mounts, heaving our saddles off our mounts. Hay is pulled from a rack, and a leather pail filled with water for each horse.

'Are you sure this is an inn?' Harding asks me when he has finished settling his horse down for the night.

'What else would it be here by the roadside? Still, there are no horses other than ours'. I stop, wondering if Harding might be right.

'That is what worries me. Would an innkeeper not have horses – if not of his own, then for guests whose mounts may be tired or ailing?' Harding squints at the back of the building in the dark, 'There should be at least someone to take our horses from us'.

'Perhaps the innkeeper's horse is being used by one of his close kin', Eirik looks around, points at a door and leads inside.

There is no-one within and we stand inside the doorway, shuffling, thinking about whether to stay or go on and trust to luck. The only light in the main room is from a flickering fire burning in the hearth. A door opens elsewhere within. Someone is coming and we shall know soon whether we have made a mistake in stopping.

'What might I do for you, friends?' asks a grey haired, bent old woman.

174

'You might tell the innkeeper we are here and are in need of ale, food and shelter for the night', I answer.

'*Innkeeper...* what do you mean?' she cackles.

'This is not an inn?' I look around us, at the tables ranged along the walls, with benches below them in a haphazard manner.

'Oh, you are right. This *is* an inn, or might be if the innkeeper had not been dragged away this noon by the outlander earl's men', she cackles again, but the laughter is short-lived. She is suddenly overcome with sorrow and buries her head in her apron.

We stand awkwardly waiting for her grief to pass but Eirik does not feel able to wait and bears down on her,

'You have ale and food, and beds?'

She backs away from him, fearful of what he might do to her, having already lived through the Northmen's raid.

'Aye, we have food... well - *I* have. Our stable lad ran away whilst the outlanders set about Ringwulf. My grand-daughter cried so long she needed to sleep, poor soul! My grandsons are with Thegn Eadric. There is no-one to see to the rooms'.

'We have been riding since dawn. When we have had our fill, drunk some ale –'I am not allowed to finish.

'There is *no* ale. They broke up the ale tuns and smashed the cups to make Ringwulf tell them if two armed men had passed. He could not, so they took him to Scrobbesbyrig'.

'Can you make a broth?' I ask.

'I daresay I *could*', she answers, 'but there are no bowls to eat it from'.

'You have beds?' Harding chides, but she pays no heed to him and looks at Eirik, scratching his chin and looking up to the rafters.

'Is there still the inn by the bridge, beyond Stochetun?' Eirik asks her.

'There is, aye, but the innkeeper there might have suffered in the same way as Ringwulf', she sighs. 'You can try there. Do you know the inn?'

'I know the innkeeper is Herfast', Eirik starts.

The old woman stops him, shaking her head she looks sadly at Eirik and tells him,

'Herfast was taken *last* week. They thought he was hiding one of Eadric's Wealshmen taking word to Earl Morkere'.

'The inn will still be there, surely', Eirik grasps at straws.

'Do I know you?' the old woman asks suddenly.

'I should think you *would* know me, a thegn with land near Scrobbesbyrig'. Disgruntled at her failing to know him, he stares down at her. Yet he did not even know this inn was here.

'I know you from *Actun!*' The old woman gapes up at Eirik and cackles, 'You are thegn Eirik!'

'I *was* a thegn, but the Northmen took that from me because I would not swear an oath to the new king', Eirik puts her right. 'How is it you know me?'

'My other daughter lives there, her name is Aethelwila'.

'Aethelwila at the mill-' Eirik begins, but Harding has a rumbling stomach, as have I, and this talk of knowing one another is getting us no-where.

'Talk about your past life when our bellies are full! Where is this other inn? We might see if they have the means to settle our hunger and need for sleep', Harding groans.

He has the look of a man who has been tested too much.Arms folded across his chest, he looks down at the stone floor because otherwise he might snap at them both.

'It is not far through Stochetun', Eirik offers.

'At least our horses have been fed and watered. They will be a little fresher for this short stop', I count our meagre blessings.

'*Do not go*', a young maiden shows from behind Harding, who spins on his heels to see who is behind him, his hand to his sword hilt.

'Herdis, sweetling, what are you *doing* down here?' the old woman shuffles across the floor to comfort the maiden.

'I heard men talking', Herdis pushes past the old woman. 'Who are these men, grandmother - where are they going?'

'We are on our way north', Harding answers, hoping she does not ask further.

She and turns back to her grandmother to seek comfort, 'What are they doing to father, *why* do they want him?'

'We shall be away', Eirik takes his leave and are about to make our way to the door when Herdis pleads,

'*Do not go.* Stay here, with us, for pity's sake!'

'We need food and ale, and sleep. You will have beds for that, but we need to fill our bellies', Harding sounds almost sorry for her. 'You do not have the means to feed us'.

'The inn does not, but you are welcome to use *our* cups and bowls. There is enough for us all as long as you do not mind drinking apple ale', Herdis sounds stronger now. She makes her way shakily across an uneven stone floor to the door of their rooms.

176

'I did not know you would allow guests to eat with us',the old woman shuffles along beside her and opens the door for her grand-daughter. 'Gladly I will make broth for these good men'.

Herdis leads us into a kitchen that is as poorly lit as the great inn room and lights a tallow candle,

'It will take my thoughts from my father, Ringwulf's plight', Herdis tells us and bids us sit at a square kitchen table.

'Your mother tells us your brothers are with Thegn Eadric', I begin talking both Eirik and Harding look nosily around. What they hope to find only they know. I shall be happy with what I have asked for, food, drink and sleep.

'My mother talks too much', Herdis chides and stands out of the way as the old woman busies herself finding tools to make ready the food, and things to put in our broth.

'I am sure she would not have told the Northmen', Eirik offers, looking down at the old woman peeling turnips. There are grubby, unwashed white tubers that ceorls leave to grow wild at the field edges and are harvested together with the turnips.

As long as she boils them long enough, we should not be plagued with stomach cramps later when we should be sleeping!

Herdis chafes at the thought of her grandmother talking to the outlanders.

'Let us hope not', Eirik agrees, 'although feelings hereabouts were against Earl Harold taking the throne after the old king died. Earl Eadwin and his brother Morkere felt the *aetheling* Eadgar should have been crowned, and guided by the earls and bishops. Whilst the young earls are guests of the new king in his own land, we will bide our time and see what comes'.

'I have heard that King Harold's following fell away beyond West Seaxe and Middil Aengla', I answer, watching the old woman scraping away at the turnips and white tubers.

She washes them together in a wooden pail, looks at me as if she is about to say something and thinks better of it, setting herself the task of chopping meat and offal. Scraps are put into the heavy, blackened pot, finally ladling water into it. She adds scrapings of rock salt, which she feeds in between forefinger and thumb.

Lastly she drops a lid onto the pot. I feel my mouth watering at the thought of the broth. A while later, as we sit side-by-side on a bench at the plank-built table across from Herdis, with cups warming in our hands, Eirik and Harding regale us with stories of their youth. They laugh about the women they chased as they grew older, and the men

177

they faced in fights. Herdis tells of young men who fought for her and I almost doze off listening to them.

'How was *your* youth?' Eirik suddenly asks me. He asks again when I start, and Harding, sitting between us, shakes me into wakefulness.

'Eirik wants to know about your early days'.

'He wants to know about *my* early days? They were spent with my half-brothers on Sjaelland, before I left with the younger one, Osbeorn to sail through the eastern sea to Holmgard and Koenungagard. I came to his kingdom and learned how to fight with sword and axe alongside Harold and his brothers –'

I drift into deep thought before I finish, only to be shaken again by Harding, who thinks I have fallen asleep,

'Go on, this sounds like a good story. You were kin to King Harold?'

'Aye, my father was their mother's brother, and he in turn was first married to Knut's youngest sister, Gunnlaug'.

Suddenly I am wide awake recalling the days when my uncle, Knut, ruled both kingdoms.

'His brother Eilaf was made an earl when Knut was made king here after Svein Forkbeard died suddenly. My mother died in childbirth and Ulf married Knut's other sister, Astrid'.

'*Go on*', Eirik presses. 'We have time on our hands'.

'He fathered three sons on her before he was slain in the church he built at Roskilde'.

I see the church when I close my eyes, even now.

'Knut bore ill will toward my father, Ulf. Tostig is very much like him, but my uncle was more feared'. When I look up they are sitting open-mouthed. This is all new to them.

'Go on, *go on!*' Harding sits, gripped.

'After my father's death, Knut made sure my half-brothers spoke of themselves as the sons of Astrid. I was not going to betray my father and went on telling folk I was Ulf's son. Knut let it be known to me that unless I left Roskilde and no longer lived on Danish land, I would be looked on as an outlaw. Astrid nursed me from childhood and, not wanting to see me harmed by *any* of her ilk, king or not, she paid for a ship fitted out, a crew and a chest of silver to buy goods in the east'.

So began my knowledge of the sea-lanes of the Svear, the Wends and the Rus. Some of the crew had served in the Varangian Guard at Miklagard and all around the middle sea against Turk and Northman alike, even Rus. I go on to talk at length of the eastern tribesmen, the Patzinak Turks, whose thirst for Rus blood led to horrifying killings east of the Volga. Finally I come to when I learned my swordsmanship from no less than Earl Godwin.

Herdis is the first to speak, having drawn a long breath,

'I feel as if I had sailed *with* you, Ivar! You took my breath away when you spoke of the Patzinak Turks', she gasps.

'You are, sorry, *were* kin to King Harold and his brothers –'Eirik breaks in and stops when I clear my throat to break his flow.

'There is *still* Wulfnoth in Falaise. Hakon Sveinson, King Harold's nephew, is at Naesinga with Harold's sons. They bide their time in East Seaxe before linking up with Eadric, teaching fyrdmen in the hope of bringing their fighting skills to match those of their huscarls. Harold's mother Gytha is in West Seaxe with Eadgytha 'Swan-neck' and her younger offspring', I set him right. 'We hope to hurl the Northman king back into the sea before he has settled in. We must be rid of his brother, the earl Odo, make no mistake!'

'Why were you riding north?' Eirik asks now,

'The king has made Copsig earl of Beornica'.

'They would find out before too long for themselves anyway!' Harding grunts and earns himself a blank stare from Herdis.

'I think he is doing the right thing!' she chides.

'It may cost him his life!' Harding grunts.

Eirik asks, staring at Harding,

'Why would they kill Ivar?'

Harding laughs hollowly and shakes his head,

'He is of Tostig's ilk. Ivar was one of Tostig's huscarls'. He goes on when he is sure Eirik is listening, 'After Earl Siward's death they wanted one of Uhtred's kindred to be earl, but Eadweard's queen, Eadgytha sold the old king on her brother. When Orm Gamalsson, one of the Northanhymbran nobles disputed one of the queen's edicts she had him done away with!'

'Is this so?' Herdis asks me.

I shrug and have to allow there may be some truth in it,

'I have heard about it, but it cannot be proved either way'.

'Was Queen Eadgytha *so* underhand in her dealings?' Herdis tries to stare me out.

'Of her brothers, Tostig was the closest to her but Harold had to agree to Morkere being made earl in Northanhymbra'.

Thinking back now seems odd. I had not thought to have to do it any more, for *anyone,* and add,

'The northern nobles had Tostig removed. Riding to Northanhamtun they fired Tostig's houses after killing his huscarls in Eoferwic', I make sure of using the Aenglish name for Jorvik. 'Harold married Ealdgyth,

Eadwin's and Morkere's sister, to keep them in check, because he feared a war within the kingdom would bring our foes upon us even sooner. Eadweard was upset at the way Tostig was ousted and fell ill. He was never fully well after that and died in the winter. The rest you must know'.

Harding growls angrily to show not all think the same way,

'Nevertheless, we all felt Earl Harold overstepped the mark by claiming Eadweard's crown for himself. He should have given his oath to the *aetheling* Eadgar'.

'Eadgar is a child!' Herdis shouts and thumps the table in her anger. 'He is barely away from his mother's breast!'

'He is man enough to bear a sword, and old enough to learn the ways of kingship!' Harding tries to shout her down. 'Ivar will tell you!'

'He did so when we stood against Duke Willelm's men at Lunden Brycg', I agree with Harding, but not in the way he behaves.

'We beat them off and Duke Willelm himself was unhorsed, as he was a number of times on Caldbec Beorg'.

'You *beat* the Northmen back?' Eirik can barely believe his ears.

'Eadgar had the following of the bishops and earls. He was later betrayed by the same men because they feared losing their lands', I tell them, 'and by Archbishop Ealdred'.

An awkward stillness fills the room.

'Morkere and Eadwin sold him *out?*' It is Harding who shouts at me now, but not to browbeat me as he wished to do with Herdis. He is unable to take in what I have told them.

'What led to this madness?' Eirik asks and wets his throat with a long draught of apple ale.

'Duke Willelm led his men around the southern and western shires, burning crops and homes, killing animals as they went before crossing the Temese upriver of Readingum. Finally, after he called a halt the earls and churchmen gave in to him at Beorkhamstede. Eadgar was left friendless. My friends and I were in Suth Seaxe and Centland spying out Willelm's supply lines for him at the time. The young earls did nothing more to stop the Northmen!' It is my turn to thump the table this time, knocking my ale cup across the table.

Herdis might be upset about me drenching her clothing in apple ale but she merely sits there, her head buried in her hands and moans softly,

'The poor young man, could *no-one* help him?' Comforted by her grandmother's gnarled hands on her narrow shoulders, Herdis rocks back and forth - the world's cares having been made her own.

'And now we shall have Copsig foisted on us again!' Harding can only think of Northanhymbran woes and earns icy stares from the women.

Eirik shakes his head in disbelief at the women's scorn and throws his hands up in the air, tired from the day's long hours in the saddle. He is at least at one with Harding when he stands and tries to stifle a yawn,

'Well, the least we can do is rid our northern friends of an unwelcome guest. We must rise early!'

Harding nods, yawns and stretches, almost hitting the side of my head with his elbows,

'Aye, sleep beckons!' He adds for my sake, 'When you can see to rise and let me out of this corner, Ivar!'

'You could climb over the table. I feel as if I had lead in my legs!' I joke and an angered Harding shoves me bodily along.

He does not stop shoving until I slide, laughing off the bench onto the straw-covered floor. Eirik's jaw drops open, taken aback by Harding's sheer brute strength, then with his head in his hands he begins to rock back and forth.

'What is wrong?' Herdis leaps from her side of the bench and goes down onto her knees at Eirik's side. She looks closely at him but cannot see any bruises as the young fellow still holds his face in both hands, 'Thegn Eirik, what is the matter? Speak, for God's pity! I shall bathe your wound but let me first see!'

Eirik takes his hands away from his reddened face. Tears stream down over his cheeks and he begins to shake his head furiously.

'What have you done to the fellow?' I bend over Eirik, trying to see what ails him, but I can see no bruises either. Finally, I yell,

'Eirik, tell me what *ails you!*'

At last, the tears wiped away and on his feet with Herdis still fussing over him, brushing the straw from his woollen shirt, Eirik turns to me and grins foolishly,

'I could not stop laughing! God help anyone who stands in his way, but I would not wish to be a Northman!' He turns to see Harding staring at him as if he had lost his wits and begins to laugh again.

He almost chokes, laughing, and asks the Northanhymbran thegn, 'Is that what passes for wit in your part of Deira?'

'It is plainly *not* your sort!' Harding growls and looks to Herdis to show him to a bed, any bed by the tired look of him. He yawns and stretches again, almost knocking a rush light from its bracket on the wall.

'Foolish man, would you sooner burn the inn down than get to sleep?!' the old woman scolds, setting the rush straight again.

'Well lead me to it, old woman!' Harding glowers at her when she does not stir. *'My bed – where is it?'*

'To you my name is Winflaed!' she screeches, thumping Harding on his right shoulder.

He winces and makes to hit back but it is Winflaed's turn to glower. She seizes a besom and thrusts the head at him, 'Just you dare!'

'Mother, behave yourself!' Herdis chides, grinning.

'I think she should come with us and frighten away any Northmen who poke their noses out of their strongholds', Eirik grips Winflaed's shoulder and the old woman pushes the head of the besom under *his* nose. Harding doubles up, helpless with laughter at Eirik's plight.

'Now we *know* what passes for wit humour near the Tese', Eirik winks at me and sneezes. He turns to Winflaed and bellows at her, 'God woman, do you never wash the thing?!'

'Who ever washes a *besom?'* Herdis, open-eyed looks to her mother, who bursts into shrill laughter. They cling tightly to one another, helpless in their mirth.

Finally Herdis dries her eyes and collects a candle holder from the table, waving us to follow her up the creaking stairs.

'There will be no creeping out of here in the morning without paying', Eirik cheekily notes to me behind the back of his hand.

Winflaed flashes him an ugly stare and we laugh playfully.

'I think he was testing to see you are awake', I tell her.

'He had better be. We have some sharp hayforks out in the stable if he wishes to try his luck at leaving with all his silver!' Winflaed stops a smile from betraying her feelings toward Eirik.

He laughs again and leans toward her as she unlocks a door,

'If you are lucky I shall give you a kiss with your silver in the morning', Eirik tells her.

'The silver will do, thank you', she tells him drily.

This draws a knowing guffaw from Harding and she turns, looking taller than him where she stands three steps above him.

'And you can give me *double* if you knock any more rushes askew!'

'She has a little something for everyone', Eirik giggles, enters the darkness of his bed closet and closes the door behind him after first taking a spare candle from Herdis. He begins to sing to himself behind the closed door and is growled at loudly by Harding.

'Go to sleep – remember we have to be away early!'

As I am the last to my bed closet, Herdis bids me goodnight, stretches to her tiptoes and plants a kiss on my ear,

'Sleep sweetly, good fellow. I shall dream of ships breaking the surf under bright eastern skies'.

Before wearily pushing the door open and dropping fully-clad onto my bed I answer,

'*I* shall dream of not having to chase fleeing Northmen all over the kingdom'.

In the morning as I stir my porridge in its rough stone bowl I ask,

'Eirik, how far can we ride this morning?' I set the wooden spoon down on the table and pick up a cup of strong, sweet apple ale.

He thinks briefly, dips his spoon into his porridge and raises it with the steaming oat bran to his mouth. Before he takes it into his mouth he scalds himself and drops the spoon on the table,

'I had best leave that to cool. As to what you asked, Ivar, our way will take us roughly east from here over hill and down dale, skirting Staefford and turning north to Aescburna', Eirik tries his porridge again and finds it to his taste, 'It is not to hot now, Ivar. Try it for yourself'.

One corner of Harding's mouth turns downward in mock loathing – or is it real? Herdis walks in from the kitchen and sees the way he looks at Eirik,

'What ails, Harding?' She looks from him to me, and then at Eirik. We shrug and look down at our bowls.

'These two babes in arms - honestly, you would think they had just crawled out from their cots'. He mimics a child sobbing, 'My porridge is too *hot!*'

Herdis looks at Eirik, her brow furrowed,

'Why waste this hot porridge I made for you?!'

Eirik and I look at one another and grin. Harding looks up at Herdis and beams broadly at her,

'I *like* your porridge, woman. What does it matter if it is scalding hot or bearably warm? Your silver is well earned, believe me'.

He is rewarded with a warm smile and she leaves again for the kitchen. Eirik watches after her and goes back to eating once the closes behind her. Harding shakes his head again, lifts his cup and takes a long draught of what is left of his apple ale, and then bangs it down on the table.

'Something is wrong, Harding?' I ask, awaiting another put-down.

'Damned *spider* crawled out from between the boards. That is all!' He stands, ready to leave.

'Seat yourself, friend. There is more to eat', Eirik assures him.

'The porridge was enough! How much do you *eat* in the morning in this part of Mierca?' Harding wants to be away.

'You go out and see to your horse if you wish. We will have what is to come – yours as well if you like', Eirik offers, grinning at me.

Herdis comes back with meat platters and Harding brushes her aside on his way to the door.

'Have you had enough?' she looks worried.

'He wants to be away', Eirik waives Harding's bad manners. 'I told him he should take care of his horse. He will be happier in the stable, perhaps he will try what the horses are eating'.

Herdis fights her laughter and leaves our platters on the table. Harding wavers at the door. He can smell what is on offer, but steels himself to fasting all the same. Who knows when we will next eat, I say to myself. It may be tomorrow before we can line our stomachs again.

Harding is in the stable, tightening the straps of his saddle when we at last tear ourselves away from Herdis' groaning table.

Eirik belches like an Arab trader I recall from strolling in Roskilde Haven a long time ago. No-one turned a hair then, but here it is frowned upon. Winflaed yells at him, giving him a ticking-off. Eirik smiles and turns his back on her.

'You missed some wonderful food', Eirik tells Harding.

He lifts his saddle onto his horse and belches again. Harding grunts something from the corner of his mouth and busies himself with his weapons.

'How *far* do you think we will get today?' I ask Eirik, forgetting what he told me earlier. I draw my axe from its sheath and take a close look at the blade for nicks. There are none that could be made worse by fighting and I sheathe it again. I shall have to make sure I do not waste my efforts hacking at shield-bosses.

'With luck, we could make Aescburna a little after nightfall, as I said', he smiles and holds in another belch.

'Oh, my God, what is happening to me? There is a burning in my chest!' Eirik groans aloud, but we are all too busy to listen.

Herdis has followed us into the stable and laughs, chiding him,

'You ate much too fast'.

'I think you should die a horrible death!' Winflaed rasps. She has followed on the heels of her daughter, like as not thinking us untrustworthy saddle tramps. She might not be far wrong!

'Mother, how could you! He is a young man, and young men are like this', Herdis looks up fondly at Eirik, now settled in his saddle and ready to leave. He bends and steals a kiss from her.

Winflaed is not happy. She curses him under her breath and says out aloud what she swore under her breath,

'*My* sons are not like that!'

'Would your sons understand a woman's needs?' Eirik answers cheekily and ducks Winflaed's flailing besom.

We file away eastward from the inn, Eirik waving until we are out of sight. He turns to me and fights down another belch as he tells me,

'She is a wonderful woman in other ways, too!'

'Who do you mean, the grandmother or Herdis?' I ask, laughing.

This raises a guffaw from Harding, a knowing wink at me and he asks,

'You bedded one of them – or *both?!*'

I am taken aback, but it is not altogether beyond the realms of the likely. I had thought of taking the young one myself, but sleep overcame me.

'She said she tried your bed-closet first, but you were fast asleep. I did not want to turn her away after her hopes had been dashed, did I?' Eirik rubs salt in the wound.

All I can do is grunt. Bemoaning my missing her would only draw some witty line from Harding. Then again, would Braenda not have sprung from nowhere as she always does? Anyway, where to God is *she* when I need to feel a woman's soft skin next to mine?

Harding laughs hoarsely,

'Think of what your friends would say if they knew you were too tired to take a willing woman?' he snorts.

'They would not believe you', I have to laugh, 'knowing my appetite for women!'

'You would never tell them anyway, Harding', Eirik calls over his shoulder, 'I thought you were not going back to rejoin Thegn Eadric'.

'I was not thinking of them. As it is I *have* to go back after all. Thegn Osgod awaits me with word from his woman. When we have seen Osulf and Gospatric, we must make a halt in Deira, near Saelgeby. He began to build a new hall where Eadwy's once stood before Harald Sigurdsson's men burnt it down', Harding stares into the air above my head as he tells me. 'He needs to know how Torfa and their young ones are faring without him'.

Harding flicks his reins at his mare's neck and she hastens into a fast canter after Eirik before he vanishes into the gathering darkness. I press my knees for Braenda to keep up with them.

Lagging too far behind might make me easy prey for any passing Northmen.

'Eirik, what is the likelihood of our coming across more Northmen around here?' Harding echoes my thoughts.

'Not great, once we cross these hills to the east here', Eirik answers, nodding ahead.

'They have not reached this far?' I hazard a guess.

'Not in enough numbers for them to be so bold as to stir up the folk of the Danelaw. They have poked their noses beyond Staefford from time to time', Eirik's horse steps out proudly and we need to keep pressing our mounts to stay level with him, to hear what he has to tell us.

'When will we be beyond their patrol lines?' I ask.

'Beyond Staefford itself, where the river dales make it hard for them to see far, there are outlaw bands bigger than theirs', Eirik finally gives the reason for the Northmen's dislike of that part of the kingdom. 'Until they are given the numbers of men they need to push further, the Northman earls will not risk ambush and loss of men'.

'What about us?' I ask.

I have a purse of silver that I need for the long ride north and back. Innkeepers anywhere are not known to give free food or shelter.

'We do not offer rich enough pickings. I never carry more silver than for a few days' needs. No outlaw would gain from stopping me. What about you, Harding?' Eirik grins across at our Northanhymbran friend, who curses under his breath and calls out, 'I did not catch that, what?'

'They will not dare rob me, *a thegn!*'

'If the purse is big enough, you will not have much else to do but hand it over. These outlaw bands number in their scores!' Eirik raises his eyebrows at Harding's bluff manner.

'Let them just try!' Harding adds, 'Let them *try!*'

11

We skirt Staefford upriver and ford the freezing river without mishap. Loose and slime-covered stones in the shallows are avoided as Eirik points them out. Nor is the climb to the next ridge above the dale of the River Treonta as troublesome as it could have been, even with fetlock-deep snow on the ground. Dropping down to the dale is more fraught, however, and even Braenda's footing is not as sure as it could be.

There is no way of fording the Treonta until we reach Sandun.

This is a settlement near the far bank of the river beyond a wooden bridge. Winter snowfalls have pushed the waters up through and over the planks, making the footing harder for the horses. Nevertheless a stop to water the horses is needed, and not before time. Even Harding nods when Eirik calls a halt at what looks to be an inn. Some women gather outside to watch as we draw up and dismount. One of them points gleefully at Eirik and begins to shout at him whilst poking the air at something or someone back down the dale,

'One of your friends has been left behind, Thegn Eirik'.

Eirik stares back down-dale, shields his eyes with his hands and yells to me, waving at someone behind,

'Is he a friend of *yours?*'

Both Harding and I crane our necks to see the newcomer across the sunlight. I begin to think he must be one of his huscarls, until I see the Northman helm that he took from the corpse of the man he killed to 'borrow' his gear.

'Saeward how come you are here, how did you *find* us?' I call out to my friend when he is within hailing. He cups a hand to one ear when he is closer, but shakes his head to show he has not heard.

'What is more, how did you get across the River Seoferna without a ferry?' Eirik stares at him, 'Did you ride through Scrobbesbyrig? What manner of fool would do such a thing?'

187

'I did ride through one burh that straddles the river, crossing by a wooden bridge after passing a lot of Northmen. They seemed to be waiting for someone of high standing and just waved me through', Saeward drops from his horse as clumsily as ever and strides across the grass to me. He clasps my hands and smiles like a long-lost brother at me. 'They wanted me out of the way'.

'What became of Theodolf?' I ask when he finally stops squeezing the life from my hands.

'Sigrid is nursing him in Rhosgoch. Eadric sent men to bring him, the two women and Sigrid's offspring to safety. You were right, Ivar, about Sigrid and her maid. They are not whores!' Saeward tells me as we come to the doorway between the gaping, giggling young women.

'Why do you have on that Northman helm when you are wearing a Brother's habit?' Harding laughs and pulls on the loosely hanging cord. The habit falls open and beneath is a Northman's hauberk. The Northanhymbran thegn stares disbelievingly and looks Saeward up and down, 'Where did you get *that?*'

Saeward quips about how he came by the hauberk,

'It was a gift from a fellow who grew tired of wearing it'.Looking admiringly down its length, Saeward smiles and pats the chain mail on his chest fondly.

'This fellow that you parted from his mailcoat would not happen to be a Northman noble?' Eirik's wide, cheesy grin tells me Saeward has won himself another friend. Saeward's look of mild hurt brings a laugh from them both.

'He did not say as such, but he was much happier to be rid of it when I pulled my sword from his midriff', Saeward winks sideways at me. This brings gales of laughter.

'I like your friend', Harding slaps Saeward on the back. 'I am not so taken with you, Ivar, but this man in the habit makes me laugh, even if he rides like God's own mother-in-law!'

'I like you, too, my Northanhymbran friend, but slap me on the back like that again and I will let you feel the blade of my sword in *your* fatty ribs!' Saeward brings a look of mock horror from Harding with his warning, but soon a hoot of laughter tells me friendship between these two could be long-lasting.

'You speak bluntly, as would a man from Northanhymbra. I like that!' Harding tells him gleefully and is about to slap him on the back again when a dark look from Saeward warns him against the folly of it and he pulls his hand smartly back again.

'I would rather speak bluntly to you as an East Seaxan, Thegn Harding', Saeward smirks, 'not knowing any-one else from Northanhymbra but Theodolf and his kin'.

'Mark my words, these hands of mine have been put to hard work in Wealtham's fields and in its mill, so I would think they could span even your thick neck', Saeward smiles in a friendly fashion at Harding as he puts across his meaning with his hands together, thumbs pulled back.

Harding knows Saeward well enough not to take his words as an empty threat. He has been told of the numbers of men Saeward has sent to their maker and smiles thinly. He will trust my friend with his life, but only so far. Eirik cheerfully offers Saeward his hand. A little hand-wrestling goes on as both men grinning madly, clinging for dear life to one another's hand.

'Come on, you two', I try to break in, 'you look like star-struck lovers'.

At long last their hands pulled apart, they both look closely at the marks left by the grappling.

'That is some grip you have, Seaxan!' Eirik pulls a face as he balls and opens his hand a few times to let the blood run freely once more.

'You are no fair maiden, either', Saeward kneads the ball of his thumb to ease the sinew of his hand, 'and to friends my name is Saeward, as Harding already well knows but seems to have forgotten'.

Harding acknowledges his ill manners and offers a hand,

'Are you sure?' Saeward asks and smiles warmly.

'We are not going to do any more than shake hands in friendship, I trust?' Harding nevertheless gives his hand trustingly. A brief trade of friendship is enough for both Saeward and Harding, and firm faith by either man that the other lacks no spirit.

'Is this an inn or an alehouse?' Harding asks Eirik as we enter the darkness within.

'I cannot rightly tell', Eirik answers.

He turns to an old fellow who has just stood up, and asks,

'Is this an inn, or is it an alehouse?'

'If I knew what an alehouse was, I might tell you', comes the tart answer.

'Alehouses offer only food and ale, whereas inns offer beds', Harding growls back, sniffing at the man's rebuff. He looks sullenly at the fellow, who stares boldly back at him, throws his hands up and snaps,

'I would say it is neither, then'.

'*Is* there an inn or alehouse here?' Eirik's eyes narrow, unsure whether or not the fellow has taken Harding's answer amiss.

The old man asks plainly,

'Well, do you wish just to drink ale and water your horses, and then ride on?'

Harding seems to be suddenly taken off stride and clamps his mouth tight shut.

'Both would be helpful, as would a bed for the night. We have a long way to go yet, so riddles are not needed right now', Eirik answers for us all, showing he knows we are being made fun of.

'In this part of the kingdom we call such a hostelry a *ghildhus*', the man snorts and pulls a rag from his sleeve, blows his nose and waves at something - only he knows what - in the darkness. Grinning toothlessly he adds, 'I can sell you ale, perhaps bread and cheese. Apples are in the barrel in the corner over there. Beds would be where you can make them in my barn'.

'Ale for four, and we would all be thankful to you for something to go with it', I call out as we stride past the man I take to be the innkeeper. Time is moving on, and the less time we spend talking the sooner we can be on our way again.

'Where are you going?' our host pries.

'Beyond the end of your nose is as far as you should know', Harding draws to his full height and pulls down cobwebs.

Laughter in the darkness tells us we are being watched. Eirik's right hand goes to his sword hilt, and Saeward thumbs the hilt of his dagger. Harding stares into the gloom as he pulls off the thick, grey mass of cobwebs from his shoulders, says nothing and turns to me,

'Ivar, do *you* know any of them? I am blessed sure I have never seen any of them before'.

I can make out men's noses and beards touched by the feeble light of a rush light burning in the middle of their table.

'You might let me know who you are, that we do not punish you for laughing at others'.

The answer comes quickly,

'I think we know one another already'. I know I have heard *him* before, now that he has spoken again. What is his name and from where does he hail? The owner bends forward to let us see him better by the light of the fire.

'You are Thegn Hereward, are you not?'

I hear Eirik push his sword back into its iron sheath. Saeward eases and takes a seat nearby.

'Who is Thegn Hereward?' Harding is still unaware of being amongst friends. He strides across the room but is halted by Eirik.

'Saeward, have we not met Thegn Hereward before?' I look sideways at my seated friend, who nods wearily.

He has ridden hard these last few days to catch up with us, I would guess, and the miles have caught up with him now he no longer feels threatened. Eirik grins broadly and ambles to the table to make himself known to an old friend he has not seen for some time,

'If we are all friends, why do we not drink to one another's errands?'

'Thegn Hereward, I welcome you to Mierca however humble the hospitality offered'.

'It is more than we were offered by this outlander king on his crowning. Believe me –'Hereward begins.

'You were *there?* There were many of us, Aenglishmen I mean?' Eirik offers a beaker of ale, which Hereward takes from him gratefully. Eirik turns to me and asks, 'You know this fellow, I understand?'

'We met not long after the bastard Willelm's crowning, not far from Ceolsey'. I add, 'Close to where it happened'.

'Hereward was on his way home and we had spent the night at an inn nearby. What he told me about the inn we over-nighted in would make your skin creep, Eirik'.

'*You* went to his crowning as well? You are not a thegn, nor a noble, so how –' Eirik is nonplussed.

Hereward's friends lean forward to listen to my tale.

'We *stole in*, clad in monks' habits, Saeward and I', I answer and smile, nodding to my East Seaxan friend. 'Well, afterward we went to an inn close by that Oslac told me of, hidden away from the road by trees and bushes, and cloaked in the river mist. He told me the innkeeper seemed to know my horse, and spent some time on her. We were not long there when an overbearing fellow by the name of Count Eustace burst in with his friends and began trying to order the innkeeper about. She –'

Eirik breaks in,

'The innkeeper was a *woman?* How odd! And you *knew* her?'

'Aye, I will get to that'. I forget we have known Eirik for such a short time and add for his sake,

'She fixed the count with such a stare he was maddened! We do not know what it was he saw, but he was so upset by it he spun on his heels and could not find the door fast enough!' I fix Eirik with a tired stare and finish,

'We spent the night in one another's arms. I awoke cold and hungry in the crumbling ruins of an old inn Thegn Hereward said had been long abandoned. Think that over...!'

Eirik asks, wide-eyed, looking around at the others,

'You were *lovers,* you and this innkeeper – how did you come to know her?' Of Hereward he asks, 'Did *you* know of this?'

'There was no time to talk. Willelm's men were all around. I had no knowledge of this then', Hereward gives me a look of puzzlement, but says nothing more on the matter, 'I had to catch up with friends after relieving myself of someone's watery ale'.

'You rode west from Thorney to ride back to Bourne?' Eirik scratches his matted beard.

'The king's men blocked the roads east, believing Willelm to be threatened by the men of Lunden Burh. We rode out through Middil Seaxe and on through what had been part of Earl Leofwin's lands. It felt odd, as though we were being followed by the eyes of the folk who lived there, without ever seeing anyone', Hereward looks into a dying fire in the hearth, chewing his lower lip, thinking.

Eirik looks from Hereward to me, but my thoughts are elsewhere. I cannot help but dwell on the loss of so many friends.

Only Theodolf is left of those who stood with me on Caldbec Beorg, and of those who we came to know from Lunden Brycg only Cyneweard is left, and he is still with Eadric.

Wulfmaer has gone back to his mill at Wealtham, having lost both brothers to the Northmen. Nevertheless Saeward is here with me still, having dealt death to many of Odo's men. He has the same luck as I for living through strife. It is the lot of those who have lost their close kin to outlive their friends. Will we be rid of this bastard king before we lose more good friends?

'Hey, Ivar, raise your spirits and sing with us!' Eirik puts a hand on my left shoulder to cheer me and knocks his beaker against mine, 'Let us sing a song of the snow melting, the leaves growing on the trees and the bees calling on the flowers!'

He laughs noisily, urging everyone to link arms – even Harding laughs like a child – and sing with him. Some young women push into the ring of men to be next to Eirik, chattering above the gruffness of the men. Saeward laughs light-heartedly without a care and suddenly the alehouse takes on the air of a feast-day.

I stand nursing my beaker, looking on, thinking of Braenda and what she might be doing at this time... Time is passing!

The singing dies down and one of the young women dances slowly around her friend, who seems more taken with Eirik.

'We must be on our way', I press, almost unwilling to break into his carefree world of laughter and song. The laughter dies as quickly as it had started.

'Aye, so must we be on *our* way', he unwillingly agrees, looking out through the doorway at the lengthening shadows, 'Harding, Saeward we must think of the road ahead. Are you set to ride on?'

Harding grunts and nods. Saeward yawns and stretches. He will sleep well when we do find an inn to rest either in or near Aescburna. Hereward and his friends stride out through the doorway ahead of us after handing over their silver.

'You have not eaten', the alehouse-keeper points to the food on a table near the hearth.

'We will take it in our saddle bags and eat on the way', I offer and feel for silver in the purse that hangs from my belt.

'It is paid for, by Thegn Hereward', the fellow tells me, and vanishes into the inn. He shows again with the leather food bags,

'You must pay for *these*'.

Harding growls at the fellow, who pulls fearfully back.

Hereward is already mounted and ready to leave with his friends when we come out once more onto the sunlit thwait the alehouse stands in. He grins when I stand by his horse, grips my outstretched hand firmly and laughs,

'Next time we meet, I will let *you* pay'.

'The *next time* – you think it likely we shall cross paths again?' I look up at him and put on a breezy smile, 'I shall look forward to that!'

Hereward salutes us, the few men with him turning and saluting as their horses climb the hill we came down not long since. I watch as they ride away, their horses carefully picking their way over the partly snow-covered, rough, stony track.

When we are mounted and on our way again, Eirik waving at the jostling women eager to be at the front of the gaggle waving him away, I ask Harding what it was he told the alehouse-keeper.

'I told him that as we had brought light to his otherwise dark little hole of an alehouse, he ought to be glad of our trade', he rumbles. 'I *also* said the leather bags he put our food in were ready to fall apart, and he should be glad we did not ask him for silver to take them off his hands!'

I am happy to leave it there. We are on our way again, with food to keep us from starving, skins of ale to wash it down.

What more could a fighting man wish from life?

We have left the Treonta behind, the river like a shiny grey ribbon below us. Up here, however, the snow still lies fetlock-deep on the deeply rutted road that we are following. Eirik warns against straying too near the edge, where it looks smoother going, but the way the ruts lead here and there we have no other way of making our way forward.

Smooth snow belies hidden dips, as Saeward finds to his cost. He is thrown into deep snow when his horse stumbles into a pit left from when men have dug themselves free of the sticky mud this road becomes in the fore- and after-year. Nevertheless he cheerfully picks himself up, brushes the snow from his habit and hoists himself back as clumsily as ever back into the saddle.

Harding shakes his head at the unwieldy way Saeward mounts, and Eirik holds back from laughing when I fix him with a stare.

The East Seaxan pays no heed to Harding's bleak look and presses his horse back onto the middle of the road. Now and then the way dips into the hillside between steep banks and the snow lies forbiddingly deep here.

'You should see what it is like beyond Aescburna', Harding warns. 'That is the way we wished to come with Osgod. I do not wonder he stayed behind in Rhosgoch. My friends and huscarls thought you mad to leave for the north at this time of the year'.

'Then why not ride east by way of Snotingaham?' I offer. Although it would be a long way around, it would make the riding easier. 'I thought that was the way you came when we came across you in Oxnaford shire'.

'Some wit put us on the wrong road through the southern Danelaw!' Harding snaps.

'That would add another day or more', Eirik nods.

'It would be Copsig's way north', Harding says, adding, 'I thought you wanted to get there ahead of him?'

'True', I have to admit he is right, 'we will just have to work our way north by way of Werchesuorthe'.

'Or north-eastward from Aescburna, do you think, perhaps?' Harding puts me right, screwing his eyes against the sharp sunlight on the snow-covered hillside. 'Where to from there, would you say?'

Eirik grins and shakes his head slowly, which makes me think that he has thought of another way ahead past Aescburna.

Before answering Harding I guide Braenda around an outcrop of rocks and look ahead to where he halts. He waits for me to catch up, knowing from the way I look I wish to seek counsel,

'Which way would you *sooner* take?'

'I was hoping you would ask. Copsig knows the land as well as, if not better than you. He has been there before. The last thing he would think is for us to cut through these mountains. We strike north for a while, then north-eastward into Deira through Odresfeld'.

194

'Are you coming on with us to Northanhymbra?' I ask Eirik. He shakes his head again as if I had said something witty.

'I have nothing to go back for, have I? FitzOsbern would have me thrown into a cell at Earl Ricard's stronghold in Scrobbesbyrig if I were to show there again. There is only one way for me to go – with you!'

I was hoping he would say that, and slap him on his back.

'Then I welcome you to my small band'. The chill air of a north-easterly wind strikes at my teeth as I grin broadly back at him.

'Come, we have too many miles ahead of us to spend our time being friendly', Harding berates us both for slowing him down.

The sun has cast its dying glow over the hills and woods behind us as we drop down along a deeply rutted road into a broad dale. The settlement through which we clatter along the snow-laden road spreads along the west side of the river. High wooden gates are jerkily pulled open for us on a wave from Eirik, and prying eyes take us in as we pass small clutches of men and women going about their daily tasks. No-one challenges us. A fellow I take to be a thegn stops as we pass him talking with a fellow burgher, but he merely waves us on. We pass through another pair of gates on the eastern side of Wotocheshethe, as Eirik tells me this small burh is called.

On we ride, at a slow trot toward a simply-built, short wooden bridge and over the river that snakes from the south-east. We follow along the eastern bank through the now fast darkening dale over a thick, though not unduly deep covering of snow.

Thick banks of cloud mass over the hills from the east, threatening to blot out the moon and free themselves of their cold white load. Smoke billows from rooftops ahead, pushed down onto surrounding fields by the strong downward gusts. Soon we will be unable to see anything; snow already falls heavily above us to our right.

'God, I am glad we are close to Aescburna!' Harding curses loudly.

'I see we still have a small river to ford before we can count our blessings', Eirik points ahead as we follow the rise to where the dale narrows and a smaller river flows into the Dof.

'Doubtless it will be cold', Saeward speaks for the first time since we left Sandun.

'Aye, although the snow should not fall deeply, fear not', I put him wise. 'As you well recall, the River Leag was high up on our horses' withers when we crossed from near Leagatun. Grin and bear it, we shall soon be warm again!'

'Our teeth will chatter but the innkeeper's wife will know best how to deal with that!' Harding bellows with mirth.

'I am looking forward to meeting her *already!*' Eirik laughs with him.

Should *I* try to bed her, doubtless she would turn into Braenda again!

'Is that all you ever think of, *bedding women?* What I am talking of is mulled ale!' Saeward sounds annoyed with Eirik.

'Oh, that too – *and* bedding them!' Eirik laughs again.

'All I can think of is the mulled ale and food', Saeward grits his teeth, trying to stop them from chattering as he head into the swirling waters of the smaller river.

'Women have a way of warming you up *out*side', Harding chortles. 'What you put into your belly beforehand will help warm your *in*side'.

'At least this riverbed is shallow here', I bring them back to what we are about to do now, having thought our mounts would be wading through deep icy water, I am grateful for this small saving.

Our horses scramble roughly in line, up to their ankles in the icy water and up the steep, crumbling clay riverbank. From there we make our way across the upland plain to the small walled burh. We let our mounts find their own way slowly through creaking gates that have seen better days and Harding asks a tired gatekeeper the whereabouts of an inn, adding, as if the fellow could not have seen it from looking at us,

'My friends and I have ridden across the hills and we are in need of some comfort. Which way is it to the nearest hostelry?'

'You asked me that only a week or so ago!''

'Listen friend, we are tired! Do not play games now. Show us the way to the nearest inn and I may reward you, or I shall see your thegn has you put on Brycgegeweorc for the rest of the year!'

'That way, turn left', the fellow answers sullenly.

Harding nods his acknowledgement and sets off again, paying no heed to the gatekeeper's balled fist.

'You said you would give me silver!' the gatekeeper croaks defiantly.

'I thought better of it', Harding calls back, making a half turn to look at the fellow over one shoulder.

Eirik winks at me and asks,

'What do you say, Ivar? Does our friend Harding not have a droll way of dealing with these folk?'

'I think he is right', I hear Saeward say behind me.

Eirik leads the way upward through the burh.

'That way, turn left'', was what he said', Eirik peers first down the narrow street, looking for an inn on the left side and then uphill,

'Ah!' is all he says, waving us uphill. None of us can see where we are headed until we have gone half the length of the street. There is little to show that it is an inn, but the front is long, a gate inset into the long wall beyond a heavily-studded door.

'Open up!' Eirik thumps on the door.

We are told by what sounds to be an old man that we must wait at the gate until someone un-bars it. After a stomach-churning wait in the cold the sound of iron chafing on wood and the dull scrape of a key in a lock signals that the gate is being opened for us.

'Forgive the wait, but we must safeguard the horses within. There have been thefts lately. Also there have been drunks pissing in the yard on their way home', an aged-looking, wizened fellow welcomes us into the yard and waves us on to the stable.

'I thank you, my good man', Harding wearily hands over the reins of his mare and presses a small silver coin into a gnarled open hand.

'I am not a man', is the answer we did not think we heard rightly the first time. On seeing our blank looks the words come again, 'I am *not* a man. My name is Rhonwen, a thrall from Ewyas up above Elwistan. Do you know it?'

Someone booms in the yard, demanding to know her whereabouts,

'Rhonwen, where are you hiding *now?*' The man booms again, 'Good-for-nothing time-waster that you are, where *are* you? That trader, what was his name? He has a lot to answer for, asking so much silver for you!'

Rhonwen is about to leave when Saeward catches her.

'Wait for us to enter. Fear not, you will be safe', he tells her. 'Our grandmother was taken by the Danes when Beorhtwulf was still too small to walk. This trade must stop one day!'

'*Rhonwen*, get in here- now!' a woman yells loudly, as loud as the man's.

'*I should go!*' Rhonwen is about to head for the door when Harding stops her.

'This fellow said you are safe with us. Wait here with us until we are ready to enter'.

A man leaves the inn by the back door and lopes toward Rhonwen. Before he can say a word Saeward has him by the throat,

'She will come in with us - *no sooner!*'

'I am here to take your horses to the stable, water and stable them', the fellow tells Saeward hoarsely when he speaks again.

'Raedmund is the man you want to speak to. Rhonwen, *you* go to master –'

'Is she a hearth-hound or does she bark for herself?!' Harding snaps at him, sending him scurrying to the stable leading our horses by their reins.

'Let us to it!' Eirik seems to delight in the moment and leads into the inn with Saeward, Rhonwen following us.

'Where have you *been*, woman?' the innkeeper's wife catches her over the ear from behind with the back of her hand as she cowers behind Saeward in the doorway.

'To whom are you talking like that?' Saeward faces the woman down, only to be accosted by the innkeeper himself.

'If you mean to be a guest here, do not threaten my woman!' A stout fellow shows from a door behind her.

'Do not talk to Rhonwen as if she were a hearth hound!' Saeward turns to look at him and balls a fist under the man's nose.

The innkeeper croaks,

'Ordwulf, see this man out of here!'

When he comes amongst the throng in the main room of the inn, Ordwulf is too tall to pass beneath the nearest beam without ducking.

'Are you are so tame you do not know you spoken to like a hearth hound, Ordwulf. Why do you *allow* it?'

Saeward stands his ground. We have to stand in awe of his foolish bravery. Ordwulf could tear him limb from limb. Ordwulf stops and glowers down at Saeward from between the beams. He rolls back his sleeves and plants his feet wide apart to take a swipe at the East Seaxan. What he hears next stops the giant in his tracks,

'You know, you could be Rhonwen's grandson!'

'Do not listen to his foolishness, Ordwulf, show him what you do to unruly drinkers', the innkeeper presses. 'Throw him out!'

'Do you know where she hails from?' Saeward asks Ordwulf, who stands squinting at the East Seaxan against the light of a burning torch on the roof post to his left. He glowers at me, and then turns back to Saeward, his master fuming. Onlookers gather nosily.

'How could *she* be my grandmother? Mine are both dead. Raedmund told me'. Ordwulf's whine tells me his master has raised him from childhood, and wants his pound of flesh from his underlings. He wants to know his silver is well-spent.

Saeward upsets the fellow further,

'Why should you believe a man who pays you poorly and holds a woman as thrall who could be your grandmother?'

He has no thought for himself, thanks to Raedmund. It only takes someone like Saeward to come along and muddy the waters a little for Raedmund's world to come toppling down around him.

'Ordwulf, what are you *waiting* for?' The innkeeper's wife joins her husband by the door, urging 'Go on, you great oaf. Thrash him!'

'Why should I?'

Turning on the woman Ordwulf finds Raedmund standing in his way.

'You do what you are told because I pay you!' the innkeeper seethes, helpless with rage, his guests standing looking from him to Ordwulf, and on to Saeward. Saeward now delivers his master stroke,

'You could be Wilfrith, my long-lost brother who was taken by the Danes'. Saeward has summoned his story-telling skills and dealt Raedmund a stunning blow without touching him.

'I see it all now, father dying in mother's arms, our home burning and the Danes leading you off to their ships, *both of you'*.

'So how come the Danes did not take either you or *your* mother?' the innkeeper thinks he has Saeward with this, but reckons without the East Seaxan's way with words,

'They thought our mother too ugly', Saeward winks at me, 'and I had my grand-father's crutch. That helped make me look a cripple'.

We watch with baited breath as Ordwulf turns on the innkeeper and his wife with a sobbing roar,

'You *bought* us both, grandmother *and* me, hoping to get away without having to pay her, feeding me *scraps* at mealtimes!'

Ordwulf pushes his master bodily out into the yard, where he falls forward into the muddied and dung-soiled straw by the stable doors, almost falling backward over his wife.

'*Go*, the pair of you. Find somewhere else to eke out your shabby way of life!'

Raedmund picks himself up and stands looking around in the darkening greyness for his woman. On finding her grovelling in the dirt behind him for the few belongings she had in her hands, they almost fall over their grinning stable ceorl on their way out to the yard door. Together they back away from Ordwulf as he glowers at them furiously, standing over them.

Their mutterings are drowned by the uproar of the guests pushing through the inn door to see them being humbled.

'Grandmother, come and watch as these unworthies crawl away - they will think again before coming *back!*' Ordwulf sneers.

'*Now* look what you have done!' Harding laughs as Saeward stands, arms folded on his chest, smiling smugly at this feat. He seats himself by the fire. A task well done, he finds his reward soon forthcoming,

'Who is for mulled ale?' Saeward asks needlessly as Ordwulf brings us steaming cups of the welcome brew, adding, 'Innkeeper, join us when time allows!'

'Well, *brother*, why ever not?' Ordwulf answers with a knowing wink, basking in his new-found glory. 'Come, grandmother, sit here with me at my other side'.

'Tell me how your wyrd led you here in years past. Do you think a trader could ever look you in the eye again? Ivar, meet my grandmother', Saeward bids me sit by him on his other side, Rhonwen still unable to take in what has happened, being patted by all and sundry like a hearth hound.

It is almost as if he really *is* the old woman's grandson. As for Ordwulf, I am sure his head must be spinning, the way everything has happened so suddenly. Is he ready to be his own master?

'We need beds for the night, innkeeper', Saeward waves Ordwulf over, 'your *best* beds'.

Ordwulf beams at him as he passes between well-wishers,

'Whatever else *could* they be?'

'What if Raedmund comes back to demand his inn?' Eirik seats himself by us on the next bench, with Harding.

'Is that likely to happen?' Saeward looks guilelessly at Eirik, as if he thinks it wholly unlikely. 'Look at those around you. *Can* Raedmund ever show here again?'

'The law is the law', Eirik warns. 'None can argue about Raedmund's right to the inn'.

'Telling them you are Ordwulf's brother and Rhonwen's grandson might have earned pity for them, and that might last for some hours - or even into the morning. Then the thegn will laugh and everyone will see the wit of it, but there is a limit –'Harding offers a few words of wisdom but Saeward will hear none of it.

'Let them taste their freedom, even if it cannot last. Dreams never do. The thegn will tell the innkeeper to treat them better from now on, but they will still be beholden to Raedmund'.

'Aye, and meanwhile who sells us the ale? I hate to bring you back to earth, but we have an early start. If the snow falls on the high ground, we will need every pound of strength to work our way through to Deira', I remind them and nod at Ordwulf who grasps my meaning and heads toward a great vat with a handful of beakers. Tongue in cheek I ask, 'Are you taking our silver, or keeping tally?'

'What do you mean, keep tally?' Ordwulf gapes at me, mouth wide open, almost pouring the drink over the rags on his feet as he scoops a measure of ale with one of the beakers.

'You need to know how much we have had from you, to take our silver after we have eaten in the morning', I tell him, smiling.

Even if Raedmund does come back, Ordwulf could learn from his hours as master of the inn and be of greater use to his master one day.

'You *could* carve nicks into the table edge', Saeward laughs evilly and takes the first beakerful from his 'brother'.

'Why would I do that? I have a stick to cut into', Ordwulf sniffs and scoops more ale. 'But I cannot count anyway'.

Harding takes this second beaker and empties it, belches and thumps it down on the table beside him and almost howls for food at Rhonwen,

'You know I could finish off a bullock on my own'.

Rhonwen gives a start, and almost leaps onto the bench she was rubbing her left leg against. On gathering her wits together she answers warily,

'We have no bulls to eat, would broth be enough – with bread and cheese?'

We seem to be living on bread, broth and cheese. Still, if that is all there is at this time of night –

'Do you have nothing better?' Eirik looks down at a lost-looking Rhonwen, bewildered by demands in a tongue she does not rightly understand.

She looks from one to another of us helplessly before turning away. Before she reaches the door to what must the a kitchen, she turns and looks over one shoulder at me,

'It *is* bread, broth and cheese for the four of you?' she asks, to be sure she has it right. On my nod she leaves us.

'More ale', Harding growls. When Ordwulf stares glumly at him he adds, winking at me, 'Worry not, I shall take my time with this one'.

'You will get us a bad name, Harding!' I chide with a sly grin, pushing him on the shoulder and earning myself a growl into the bargain. 'These good folk will think we are sots'.

Harding straightens and snaps back.

'We will be *tired*, hungry sots if that Rhonwen woman takes much longer with our food!'

'Ah, *here* she comes at last!'

I turn on the bench to see Rhonwen struggling through the kitchen doorway, a platter laden with bowls and a pot slopping broth over her hands as she fights to keep it from sliding off onto the straw-strewn floor.

Saeward sees her and strides across the floor to save her from ruin and almost trips over someone's outstretched foot.

'What is this, some brave-heart wishes to *test* me?' Saeward stops dead and follows the foot upward to coldly stare the foolhardy prankster in the eye. 'Say you are sorry or I call you out!'

'What will you do, priest - *pray* me to death?' the fellow sneers.

'No I will cut you into *wolf-meat!*' Saeward pulls down the neck of the habit to show the hauberk, the sword half drawn before gasping onlookers know what it is they are looking at.

'Do you know how to *use* that?' the fellow asks, guffawing, and pulls apart his own coat.

Also clad in chain mail, the newcomer is cross-belted, a fine craftsman-worked silver inlaid belt-buckle showing him to be a man of some standing.

When one of the onlookers is about to speak to him, the fellow puts his mail-gloved hand across the man's mouth and puts a finger to his own to show he wishes to speak.

'Can you *use* that trinket on your belt?' Saeward is asked again.

Sword fully unsheathed, my friend upends the table nearest to him to make room for a fight.

The newcomer smiles coldly, drawing a sword at least two hand-widths longer than Saeward's but my friend is not put out,

'Plainly, you know I am calling you out'. He knows there is more to handling a sword than merely showing its length, adding,

'I can show you more than just how to answer your foolhardiness, if you know more than to stand yapping like the young pup that you are', Saeward bares his teeth in defiance, 'Let me show you how we dealt death to the Northmen in the southern shires!'

'Then you have come a long way to learn a lesson', the fellow threatens.

I feel I should know him but he wears a hood low over his eyes, as if hiding his hair.

One of the fellow's followers laughs out aloud and mocks, a Fleming by the way he speaks.

'We will be riding further, to teach another fool a lesson!'

'We take him one at a time, Dirk. I come first!' the fellow holds his sword with both hands, and cuts through the air in front of Saeward's nose, 'if there is anything left of him when I am done!'

'You will have to do *better* than that, braggart!' Saeward brings down his sword onto the newcomer's blade, the clash echoing throughout the inn.

'Hey you, fight outside, not in here!' Raedmund has found his spirit, having come back with others. Behind him another newcomer, a thegn perhaps, rests one hand on the pommel of a finely crafted sword.

Saeward's challenger warns,

'Stand back if you wish not to be struck down'.

The one I take to be the thegn breaks in and bravely stands between Saeward and his challenger,

'Fight away from this burh or part friends!'

'Damned spoilsport, coming between us like this – you could have waited, surely?' Saeward rams his sword back into its sheath and almost knocks the thegn over as he recalls Rhonwen with the broth, 'God, I forgot the broth!'

'Be a good fellow', the thegn asks of the newcomer. 'Take down that hood when you are in an inn, that we know who it is flouts the common good!'

'Must I?' the fellow growls, sheathes his sword and stands, arms crossed over his mailed chest, daring the thegn.

'Aye, you *must!*' Harding bellows, then softens, almost as if he were begging, 'To put us all at our ease, I must know who is foolish enough to cross that Seaxan hothead!'

Harding prods the air at Saeward, who now helps the ageing Rhonwen bring our food. Having set the platter down on the table Saeward seats himself and she heads back to the kitchen.

Raedmund snaps,

'Have you paid for that?' he almost dips a grubby, unwashed finger into the broth.

'It *will* be paid for, as long as you keep your filthy fingers to yourself!' I berate him, and beckon the thegn over to our table, 'What has he told you?'

'He wailed at me that his inn had been stolen from him by outlanders', the thegn answers.

'We are *outlanders?*' Saeward sprays broth everywhere.

'*I* did not know who you were!' Raedmund whines. His wife grinds her teeth behind him, maddened by his lack of mettle.

'We are riding north to rid Northanhymbra of one of its worst woes!' Saeward rants.

'Say nothing more', the newcomer lifts his hood. 'I am also on my way to Northanhymbra with my men. Perhaps we can ride together?'

'Who are *you?*' Eirik eyes the fellow warily.

I swear I *should* know who he is. Then it dawns on me. I *do* know. When I saw him last, Copsig was grey, unkempt, and walked with a limp from the wound I had inflicted on him. This man is dark-haired, straight-limbed and younger than Copsig could be... But he *is* Copsig. I *know* it.

I must still be suffering from the blows to my head. Can a man grow *younger?* The way I hear him speak now is how I first heard the lies from his own mouth all these years ago.

12

The night wears on and we have taken our fill. Ordwulf, still Raedmund's ceorl by the thegn's word, leads us to our rooms. We leave the newcomer downstairs, being regaled by a gleeful Raedmund. The innkeeper and his wife may be known to him, but never speak to him by name throughout the evening. None has asked him about errand to Northanhymbra, and why he would wish us to ride with him and his men.

It is still dark when I wake sweating. Sleep did not come easily, and I have been robbed of it again by my thoughts.

In the time I should have been asleep I have been on my back, staring at the gutting candle on the chair by the foot of my cot bed. I saw a grey-haired warrior, once fox-red haired, laughing and taunting –

'He *is* Copsig!' I awake with a start and Saeward snores on.

I pull on my boots and fumble through the darkness to the room Harding shares with Eirik. The door to Harding's bed-closet is already half open and I draw it a little wider to enter. When I put my hand over his mouth he opens it wide and bites down on my knuckles and I need all my strength not to yell out. When he opens his eyes he looks bewildered at me and hisses so as not to awaken Eirik,

'Ivar, what are you doing *here?*'

'*What is it?*' Eirik hisses and I hear the creaking of his cot-bed. He is on his feet quickly and hurries sword in hand to Harding's bed-closet.

'The newcomer who challenged Saeward earlier', I begin breathlessly.

'*What of him?*' Harding groans, angered at being roused from much-needed sleep. Eirik stares at me.

'He is *Copsig!*'

Harding is up on his feet as if stung,

'What makes you think it is *him?*' Harding is up on his feet as if stung, trying not to shout and wake the whole inn. 'I would be hard-put to know him anyway!'

'My head has been whirring all night, thinking about him. He is darker somehow, and the short plaits over his ears have been shorn, but what he can *not* hide is the way he speaks!'

'Your head must still be whirring!' Harding scolds. '*How* can he be darker than when you last saw him? We do not grow younger!

'Women use henna to darken their hair when they grow grey'. Eirik assures Harding, 'Why would he not do so, to show this Northman king he is able to rule an earldom like Beornica?'

'He would have lied, as he always did to save his neck, or when he thought he could smell gain. We must be away early, before he and his friends awaken. I do not know if he has any on watch outside, so we must leave by a side door somehow', I go over our ride north with Harding, which tracks and moors or hills we cross.

'He knows his way, aye. Any road north that is not blocked will be useful to him. There must be some tracks he does not know as well as you', I tell Harding.

'True, but I do not know *him* as well as you seem to', Harding answers, trying not to fall asleep again.

'He has crossed my path only once'.

'He is a wily old wolf, we know. Will he halt in Jorvik, or go on to Beornica? He cannot go to Baebbanburh, because he knows he will be hunted down there. Where else does he go?'

I am trying to fight off a growing tiredness that threatens to engulf me, and the likelihood of combat with him crosses my thoughts. It is all that keeps me awake.

'Should he ride by way of Jorvik, Copsig might take more men from there', I warn.

'You think Gospatric would fret about a handful of men from the south, even if they *are* backed up by men from Deira? Lose no more sleep over it, Ivar. Go back to sleep. We will shadow Copsig and if he leaves the highway to ride east – *if* that is what he means to do - I will think of something', Harding tries to cheer me.

'Having fought with me by the Deorewent, and lost, I doubt he will calmly ride north without trying to cut me down as soon as he thinks I am not watching out for him', I warn Harding again.

'*You* – fought with Copsig? How come he has not tried to take your head off yet?' Harding stares at me.

'Are you *sure* it is Copsig?' Eirik asks. He may think I have lost my wits since I told him of the times I have been bludgeoned.

If only to keep an eye on him, we must press on. It is not for nothing he is known as the 'wolf', not because of his shaggy grey hair.

'He is wily', I answer Eirik, 'always looking to best his foes. He knows me better since we fought, and will find a way of dealing with the three of you if I can be dealt with quickly'.

Harding and Eirik look bleary-eyed at one another, the older thegn shaking his head. We *must* leave early, if only to stay alive. He could even try to do away with each of us in the wilds of the peaks.

'He will claim he is only redeeming his good name by killing me, and his men will not waste too much sympathy for any of you, merely for being with me. We have to leave now, and be far enough ahead of them that they will not think it worth bothering to catch up with us'.

'You had better be *right*, Dane. Losing sleep to save *your* skin would not sit well with me! If we are outnumbered out there, as you say we will be, there will be little we can do to save our*selves*. His men may or may not be untried, but they could overwhelm us in the upland passes, aye'. Harding nods at me, then looks to Eirik, telling him, 'We can make up for lost sleep tonight, close to friends of mine. The innkeeper in Dereleag would send a rider to summon help if needed when we reach there'.

'How far is that from here?' Eirik rasps, leaning forward. When no answer is forthcoming he shrugs, looks at me and pulls on his boots.

'It is near enough for us to ride in one day and perhaps not the way Copsig's wishes to ride north', Harding growls an answer under his breath.

'Surely our tracks in the snow would show him the way', Eirik smiles smugly, then looks down at the floor when Harding glares up at him. '*Still* - perhaps if it goes on snowing we *can* lose them'.

'That was what I thought', Harding stands suddenly and looks around at us.

'I had best stir Saeward from the depths of sleep', I tell them and make back for the door.

'We will see you at the stable door. I will get food from Rhonwen, not the innkeeper. Be as quick as you can without giving yourself – or us - away', Harding tells me.

No-one else seems to be awake as we lead our horses out of the yard, north uphill before we mount. Harding, true to his word, has sworn Rhonwen's to silence about our going, and brought enough food for the four of us, with a skin of ale each to wash it down.

The snow on the track deadens the hoofbeats as our mounts climb to the dale head above Aescburna. The first streaks of grey in the eastern sky shine back up from the burbling River Dof to our left where it winds to the west.

'Look ahead', Harding warns in a breathy whisper. We halt and he nods at the cluster of riders ahead of us, dark against the light snowfall. 'Copsig thought as you did about gaining a head start'.

'They will not see us as long as we keep them within sight', I offer, although sooner or later one of them is bound to look around to see if they are being followed.

'There is a crossroad ahead, at Torp', Harding assures us, 'and we shall see which track they take from there. If they follow to the east, we go on north and bypass Dereleag. If they go on, they will not backtrack for fear of losing ground'.

'Where do we stay if not at Dereleag?' Saeward asks, yawning still even though we have been underway for nearly half the day. To stay awake he rubs his eyes and shakes his head like a hound.

'I will find somewhere, fear not. But fall asleep here and no-one will find you until the thaw'. Harding grins at the East Seaxan. 'Rest assured, you will have a bed with deep down to help you back to your slumbers, perhaps even a woman to keep you warm'.

Saeward nods meekly, giving in, and dismounts.

Eirik has seen him and reins in hard. He demands to know why Saeward is on the ground,

'Hey, what are you doing? This is not the time to dismount - get back on your horse!'

'Hush, do you want to warn Copsig?' I try to keep my voice down, only to bring Harding's wrath down upon me.

'*You* are as bad as he is!' Harding growls first at me, and stares at Eirik as if he were to blame for my deeds, adding, 'Stay with him. Whatever he is doing, he should not be long'.

'I only want to rub snow into my face, to keep me awake', Saeward almost whines, like a child, earning a look of scorn from the three of us. Harding sets his teeth, maddened by Saeward's show of awkwardness at this of all times.

'All right, do it then - *without* whining!' Harding hisses, turning in his saddle before loosening the reins to ease his horse into a walk. He and I are side-by-side now, with only the girth of a man between us when he warns me,

'I can do without his foolishness. In Christ's name, make sure he does not stay like that for long – jerk him out of it!'

'This is not like him', I turn in my saddle to look over my shoulder and see that he is back in his saddle.

'If this is how tiredness takes him, he should think again before coming on. Gospatric and Osulf would not stand for it if he is in their company for long', Harding stares hard at me after giving me the warning and looks back to see that Eirik and Saeward catch up before kicking his horse into a trot.

'They are out of sight now, thank God!' Harding says shortly when our friends are with us again.

'We rode through Earl Odo's lands for days without so much as a hint of weakness from him. I will have words with him when we are abreast of one another', I offer. Saeward could be trying on me, too, if I allowed him too much leeway.

'All *right*, Ivar! Say nothing more about it. We can forget this for the time being. We need to keep our wits about us when Copsig is about, you ought to know. We have to be wary lest he has left any of his Flemings behind to watch for us'.

At Torp Harding dismounts to look at the tracks left by Copsig and his men to see which way he has taken.

'There are some droppings on the road north from here - still steaming, look. We could turn east now', he tells us and hurls himself back up into his saddle. His horse turns skittish and Harding struggles to keep her from hurtling off after Copsig and his men. When she settles down again he tells us,

'In riding through, it shows he does not know the lie of the land as well as I thought. That road veers north-westward. Unless he means to come off the road to head north for Tadintun, the way beyond will be hard as on their horses as on them!'

'That means they will be climbing steeply?' Eirik asks, trying to strike Harding with his knowledge of the land here.

Harding blows out his cheeks and rolls his eyes by way of an answer, meaning 'what do *you* think?' Eirik turns his horse to ride eastward and we follow him, with Harding taking up the rear after looking along the road at Copsig's tracks in the deep, ice crusted snow.

'One thing is plain, they will be walking their horses before long', Harding tells me as he draws level with me and takes one last watchful look northward.

Yet Harding's chosen way is threatening to tire our horses. He says nothing yet about dismounting and walking them, as he says Copsig's men will have to. Perhaps the going will soon be easier – I hope so for Braenda's sake.

There are more snow clouds over the eastern foothills to our right. Only Harding knows whether the hills this road passes through are high enough to break them and unleash more white hell on us. In a hamlet known to Harding as Werchesuorthe, he calls a halt outside a small alehouse.

'We can stay in this inn', he tells us, but it is plain the building has no rooms for anyone but the owner. There are few about who would challenge him, such is the strength of his will. Alehouse or inn, it is all the same to me. It means water for my horse and ale to ease my own thirst. There may be more for us, both in the way of oats or bran for her and broth for me, but no beds.

I seem to live on broth these days. Much of the harvest would have been gathered in the north and west of the kingdom, but in these parts the only harvest is of wool. At this time of year the sheep are well sheltered, better than we are. They may also be better fed, as when we enter the building and Harding asks about food, the owner shakes his head,

'I sell only ale', he answers grimly, tersely. 'If you want more, there is an inn further down the road to Maesteslach'.

'*Further* down the road?' Harding rumbles, looking into thin air as if in a dream. He is given a sharp nod by our host, who turns to us, looking us up and down.

'Well, my friends, the man says we have to go further down the road if we wish for something to line our stomachs. We have more riding ahead of us', Eirik groans, puts on a look of anger and sucks air through gaps in his teeth.

I look around in the darkness of the room before leaving and note that the room is empty. There is little trade in winter for ale only. I dare say even the rats have passed by this hostelry and turned their noses up at the fellow's scanty hospitality.

'A little further', I tell Braenda. Just a *little* further, I hope. Harding is disgruntled at the rebuff, I know. He shows nothing outwardly. Inwardly he may wish to strangle the fellow, but that would only start a feud with the man's kin. They could be all around us, watching.

Harding has enough in store ahead of him, what with keeping his head when we meet Gospatric and Osulf. They will ask themselves why he has chosen to guide *us* to them, when he only had to agree with Osgod that warning them about Copsig was a waste of time.

'A little way down the road, he said?' Saeward laughs hollowly to me. Our horses can do no more than walk downhill in the snow, and the sky is darkening ahead of us.

'Are you still whining like a wet-nosed child?' Eirik sounds like Harding now.

Looking back at my East Seaxan friend his brow knits with poorly hidden dislike.

The snow has drifted on either side of the road and we are coming to a bend on a steep hill. There is no bank or wall to our right to stop us from sliding into the buildings below. One of them may be the inn we were told of.

'Is one of these hovels an inn? Somehow I cannot see it', Eirik laughs as we pass between scattered homes.

'We are almost in Maesteslach', Harding answers with a scowl. 'Believe me'.

'Eirik nods after Harding and turns to look at me over one shoulder.

'Harding thinks there is an inn in the hamlet ahead'.

I can only summon a weak smile. My feet feel sore from hours of walking beside Braenda. The boots we wear are not made for marching, I have been told. If I ever doubted it, I know now for myself. Another mile or so beyond the hamlet is a building that looks big enough to be the inn that the dour fellow in Werchesuorthe spoke of.

'This looks like it!' Harding seems to have read my thoughts.

Eirik calls out cheerily,

'We can down some mulled ale and fill a corner of our stomachs until we halt for the night in Dereleag'.

'You will be hard put to reach Dereleag!' a woman cuts in from our left.

'You mean *you* would be hard put to reach Dereleag!' Harding answers without looking around at her.

'I mean *anyone* would find it hard', she brays and steps out of the shadow of her home.

'Who are you, that you are so wise about the roads above here?' Harding seems annoyed that she is so knowledgeable, 'What makes you so sure of what you say?'

'Who I am is of no matter to you, but for the sake of manners I am Sigrun. My man came down from Dereleag this morning – *downhill*, mark my words you lunk-head – wet with sweat and worn *out*! He barely had the time to eat a few spoonfuls of porridge before falling asleep', Sigrun stands like a man, a pipe in the left corner of her mouth, rough hands on well-padded hips.

'What was he doing, that he was so *spent?*' Harding's voice lifts, he is taken aback by what this woman has told him.

'He was trying to find some of his ewes'. She is about to step back into the shadows when I raise my hand to catch her eye.

She turns to look at me as I ask,

'Are *all* the roads on these moors so beset with drifts?' If the road up to Dereleag is so bad, the road Copsig followed would be harder to follow.

'Think about it', is all she says and leaves us mulling with Harding about another way around, to steal the lead on Copsig.

'What other road can we use?' Eirik looks to him.

'Hush, I am thinking!' Harding scratches the thick beard growth on his jaw.

We nudge our mounts closer around him. Fresh snow falls like eiderdown on our heads and shoulders. Saeward pulls up his hood to shield his neck from the biting easterly wind. At least he *can*. Wearing an iron helm, even were it well padded, would be asking for a cold in the head.

'We could ride some way uphill and see for ourselves?' I offer. 'We might not be too sorely tried'.

'These folk live here. She must know how bad it is', Harding answers. Scowling, he sits back on his saddle. He takes a long look northward and shakes his head. He looks eastward over Saeward and shakes his head again. As if pleading for better insight, he looks heavenward, then turns to look at me with snowflakes on his beard.

'Northward is best. That way, however', he tells us, a long, bony finger prodding at the air eastward, 'although it looks from here to be the easier road, it soon climbs and could add a day to our ride. Copsig would not allow *his* men to hold him back, even allowing for the hard road he has chosen to follow. North-eastward the road would be even worse, over the brow of a steep hill. The nearest settlement that way is Ceasterfeld and we might not reach it before daylight. We ride on to Dereleag!'

Eirik nods, not knowing better,

'You know the lie of the land'.

Saeward shrugs, holds up his hands with the reins held loosely in them and purses his lips as though ready to question Harding's wisdom.

'Do you know better?' Harding growls to Saeward's head-shaking.

'Whatever you say', Saeward backs down from a fruitless argument. He looks to me to take Harding's glowering eyes from him.

'We will bow to your greater knowledge', I am at one with Saeward. Harding grunts. I feel he would fight his corner like an angry bear even if he were knowingly wrong. As it is, never having been this way before I know no better.

One by one we strike out northward, with me the last in line. Sigrun leaves her home again and stares balefully at Harding. I fight down a smile. Whatever she thinks she keeps to herself this time, knowing her words are wasted on him, or us.

Dark shapes of buildings loom out of the darkness as we fight our way on foot again through deep snow, our horses struggling behind us with their heads low in driving snow through a knee-high drift. I am grateful our climb to Ewyas was not made harder like this, even though it was much steeper. Had there been snow on the hills of western Hereford shire, our way to Rhosgoch would have been hard enough to make us think twice about joining Eadric.

'This is Dereleag', Harding assures us.

'Thank God for that!' Saeward breathes out, 'Think what it would have been like going east!'

For want of knowing better, Eirik agrees with what Harding told him earlier,

'We would still have been due for a long fight on foot against the snow, had we taken that way'.

I keep my thoughts to myself. When we have taken care of our horses and seated ourselves around a blazing hearth fire I will be happier. First we must see that there *is* an inn to shelter in.

Eirik asks artlessly,

'When you came last, where did you stay the night?' Eirik innocently asks a beaming Harding.

'We rode *through*', Harding answers, then adds, 'On our way south we stayed the night in Maesteslach. There was hardly any snow at all then. We thought winter was over early!'

'Did you see an inn then?' Saeward asks, risking Harding's wrath.

'We saw an inn, aye. But as we made no halt there, I see no sense in trying to think back on it', Harding answers haughtily. From the way he answers he is unsure whether there is one at all.

We wade manfully through the drift between the buildings, our horses faltering. No-one stirs, although a dog barks somewhere in a back yard. Our eyes strain in the darkness to see a house that looks something akin to an inn. I am beginning to despair of finding somewhere to stay the night. We are almost on the far side of this hamlet when he points to a lone building piled to the eaves with snow on its eastern wall.

'Ah-*hah* - you thought I must have been dreaming when I told you there *was* an inn here!' Harding laughs, relieved at having found it, but I see nothing about the building that tells me it is an inn.

'If this is an inn', I ask him, 'tell me, where are the stables?'

'They must be at the back!' he answers gruffly.

'*Where* is the back?' Saeward asks, looking through the flurrying snow.

'Bang on the door', Eirik tells Harding.

'Hold the reins of my horse!' Harding reaches to him and stamps up to the door.

Before he begins to thump the snow from the iron studded oak door, someone opens it and stands in the doorway. Lit from behind, the fellow squares up to Harding, hands folded across his chest.

'What do you want?' the fellow demands. He would make a good match for Harding in a fight, I would warrant.

'We wish for rooms for the night', Harding straightens.

'You wish for rooms for the night', the fellow half smiles, having thrown Harding's own words back at him. This tells me that Harding must be mistaken in thinking this man's home to be an inn.

'Aye, *do you have any?*' Harding sounds wearied by the householder.

'I *have* rooms, but this is no inn', is the answer I have been dreading.

'But –'Harding is tongue-tied.

'*But* you are wrong. If I were an innkeeper, where would I stable your horses, *in the swine-sty?*' The fellow's laughing, mocking answer tests Harding to the utmost, yet he holds his temper and asks,

'*Is* there an inn in this God-forsaken shit-hole?'

'As to this hamlet being forsaken by God, you might be right. We have no church, nor do we have an inn. You could try Thegn Gudbrand's hall, back that way', the householder offers Harding a way out of his misery. 'Tell him Alwig sent you. His men have mostly left, only two or three have stayed since Earl Eadwin took the rest to fight Tostig. He *has* rooms, I would say. Being a friendly soul, he would be glad of your company for the night'.

'We thank you, Alwig. How do we come to Thegn Gudbrand's hall?' I ask, before Harding loses his temper and regrets it.

'Go back the way you came, turn right halfway along. You will see by its greater size between the dwelling houses around it', Alwig answers me with a sly grin.

By what little light there is from the doorway that escapes past Alwig, Saeward looks smitten at the thought of having to trudge back the way we came.

'Bear up, friend. We will soon be warm', I comfort him and turn, Braenda turning behind me. Eirik leads this time, with Saeward trudging wearily behind him. Harding and I wade slowly side-by-side through the snow that we have already trampled down on our way to what Harding thought was the inn.

Thegn Gudbrand's discthegn answers Eirik's banging on his master's huge oak door.

'Why do you wish to see Thegn Gudbrand for something that can wait until morning?' The thegn's house-warden is a thickset, balding fellow. Lank dark hair falling on his shoulders, he sports a dense growth of hair in long, elf-like ears. He has seen better days, as has the jerkin he wears over a much-patched woollen tunic. A sometime worthwhile garment, it has been mended than once around the ties at the front. Nevertheless, he is clothed for the cold, rather than to show the thegn's wealth – if there is any to show. Eirik shows the three of us to the ageing retainer and answers,

'We were told to say that Alwig sent us'.

'*Alwig* sent you?' He seems to be laughing at us.

'Something is wrong?' I hear a man boom within.

The house-warden looks askance at me, turns and calls back to his master,

'There are men at the door who claim to have been sent here by Alwig, Thegn Gudbrand', he calls out, still snorting with laughter.

'They were sent by *Alwig?*' Thegn Gudbrand, still out of sight from us thunders and begins to laugh, 'Bring them in Arnkell!'

We are shepherded into the hall where a huge fire burns in the hearth, the flames throwing dancing shadows around the walls and carved wooden pillars. A scruffy, heavy-jowled fellow stares at us as we near him on his dais. He looks under his bushy brows at us, for the world looking as though he might be Arnkell's older brother. He rises slowly as we are led to the dais and greets us one by one with a warm hug.

'Welcome, I am thegn Gudbrand. So *you* are Alwig's guests – or might have been. Tell me your names, each of you. I would like to know who it is thinks I am an innkeeper?' Gudbrand laughs himself hoarse at his own wit and his few men join him. Whether they do so to keep their places at his hearth, I do not know.

He looks first at me.

'I thought we *were* at an inn when we stopped at Alwig's home', I tell Gudbrand.

'It was he who told us we should come here and sample your good hospitality, Thegn Gudbrand', I tell him. When he winces, having to wait for my name I add, 'I am Ivar'.

'Welcome Ivar. We find life boring in the winter time, so we like to see someone new. I told Alwig to send anyone here who seemed to be at odds with their surroundings. From afar his home does look like an inn, I grant, but did you not think to yourself that it could not be such when you failed to see stables, or even an inn sign?'

'With snow everywhere, and it being dark, there was no way of knowing whether his house was not an inn. My friend Saeward thought that it could not be an inn without stables at the back', I am bending the truth a little here, but what does Gudbrand know – or even care – who thought or said what?

'Which of you is Saeward?' Gudbrand laughs and holds out a hand in greeting for my friend when he steps forward, 'I want to meet the only man with the wit to know you cannot stable horses in a swine-sty!'

'Oddly enough, these are the words Alwig used when we stopped there. Is there a binding spirit about these parts?

'Welcome Saeward', the thegn's wife echoes her husband's greeting and holds her hand out for Saeward to kiss her ring.

'Who are the others -?' Gudbrand begins, only to be stopped by Harding.

'I am Harding, Thegn Gudbrand', Harding speaks out of turn, kisses the ring on the lady's finger and looks to our host. 'It was I who thought Alwig's home was the inn, not Ivar. He takes too much on himself! I am a thegn from the north of Deira, almost overlooking the River Tese, and we are on our way to see Earl Gospatric'.

'Why ride to Beornica at this time of year?' someone asks gruffly from the back of the hall, behind one of the pillars.

'We are riding to warn Earl Gospatric of the coming of the new earl of Beornica, Copsig, who was chosen by King Willelm', Harding foolishly blurts before he is stopped by Eirik.

'I am Eirik, from the Danelaw, but King Harold made me a thegn of lands near Scrobbesbyrig. Earl Willelm fitzOsbern took my lands and I was made to ply for trade ferrying folk across the River Seoferna. That is until my friends here came across with me, leaving Earl Willelm fuming on the western bank!'

'They have done you a good turn, friend Eirik', the man behind the pillar calls out again.

'Aye, Ivar and Harding you have done Eirik a good turn', Gudbrand beams broadly at Harding.

'But I would say Eirik did the two of you an even better turn taking you across the river, because, my friend, you would otherwise have been rotting in that new earl's cells by now, and I like an honest man as much as I like a man who is willing to take the blame for his friend. You are each welcome!'

Gudbrand looks down the length of the hall to where the fellow still sits out of sight, who asked Harding his business.

'Come out from behind that pillar and join us on my bench, Thegn Wigod', Gudbrand waves him to come to us.

The tall, dark-haired Thegn Wigod shows from the dark and walks half the length of the hall from near where we entered. We must have passed him by in the darkness. Earl Copsig, as we should call him, strides slowly up to Gudbrand's dais. He grins wolfishly at Gudbrand's wife, takes her slender, outstretched hand and kisses the ring. He kisses her hand next, at which she withdraws it and looks sideways at her husband. Luckily for Copsig, Gudbrand was listening to Harding's tale of our ride from Rhosgoch, and of the monk Aldo who tried to betray us to his Northman masters.

Copsig eyes me warily and weighs me, plainly unable to understand why I have not betrayed him to Harding or Thegn Gudbrand. That he is not Thegn Wigod should not matter to Gudbrand, but he has broken the rules of hospitality in lying to his host.

What would matter even more would be in knowing that Copsig overstepped the mark with his wife, and that she is afraid to show her true feelings. However, my thoughts lie in stealing the march on him without flouting Gudbrand's open-handedness.

Eirik and Saeward sit further down the bench from me. Harding sits between Gudbrand and me, and the thegn's wife is seated beyond her husband. Copsig sits, hawk-like, perched on the end of the bench, watching us. Any fighting they may have in mind has been forestalled. We have all handed our swords to Arnkell and his ceorls. Copsig will not act rashly, bringing down the thegn's wrath upon himself, even though he has been made an earl. Here he is a guest, as we are, and he does not want Gudbrand to know who he really is.

I believe Gudbrand is loyal to Eadwin, but does not know that the earl is with Eadgar, Morkere and Waltheof in Northmandige as the new king's unwilling guests. I will not be the one to try to break his trust in his earl, because I want Gudbrand on my side. We may need his hospitality on the way back to Rhosgoch, and he may offer the few men he has left for Eadric's fight against the Northmen.

We are like the pieces on the board in the game of Hnefatafl, or Nine Men's Morris, with Gudbrand in the king's square, set for play to begin.

Copsig has gone back to his corner, to his men. Whether the ale will loosen men's tongues enough for Gudbrand to call them into the firelight, I cannot say. I would say he and his men will do much of the drinking, safe in the knowledge that they are on their home turf.

Copsig's men would then be free to deal with us in their own time. With us short in number, we will have to be on our guard, perhaps act drunk for Gudbrand's sake.

It would help us to deal with Copsig's men, should they also take us for drunk and make for their weapons. Arnkell would be unable to stop them taking their weapons, and helping themselves to the host's silver, making free with the women in their own time. What happens tomorrow, after we leave here, is for the Norns to cast their runestones.

The morning brings bad tidings from Gudbrand about the worsening weather.

'My friends the way north is blocked. Deep drifts have filled the hollows. Your horses would sink in beyond your help'.

He watches Copsig shifts awkwardly on the bench, put his spoon to his lips and blow softly on the thick porridge before tasting it on his tongue.

'You will not be able to ride either, Thegn Wigod. Walking your horses over the tops could lead to slow death through cold. Can you hear the groaning of the wind in the eaves?' Gudbrand jerks his head. 'It is the wind telling you that you must sit out the storm about to break! My wife, Sigeflaed, tells me she has food aplenty in store. Thegn Wigod, you do not mind staying here with us?'

'We will gladly take your offer of further hospitality, Thegn Gudbrand. My men and I were exhausted yesterday, coming across the moor. In the whiteness my guide lost his bearings. Your wife Sigeflaed has twelve grateful guests that I can speak for, and I add myself to the list', Copsig smiles, his thin lips drawn down in one corner of his mouth. I would guess that the grey wolf is up to his old scheming ways. Did he tell me the number of his men to make me wary of leaving here? Although I have faith in the fighting skills of my friends, in this winter weather it is he who strikes first who has the upper hand. I have to think of a way of getting around this hazard.

'Aye, and *we* too shall be glad of your good ale, Thegn Gudbrand', Harding tells him.

Forgetting that only last evening Gudbrand told him all are friends under his roof, he checks himself and nods humbly when the thegn stares forbiddingly at him from beneath those bushy eyebrows.

'I beg your forgiveness', Harding sniffs meekly.

'Take your fill', Gudbrand tells him. He points cheerily to Saeward, attacking a bowl of porridge with renewed zeal.

'Look at the way *he* goes about it!'

'When there are so many good things on offer in this household, I cannot deny myself', Saeward answers, throwing his arms up in the air, stretching his limbs. The spoon in his hand slips from his grip and sails over everyone's heads, prompting a laugh even from Copsig.

'Arnkell, bring this fellow another spoon. The hall ceorls will find that one when they sweep the old straw. It is good he takes his fill in this gnawing cold', Gudbrand's eyes twinkle, as if he had found a long-lost son. 'We have a swine's belly slices, if you want some after that porridge. Eat up all, follow Saeward's lead!'

I have not eaten this well in weeks, and can feel my belt tightening. If I am not careful I will fall asleep, enabling Copsig to steal a march on us. However, if Gudbrand says the moor roads are blocked, *how* is he likely to get away? However wolf-like he is, he can never hope to reach his goal in the time he wanted to. I wonder he did not ride north along the Great North Road on being given his earldom.

For now Copsig behaves like the good guest he should have been elsewhere, overstepping the mark when gathering tithes.

In Beornica he forgot his manners with the blade of a dagger. Harding knows that from being told by his kinfolk. Now they are seated side-by-side, Harding not knowing who his bench-neighbour is.

The slurping, belching and smacking of jaws begins to overcome me. I want to catch some fresh air in my lungs and clear my head. I think I must have overstepped the mark with the ale. As I take in the wintry landscape to the east, the sun only lifting itself above the sparse trees that break the skyline, I am suddenly aware of someone standing beside me.

'It has all become too much for you too?' Sigeflaed makes me jump. I look around and see her standing by the hall's yard door.

'I must have had too much to drink', I answer truthfully.

'Everyone drank well last night, Gudbrand more so than others, as you well recall. To think that he almost called out Thegn Wigod –'she breaks off when one of the serving women comes out to throw stale bread for the birds. 'Cuthfleda, you could have done that later, when there was more bread to throw for the ducks, too'.

'I am sorry, my Lady', the woman, Cuthfleda throws her mistress a hurt look and stares at me. She bobs quickly before adding, 'Arnkell said I should throw out last night's bread now, rather than wait'.

'Well, Cuthfleda?' Sigeflaed challenges. The woman lifts her skirts and hurries back inside. Sigeflaed then turns to me,

'You have to forgive me... I do not know your name?'

'My Lady, my given name is Ivar Ulfsson', I answer without giving away much else about myself.

'Well anyway, Ivar, my husband almost called out Thegn Wigod when your friend Harding asked him what his thoughts were on killing guests over me. Gudbrand went a very deep red at that. Who would have thought it fit to be under the same roof as a man who had killed a guest over his own wife?' Sigeflaed stifles a giggle, shaking her head with mirth she can hardly fight down.

Looking sidelong at the woman my thoughts flit unwillingly to Braenda. Much like her, Sigeflaed stands about shoulder height to me. She has seen her best days, yet holds some of the youthful bloom in the set of her cheekbones. Her finely chiselled, upturned nose tells me Thegn Gudbrand chose well when he was young. I could go long or far to find better for her years.

Even Braenda would have been hard-pressed to hold her own with Sigeflaed at her best. Her faded golden hair straying across her brow from beneath a tightly tied head cloth, well-shaped breasts rising and falling beneath a long overcoat give me thoughts I should best not have.

Besides, Copsig is set on her. One man other than her husband paying court will turn her. I want him to think he has a clear field for his chase. That way he may make a mistake and give us a head start when the weather clears. My woman will be with me again before too long, I am sure.

On turning I take in the glistening white hill in front of me, fold my arms across my chest and look yearningly for a road that has not been covered by snow.

'Who are you thinking of, is she good-looking?' Sigeflaed asks.

'What?' I answer gruffly, forgetting who it is I am talking to, 'I am sorry, I was far away – I was thinking of our way north'.

'Do not be awkward with *me!* I asked whether you were thinking of a woman, and if she is good-looking', Sigeflaed is hurt and turns on her heels to leave.

'Forgive me, my Lady. I really was deep in thought. What was it you asked?'

She stops, looks crossly and shakes her head at me, lifts her skirts to walk away and shuts the hall door hard behind her. I am left standing there, arms folded still and watching the hilltop as it gains shape against the steadily rising sun. Dripping water on the stony, puddled yard behind tells me that the snow will not last.

In the yard it has been well-trampled, patchy and muddied. The mud will spread where last night there was deep snow, and before long the road up to and over the moor will likewise be mired. A new threat will slow us on our way north. We will have to keep to the middle of the tracks because at their sides the ground underfoot will be water-ridden and boggy, enough for our horses to sink to their withers!

'We should be able to leave in the morning', I hear Harding's heartening words.

'Not before?' I ask, hopeful of being on the way again before Copsig has the same thought.

'It would hardly be worth the struggle. Tomorrow much of the snow will have shrunk back away from the middle of the track out of Dereleag. We can then make for Totingeleag, which would bring us to within Deira. Whether Copsig will go that way is for the Lord to know', Harding crosses himself and stands there, quickly taking in the cold, sharp morning air through his lungs, 'I am told Gudbrand will give us food and drink for the way'.

'He is an open-handed soul, I will give him that. He has pluck, although fighting Copsig would be well beyond his skill'.

When Harding laughs I begin thinking of the sound of men marching across gravel,

'You know he almost called out the grey wolf, Copsig?' he asks, grinning broadly.

'Aye, his woman, Sigeflaed gave me her thoughts on it just now. She seems to be taken with the thought of two men fighting over her. What was it about?' I ask, 'I recall it only dimly, through a fog brought on by the ale that I drank last night'.

'You did lay into it somewhat strongly. You are getting old, Ivar. It was about her', Harding stretches, as if to reach for the sun, 'although what I said was about the likelihood of Thegn Wigod killing his host over a woman'.

'He knew really that Copsig was making a play for her?' I look at Harding, searching him for a show of pity for Gudbrand, having to stand for his guest having caught the eye of his wife. There is no pity forthcoming. He may have the same thoughts about her as Copsig – and me. Speaking of the 'grey wolf reminds me. I elbow Harding and ask, 'Where is Copsig now?'

'Out by the side of the stable, with his men, readying to take the hill', Harding would not have spoken of it, had I not asked.

'You would have kept that to yourself?' I ask, taken aback by his half-heartedness.

'Where could they go in this? They will be back before midday, beaten, cold and hungry. It was hardly worth telling you'.

Harding looks at the dirtied yard floor and spits into a pool of melted snow water.

'What if they *did* gain the top of the hill?' I feel angered, dismayed by his lack of unease.

'They would - *will* not! Believe me, Ivar, I *know* these hills. I have come this way before riding west with Osgod. I led our men this way on our way to Northanhamtun before we struck west and met you. If I tell you it cannot be done, I swear, it *cannot* be done!' Harding's eyes burn like hot coals with anger at my lack of faith in his understanding of the land.

'He is right, Ivar. Copsig would be a fool to take on the moors with the deep snow', Eirik has come up behind us, not even bothering to speak of the new earl of Beornica as Thegn Wigod with Gudbrand's ceorl standing close by.

Copsig and his men have mounted and are making their way out of the yard when thegn Gudbrand bursts out through the door behind us, cursing Copsig's maker and all those with him,

'Lying turd, come back and tell me why you could not give me your real name! I call a pox on you and your henchmen!'

Copsig looks back and grins before passing through the gaping gateway to the foot of the hill. He looks on ahead again and thrashes his horse into a startled trot, his men bunched behind him.

'You *knew* who it was and failed to tell me?!' Gudbrand rails, howling his anger at us, 'Go *with him!* Go, *all of you!* By Christ you will not be allowed back through *my* doors again!'

'Hold still, Gudbrand!' Harding barks at the elderly thegn, 'We did not tell you because we did not want to *upset* you! What you have done anyway? He has these fully armed men with could him. Were we to grapple with them on your behalf, in your *hall?* Even with your few men, we would be no match for them. He is battle-hardened, wily. Go back to your wife, keep her company. We will take the food you offer, and ale for the ride, but no more than that. God help you, if you ever cross *me!*'

Before Gudbrand vanishes into his darkened hall he makes a fist at Harding. The thegn stares down at him and then turns to us with a broad grin,

'As we are out on our ears there is nothing left for us but to ride after Copsig. Where is Saeward?'

Sigeflaed stands at the door, barring our way back into the hall for our weapons and gear. Anger knits her otherwise finely shaped brow. As we pass she rains blows on both Eirik and Harding ahead of me, her high-pitched yelling unlike the woman I took her for.

'Can you not see what you have done to Gudbrand?!'

She wails, anguished,

'He will be fevered now that you have slighted him, telling him that Thegn Wigod and I are past lovers! What were you thinking of? I can only hope you have what you want, now that you have made him ill!'

'He will be well enough', Eirik assures her. 'Keep him sweating by the fire and his fever will go down again. Be glad we did not tell him Copsig had you last night'.

Sigeflaed darkens yet further and splutters,

'What – *what* did you say?' She scurries to a dark corner of her kitchen and shows again with a butcher's hatchet, asking again, '*What* was it that you said to me?'

Eirik sees her pull her skirts up and make for him, sidesteps and pulls the hatchet roughly from her hand, holding the tool down by his right thigh,

'He is Copsig, erstwhile tithe gatherer for Earl Tostig. You know full well what I said. Deny creeping into Copsig's room, if you can', he holds up a warning finger, hissing a warning to her, to let her know she is at risk of making a fool of herself for her lover,

'You gave more than your tithes when Gudbrand was away fighting the Wealsh!'

Sigeflaed screams in anger at Eirik and balls her fists, the flesh on her knuckles stretched to breaking,

'Just because I would not let *you* bed me, you lank-haired *beanpole*, you do not need to spread your gossip around *my* house. *Go now* - take your food, but go – *now!* I never want to see your ale-blotched cheeks in this hall *ever again!*'

Gudbrand must have heard his wife raving but he will be hunched on his high-backed chair by the hearth. He has had his say, and Sigeflaed has banished Eirik – and no doubt we with him. We now have a hard day's climb ahead of us in the mud and snow after Copsig, some of it on foot. I would stake my sword on *that*.

Eirik brings the hatchet down onto the oft-notched corner of the butchering bench, the sharp blade cutting another notch across the others and stuck fast in the worn oak. He leads the way, speechless with fury toward Arnkell, who wordlessly bags food for us as told.

We are making ready in Gudbrand's stable yard, Eirik being within the stable saddling his mount, when Sigeflaed shows at the doorway again, arms folded. I try to hide my smile when she looks my way and her mouth twists down in one corner. As she turns for her kitchen once more I go back to what I was doing, seeing my axe is in its sheath, sharp enough to draw blood on my thumb.

13

The going is heavy uphill, not only because the road is bad but ice has built up at its side. Harding curses loudly, blaming Eirik for our plight. Saeward looks glumly up at the distant hilltop, across the back of Harding's horse at me and scowls. Eirik is with us to make up our numbers, no more – unless he proves himself before too long.

None of us has spoken in the last hour or so since we left Dereleag. Harding glares at Eirik as his horse picks her way over rubble and stones, and clears his throat,

'I hope you are *happy*, my Danelaw friend. We have to find another way back, you know that? Are you even *listening*, or am I talking to myself?'

Well at least I know now that Harding *means* to ride back with us to Rhosgoch, despite his utterings to me that I will be on my own. As Saeward has joined us again, and we have Eirik with us, he knows my hand has been strengthened.

Eirik may or may not be listening, but before Harding asks again he nods without taking his eyes from the still snow-bound track that Harding has led us onto.

Saeward tries to take our thoughts from the gruelling ride,

'The way leads... where?' He wades on through almost knee-deep snow and looks across at Harding past his horse's bridle. We have had to dismount as the going is steeper now, and there is an ice-cold wind pushing against us where the track leads in a horse-shoe around the head of another dale. Harding pants with the effort of climbing through the mix of slush, ice and mud. Although Saeward meant well no answer is forthcoming. He shrugs and puts more effort into his stride.

'We are headed for somewhere called Totingeleag', I tell Saeward, 'hopefully a day or less away from here. We may look for somewhere to rest our heads earlier if the going is too hard. There should not be much more climbing through the snow –'

'There are men ahead!' Eirik warns and points up the slope.

'*Quiet!*' Harding hisses back at him.

'I doubt they can hear either of you over this groaning wind', I try to dampen Harding's anger but he will have none of it and shakes his head, upset that our way north is not as smooth as he had hoped – no doubt wishing for me to call off our long ride north.

Thankfully the wind blowing down at us from over the pass is not laden with snow, or else our climb would be unthinkable.

Copsig and his men have to be the only others on this forlorn track. If they have seen us they could waylay us. What would happen if they did so, I do not know. Were we to fall foul of him, our bones would be picked clean by the crows before anyone else came this way. However, I think the newly-appointed earl wants to push ahead, to reach his goal and gloat over his new standing.

Halting to wrongfoot us might lose him men before we are beaten, and those men would be sorely missed if he were to be met by a much greater number of his many foes. Copsig is too sly to risk a needless fight. If he had wanted to get us out of the way, he could have done so in Aescburna, when he could have turned Gudbrand's men against us with clever word-play. We are safe for now and all we need do is keep him in sight and when he has tired his men and horses, we can catch up and pass him in the night by another track. He will soon wish he had stopped us.

I can only guess at what he has offered them for their swords, but he will not have told them their lives are forfeit if seen by Osulf or Gospatric before they gain the hearth of a friendly thegn in Deira. Copsig's kindred and allies are thicker on the ground in the east, between Jorvik and Beoferleag.

His tithes will be higher than Tostig's to reward his men, to keep them from turning on him, and because our new king will demand them for *his* coffers. He must rob the folk of Beornica again.

Keeping Copsig and his men within sight is tiring, however. It is hard on the horses, although we have not been riding them for the past two miles, or so it feels - and the wind is still driving at us from the north east.

If I have not misread the clouds and the waning wind, there is the added threat of heavy snow. Lighter grey clouds scud across the moor tops to our right, bringing harder, drier snow in tiny pellets that run off our cloaks but drives into the horses' eyes. Eirik's and Saeward's horses are not used to this sort of weather, shying, rearing and backing onto Braenda. Harding's mare grunts like an old sow, fearful of being knocked into.

'Have you no strips of cloth to bind over their eyes?' I ask Saeward. Harding scowls, annoyed at Saeward and Eirik for losing us time.

Copsig's tracks may be lost with the new snowfall as we struggle forward. Now, with this pricking, dry snow maddening the two horses he and his men have gained on us. Luckily Saeward has rags he uses for dressing wounds, and whilst we turn the horses away from the driving snow he rips one in half lengthwise. One he gives Eirik, the other he binds around his own horse's forehead, over the eyes, but not so much that she cannot see the road under her hooves. She quietens quickly. Eirik, having seen how well it works, sets to copying Saeward.

'Perhaps *you* should do likewise?' Saeward asks Harding, who shakes his head and grasps his mare's bridle tightly. There is only a fist's width of loose rein in his hand. The East Seaxan looks to me but all I can do is shrug and raise a hand, dropping it to my side in hopelessness.

Understanding I am unable to coax Harding into following his lead, Saeward hands me a strip of cloth and I tear it, tying one half around Braenda's forehead, hoping for Harding to do likewise.

The dry, pricking snowflakes die away anyway and we pull off the make-do hoods. Harding hums, thankful for this turn of events and we struggle forward, mounted again and dropping into a new dale in the failing light. There are scattered homesteads, and a small church nestles amongst trees to our right. Nothing stirs as we near the houses, not even the hounds bark to warn of our coming.

Harding puts a finger to his mouth and waves us to stop where we are in the lee of the first two homes. Darkness grips everything now, with no moon above to give even the weakest light. He dismounts and makes his way further on foot.

Saeward's mount has turned skittish and he only keeps the animal from giving us away with great effort, stroking its muzzle and whispering into its ear. He has come a long way with horses since I left Braenda with him at Wealtham a few years since.

We are seated astride our horses in a deathly hush, waiting. Harding has been gone for some time when we hear crunching footfalls in the cold, dry, settled snow. Saeward is still calming his horse, but cannot stop it snorting. It is then that five men show from around the nearest homestead. One carries a crackling torch aloft at arm's length.

Two others stand behind, spears pointing threateningly upward at our heads.

'Do not put up a fight', one tells us, 'or else Lord Copsig will kill your friend'.

'What if we are not bothered by your killing Thegn Harding?' I answer rashly.

'Come now, does he mean so *little* to you?' the fellow mocks.

'Try us', I dare him, smiling coldly, pulling my axe slowly from its sheath. Braenda's flanks are in the way and he does not see what I am doing until he stands speechless with the blade of my axe in his chest.

Before he drops, blood bubbling from his lips, another axe embeds itself in the next man's forehead. He falls backward onto a comrade, who pushes him out of the way and draws his sword. Eirik comes at the fellow from beneath the belly of his horse.

Knocking the man into the wall behind, he thrusts a long dagger blade upward into his ribs through a long mailcoat. Saeward pushes his horse toward the fourth man, the one carrying the torch. This one backs away, and screams in fear, still holding the torch aloft. The fifth has already left for the safety of darkness, to warn his master.

'Where has he gone? Answer me!' Saeward has his captive by the throat, his thumb on the man's windpipe.

When Eirik pulls Saeward's thumb away and loosens his grip, allowing the man to gurgle an answer.

'What was that you said?' Eirik demands.

'*He has gone* - to the second house along the road!'

Saeward tightens his grip and the fellow croaks feebly.

The torch falls onto the crisped snow, scattering burning embers. The flames fizzle harmlessly in the cold ankle-deep snow as I bury my sword blade slowly, up to the hilt in his stomach, through loosely linked chain mail. Dying, he stares in disbelief at me until he rasps his last.

'Did you *have* to do that?' Eirik asks.

'We do not want our foes coming out at us from the shadows', I tell Eirik as I clean the blade on the dead man's cloak.

'Best see them off, out of harm's way', Saeward agrees with me.

Eirik stares down at the dead man, shaking his head.

'They are Aenglishmen', he tells me baldly, forgetting that he has just killed one himself.

'All the better to kill them', Saeward tells Eirik, pulls his axe from the second dead man and wipes the blade back and forth carefully in the folds of the dead man's cloak. 'The fewer there are of them, the better for us. Aenglishmen who do King Willelm's bidding for silver are no better than any other freebooters'.

'We press on and chase Copsig from this hamlet', I beckon the others and lead into the shadows. As Saeward and Eirik make their way to find Copsig I wrench my blade free.

'There are more of us than there are of you', Copsig boasts, calling out to us from the safety of darkness.

'Not so - not *now*', I answer boldly. 'We are almost even in number, and by the fools you sent I would say we are more than enough for you!'

'What, even if I kill Harding - I *hardly* think so!' Copsig sniggers.

'I will tell you what', tongue-in-cheek I offer him a way out, 'if your men do not kill Harding, we will kill no more of yours'.

Copsig's laugh is deep and throaty, as in the old days when many a ceorl who pleaded for his life was sent to his maker with an upward thrust of Copsig's short sword into his gut.

'Ivar, you remind me of Harold. He would offer a way out that was not really a way out, just a way of putting off what will happen anyway once he caught you', Copsig sounds as though he had once been dealt his come-uppance by Harold, although *when* I cannot think.

'You bring out the best in a man, Copsig. Perhaps he had your measure?' I call out.

'More likely Willelm had the measure of *him*', Copsig calmly walks out from behind the corner of a homestead.

He stands, smiling in the dancing light of the torch that he carries. Still smiling, he asks me,

'You think I would let you get the better of me again, Ivar?'

'I think you still fear my axe', I answer with a crooked grin. He waves two of his men out from the shadows, who lead Harding into the light, a knife held hard at his upturned, heavily bearded double chin. The thegn smiles, unafraid to die – no doubt his lust for life will carry him to an early grave yet.

'You wielded your axe well enough for me not to want to risk another arm. This arm is good enough now to do just that! I have had to learn to fight left-handed, thanks to you. You say that you do not value Harding's life? Very well, I shall put it to the test. Bring the fool here, Saewold'.

One of Copsig's men pushes the still smiling Harding forward, his hands tied behind his back. He must know – or thinks he knows - something that the rest of us are unaware of.

'Thegn Harding, you have kinfolk on either bank of the Tese, am I right?' Copsig prods Harding with the tip of his sword, still in the sheath.

Harding nods, not knowing where this will lead. He looks at Copsig and his jaw is pushed our way with the knife.

They want to make sure it is us he sees if we let him down. Copsig is quick to anger. Sweat runs down over his grey-bearded cheeks from his forehead even in this cold evening. Be it from fear or anger, it looks the same to his underlings. I would say Willelm has picked the wrong man to rule north of the Tese.

'Look at *them*, not at *me!*' he yells shrilly at the thegn. Harding shows no pain as the point of the knife is pressed harder against his jaw.

We have killed several of Copsig's men, but as yet none of us has been so much as scratched. Harding may think that if he can hold his head high, the Aenglishmen amongst Copsig's followers will waver and leave their new master to his wyrd. Men have often gone over to a bolder foe when their own leaders have shown weakness. We may see a turn of fate here, too.

Harding shrugs and shakes his head in disbelief. This is not the Copsig we know of old. Could his strength really only have rested in the numbers of huscarls Tostig sent with him to press his demands?

'You think you will be as forthright when your kinfolk are threatened through your foolishness?' Copsig brightens, but only his Flemings are still grinning. Saewold looks grimly at Harding. 'The new king will not be as easy to fool as Tostig once was, taking men at their word they would not bear arms against him'.

'You are not yet out of this wapentake', I remind him. 'There are many miles yet, and folk here have long memories'.

'Are you *threatening* me, Dane?' Copsig's lopsidedly smiles, the right corner of his mouth drawn down. 'Might I remind you, Ivar, that you have few men who can enable your escape? Do not forget we have Thegn Harding'.

'*I* have Thegn Harding, Copsig'.

Saewold takes his dagger from Harding's chin and makes to threaten Copsig.

'Whatever you wish', Copsig's sword is embedded in Saewold's stomach in a flash of steel in the torchlight. The fellow drops, ashen, onto his knees and falls forward. His two fellow Aenglishmen stare sullenly at their paymaster, yet do nothing to avenge their friend's death.

'You are next, Harding, if Ivar gives me a wrong answer to what I ask next'.

'Do not listen to *him*', Harding laughs. 'He is bluffing'.

'*Try* me!' Copsig hisses into Harding's right ear with Saewold's dagger in his left hand, having rammed his sword back into its scabbard. 'Now you *have* to talk to me, Ivar Ulfsson!'

'*To what end?*' There is nothing I can add to what I have already made plain to him. If he wishes to make his way north, there is nothing we can do to stop him, but he will not be long there before either Gospatric or Osulf catch up with him.

His Flemings and the other two of his Aenglishmen, seven in all now, will assure his safety only as far as Jorvik and keep us at bay with Harding at blade's length away from him. He can make his way safely on unless Harding somehow forfeits his own life.

Copsig's horse is brought from the shadows by one of the now mounted Flemings, another has Harding's mare ready. Gleefully he calls back as his troop files out of the hamlet,

'*If* you catch up with us, perhaps we can talk again, Ivar?'

'Why would I *bother* to talk to you if we catch up again?' I do not even look at him as he and his men fade into the darkness. I am tired, drawn and hungry, but I tell myself this, if we do catch him up again he *will* lose his smugness.

Gladdened by my sourness at losing him again, Copsig laughs out aloud,

'Ride well. Ride *hard* - if and when you find your horses!'

'What in Jesu's name does he mean by *that?*' Saeward knows the answer almost as soon as he has asked.

Copsig crows with laughter out of the hamlet.

'How do we damned well *find* them?' Eirik curses, looking forlorn around where we left our mounts. I had thought of leaving them with Saeward or Eirik, but we were overtaken by our wyrd.

'They cannot have gone far', I try to ease my friends' fears. 'I heard no-one chase them off'.

Saeward stares dully into a thickening mist and asks,

'Still, *which* way do we go to look for them?'.

'Be not defeated!' someone answers from nearby.

'Who was that?' Eirik draws his sword and braces himself for another attack.

'I am a friend, my son', we hear from behind. On turning our gaze is met by a brown-habited young fellow leading two horses. 'One of the outlanders was told to scare the animals, but they only trotted away and began grazing at the top of our settlement'.

'Where is *mine?*' Eirik blurts, angered that of our mounts, his is the one that is still lost.

'It cannot have strayed far', I put a hand on his back, trying to put him at ease.

'I shall slay the turd when I see him!'

Eirik ignores the priest's disgust and shakes my hand off his back.

'You mean your horse - or Copsig? We will have to find you another horse, unless we find yours. 'Did you see a third horse, father?'

'*Alas no*, my son', he answers, nonplussed. It feels odd to me, speaking to a young man who could easily be *my* son, as 'father'. This is one side of Christianity I do not think was foreseen by the church elders a long time ago.

'Look for hoofmarks in the snow', Saeward offers.

'Well, are you not the brightest star in God's heaven, Saeward?' Eirik shakes his head as if pained at his lot. He stifles a yawn and finishes, 'Meanwhile the turd Copsig vanishes over the hills and far away'.

'Being bound, Harding may slow them down', I ponder aloud as Saeward and I mount. Braenda looks none the worse for having been parted briefly from me. I add, as if Eirik were not with us, 'We can ride at a walk until either we find Eirik's mount or another horse for him. We will have to stop soon anyway to feed and water our mounts'.

'*There* she is!' Eirik jabs the cold air with a bony finger and strides away to where he has seen her.

Saeward has been dozing in the saddle and gives a start,

'God, *what – where* is she?'

'She is munching on someone's shoots!' Eirik looks over his shoulder at the half-asleep East Seaxan and growls,

'I hope no-one sees me taking her, or else I will have to pay some sort of wergild for the man's crop'.

I see her through a broken wicket gate, feasting on young green shoots. Saeward and I halt for Eirik to haul his mare away.

As Eirik leads his mare back out of the field an angered ceorl bears down on him from the nearest dwelling, brandishing a cudgel in one hand and a sickle in the other. The man means to do harm, and could well be harmed himself if he does not handle himself well. Having thought better of setting about us when he sees we are well-armed, he yells from beyond the wicker hurdle outside his home,

'What are you *doing*, trampling my early barley? There will be hell to pay if I cannot supply the innkeeper for his ales!' he yells loud enough to wake his neighbours who crowd around him, half asleep at this late hour and angered at being awakened.

'Is it any fault of mine if my horse alights on your barley when he has been driven away from me?' Eirik snaps back.

'Your horse trampled my barley, as you are doing right now, flattening it. You are as bad as one another, but your horse can be forgiven!' the ceorl snarls, still brandishing the sickle. 'Offer me silver or my neighbours will help as I take her from you!' The fellow is not shy about demanding payment for his loss, but I see no-one coming forward to help him.

'I did not drive her onto your land', Eirik shouts and draws back when the fellow draws a knife from the folds of his tunic.

'Your horse for your silver', snarls the ceorl, emboldened by his neighbours' braying for Eirik to be brought to book.

'We have to catch up with the men who drove his horse onto your land, to rescue Thegn Harding', I try to argue with him.

'Whoever - *whatever*, I want silver to keep my kindred from ruin. *My* thegn will be taking his dues soon and what will I have to offer *him?* Thanks to you, I will have to plead for time to grow a new crop. You must know how long barley takes to grow – *now* what?!' the fellow stops suddenly when I put up my hand.

'What would your crop be worth to the innkeeper?' I ask. He brightens, thinking I am going to pay him.

'He pays me either two or three pennies, going by the size of the harvest and the thickness of the ears...' the fellow falters when I beetle my brow, seeing that I know him to be a liar.

'It is usually two silver pennies, *if I am lucky*, my Lord'.

'That *much* – you take me for a fool, or what?' I fight down a smile. Eirik comes closer and the ceorl raises his scythe. When I frown he lowers it again and Eirik draws up to stand by my horse. 'Would you believe, friend, this plucky fellow wants *two* silver pennies for his crop you have robbed him of?'

'Two, for all *that* -', Eirik reaches out with both hands as if to measure the field, 'do I look as if I am rich?'

'Who knows *what* he thinks, or even *if.* He knows you robbed him of more barley, trampling over more than your horse ate'.

I stop there and leave Eirik to mull over the ceorl's demand without adding that I think him to be asking too much. As a thegn he would have known the value of a crop of barley when he bought it in for his own household's brewing, unless he sent one of his men to buy it. He seems to be having trouble working out how much he may have ruined and reaches for his purse.

'Do not let anyone say I am mean', Eirik fumbles with two fingers in the folds of the leather bag he keeps on his belt. He adds ruefully, 'My ferry earned me enough to pay for my mistakes'.

So saying, Eirik hands over the pennies to the open-mouthed ceorl. He slaps them down onto his shaking, grubby, sweaty palms.

The ceorl stares agog at me when Eirik walks away again toward his horse and I wink, telling him under my breath not to be as greedy with anyone else,

'Another man may not just beg to differ. He may cut you down for your cheek. This time you were lucky – now go *home* and gloat!'

232

The fellow touches his forelock hastens back to his dwelling before Eirik finds he has been made a fool of. The ceorl dances out of sight and Eirik still seems none the wiser. His underlings must have robbed him daily by the bushel. Harold may not have thought me worthy of being a thegn, yet I know the true worth of barley.

With his earnings from the horse ferry, Eirik will not miss the pennies.

'Now we shall have to free Harding before Copsig tires of him', I tell them. He will no doubt share sweet words with the erstwhile bane of his life - nor is Copsig well known for being forbearing, so the air could be well laden by the time we catch up with them.

We are on our way again, climbing, stomachs rumbling fit to hear across the high hills. Thankfully there has been no more snow and Copsig's trail can be seen plainly in the bone-chillingly cold, moonlit night. We may yet find them before more snow falls and dims Harding's hopes of being freed.

Following the track that has been bending downhill between cliffs leads into a widening of the dale ahead and below us. Here the shadows under a cluster of trees almost hide a beck that runs alongside the track we are following. Saeward reins in and points down,

'I saw something stirring, amidst the trees - *there*'.

Briefly the moonlight flashes on a polished blade amid trees and bushes, and then it is gone again. Have they seen *us?*

'They know we are here, surely?' Eirik rides up to me.

'They may, or not', I answer, looking levelly at him.

'I can ride down to look –'he begins.

'You can *walk* down', I tell him and take hold of his mare's bridle. Nodding slowly, he dismounts and strides toward the nearest clump of bushes.

'If I meet someone less friendly than Copsig, I may have to use it', Eirik gripes.

He vanishes between laurel thickets and coppiced willow. Soon after the bushes shake furiously, causing Saeward and me to dismount to make ourselves smaller as targets. There is more shaking of bushes and willow boughs, and Eirik shows grinning broadly with Harding behind on his horse.

The thegn is still bound with his hands behind him, and has been given a gag. Copsig must have thought that, unable to talk he would be easier to bear. Saeward and Eirik between them bundle Harding down from his saddle and loosen his bindings for him to pull down his gag.

'*You took your time!*' Harding curses under his breath.

'Are they far away?' I ask Eirik, who has come forward from behind Saeward. He has been listening out for Copsig's men.

'I could see only two of the Flemings', he answers. 'They were far enough away from Harding here for me to lead his horse away without them hearing. They were looking the other way, waiting for their master –'

'He took the Aenglishmen into the hamlet to look for food', Harding tells me, rubbing his cheeks for warmth.

'Feeling his Flemings were more trustworthy looking after you', I chuckle. 'He left them to look after Harding and lost him anyway! He will learn, by and by, but he will no longer be with us when he learns his most weighty lesson'.

'What is that lesson?' Saeward asks, looking over one shoulder for anyone following.

Harding waits until Saeward turns back before telling him,

'That he should never have talked this Northman king into giving him an earldom', Harding laughs. 'When Willelm offered him Beornica he should have run as fast as his legs could carry him!'

Eirik stifles a laugh and points to somewhere behind me.

'*What* – is there someone there?' I rasp and turn to look.

'*Get down!*' Saeward hisses, dismounts and pulls me down. Two of the Flemish riders crash through the undergrowth past us, yelling loudly in their own tongue, out of sight and unaware of our being there.

'Let us away from here', Harding grunts, 'before Willelm's new earl comes back with the Aenglishmen!'

When I am sure Harding's guards have gone far enough away through the trees I nod to Eirik and Saeward.

They mount quickly causing birds to take flight at their sudden movement. Saeward draws Braenda to me by her bridle and Harding jumps into his saddle. We will be away before Copsig shows to berate his Flemings for the loss of his hostage. We should be in Beornica well before him, by way of Jorvik and Treske.

We have seen nothing of Copsig for days. Each hill we round, each ford we cross I look back, but all I see are bare trees - and whiteness, for miles. Knee-deep drifts dog us on our way through southern Deira, but each day there are also signs of the thaw. Fords are deeper, and drips from overhanging trees shock as they slip down the backs of our helms down onto our collars.

'We need to stay clear of these trees', I hear Saeward call out in his misery.

'We need to keep to the trees, Saeward. Be like a green man', Harding answers gruffly. 'Our foes would see us mid-track!'

Saeward does not understand and demands to know,

'*What* foes? I thought we had stolen a march on Copsig?'

Eirik grins lopsidedly at me, showing foul teeth. He shakes his head and laughs, telling Saeward,

'I think Harding is telling you that you should grow your hair a little longer'.

Harding laughs hollowly and snorts,

'If he grows it long enough, he can use it for bedding at night! I have seen men do that'.

I try to think of Saeward enwrapped in his own hair and almost fall from my saddle laughing.

As I throw my head backward an arrow hisses past the bridge of my nose and embeds itself in the tree trunk to my right.

'God, where did *that* come from?!' Riding close behind me, Eirik has seen it and is as taken aback as I am.

'Where did *what* come from?' Harding draws sharply on his reins and Eirik shows him the arrow flights. '*Jesu*, who can it be loosing off at us here?'

We are not kept waiting long before men show from the trees all around. They look to me like outlaws.

'Who are *you?*' Eirik asks the fellow nearest to him.

Another arrow at the ready to loose off at me, the bowman sets his jaw but says nothing.

This is like meeting Hrothulf again by the Hvarfe. The man's friends are armed to the teeth with spears, billhooks, scramaseaxes and axes, each watching us closely lest we try to draw our swords.

'*Who are you?*' Harding demands.

They stare dully back at us until another fellow shows from the undergrowth, walks around us admiring our mounts and tells us to step down,

'If you value your lives, you will walk on into Aet Hripum and let us have these handsome mounts. How does that sound to you?'

'Is that the way to talk to Aenglishmen who have been skirmishing with the outlanders?' My call for loyalty falls on deaf ears. His fixed smile tells me my efforts are wasted. Something else is needed so I tell him, 'There are outlanders led by Copsig on their way north to help him claim the earldom granted to him by the Northman king Willelm –'

'*Copsig*, you say?' his eyes open wide. 'With his grasping ways, he robbed me of a good living! Where is he now, do you know?'

'He cannot be far behind, a day's ride or less', I think back to the last time I saw his men, worried about losing Copsig's hostage.

'You will abide with us until they are within sight at least. Tofig, take these men and give them something to keep their stomachs from growling and warning off Copsig! You had best be right, whoever you are', he stares at me and nods to the bowman to lower his weapon.

'I am Ivar Ulfsson', I hold out my hand in friendship but am rewarded with a surly grunt, followed by a threat.

'You are ours until Copsig shows, then – and only then – are you free to leave. If he does not come then we will take our due from you for the food and drink we give you, and your horses. Water for all, Tofig, *them as well*', he waves at the four of us before leaving for the woods.

Darkness is almost upon us when Tofig stirs.

'You *owe* us', he tells me with a lopsided smirk.

'He may *not* owe after all', the outlaw leader comes out of the lengthening shadows, a dagger clenched in his right hand. 'There are men coming from the south on the river road. Tofig gather everyone, we have to be ready to meet the great man, Copsig! Will you help us catch him, Ivar?'

'If I know the name of the man who leads this band of green men, I can lend my sword to his task', I tell him. 'Otherwise he will have to do without my help'.

The fellow chews his lower lip thinking, whether he needs us badly enough to warrant giving me his name. I can see he has misgivings, and is at odds with himself. On the one hand he needs us because on foot they may be unable to stop Copsig on open ground.

On the other hand he can use us to lure the man into the woods and drop onto him and his men. Which way will he jump?

'I am Ketil Bersason', he finally allows.

'Where did you scratch out a living, that Copsig could rob you of it?' I ask, never having heard the name before. Hrothulf never spoke of the wretches his master ruined.

'Ask *him*', Ketil nods toward Harding, who, munching on a juicy apple is unaware of our talking about him.

'Have you heard of Ketil Bersason?' I ask Harding.

'Ketil Bersa-' Harding jerks his head back at me. 'Oh, *him*, he ploughed land across the river from me'.

'Was that across the Tese, or the Leofen?' I ask, trying to be helpful, knowing he is struggling to think back.

'What does it matter? Aye – he was across the Leofen'.

236

Harding stares hard at me before finishing and winks at Ketil, 'at Rudby. He was run off his land by Copsig's men'.

'There *was* one with Copsig, Hrothulf, who was so good at what he did he revelled in making men's lives a misery. I cannot think what happened to him when Morkere was made earl', Ketil remembers, and spits.

It would be foolish to say that my friend died a hero by his king's side. Ketil may merely think it rightful that Hrothulf died by the weapon he outshone us all with. Saeward says nothing, being the only other of us who knew the man well enough. I am glad for Theodolf's sake he was unable to come with us. Harding's damning words about his father would have brought him to bloodshed – his own. Had we been able to take Theodolf north into Beornica, Hrothulf's name would have been no less besmirched by Gospatric, and crossing *him* could bring death to all three of us.

'Harding - you can go', Ketil waves him away idly with the hilt of his dagger.

'You are a good man, true to your word. As for these three', Ketil looks at Eirik, Saeward and me in turn, 'they will have to wait until Copsig shows'.

Harding gazes unwaveringly at his erstwhile neighbour, and shrugs before warning,

'Copsig *is* coming. Ivar wants to warn Earl Gospatric. We must speed word to him and Earl Osulf that he has been made earl of Beornica'.

'Is he alone?' Ketil demands to know, waving his dagger carelessly around in mid-air.

Harding snaps back,

'He has with him some Flemings and Aenglishmen'.

Ketil will not be put off his sport. He grinds his teeth at being told of Copsig's bodyguards, and then laughs loudly, as if there is nothing for him to be afraid of. He must know of Copsig's name for fighting. Knowing as I do that Copsig is still smarting at my wounding him, and that he is no longer as much of a threat with one arm, I would not flinch at his coming. But he still has horsemen with him, on open ground. The river track is well away from the woods and Ketil's men could well be ridden down if we are not out there to drive Copsig toward the trees.

'Copsig may shed some light on this one', he points to me. 'I swear I have seen *him* with them'.

'Ivar would do nothing underhand!' Saeward snaps. His outburst draws stares from Ketil and his men, who draw a tight ring around him and wait for their leader to give them some sport.

'*You* are an outspoken fellow', Ketil grins sourly.

'Who are you to say what your friend Ivar might have done? I think I have seen him with Copsig and do not want to hear an outsider, a fool East Seaxan telling me I am wrong! Who are *you*, anyway?'.

'He is a friend –', I begin but Ketil purses his lips and puts a finger to them,

'Your friend has a mouth of his own, I have heard him well enough already, *Ivar*', Ketil snarls at me, rolling the 'r' of my name, looking back at Saeward. 'Well, who are you, friend, that you know him better than I?'

'I am Saeward, one-time lay brother of Wealtham and good friend of Lord Ivar', Saeward leans forward, almost towering over a much shorter Ketil.

'Saeward you should by rights be dead by now, with an arrow in your gut, but somehow you have shorn Arnbern of his duty to me. *You have spirit!*' Ketil steps back from Saeward's shadow, and wipes his brow, saying quietly as he does so, 'But be a good man and do not bathe me in your spittle!'

Eirik laughs behind me, drawing Ketil's eye,

'*You* seem to think this is something to laugh at. What claim do you have on this life that we do not part you from it?' he looks up at Eirik, about to add something when a lookout calls down from his perch on one of the upper limbs of a nearby sycamore.

'I see riders - a half mile to the south, and closing at a steady trot!'

'That cannot be them already', Harding's brow knits as he looks at me. He must think we were that much more ahead of them, 'Surely not?'

'What would you say, Harding - do we dive down behind the bushes and let him past, or do we make him feel welcome and as beloved as the friend we knew him to be?'

'I would say we fan out toward the river and drive him and his men onto you. He has only two or three more men on horseback than we are, and would be hampered by fighting us. His best way forward has to be to ride ahead, hard by the trees. You could take them there with an arrow hail', Harding lets know his thoughts, and the outlaw nods almost before it is too late to act on Harding's counsel.

'Then you should be on your way', Ketil answers, on cue.

The four of us mount hastily, pulling our horses' reins hard away to the right to put ourselves by the river just as Copsig shows around the bend of the river bank track with his bodyguards. He reins in his mount, jabs his hand toward the woods and the six of them veer toward the waiting Ketil.

238

Pushing these horsemen toward the trees until Ketil's men can deal with them is another matter. Harding has the same thought and signals to ride after Copsig.

Mounted skirmishing is something not altogether new to me now, and Saeward has taken well to the way the Northmen fight on horseback.

Harding and Eirik, however, still dismount and tackle the foe on foot, giving them an edge we can barely afford to lose.

The Flemings are skilled at fighting in the saddle, seeing them wheel, cutting into Ketil's men with their slashing swords. Copsig brings down his own short sword left-handed onto the men's bare heads, plainly well taught by his Northman masters. A horn is blown loudly and Ketil's men melt away into the trees, leaving us to tackle the lone Aenglishman and three Flemings.

Harding and Eirik are still fending off blows that threaten to split their round shields and I am closing on Copsig, when arrows begin to rain down on them and us.

'Pull back!' Harding yells, trying to shield himself both from sword-blows and arrows and Eirik bumps against Braenda's flanks in trying to shelter from the arrows behind my longer shield. Harding roars at the Fleming above him and grabs at the man's arm, yelling to us again, 'I said pull back! These outlanders know how to fight in the saddle!'.

Saeward swings with his axe at the Fleming nearest to him, felling him with one blow just as an arrow thuds into the saddle behind his right leg,

'In God's name, who is the fool aiming arrows at *us* whilst the foe is at such close quarters?!'

Copsig wheels his horse around, using his knees to steer his mount, holding his sword out to catch Harding in the back.

From the corner of my eye I see Saeward's axe blade clash onto the blade of Copsig's sword, knocking it from his hand and rendering the earl weaponless. With a sharp cry, Copsig snatches back his left hand before Saeward's second blow severs it at the wrist. It is time for him to head away onto the river track once more, to flee northward for Jorvik.

With him flee his two Flemings and the last Aenglishman, his other two bodyguards left to bleed to death by the trees. Three of Ketil's men lie twisted in their death throes, shoulders and necks gashed.

'Harding, Eirik – *mount so we can hunt him down!*' I scream at them and hoist Harding roughly onto his mare. Eirik looks around for his horse and shrugs. We are losing time! In turning to my tight in my saddle I catch sight of her cropping the grass again.

'There she is!' Eirik is the last away, thrashing the flanks of his mare with his boots to narrow the gap. We have to chase Copsig, to catch him and bind him to his horse to bring him before Gospatric. But Copsig and his last three bodyguards have made headway, thanks to Harding and Eirik. He will find more followers amongst his friends in Jorvik.

Riding north with just three followers would not cut much of a dash at Monkceaster, or wherever it is he is heading near the Tina. Morkere would not be able to stop him, having been taken by Willelm to Northmandige, along with his brother Eadwin, Eadgar and Waltheof.

It should be easy to follow Copsig and his few followers. The snow is still fresh on the track and on the grass nearby. They rode away in line abreast, each man as much afraid for his life as the other.

Ketil and his men were no help, fleeing when the fighting overwhelmed them, and his bowmen almost cut us down with their arrows when they did turn back to the skirmish. Luckily they melted away again just as quickly as when the horn blew, leaving us to deal with the foe in our own way. Now we have the unwelcome task of rooting out Copsig again before he can reach Jorvik.

14

Our road is clear from the banks of the River Thona eastward when we leave Sceafeld the morning after our skirmish. We have still seen nothing of Ketil since then, either. His humbling will be forgotten with the help of a whore in an alehouse, like as not stretched out on a grubby rush-strewn floor. There is nothing lost there. Harding has said nothing about him all day, unwilling to share in the outlaw's shame. I can understand his wish to forget what happened. We must all put this behind us.

We are looking for a ford amongst these wooded hills before the river widens. Any bend may offer a way across within the next few miles. Can there be somewhere Copsig crossed? If we are unable to find his ford, he will be well ahead of us and beyond our reach by the time we enter Jorvik, on his way with a new bodyguard.

There will be men who held him in high esteem, helped him flee Morkere and hid him until such a time as he could meet with Tostig. They would most likely stand to gain from his being earl north of the Tese.

Harding raises a bony finger towards the right, at a road fork south of Swintun,

'There is a wooden bridge, built to allow Morkere's fyrdmen across the river to Coningesburh', he stops and it looks as if he had been hit by lightning when he finishes, 'that way'.

'That would make life easier, a *lot* easier. Would Copsig know about it?' I ask, my hand pulling to the right on Braenda's bridle.

'I very much doubt it', he answers, grinning. 'He would have been out of the way, hiding in some stew near Coningesthorp outside the walls of Jorvik. If he had wanted to, he could have gone east to the coast to await Tostig. That would have meant he would have been out of the way with no knowledge of what Morkere had done in the way of brycgeweorc in the West Thirding'.

'You know the feeling you have when you have the edge on your foe?' Saeward laughs lightly.

'I *know* that feeling', I answer to laughter from Harding.

'It would not be the first time *I* had that feeling myself. That one has a bad habit of showing when you least wish to see him', I tell them, speaking of Copsig.

'What made him want to be earl of Beornica?' Eirik asks.

'Greed is the master of many', Harding answers on both his and my behalf. 'He was at the hub of Tostig's tithe gathering undertakings. He would miss that and this new king needs a buzzard to watch over his meat, so no-one steals what he sees as his. What better could he do for a buzzard than one who knows his way about this corpse hall of a kingdom?'

'Surely Willelm knows he is tainted?' Saeward raises an eyebrow, taken aback at the thought of our Northman king giving a known villain the task of overseeing the northern half of this great earldom.

'He is using Copsig', I answer for Harding. 'Either that or Copsig has painted himself into the Northmen's dream of how the kingdom should be run'.

'Aye, well sooner than set one of his own over Beornica's unruly nobles, if Copsig is killed he will be missed neither by King Willelm nor by us', Harding further enlightens Saeward, who knows little about the north.

'He would have offered himself and in the way of the welcoming host, the king would have made fitting utterings. Copsig would not have seen himself as an offering, to give the king grounds for coming north when he lands at Dofnan, back from Northmandige'.

As we cross Morkere's well-built bridge from Swintun, Harding waves down traders riding westward.

'What gives, friend?' one of these fellows jerks his jaw, angered at the hold-up.

'Have you seen four men on horseback this morning, riding eastward toward Eoferwic?' Harding offers a smile to allay the trader's fears.

'We have seen no-one, friend. Are you sure they would have come this way? There *are* other roads to Eoferwic, you know', the fellow squints at Harding.

'Do you know your way about in these parts?' another of the trader's party asks.

'I do, very well thank you', Harding answers curtly. 'I was only asking if you had seen –'

'What do these men *look* like?' the first trader asks again.

Without giving away who it is we are chasing I offer,

'They are outlander warriors, well-armed, with mounts that are differently saddled to those we know'.

'There *were* four such men. We could see them from across the meadows as we followed the road south from Denegeby. They seemed to be looking for a ford'.

'*Are* there any further north near here?' I ask. Is he going to steal a march on us after all?

'There is no need for them to cross the river at all, as you will see when you come to Coningesburh. You will have to cross the river again yourselves over another bridge when you reach there', the fellow leaves the best for last. 'This road leads eastward, not north'.

'*God*, why do I always have to make such an ass of myself?' Harding beats his forehead with balled fists. '*I could kick myself black and blue!*'

I try to calm him,

'You were not to blame'.

'I *wish* that were true!' Harding rubs his brow and calls out to me for forgiveness, 'I am sorry, Ivar, really and truly! There is nothing for it, but we need to try and overtake him somewhere before he reaches Jorvik'.

To a stifled laugh from Eirik, Saeward adds,

'We trust to your guidance'.

'Go on, *laugh!* As it happens I *do* know now where I went wrong', Harding sets his teeth and whips his startled mare into a gallop before we can draw breath. Some way further he turns in his saddle and yells back at us, '*Come on then!*'

There are other traders setting up their stalls in Coningesburh when we round the last corner into the market square, blissfully unaware of us until we sweep close by them on our way north. Chickens scatter, squawking, young swine scurry out of our way and cattle roar in fear on either side of us. Ceorls, their thralls, wives and children dart out of the path of our horses as we thunder between them, hooves striking sparks on gritstone blocks.

Thankfully the armed men watching from their guard posts do not take us to task for unsettling their everyday calm as our mounts' hooves drum across the broad bridge. Old men, women and their offspring cling for dear life to the railings on either side to allow us through, back again across the Thona.

Once out in the open we can let our mounts run freely. I can feel Braenda's stride lengthen as she gathers speed on the snow-covered, hard-packed road.

'Ahead is a crossroad, where we will see whether Copsig *is* far ahead of us!'

Harding's shouted words are almost lost in the wind. There is no need to answer – he could never hear above the drumming of iron-shod hooves on old, worn stone blocks. On reaching the crossroad Harding leaps from his horse and hastens to the middle of the road. He strides northward a short way before standing straight, beaming proudly at us. All is well again.

'*This is the way they came!*'

'I would say, by the state of this road, that this is the way *everyone* has come since your fore elders landed in Northanhymbra'. Eirik grins sideways at Saeward and adds, 'Which has to be why the road is in such a mess'.

'Leave me out of this!' Saeward rumbles. He may be hoping for me to step in and throws up his hands hoping to be left out of Eirik's dig at Harding.

Harding pays no heed to the back-biting and shields his eyes against the sun. He looks across the land from east to west before telling Eirik,

'Mess or not, it will take us to where we need to go. Once we sight Copsig we will know which way to take', nothing will cloud Harding's cheerfulness now, not even Eirik's double-edged wit.

I cannot see the wisdom of following Copsig into Jorvik. For some time now, ever since we slowed down on nearing this crossroad, I have been mulling this over. It seems to me that there are few wise men he could hope to call to his banner, once he tells them where he hopes to take them. Gospatric and Osulf are not known to be friendly toward men from Deira, and their strength stems from a broad following both north and south of the Tina. Nyburna, where Tostig will be heading for, is at the heart of Gospatric's lands. Would Willelm know that?

'Why do we not ride straight for where Gospatric dwells?'

My asking this jerks Harding in his saddle as we set off again at a trot. Why do I suddenly wish to strike north before trying to cut Copsig off from his hiring grounds?

'Not so long ago you wanted to keep him from entering Jorvik – why the change of heart?' he pulls at the reins and brings his mare to a halt again. Eirik and Saeward slow their mounts and halt a little way away, lest Harding loses his temper again.

'Think about it, Harding', I put to him, 'what man would be foolish enough to take on Waltheof's kinsfolk? Few would dare, unless their appetite for silver overcame their fears. When they think of what must be forthcoming, they may lose their taste for reward and think of saving their worthless skins!'

'You are right', Harding scratches his nose whilst he thinks it through. 'We ride on for Baebbanburh'.

'Aye', I nod, looking levelly at Eirik and Saeward before finishing, 'we ride on for Baebbanburh'.

'You are Tostig's kin, yet you will have me believe you have bethought your standing on his rule – why *should* I take your word that what you tell me is true?!' Earl Gospatric stares mistrustfully, awaiting my answer, hoping I have none.

Gospatric, taller than Osulf, stands side by side with him in the earl's great hall, warming their backs by the hearth. The earl's dark Celtic looks are striking. He is only kin to Osulf through his mother, sharing little in the way of looks. Whereas Gospatric has the lean look of a Celt from his father, Osulf has filled out in his middle years, greying fair hair and reddish cheeks telling of his Aenglish blood line. Osulf glares at Harding for having dared bring me, a Dane onto their hallowed ground, whilst Saeward and Eirik are held back, out of hearing, out of sight around a darkened doorway.

Crossed spears held by Gospatric's household warriors keep them from crossing a cold stone floor into the welcoming warmth, but for the white heat of Osulf's hatred for Harold's kin.

I think they are better off where they are, for now. Harding throws me a look as if to say 'I told you so'. He may be right, but I have to talk Gospatric over to thinking of Copsig as a useful tool. To all but me Copsig is a dead man, of no earthly use whatsoever. That he should wish to show here in Beornica at all rankles with them, in view of his deeds as Tostig's tool.

'*Why* should we fear what Copsig stands for, if he is merely this king's lickspittle?' Osulf demands, steps aside and empties his ale cup into the dancing flames. The ale crackles on the hearthside where it splashes onto the hot stone.

'There *is* no need to fear the man', I begin to answer, thinking carefully about the words I should use. 'He is in Eoferwic now, looking for men foolish enough to take his pay and come north with him as his hearth warriors. King Willelm gave him the earldom before sailing for his homeland. You may not wish to talk with Copsig, but you must hammer out how to raise tithes for the new king –'

'You wish me to *talk* to him?' Gospatric smiles wryly. 'Why do I hear you ask that of me, when I can have you cut up with your fellow Dane and fed to the gulls out there?'

Osulf cackles harshly, like an old crone. He nods to a small arrow slit, seaward, to make sure I understand Gospatric's meaning. I can hear the gulls' screams through the arrow slit as they battle with the bitter-cold winter wind. They are both wreathed in smiles, but there is nothing friendly about those smiles.

Harding warned me of their hatred for all things linked with Harold *or* Danes. I am both, and I feel an icy trickle of sweat down my back beneath the woollen tunic and chain mail of the Northman's hauberk that I am still wearing. I cannot allow fear to push me into a dark corner and let Gospatric see me beg for freedom.I shall stand my ground and share my thoughts with them. Willelm can wreak no harm through Copsig if they stand their ground.

'You can tell this king through Copsig that you will pay no more than what you gave to Eadweard. Copsig may have lied about what geld he could wheedle from you, but he would have to give Willelm the shortfall from his own boxes and he would soon see this earldom is not worth holding on to. Willelm would send another earl and you have Copsig for the asking'.

Gospatric folds his arms and stands, feet wide apart.The way he looks at me with a wry smile, he thinks I take him for a fool,

'We can tell the king to take his tanner's hide home'.

Gospatric laughs hollowly and Osulf shakes his greying head, grinning. The younger man adds, lest I cannot think for myself,

'We will have Eadgar for our king, and this sly red fox Willelm can stare down his men's lances at us as much as much as he likes. What did that old fool Ealdred think he was doing, putting Eadweard's crown on the Northman bastard's head, by all that is holy?'

'The Witan together took the step of asking Ealdred to crown Willelm', I have to tell him, 'although Ealdred would have crowned him anyway, come what may'.

'Who else took the step of denying the crown to Eadgar?' Osulf snarls. He does not wait for me to list the names, 'You need not tell me, Eadwin, Morkere and Waltheof were at the forefront of those fearful of him taking their lands and giving them to his lackeys',

'Waltheof added weight to their following for Willelm', I tell them.

Waltheof is kin to Gospatric through a common forefather, Ealdorman Uhtred, whose granddaughter Aelfflaed married Earl Siward, Waltheof's father. Had the elder son Osbeorn not been killed by King Macbeothen at Dunsinnan, Tostig would not have been given the earldom.

Northanhymbra would have been kept safe under the rule of a mighty clan with links to the Scots' nobles. However, life does not follow the lines of man's thinking, and Tostig was for ten years able enough, with a tight hold on Northanhymbra until Aelfgar's kindred cast their eyes about for something to give Morkere. Eadgytha did not help her brother, either. She became entangled in a web of her own making in the murder of Gamal, one of the greater landowning thegns who had misgivings about her brother's handling of tithes.

Now I am here, trying to talk Gospatric and Osulf into keeping Copsig alive as a tool and go-between with Willelm. The spider's web tightens! Waltheof's part in taking the throne from Eadweard's rightful heir could be seen as treachery by Gospatric.His kinsman leaving Harold on Caldbec Beorg might not be seen as shameful.

'By the time the tanner's grandson hears of Copsig's end, it will be too late for them to do anything-'Osulf begins, but is stared down by Gospatric.

'He will send another, one of his *own kind*', Gospatric acknowledges what I have told them. He looks at me, for the first time as if I can be trusted 'Do you *really* think we can steer Copsig whichever way we want? He went beyond his master's brief when he was with your kinsman, Tostig'.

He seems to relish reminding me of the failings of my kinsmen.

'You do not want the likes of Odo or Willelm fitzOsbern trampling all over Beornica, believe me. Leave Copsig at Nyburna. Make it plain to him, however, that he is only earl as long as he does *your* bidding', I would sell my soul if I believed I could win peace by doing so. Finally Gospatric sees sense, but I am not sure Osulf is sold, not yet.

'What that would tell him, far from putting him where we want him to keep his masters at bay', Osulf has the ear of every man in the room when he makes a break here, 'is that he is our lord. Do I read this right in your eyes?'

Everyone here begins to talk over one another, unsure about whether I am in deadly earnest, or whether I have lost my wits in the years since they last saw me. Osulf is gloating and Gospatric cannot help me. He understands what I mean by trying to talk them into keeping Copsig as a sop. Alive, Copsig would hold the Northmen at arm's length. That much he knows. He also knows that his kinsman will brook nothing that allows his earthly foe even only token rule.

At length the babbling stops and I am left with Osulf's glare burning into me. He is never as happy as when he can see a kinsman of Tostig's writhing on his spit.

I am now the beast on the spit, being turned slowly, roasting in my own sweat. Until I think of an answer – and that will have to be soon – my pain will sharpen. It will not matter how well I put my answer because my time on this earth will be shortened.

'Well -? I am waiting for my answer, or has your head taken too many hard knocks over the years?' Osulf folds his arms over his barrel chest, his glare still etching hatred upon my damned soul.

'Then I can only pray that you do not outlive your fellows', my answer is taken as if I had spit on his mother's grave.

That Gospatric is quicker with his sword point at my throat than Osulf means no less of a threat. He shakes his head and swears under his breath at my cheek,

'Fool Dane, *are* you really trying to get yourself killed?'

'*Run him through!*' Osulf hisses through clenched teeth to shouts for my grim end from all around.

Saeward tries to speak up for me before being howled down,

'What he means –'

'If you are still here when the Dane breathes his last, you can enter hell with him! Leave while you can, with this fool here!'

Osulf brandishes a long-handled dagger under Eirik's nose when the poor fellow makes to stride toward me.

'What he means is that you do not want Willelm burning through your lands in the way he did through Centland. You should see the ruin the Northmen wrought upon the southern shires!' Saeward croaks the last few words with a sword point at his neck.

'Why would he do that here when we have not lifted a sword against him or his kind?' Osulf snaps back at Saeward, who finishes what he wanted to tell them.

'The folk of Bearuc shire, Suthrige, or Suth Seaxe had never laid eyes upon the man before he laid *their* lands waste!' Saeward finds Osulf's dagger pressed against his lips to put an end to his talking out of turn, but he goes on bravely, 'We saw to what lengths the Northman king's brother Odo went, in order to have his stronghold built at Hrofesceaster'.

Osulf still glares into Saeward's eyes, but he lets him finish all the same,

'Half the settlements in Centland and eastern Suth Seaxe were emptied to give him enough hands for the task. When we rode through Hereford Shire the Northman Willelm fitzOsbern was building strongholds up to the bounds of Wealas'.

'That is what I was trying to tell you', I enter the talking again. Gospatric and Osulf stare balefully at me but now they lower their weapons to their sides. 'Kill Copsig, but when Willelm hears of it, you will barely have time to make your peace with him before he brings down his wrath on your heads. Copsig means little to him, no more than

248

a hammer to a smith, but he stands for Willelm's right to rule every part of his kingdom'.

'*His* kingdom, you say? We shall show Willelm whose rule is acknowledged in Northanhymbra, and it will not be *his*', Osulf sneers. 'What can they show *us* about fighting?'

'They can show you how they beat King Harold', I offer.

'King Harold was a poor leader!' Gospatric glibly waves away my warning.

'He was such a poor leader he took the west Norse king Harald unawares – and thrashed him', Eirik throws in jokily and is rewarded with a withering scowl from Gospatric.

Both Gospatric and Osulf stare at me now, no longer balefully, but still there is no friendship when Gospatric tells me,

'We will not keep you against your will, any of you – *and* that goes for Thegn Harding, *are you listening my friend?* However, by the same token we cannot let you warn Copsig'.

'We are your hostages?' Harding asks.

'You stay under our watchful eye until he has been dealt with. Do you understand me, Harding, Ivar?'

'It is plain enough to me', I nod to underline my understanding. 'I am no friend of his, either, and I do not wish to warn him. I hope you understand, my Lord Earl, it was I who made him learn to use his left hand for fighting when I fought him on the following morning after Harald Sigurdsson's downfall'.

Osulf stares at me in disbelief. He looks to his kinsman and bursts into laughter. They both begin to laugh until Gospatric breaks off and gazes earnestly at me, asking,

'Was that *you*? I had heard tell of that. The stews and alehouses in Eoferwic were still full of the tale weeks later. We thought it was idle Deiran chatter just to make *them* feel better. After all, when your strength comes from drinking cups of ale –'

'I know someone who saw it', Saeward breaks in fearlessly.

'Oh, and *who* was that?' Osulf glowers at the East Seaxan before looking over his head at me, as if being spoken to by a child.

'My brother, Beorhtwulf saw the fight!' The anger in Saeward's sharp answer seems to take him aback, but not for long.

'Is he here to attest to that?' Osulf closes one eye, hinting that Beorhtwulf might have made up the tale.

'Thegn Osgod told me of the monk's killing by an ale-swilling oaf named Garwulf outside Morkere's hall in the Earlsburh', Harding solemnly tells Osulf.

'Your brother was a monk?' Gospatric breathes out, pouts and turns to Osulf, 'You do the fellow wrong'.

'He was a layman, as was I', Saeward puts Harding right, 'but he was close to making his vows and taking the first step to becoming a Brother of the cloth'.

'We will not go into that', Gospatric tells Saeward and sheathes his sword. As Osulf slides his dagger back into its hilt Harding breathes out.

'We eat soon', Gospatric becomes friendly suddenly. 'You, Ivar, and your friends are welcome to stay here until word comes that Copsig has shown with his men at Nyburna. Drink your fill, each of you. Harding I want to speak with you before then, if you will'.

Harding casts Gospatric a forlorn look, as though he knows the earl will berate him for leading us to Baebbanburh. Osulf stands back and allows us to leave, waving the guards aside.

Eirik tests Harding's mood lightly,

'You are heavy-hearted, friend Harding'. Only a few mumbled words can be heard in answer, nothing that we can understand, nothing that worries Eirik as we follow Gospatric's discthegn to where we can make ready to eat, and where later we are to sleep until Copsig shows.

Saeward and I share a small room overlooking a now wild, iron-grey sea. Snow clouds are chased along the coast by a wind that buffets the outer walls where it cannot find a way over the top, groaning wind sent by the ghosts of the seas to keep us awake. I shall not find sleep easy to come by. Braenda has not shown herself to me since before we left Naesinga. Perhaps she has something to keep her in Elmete, or some*one*. I must find something else to think of. God knows we will be tested in the days to come.

Saeward has been watching me stride to and fro, aimlessly across the stone floor.

'You are thinking of your woman?' Saeward asks after some time. 'She has not shown herself to you during our ride?'

When I have crossed the floor twice more I stop and turn to look at him, telling him,

'We may see the worst of one another. We have the skills to keep us above the wolves and kine, but do we use them?'

'You think you might be dragged down by the others in their thirst for the settling of scores? Copsig means more to you alive than dead, is that because there is a bond between you?' Saeward looks me in the eye, searching again. He has shown a cruel lust for blood, but risen above it again. Perhaps he is meant for higher things than killing, after all. Waiting for an answer may try him, but he will have it soon. When

Copsig shows in Nyburna, Saeward will have his answer without my having to open my mouth. However, my soul will be laid open for him, as long as he is not afraid to look into the pit for what he wants to know. He shakes his head and drops his saddle pack into one of the bed closets and I hear him drop heavily onto the cot-bed.

'She may seek you out tonight', he yawns. 'Wake me when it is time to go and eat'.

'Do not fear, you will not be left behind. If you need rest, pull your boots off and lie flat out on the bed', I answer the second part gladly. As to the first, I hope it comes to pass but I shall not let myself feel let down if she stays away one more night. She would want me rested, I should think.

The evening follows without mishap. Osulf smiles once or twice, a childlike smile, open, welcoming. With the smile he shows teeth that have been blackened by a liking for strong, sweet ale.

Gospatric spends much of his time at the head of his table talking earnestly with men we did not see earlier when Harding brought us here. He laughs loudly without showing warmth, his underlings laughing with him - but uneasy at what is to come. Their laughter stems from wishing to be at one with their lord, not out of understanding for his dark wit. His kinsman is more able to take comfort from the moment, no matter what threatens to darken the morrow.

The day dawns, ragged sleet clouds pushed inland by a stiff easterly wind that buffets Baebbanburh's thick walls. To the west blue skies that passed inland withdraw until the dark mass covers the land. Offshore the Fearna isles are hidden by spray blown by stiff gusts. This is not the time I would wish to be a herring gull or kittiwake. Above me a chough fights to make headway across the merciless blast, but gives up the struggle and allows the wind to carry him some way inland.

Saeward shuffles behind me and coughs to let me know he is still there,

'What are you thinking of, Ivar? Did she not come?'

'She did not, no, Saeward. I was thinking of how Copsig would see his wyrd, Braenda was the least of my thoughts. Another time, perhaps...'

'Aye, you have much else to think of. Today will be a devilish mess, I do not doubt –'

'Are you ready to ride, Saeward?' Not that I wish to be rid of him, but sometimes he worries me with this childish babble.

'We were thinking you might not be', Saeward answers tartly. Plainly the others sent him to speed me on my way.

251

'*We* were thinking? Eirik and Harding sent you - are they waiting for me in the yard?' It is now my turn to babble.

'Lord Gospatric sent me. He and Osulf wish to reach Nyburna before dark, and there is a gathering of men waiting with them below. Harding has Braenda by her bridle, ready for you to mount'. So saying, he makes his way back down ahead of me as I search the sky for the lone chough.

'*What kept you?*' Harding hisses at me, chewing his upper lip, waiting for me to say something. When no answer is forthcoming, he nods to Gospatric.

Two score men ride south behind us. Hooves clack noisily on the greasy, hard stone causeway that leads down to the road washed clear of snow by salt spray. Men's mounts skid on the smoother rocks, bringing loud curses. To hide my laughter I look skyward into the wind and see my chough overhead again, trying to wing his way across the coast.

Gospatric has been talking loudly with Osulf over the noise of the horses' hooves. Their banter brings laughter, scooped up and hurled inland by freshening gusts of wind. Someone else laughs with him and then all is still again but for the noise of hooves and the gulls behind us, fighting one another for mouthfuls of herring, mobbing Fearna's puffins for their hard-won scraps.

A halt is called once on the long ride at a thegn's hall, to slake our thirsts and dent our hunger with mouthfuls of cooked game. And then it is back to the road to the Tina again. Nyburna beckons.Long strips of feathery light grey cloud scud overhead beneath greater, darker banks. It is like looking at hills behind far woodlands. Gospatric holds up a hand and we draw to a halt behind a hall above the river.

He beckons Osulf to him and they huddle together with a few trusted thegns and huscarls, no words carry across the still gusting wind back to us. No-one wants those within to know we are here.

Ahead are outbuildings behind a high wall. What must be a stable takes up the length of one wall of a thegn's garth. The smell of cooking food is strong, even with the wind stiffening again, teasing us with the smells when it drops.

'Copsig is not here yet', someone is sent back to tell us. 'He may not come until later'.

'Later...?' Gospatric casts his eyes heavenward as though someone up there is likely to give counsel. 'We will have to wait out of sight behind the back wall and keep a man posted to watch out for him'.

Osulf nods, silently cursing Copsig. Even behind the wall we are gnawed at by the now groaning wind.

'You, Eirik, you are trustworthy. Stay just out of sight below the watchtower, and warn us once he has been welcomed', Osulf beckons the young fellow, glowering at me when I look his way. If he does not trust me not to warn Copsig, what would make him believe we are not the foes he takes us to be? Even if I kill the man myself it could be read as wanting to hush him up before he tells Gospatric something I would not wish him to hear.

So now we have to wait in the gnawing cold - until *when?* Does Copsig know we are here, waiting for him, or is he late because he has had been hard-tried raising the numbers of his bodyguard.

On learning that they stand to be cut down for daring to hold with him, will they just melt away in the half light?

Our horses grunt with the cold. Rubbing them lets them know their needs are not forgotten. Knowing how cold *we* are this late winter's evening, there is little comfort to be offered. There is more bone-chilling wind to come, I would say. Many of the Northanhymbrans huddle together, their mounts shoulder to shoulder a little way behind us. Harding is halfway between them and us. Saeward looks idly over his shoulder and asks,

'We are like lepers here, Ivar', he groans and finishes, 'what do they think they will catch from us?'

No-one else speaks. Osulf stares up at the heavens and nods as if in answer. In raising my eyes I can see the clouds hastening in. The wind has come about a little, more from the south than east but the chill will stay with us all the same. We have to bear it for longer.

An owl hoots, and again. This is our signal. Copsig is near.

'He is here', Gospatric murmurs, and spurs his mount to a walk, followed by Osulf. Harding, Saeward and I ride on in mid-column. We may be warm soon, yet for how long before riding back?

When we see him next Copsig is seated at the head of the long table that runs down the middle of the great hall. This is the earl's garth, after all. Just as Jorvik has the Earlsburh, this garth at Nyburna was built as the earl's home from home. Gospatric leads, with Osulf at his side when we enter.

The earl's discthegn is brushed aside when he asks us to yield our weapons and stands looking up toward Copsig with his arms held wide, anguished. He shrugs and steps back into the shadows, knowing well not to nag. Osulf passes the fellow, frowning, and leaves one of his own men standing by, should the discthegn be told to call for help.

'*Be seated*, friends! Drink, eat – be my guests', Copsig greets us bravely. Unable to see who we are, he squints through the smoke and his jaw drops when he sees Gospatric and Osulf. Nevertheless he hides his anger with a shallow smile.

Gospatric takes a cup of ale from one of the hall wenches, drains it and plants the empty cup upside down between two seated bodyguards,

'You know why we are here, Copsig'.

'Gospatric, as you are here you are welcome to speak to my guests, to tell them what you have come here for. I am sure we behold one another in warm friendship'.

Copsig knowingly misreads the mood of his new guests, or else he is buying time. As he speaks he rises to his feet and strides slowly to the back of the hall. Osulf sends men around both sides of the long table to cut off Copsig's flight, but he and a few of his foolish bodyguards are too quick for them. As our prey vanishes through a door hidden by tapestries, Osulf and his men chase after them.

Eirik, Harding, Saeward and I hasten to the door after the others, not knowing where we are headed. Outside in the cold again I can barely make out Copsig slipping through a side door of the chapel some two score yards away, wall-mounted torches on the hall giving little light to see well by.

'Go on, *after them!*' Gospatric yells at his men, holding back. They are waiting for their lord to lead.

'No, kinsman, we *burn* them out!' Osulf barks, 'Torches, *bring torches*, pull them down from their *mountings!*'

'*What* – and bring damnation onto our heads?!' Gospatric is less sure, but his fears are dismissed.

'Copsig would never have drawn back from killing in a church, not man, nor woman, nor even *children* - here, *give* me that torch, man!' Osulf wrenches the burning, flickering torch from the hand of one of his men and throws it through a small window by the door of the chapel, shouting, 'More torches, quickly, *bring more!*'

Soon the whole chapel is ablaze, flames licking at the garth walls, shooting up to the heavens and lighting the yard brightly enough to see the side door open again and Copsig – followed by fearful bodyguards – hastens toward the garth gates.

'*Seize him!*' Gospatric howls, fearing he may lose Copsig again so soon.

Some of his men throw themselves into the hunt, almost falling over one another in the effort of catching Willelm's unwanted earl. A line of Osulf's warriors forms in front of the gate to stop Copsig's flight and a tussle breaks out. The bodyguards make a brave stand but their bravery is short-lived, as are some of the men who bodily try to shelter Copsig from harm.

'Yield, and stand *away* from him', Osulf orders, 'and lower your swords. You are free to leave and we here acknowledge your fighting spirit, but you are mistaken in following him here from Eoferwic. He is a wanted man, a haunted man answerable for his graft in a selfish search for wealth. *Go*, and do not come back to claim the reward he assured you or your lives will be forfeit!'

Some of Copsig's men look to Gospatric to bear out Osulf's offer. He nods gravely and calls out to his own men in front of the stable door behind us, a smile on his lips now he has Copsig,

'Bring their horses. *Warriors* do not walk!'

'*You two*', Osulf calls to a pair of his men keeping Copsig in check, 'bring him here!'

One of Copsig's men looks back at their lord, the one Aenglishman who outlived their first clash with us. He stares dully at me before mounting and leads the others away. None of the Flemings has lived through the fight. Count Baldwin has paid dearly with men for the duke his overlord, now king, and for Tostig's hopeless cause.

Before Copsig's men from Jorvik leave through the wide-open gates, his last southern Aenglish bodyguard turns in his saddle to look back at me, shakes his head and frowns. Silently he kicks his mount into a trot. The darkness swallows him and his new-found friends.

'What do you say now, Copsig – are we *still* welcome at your feast?' Gospatric asks, arms crossed over his chest. One finger strokes the neck hairs of his beard as he awaits an answer he knows will not be forthcoming.

Copsig says nothing, but stares at me, his hands bound before him. Gospatric asks again, keeping Copsig's eyes on him now as Osulf slowly walks around behind,

'You have no words at all for us, my Lord Earl?'

'Copsig, what do you fear most?' I ask, drawing his eyes to me.

He begins to turn to look over one shoulder, as if to acknowledge his wyrd. Osulf brings his long-handled axe around at shoulder height with both hands and Copsig's head drops with a dull thud onto the straw-littered yard floor, into a pool of muddied water.Arms splayed out wide, the headless body drops to its knees where it stays, still, as if in prayer. Osulf strides slowly toward me, kicking the corpse on his way so that it falls forward.

'I hear a friend of yours rode with him', he spits onto the muddied head, phlegm hitting the dead Copsig's forehead.

There is no point in denying I knew Hrothulf,

'Aye, Hrothulf was given the task of guarding Copsig', I keep my answer short, adding nothing that might rebound at me as his friend.

'I also hear that Copsig knew Hrothulf's woman and fathered a son on her', Osulf adds. Why he is telling me this I do not know but no doubt soon will. 'I believe her name is Aethel, is it not?'

'That is her name', I answer, aloof, still not sure where this will lead.

'Might she be saddened at his killing?' Osulf prods.

'She loved Hrothulf deeply. He died fighting by King Harold. His son lives, wounded fighting the Northmen in the south'.

'Heroes breed', Gospatric chews his upper lip and grins crookedly, 'like *lice, eh?*'

'Hrothulf earned his standing as huscarl. Had it not been for him, many might have fared worse when this scum went gathering their tithes', Osulf tells me at last, 'and Tostig may have been spared *his* humbling if Hrothulf had not missed with his bow'.

'What are you saying?' Gospatric asks nonplussed.

Osulf allows a smile to show before answering.

'One day, when Copsig was in southern Beornica, near the banks of the Tese at Ulnaby, Hrothulf aimed an arrow at his head but Copsig rode on suddenly. The arrow hit a tree instead'.

'How do you *know* this?' It is Harding's turn to be taken aback.

'Copsig's woman Aethel told me. He knew somehow that his days on God's earth may be foreshortened. In a way they were, but he lived to do more harm than his worthless carcase was worth before I cut short his new calling. *We* were abed together, Aethel and I, before she let Hrothulf into her life. Copsig had already let her know he was tired of her. He had unburdened his heart to her when she had taken care of his needs for the last time', Osulf is happy now that he has told me, and plainly sees that I also had come close to her. 'You have a woman anyway, a spay wife'.

Who in this world does *not* know?

'Last I saw of *her* was in East Seaxe', I murmur, 'weeks ago now. I have no knowledge of her whereabouts'.

Osulf gazes steadily at me, winks and treats me to a belly laugh,

'You are a lucky man, Ivar. The last I saw of *my* woman was early in the after-year!'

Gospatric grins hugely and elbows Osulf before telling me with a sigh, adding,

'What would I give to see as little – *or less* – of mine?'

Osulf and Gospatric share a laugh, slapping one another's backs before Osulf turns to me,

256

'Pay no heed to this fellow, Ivar. Were she mine, I could never tear myself from her side –'

'Were she yours, her talons would be in your back and you *could* never tear yourself from her side! Where are you headed now, Ivar, with your three friends here?' With this Gospatric suddenly brings me to thoughts of our ride back to Rhosgoch.

'I have told Eadric 'Cild' we will be back to teach his men how to fight Northmen. Come summer he wishes to take on the new earl, Willelm fitzOsbern in Hereford'.

I stare up at the still angry clouds before adding,

'Hopefully the passes will be clear of snow on our way west again'.

Saeward adds his share of wisdom, earning grave glares from both Gospatric and Osulf,

'In a way the hard weather helped us. Copsig may have been here longer and had the time to put together a better bodyguard!'

'True enough', Osulf allows. 'What of Harding – are you riding back with them?'

Gospatric laughs that I am dumbstruck. He clasps Harding's left shoulder and slaps his back,

'Harding is our eyes in Deira. He knows everything that stirs between the coast at Redekarre and Maerske, and the higher dales near Hafocswick and Medelham'.

'If I had told you I am kin to these two, would you have trusted me to bring you to them?' Harding looks at me levelly. He turns to Osulf and shrugs, bidding him farewell. He and Gospatric take their farewells next, slapping one another's backs. He tells them both, 'You have a long ride home with your men, Gospatric. I will take these three back by way of Rudby, where they can rest for a couple of days before riding on back to Osgod'.

'You are riding on back to Wealas with us?' Eirik asks, tongue-in-cheek.

'I should by rights, aye', Harding nods slowly and strides back toward his mare. He turns back to look me fully in the eyes when I ask him,

'Do you know what became of Thegn Eadwy?' I wonder. My brow knits, thinking back on when Osgod told me himself that Morkere had bestowed the land and title on him.

'He was fished from the Ose near Richale', Harding answers flatly. 'His land was then given to Osgod, but Willelm may give that land to someone else when he comes this far. Even my own land could be taken from me, although it was King Eadweard who gave *me* my deeds. I also hold a few carucates of land from the church at West Lith near the coast at Redekarre. Earl Morkere has been taken to Northmandige with his brother, and Waltheof. Do you think this new king will leave us alone now if he thinks he can draw our fangs?'

Eirik feels unable to hold in his ill luck and pours out his woes in a stream,

'My lands were made forfeit because I was given them by King Harold. Earl Willelm told me his young friend Ricard fitzScrob earned them with a show of skill at arms near Haestingas'.

Eirik draws himself to his full height and laughs lightly,

'I was given little time to gather my few chattels, sent my wife and sons to her father's home in the Danelaw and left without looking back at my new home. You saw what I was doing to keep body and soul together'.

'You kept your *life*, friend', Harding wishes to hear no more from him and sets his jaw. Eirik is made aware of the wall the older thegn has raised between them and purses his lips.

'Harding is right, Eirik', Saeward tries to comfort the young fellow but is rebuffed.

Eirik plainly feels he has been hushed like a child and stubbornly turns his wrath on the east Seaxan,

'Who asked *you?*'

'Try to be cheerful, Eirik', I feel I have to pour oil over troubled waters. 'You have your life ahead of you. Where are your wife and young ones?'

'They are in Deoraby, why?' Eirik asks in turn.

'They could come with you to Rhosgoch', I offer.

He looks to Harding and asks him,

'Could we do that – ride by Deoraby?'

Harding's mouth twists and he shrugs before asking,

'It is not for me to say. How *old* are your sons?'

'They are seven and nine summers old -', Eirik answers. He is hopeful for an answer that will make his life easier.

'Would it be fair on them to be dragged from pillar to post?' I ask. 'Better to know they are safe with her kinfolk than be beset by hunger and cold with us. We must not be slowed down'.

'Think of this also, that should your woman and offspring be caught by the Northmen or anyone serving them, they could be used to make us give ourselves up', Saeward warns.

Harding looks up at my East Seaxan friend and agrees,

'The Seaxan is *right*. Leave your wife and sons where they are. They are much safer in Deoraby'.

Eirik screws up his nose at our counsel, but I go on to try to talk him over to our way of thinking. He has to try to foresee their dreary lives if they are asked to come with us.

'We will not always be fighting the Northmen. One day, when they have been thrown back into the sea, we can go back to our lives', I suck my teeth, hoping he sees the wisdom of biding his time until he can be with his brood in happier times. 'King Eadgar may give you back your lands with a writ of his own'.

'Will we be at least able to stop by in Deoraby to see them?' Eirik pleads, looking first at me and then at Harding

'I do not see why not', Harding allows, turning to look at me, as his peer. My nod brings a smile from Eirik and as we ride south to the Tese there are grey streaks in the south east where the rising sun struggles to shine through incoming low snow clouds. There will be a fresh dusting of snow before this day is out.

The road narrows at an old stone-built bridge, the ramp undermined by the new path of the river. Since the bridge was built, long before even the Aengle came to these shores, the Tese has been pushing northward around the bridge. Silt has built up around the bend of the river here, and the waters have tried to find a shorter way, chewing at the northern riverbank and in turn weakening the road bank.

Harding curses as his horse stumbles, almost pitching him into the swirling waters below to our right

'I thought Morkere's brycgeweorc had taken care of this damned crossing!' The thegn dismounts, looks over the low wall and pulls back quickly, fearful of falling into the river. 'We should tell Maerleswein before someone is swept away and drowned! Before long this road will not be usable without hard sweat being spent!'

'Is Maerleswein answerable for work this far north?'

I only ask as Harold told me at the Earlsburh that the young shire reeve would take southern and eastern Deira from Morkere. Copsig would have ruled for the king this far north, but he was only given the earldom a month or so ago.

'*God*, man – Morkere lives the life of an idler with his brother under the king's nose! What can *he* do? Anyway, his time will be taken up with fighting, never mind rebuilding bridges! No, it is *Maerleswein* I must see for timber to get this work done', Harding clambers back into the saddle, using the bridge wall to set himself straight.

'Where is *your* garth?' I try to take Harding's thoughts away from the maelstrom of statecraft.

'Oh, you will not see it for a while yet. We must ride some way toward the coast by way of Gearum before we come to the banks of the

Leofen, and even then you will not see it! Rudby lies in the deep dale, below Huttun'.

'What is to stop the Aengle there from showering you with weapons?' Saeward asks.

'There is no bad feeling between *us* any more', Harding flashes me a knowing smile. 'Anyway, we could just as easily have attacked *them*. They had to get to the river to water their kine, and we owned the land for miles on either side. Think on it'.

Eirik nods, grinning broadly but adds nothing that we do not know already. The Seaxans had no love for the Danes who lived around the River Leag, whereas there was a closer tie between us and the Aengle. I think Saeward will learn as much as he needs to know in the fullness of time.

15

Evening brings snow, blotting out what little we could see of the sunset with its thick whiteness. When we come to the banks of the Leofen the track down to the river is almost hidden under a thick white carpet of long, frost-hardened grass.

'Keep to the inside of the track', Harding warns, 'there is a rock-fall near here. If your horses stub their hooves against the hidden stones, they will be lamed'.

A great hall looms in the darkness, barely made out through white flakes that flurry upward and around our heads as we near the building.

'The stables are here', we hear our host tell us, pointing to our left. In the same breath he roars, 'Open the gates, someone – we are freezing out here!'

'Who is '*we*'?' someone calls testily back from within the high timber baulked wall.

Harding shakes his head in disbelief, and beats the snow from his wolf-skin coat as he roars and bangs on one of the wooden gates with his gloved fist.

'*Toki*, is that you? Get these damned gates open before I have to leap over to them tell you who we are! Have I been away so long that you no longer know me?'

'*Master Harding*, forgive me!' Toki yells fearfully, 'Arnbern help me with the gates!'

Whilst the two men struggle with the gates, Harding champs like a horse and cannot hold his anger for long before yelling out again,

'Come *on* - Toki, Arnbern, the wolves out here are beginning to eye our horses for their evening meal!'

'*We are hastening*, Lord!' someone else answers and suddenly the gates swing open, heaved back by a pair of elderly fellows who are plainly past their best years. As Harding rides past followed closely by us one of them asks 'Where are the men?'

Harding scowls at the fellow and grins over his shoulder at us. The scowl comes back when he looks at the fellow again,

'They are still in Wealas with Thegn Osgod, Tofig. Anyway never mind them, help me off this mare, man! I am stiff with cold, what about *you*, Ivar?' Harding turns aside to me once he is on his feet on the yard's earthen floor, still unsteady after many hours in the saddle. How he stopped himself from falling into the freezing waters of the Tese when he mounted from the bridge wall will always be a mystery to me. 'The Lady Torfrida and my little ones are well?'

'Aye, Lord Harding. The Lady Torfrida is taken with her needlework, seated with her women', Toki answers brightly.

'Lead *in* then', Harding follows Toki and Arnbern through the hall door, the three of us trailing slowly behind, agape at what we can see of our surroundings through the murk of wood fire.

'It leads me to think of the hall we stopped at near Akeham. Thegn Osberht had already followed Earl Gyrth to Lunden', I say out aloud. I do not say is it was burnt down by Brand and his men in trying to catch Hrothulf, Theodolf and me.

'Did Thegn Osberht live through the fight against the Northmen?' Saeward asks, not having been told about any of this.

'I really would not know –'I begin to answer when Harding bellows for his woman. Having likened his hall to Osberht's, I would like to be able to see if his wife is anywhere near as good-looking as the Lady Aelfrida.

'Aethelhun my love, I am home! Where are you?'

'Your wife is with her women- 'Tofig tries to tell him again.

'I know you did – ah, Aethelhun, my good woman'. Harding strides forward to greet a short, plain, plump woman with watery pale blue eyes and up-thrust nose.

'Who are *they?*' she peers at us in the gloom. 'Why do you need to bring outsiders when the harvest has been so grim? We have little enough food for ourselves since your huntsman Valdemar rode off with you - where is he, anyway?''

'He is with Thegn Osgod. I have with me Ivar and his friends'.

Harding only has time to tell her that much before she breaks in to upbraid him, arms crossed on her ample chest, feet spread like a man in the shieldwall,

'Do not tell me Valdemar is with that upstart if I do not know where any of them are. How come you are back so *soon?*'

'I took Ivar to Earl Gospatric, my love', Harding is hard-pressed. Her kin were well-blessed with her leaving them to wed him.

'You *really* annoy me, Harding! I know nothing of any Ivar', Aethelhun crosses her fleshy arms across her chest and pouts.

'I am Ivar', I offer, and find myself lying, 'I am happy to meet you'.

I am not happy, far from it. She can see through me as if I were daylight. I am glared at, icily. Nevertheless, she reaches out a hand and heralds her husbands' lack of class,

'...At least your friend Ivar knows how to lie', she finishes, smiling crookedly at me.

Harding looks as though asking for forgiveness. For the first time since we left Rhosgoch he is at a loss for words. I smile, and shrug when she turns back to him, to belittle him before his guests. He has plainly forgotten what she is like, since leaving her some weeks ago with his men. In yielding to his wife he shows at least that he does not master her as many men of his build do, although many women seem to like that in a man. *She* would soon let him know when he has overstepped the mark should he try to throw his weight about. Then he would be under her yoke again. Life is not always kind.

'I have seen you before, somewhere', Aethelhun spins on her heels to look up at me again. 'Were you not some time in Eoferwic – at the Earlsburh, in Tostig's day?'

'That is true, my Lady', I may or may not be ready for what she asks next.

'Forgive me if I am wrong', she begins once more, 'but I am told you fought with Copsig at Staenfordes Brycg. Later, I heard, you showed again at the Earlsburh with this one after Sigurd was killed'.

She looks up at Saeward with round eyes. He looks at her blankly as if not knowing what she is talking about.

'Your brother, *the monk* was killed by that sot – ah! I forget his name'.

'His name was Garwulf, my Lady', Saeward reminds her, the pain of the memory showing in a wince, 'and Beorhtwulf was only a lay brother, as I was'.

'It surely *was* Garwulf – and you were whipped for killing him!'

For the first time since I set eyes on her she gives a broad smile, as though she *meant* what she told Saeward,

'You should have been rewarded for ridding the burh of the most foul back-stabbing cur I ever had the bad luck to meet'. Aethelhun warms to Saeward. 'What is *your* name?'

'I am Saeward, my Lady. I am an erstwhile field worker at Wealtham in East Seaxe, of late at the side of my friend Ivar!' Saeward proudly avows with a firm right hand on my shoulder.

'Well, Saeward, you shall sit by me at table this evening, and tell me all about yourself when you have eaten', Aethelhun puts a hand on his elbow, not being tall enough to reach his shoulder. I feel his writhing, trying to pull away from her.

'I thought you said we did not have enough food!' Harding snaps.

'Husband, we have enough for a light supper, but no more. We can send out Toki for more in the morning before you rise'. Aethelhun has not finished yet. She asks Eirik, 'What is *your* name?'

'I am Eirik -', he gets no further.

'You are. You sit next to Ivar on my other side and talk to my husband. I have many things to talk over with these two', she smilingly tugs at my tunic sleeve.

Cold sweat runs down my back. Is something afoot here? Is Braenda already up to her tricks again? For the time being I have to make out that I am happy to be Aethelhun's guest, and Harding – her forbearing husband – must sit some way away and bide his time until he is allowed into their bed closet.

As the night wears on, and Aethelhun becomes friendlier toward me, Harding shows he is irked. Saeward and Eirik watch between mouthfuls as she draws closer to me, gazing at me as I tell my made-up tales of rowing ships on the Dnieper.

'How *wonderful* – I wish I could have *been* there!' Aethelhun gushes when I finish the telling, of how my half-brother Osbeorn pulled me from the rapids. Under his breath Harding says he wishes I had been drowned, but his mumblings are lost in the uproar when Toki stumbles up to the long table.

'Thegn Harding, *Earl Osulf* is at the gate!'

'What does *he* want?' Aethelhun yelps as Harding rises quickly from the bench to stump toward the door.

'God knows – *he too may want to sit beside you!*' Harding bellows. Raucous laughter from a drunken Arnbern stops his master in his tracks.

'Lay off my good ale, fool!' Harding glares before stumping away to the door. 'It is for my guests. Yours is at the back of the kitchen, in the *small* vat!'

Arnbern turns sheepishly to the wall and thumps it silently. Toki stares disbelieving at his friend and is brushed aside as Earl Osulf breezes through the door toward Harding. Osulf greets his wife first,

'Ah, the Lady Aethelhun is here!'

Her answer, 'At this time where else would I be?' rocks the earl with laughter.

Aethelhun laughs at her own wit but Harding is befuddled, wondering why Osulf is here at all.

'Ivar is the man I want to speak to', Earl Osulf heads straight for me and I brace myself for the unknown. There is no attack, instead he tells me,

'Your woman, Braenda is outside', he beckons me breathlessly. I would guess they have been riding hard to catch up with us – but from *how far?*

We stride across the stone floor to be met by a flurry of snow blown in through the door. Beyond, in the dark are riders huddled against a bitter, cold northerly wind. One of them loosens the reins, dismounts, and into the light of a wall-mounted torch comes Braenda. My heart leaps at seeing her, but all I can think to say on greeting her is,

'God, woman - could you not have *rested* the night somewhere?'

She looks pale and drawn, tired from a long winter's day ride. The gnawing coldness has taken its toll on her youthful looks. Instead of her flushed, full cheeks, she wears the look of the haunted. I dare say something troubles her deeply, and that even with her own powers she is hard-pressed to cope with something evil.

She looks sideways at Osulf and tells him curtly,

'I must speak with Ivar – *alone!*'

Osulf backs away hastily and she whispers into my right ear that she wishes to get out of the wind, taking care not to be overheard by someone she fears.

'We can go over into the lee of the hall, out of the wind', I offer. A nod tells me this is good enough for her and she follows me into the darkness, away from prying eyes. Flakes are still being blown upward into the cowl of her hood, and she brushes them away with a thin, un-gloved hand. I ask, 'What bothers you?'

'*You* bother me, Ivar', she hisses. 'I wish I had never met you!'

'What has brought this on?' For my life I cannot understand the way women think. 'You know I think of you all the time, you *must* know! Hardly a day goes by without my wondering when I will see you next. Only this evening when I was seated by Aethelhun I thought you cannot be far away'.

She broods in the darkness, her hood pulled low over her eyes. Either that or she is busy casting spells on me that will bring me lurching to an early end. A long time passes before I hear a welcome answer,

'You cannot know she has powers. You see how she holds Thegn Harding in her grip? She is *hwicce* - like me, but *bad!*'

'How is that, come again – *what?* Aethelhun is a *spay wife?* Never have I heard anything so foolish - I mean, *look* at her!' There is nothing in the world I would like better than to be able to believe Braenda, but telling me Aethelhun is a spay wife - do I look so sadly witless?

'I knew this would happen when Harding offered rest for a few days at his home. She has *you* in her grip, *too!*'

Braenda turns to go, but I catch a corner of her cloak and ask her to cast her thoughts back to being with me in the bedding store,

'Think back, when we were together at the Earlsburh, when I talked Sigurd into thinking I was alone? That was only the second time we enjoyed one another, but I felt more than the man I was. I felt as if some of your powers had come into my soul and I was able to spirit you away for the time he was there, ranting'.

'I do. I was proud of you', her smile assures me.'Few men had ever spoken to Sigurd the way you did then. I felt you needed help when he heard me amid the bedding, and sent that rat scurrying across the floor'.

'That he had seen me fight and beat Copsig helped greatly', I grin. 'Did you know Osgod was given Eadwy's lands by Morkere after Eadwy was found floating in the river Ose?'

'You think that was *my* doing?' Braenda chokes back tears. Is she losing her powers? The Braenda I knew once would have laughed off any blame for meddling with men's spirits. I have to look away from her, to gather my wits and offer myself as her willing thrall,

'I have never blamed you for anything but bewitching me so that I cannot think straight. Your charms are well-known in the north, I know. Everyone seems to know you have me in your grip, now even in Naesinga. I have never found fault with you, believe me, Braenda. You would know if I felt bitter about your power over me. Now come inside before we both freeze!'

'Bring your friends out here with you - tear yourself away from here. I am powerless against her in her own home!'

'How do I talk Saeward and Eirik into leaving good ale, a warm fire and an open-handed host?'

'*Do it*', Braenda hisses, 'before I too am enthralled!'

'They will stare at me as if I had grown two heads!' I find I have to look away from her, up at the light falling snow, anywhere to take my eyes from her to hide my own weakness. When I look back again she is no longer there. There are no prints in the snow to show she had ever been here.

Was Osulf's coming a dream? When I come back to the doorway everyone has gone, ridden away again or indoors. Arnbern looks sullenly at me when I enter and asks with his eyes, 'Where have *you* been?'

Harding looks oddly at me when I stride past him. I take it Saeward and Eirik have been shown to their room as neither of them is at the table. Nor is Aethelhun anywhere to be seen.

'Where did *you* go?' Harding asks, putting into words what Arnbern's eyes asked. Everything has been a dream. 'Lord Osulf asked if there was bitterness between you and her. You wandered off as in a dream and the woman Braenda vanished into the night'.

'I should go to my bed, if anyone can show me where it is', I mumble.

'By all means – Toki show Ivar to his bed. I think I should find my way to rest before I too lose my wits'.

I stand there swaying, half asleep. Something Harding has said jolts me and I am suddenly wide awake.

'Why do you say that?' I ask, staring at him.

Harding yawns, bleary-eyed, worse for wear, hung over with his own ale. His hands drop to his side and he stands staring down at the straw at his feet before looking across the darkness at me.

The words he says burn their way into me like hot coals,

'I say that because Aethelhun's eyes lit up, like ice-fire when Osulf told me your woman was here. There was something uncanny about her just then. I have never seen her that way before. I bid you good-night, Ivar'.

Braenda does not come to me in the night as I had hoped. She jerked my thoughts when I saw her with Osulf's men. Where she went after that no-one knows. It is no use asking Harding what became of her if his woman is a spay wife, as Braenda tells me she is. In the early morning I tell Harding that we are ready to ride on.

'*Must you?* We have deer meat this evening', he has been told that I have a weakness for its rich taste. Yet I have begun to fear for my safety now. Is this is a sign that Aethelhun is hwicce? She might dearly want to keep me longer against my will, perhaps to use me against Braenda – or am I misleading myself? Perhaps I only dreamed everything.

When I fall as if drugged into the bed Toki shows me to, my head feels heavy. Were herbs dropped into my ale?

'It would be as well to ride on', I try to talk Harding into believing nothing either he or Aethelhun might have done has anything to do with my drive back to Rhosgoch. One night in that hall is enough for me. 'Are you *coming* with us?'

Harding holds out his arms, palms forward as if pleading with me,

'I told Aethelhun we would be staying a few nights until we were rested from our long ride. Do not make a liar of me, Ivar, *not to my wife!*'

'You can tell her a white lie, surely? *You* know what she is more likely to believe', I am halfway out of the door, my axe in one hand, my hauberk over my right shoulder and my helm in my other hand. Eirik and Saeward are already outside the door in the weak sunlight, looking bored with waiting for me.

'Have it your own way, but I cannot come with you right now. Wait for me in Jorvik, at the White Boar on Mickel Gata. Ask for Sigwulf. He will tell you when I am there', he waves me away.

'We have little enough time to waste, *you* know', I call back as I head for Braenda.

'Wait for me!' Harding snaps, I shrug and hear him grind his teeth.

'We can wait', Eirik tells Harding as I mount Braenda. 'I, for one, would like to look around. I am sure Saeward wishes-'

'I would not be bothered if I did not see that burh ever again!' Saeward growls sullenly. Why does he stare at, or past me?

'Best we *bypass* Eoferwic! I shall not be safe there if Garwulf's kinfolk see me', he adds.

Eirik turns to Harding, shrugs and throws up his hands.

'What if we ride by way of Tadceaster?' I ask.

'To stay at Aethel's steading? I am all for *that*', Saeward brightens. 'I should like to see her homestead again'.

'Would Harding know where to look?' I ask, not looking at the thegn.

Aethelhun shows at the door with arms folded across her chest. Her purses her lips and turns to her husband to ask him,

'Why are they going *now?*'

He answers, half believing his own words,

'Ivar seems keen to join Thegn Eadric again'.

Hopefully she does not see through the lie. Her mouth twists downward at the corners but her eyes show she sees us as fleeing from her. Whatever her feelings or however she sees me, I am not about to let her see any gain from arguing. However, before I can say anything she makes her way indoors again, ready to allow us to withdraw without her asking why I wanted to leave so soon when she was led to believe we would stay at least until the end of the week.

Were I foolishly raw I would read this as not caring whether we stayed. We are, after all, our own masters. I shall have to look through my belongings before we reach Tadceaster, to see if she took anything from me as a bearing.

'Would you know where to look?' Saeward asks Harding. 'You have never been there before - *have you?*'

Before the East Seaxan foolishly tells the thegn how to reach Aethel's home, I stop him,

'We will look out for you', I look past Harding to see if Aethelhun is nearby – by the doorway, perhaps – listening. Aethel would never forgive me for bringing down a curse on her steading through my foolishness.

'Very well', Harding puts on an assuring smile. He does not believe we will wait for him. Saeward is right not to want to stay in Jorvik, even briefly.

Any of Garwulf's kin might know him and risk punishment at the Thrijungar Thing for carrying out their blood-feud. Even knowing it is against the law few would grieve for a man who cut down a fellow in full flight, even one such as Garwulf.

'Fear not. We *will* look out for you', I assure him. 'Ride west from Eoferwic to the Hvarfe and believe me, we will see you'.

'Why *should* I fear?' he scoffs. 'I can ride on my own, even though outlaws such as Ketil abound along the tracks of southern Deira. After letting Copsig slide through his fingers, Ketil would never dream of showing himself to me'.

Snow begins to fall again as we leave the Leofen below us in the deep dale and ride along the high road past Huttun. Harding has wisely taken shelter in his hall and the flakes are being blown down at us on our way south. Soon even the upper hamlet is lost behind us in the whiteness. Our way will hopefully lead us south-westward to Aluertun, then on southward past Jorvik. With luck then, for much of the way the wind and snow will be behind us.

Although Aethel left the steading in the afteryear, the snow-laden grass has been kept trim around the house and outbuildings. The paddock where the horses were kept has been left un-barred, yet it is not overgrown as it should be. By rights the nettles and thistles should be chest high, at least. The grass would be flattened by weeks of snow.

Someone has taken over the steading on her behalf, or Morkere awarded the lease to one of his thegns before leaving for Thorney with his brother to seek out Eadgar.

Saeward is first down from his saddle and to the door,

'Ivar, look at this!' he calls, beckoning me across. A token hangs from a silver chain nailed to the door - Hrothulf's silver hammer. 'What does it mean?'

'Thor's hammer, Mjollnir', I tell Saeward, trying not to laugh at the way his mouth curls down in the corner.

'*The heathen –*' Saeward is about to rip the chain from the nail when I stop him.

'*No*, leave it! Someone has been looking after this steading, dwelling and land. They may wish this token to be kept here. Is there anyone within?' I ask Eirik to look.

He is gone for some time before he shows again at the door, waving his right hand from side to side,

'There is no-one here *now*', he shakes his head, 'but there has been of late. This dwelling is being kept in good order by someone - a woman I would think. Everything is neatly stowed, pots and bowls on their shelves, and so on'.

'We wait', I answer, looking at him over one shoulder.

'We have nothing else to do but wait', I pull the saddle and all my gear from Braenda's back, giving her well-earned freedom to dig the snow with her hooves to find the early shoots of grass.

'This is eerie', Saeward looks around the empty thwait as he walks up to the forlorn dwelling. 'On the one hand no-one seems to live here, yet on the other it is not cobweb-hung or dust-laden. Are we going to find the dwelling and outbuildings in a shambles in the morning, as we did at the inn near Ceolsey?

The light in the west has faded, the snow lies pricked out by moonlight on the paddock, and I begin to think a charm has been put on Aethel's home. Although I hardly think elves have been keeping watch over her steading, what *has* been happening here is beyond me.

It is only when I turn to walk slowly back into the dwelling that I know I am not alone. Someone is watching me from amid the trees.

'Come', I beckon, 'I will not hurt you'.

'It has not dawned on you that I might hurt *you?*' a woman asks. I do not think I know her, but I have a feeling we have met before.

'I am willing to risk your wrath if you show yourself', I beckon her again, smiling.

'You take too much upon yourself, Ivar Ulfsson', she answers, and slips quietly, eerily across the snow-spangled paddock as if she were gliding on the slight breeze.

'Have *you* been caring for Aethel's steading?' I ask when she stands before me, looking up into my eyes. A woman of some years, she nevertheless bears herself well, her dark eyes taking me in just as I am her. Grey hair is swept back under her wide hood yet the skin on her brow is still un-creased.

Her cheeks are full, eyes clear, chin smooth - as the brow that bears a narrow band of unadorned silver.

She asks testily by return,

'I take your meaning to be that you think I am not the holder of this fair steading and the land it rests on?'

'Are you?' I can think of no better answer.

'Would you think I *could* be?' Her wary answer leads me to wonder whether she is playing with me.

'This is neither the time nor the place for games', I answer, shaking my head and folding my arms over my chest. I am now standing in the way of the door she now makes haste for.

An un-womanly hiss makes me look again at her. With viperish eyes Aethelhun tries to startle me into allowing her past me.

A lifetime seems to pass and my days are laid out before me. Aethelhun cannot go forward, not can I step aside to let her into Aethel's home.

'*Stand aside, Ivar!*' Harding has shown in the thwait at the far side of the paddock, bow raised, an arrow aimed at his wife.

I feel rooted to the earth, unable to stir either way. Even when Harding summons me to stand aside again I cannot do so. Behind me Saeward and Eirik watch horrified as Harding nears, bow held in one hand, ash-shafted spear in the other. He roars fit to burst, his bull neck stiff with sinew,

'For God's sake, Ivar – *stand aside!*'

Somehow I find within me a willingness to do as he orders and take three steps to my right. Seeing the way clear Aethelhun rushes forward to claim Aethel's dwelling and her husband's spear hurtles silently through the cold night air, into the small of her back.

'In God's name this cannot be true!' Saeward drops to his knees, hands clasped, fearful in prayer.

On the cold earth beside my feet Aethelhun shrinks within her cape, the hood falling over the shrivelling head and a rank smell rises. I might have begun retching, but I am too shocked even for that. Eirik closes his eyes tightly, his hands cover his nose and he turns back into the warmth of Aethel's main room.

Only Harding seems untouched at the killing of his wife. And then he groans, a long, dry, racked groan that sounds like a death rattle,

'*Why*, Aethelhun – why does it have to be *you?*' Harding throws down the bow, the arrow dropping harmless to the ground and he drops to his knees, pulling on the cape. The hood lies crumpled where I thought the head to be. He lifts the cape and screams, 'God, woman, you filthy hag I *loved* you!'

The packed earth beneath the cape is charred black! When flesh is left too long in an oven it burns to cinders. This is all we see where the cape had been. Harding stands and stares upward into a star-pricked heaven.

'Why did you not step aside when I *told* you?' he asks, his breathing hard, rasping almost. 'You made it harder for me to do what I should have done long ago when I first knew she dabbled in her black art. I misled myself into thinking I still loved her despite holding the proof I needed that my love fed her evil'.

'I *could* not step aside, rooted to the step! How did she find us?' I ask. When I stoop to pick up the cape he brushes my hand aside and tells me to set fire to it.

He glowers down at the black-scorched earth where his woman had been and scowls, telling me in a growl to leave it be,

'*Touch it and be tainted!* Your woman will never come back to you and you will be marked against God, as was Cain! Bring an ember from the hearth within in a shallow earthenware cup, if your friend Aethel has one'. I stand, staring down and he tells me again, 'Go, Ivar. Find one, bring the ember and drop it onto the cape. We will find nothing in the morning when we come out, Ivar, take my word for it!'

Harding's breathing is slower again now. He had thrown his spear with as much strength as he could summon to render harmless the fetch that was his wife. Saeward brings a cup from within and Harding takes the cold ember from the cup, dropping it onto the snow-dusted cape. All that happens is that the cape smoulders, nothing wondrous, nothing vanishes suddenly as I thought it might.

'*Leave it!*' Harding barks at Eirik when he tries to prod the ember with a stick from the woodpile. 'I promise you, nothing will be here in the morning to show Aethelhun ever came'.

All I can think of now is sleep. I had been sapped by sudden fear for my own life, my soul threatened by Harding's woman. Until now I had never really thought of having a soul. Being eye-to-eye with the serpent's handmaid drained the warrior from me. It was as if I had been traded with a foolish ceorl. Now, until I feel the warrior within me again I must rest.

The hairs stand stiffly away from the back of my neck when Braenda whispers into my ear,

'Harding was very brave'.

'He was', I nod, adding half aloud, 'I was turned to rock with fear.

Saeward snores in the cot to my right, the cot-frame creaks and he turns onto his side toward the wicker wall and all is silent again.

'*You* were brave, too, but his was the greatest forfeit. Between you, Harding and yourself, you did us all a good deed. Elmete will be grateful to you both, having banished Aethelhun to the netherworld. How did you know there was something wrong, to hold her back from entering our - Aethel's – haven?'

'Entering *our* haven?' I ask. Was I being used as a barrier between warring powers of hwicce for Braenda's own ends?

'In fairness you *were* a barrier, Ivar. Harding had to call on you to stand aside because only *his* arrow or spear could render her harmless', Braenda adds. 'Only *her* lover could bring her down! You spared him the misery of suffering. Had you not stood away, her strength would have gathered enough to throw you bodily out of her path and Aethel's soul would have been rendered wherever she was'.

'He would have been powerless to stop Aethelhun when she had taken my powers and added them to hers'.

'This is *your* home, then? You kept it, looked after it until Aethel came back', I caress her back with one hand and wipe away a tear from her cheek with the crooked finger of the other. 'The bed I slept in was yours'.

'My bed is wherever *you* rest', she kisses my forehead and runs one hand through my hair. Her other hand rests fleetingly on my manhood to give me fair warning of the lovemaking that is to come, 'Rest comes after reward'.

'Pack your things – quickly!' Harding has been out of the dwelling. Panting he looks around the door to the room I shared with Saeward to tell me there are men on their way here.

'What men can they be that frighten you so?' I laugh. 'You are red with running!'

'They do not frighten me, their numbers do!' Harding purses his lips, 'I fear no man on God's earth, but four of us on horseback will make no inroads on men with bows and spears!'

'Duke Willelm's mounted men made inroads on the shieldwall on Caldbec Beorg', Harding tells me. 'They failed to hold the Northmen because Willelm knew he could draw the Suth Seaxan fyrd from their shieldwall! Had they held together like –'

He is unable to finish because Eirik asks cockily, tongue in cheek.

'You mean in the way Morkere and Eadwin held Harald Sigurdsson's Norsemen at Gata Fulford?'

Harding reddens again, nevertheless finding the time to hiss at me to hurry, as if we were being stalked,

'We must hasten!'

I wave them away and begin to ready myself.

'Go to your mounts and wait for me in the paddock. I will be with you sooner than if you stand here hustling me!' A hurried look around the small room shows me that Saeward's things have gone. I ask Harding, 'Where is Saeward?'

Eirik answers first, grinning,

'Saeward has the horses ready for us to ride. He was grumbling about not sleeping very well because your cot was creaking throughout the night. Ivar, are you a restless sleeper?'

'You could say that, aye'.

I smile back at him and Harding cackles. He must know I had Braenda with me. 'Saeward will one day know what life is about. He is like a child still'.

They share my wit and laugh uproariously,

'What was the joke?' Saeward asks when we join him.

'Oh, nothing – *really*', Eirik raises an eyebrow when the East Seaxan stares at us each in turn.

Saeward growls, his eyes resting on Eirik,

'Only fools and children laugh at nothing, Eirik! Which are *you?*'

'We may be fools, but as men of the world we know a thing or two', Eirik murmurs at me behind his left hand.

'Men of the world', Saeward repeats Eirik's words drily and nods toward the shaking bushes at the side of the paddock, 'which world do you live in? Anyway, Harding, why are we running from these flea-ridden outlaws? We could deal with them in our sleep. Leave that fool Ketil to me'.

Ketil stretches to his full height close to the paddock railings by the gate and pats the air as if praising an obedient hound. He means us to slow before we are drilled by his men's arrows,

'Harding, you really ought to be more welcoming toward us'. He shows blackened teeth in a smile that speaks more of threat than friendship, and we must do as he says lest he give his bowmen leave to cut us down from our mounts. He half-turns to take me in, and hails me mockingly,

'Ivar Ulfsson, how wonderful it is to see *you* again. You brought Copsig back with you, I hope. We have a reckoning to settle with him!'

'Earl Osulf settled *his* reckoning when they met at Nyburna', I slacken Braenda's reins as I draw level with Ketil, who now leans against a tree, one foot resting on the other.

'The bastard could not cheat *his* wyrd, then?' Ketil shrugs and straightens to walk the few yards to my side. 'Will you cheat *yours?*'

'How do you see my wyrd to be, Ketil?'

'I was thinking of keeping you hostage, to raise silver on your head', Ketil puts to me, whether in earnest or not he does not let on.

He scowls when Harding asks.

'How long are you willing to wait?' Harding asks him, a smile growing.

Eirik knows what Harding is thinking of and cannot help laughing uproariously. Saeward winces at the din, unable to believe his ears.

'*Why do you ask?*' Ketil raps, still scowling, annoyed now because he does not know what there is to laugh about. He wishes to gain from meeting again, but has no thought as to *how* he could gain.

'I am sure the king would like to lay his hands on us', Harding offers, trying hard to hold back the laughter, 'but we do not think he will be in the kingdom much before Yuletide, if at all then'.

Ketil stands open-mouthed, deep in thought. He looks up at me as though stunned to have found an answer,

'We keep the four of you until then!' Ketil would have us believe he can find enough supplies to feed his own men on besides us, his hostages through almost a whole year, summer and winter.

'Have you asked your men what they think of that?' I follow his eyes to the men around him, and us.

They share odd looks, some even laughing off his aims, if they are aims or merely plucked from the air for want of anything better. Few of them look as though they agree with him, shaking their heads when the senselessness of it all is made clear to them. Ketil looks across the thwait at the fellow who must be his right hand man, and throws his hands up,

'Very well then, *you* tell me what is so bad about keeping them hostage until this new king comes back'.

'I am glad you sought my counsel, wise Ketil. Think about this, what do *we* eat when they are stuffing themselves on our food for all that time? *And* Ketil, answer me this, how do we get anywhere *near* the Northman king even if we *can* keep them that long?'

'Hunding, have you no *faith?*' Ketil wheedles, casting his eyes over one shoulder at Harding and us to see whether he is the butt of everyone's wit.

'I *have* faith, but you are a long way short of being a god. We saw that when Copsig and his men ran through us. *They*', he points at Harding and me. '*They* must have thought it a great laugh to see us being thrown aside like skittles by a mere four men on horseback!'

'Hunding is right', I stretch my arms against the pommel of my saddle and use this rift within their number to our gain. 'Where is the leadership they look for if you cannot think far enough ahead to ensure their wellbeing? If we stay here under guard, feed ourselves by hunting and whatever root crops we can find, we will look well enough for our new king to reward you for your undertaking'.

'Do you think he *would?*' Ketil briefly shows unbridled eagerness until something jars within him.

'*Hah*, you thought you had fooled me, eh? I do not trust you, Dane! Do we trust him, lads?'

He looks around his followers and sees I have sown the seeds of doubt in their minds. On turning back to me he snarls,

'*Now* see what you have done!'

'You did it to yourself, *fool!*' Hunding chortles. 'You are of Danish stock yourself, as am I. As it is the only one here who *is* Aenglish, through and through to the tips of his boots, is Ingenwulf, the brightest amongst us. He was the first to shake his head when you spoke of holding these four to hand them to the Northman king!'

'Aye, we do not sell our own kind!' another agrees.

One more of his followers growls, saddened at Ketil's shaky leadership skills,

'The *N-Northman* is our f-foe, *not them!*' he stammers, waving a hand at us.

Ketil has been angered by the lack of following and puts to his men the matter of leadership,

'You want another leader, eh?' Somehow I feel he should not have raised the matter.

'Aye, we do - *not before time!*' Hunding stares sourly at Ketil, and away again in loathing.

'Who says we need a new leader?' one man barks, laughing at the discomfited Ketil's helpless scowl.

'*Hunding* should lead us!' some chorus.

'*Ivar should lead us!*' others shout and clap their hands. The rest agree, shouting loudly when I raise my hands to quieten them, 'Ivar, *Ivar!*'

'I thank you for your wholehearted backing', I begin, to shouting and laughter from both Ketil's men and my friends. *However –*'

There are groans from left and right now, feigned scowls are cast at me. However, my friends and I must be on our way back to Thegn Eadric at Rhosgoch. If you had horses-'I am not allowed to finish.

'Ah, but we know where we can *find* some!' Hunding smirks.

'I do not mean you to steal them –'I begin again but my words are drowned by the chorus of gleeful laughter and shouting.

Amid the shouting Harding yells into my right ear,

'Who cares *how* they get them? The more men we take the better. They are outlaws, do not forget. Ketil is good with his bow; they would not stand for his bluster if he was not!'

'You know where to find these horses?' I ask Hunding, as he now leads Ketil's outlaw band.

'Leave that to me. Best not ask, eh?' he taps his nose with one finger and turns to one of the men. What he says I cannot hear; nor am I meant to - the less I know, the better for them.

'Midday', Ketil tells me with a sly grin, 'will see the finest mounts this side of the Hvarfe gathered in this paddock.

True enough, when the light is strongest I hear the shrill whinnying and drum of hooves behind me. These horses are being herded toward us from Tadceaster from *Morkere's* stables, saddled!

'*They have stolen these mounts from the earl!*' Harding almost chokes with laughter.

'Aye - so what if they have? They are ours now', Ketil stands admiring the horses and points to one. 'That one is *mine!*'

'Take your pick, Ketil. I will allow you that much', he smacks a big hand on his friend's back, only to be stared at blankly. 'What need has *he* of them? Anyway, they were Tostig's before that. He had a good eye for a horse, he did! Some of *these* come from Gwynedd, where we cut off Gruffyd from his friends'.

'You were there, too?' I ask.

Hunding flashes a quick smile and answers quietly,

'Aye, I also know all about you and that strumpet maid of Ealdgyth's... Never fear, all is fair in love and war, so they say. My lips are sealed', Hunding flashes another smile and strides to the paddock to oversee the sharing out of horses to men.

'A shame the others did not think that way', I mutter to myself.

Ketil was listening in and answers,

'You gave us all something to natter about, Ivar. Never mind, you can bet the story has spread across Wealas by now. Nothing can be kept quiet amongst men of the sword for long. Who said the womenfolk had to have the biggest share of idle chatter?'

If I had fostered hopes to keeping the lid on that tale, I would have been bitterly let down. It is just as well my skin has become thicker since coming to this kingdom as a youth.

Soon everyone is mounted and waiting for Harding.

'What is everyone waiting for?' he senses our idleness, all eyes are on him,

'You are the thegn here', I smile kindly, as if talking to a child. 'We await *your* orders, even though we know where we are going. You have the last word'.

'I have, have I?' Harding grunts, nodding westward.

We set off, heading for Ceaster. For the first time since spearing Aethelhun he smiles, seemingly at one with himself. When he sees me looking past Eirik at him, he tells me,

'We bypass Scrobbesbyrig, Hereford and Staefford, where the Northmen have settled in. Our road will take us along King Offa's trench, cut to keep out the Celts'.

'It does not seem to have overawed them', I ride, looking around me at the neighbourhood.

'We rode this way three years or so ago with Tostig, remember?' Hunding senses my feeling lost in these back-hills. 'Ceaster is not far now. From there we ride south instead of west as we rode before. Do you miss Tostig?'

I had not thought of my kinsman of late. When I shrug he looks away again, thinking of something else to say. I am lost in thought about Tostig for the first time in weeks, wondering what he is doing in Flanders. My last sight of him was on the steering deck of his ship, looking out to sea. Then he was lost in the early morning mist that came rolling in off the Hymbra.

16

'We will be in Rhosgoch before long', Harding reminds me. My back aches from riding and it feels as if Braenda is limping. 'Our guide says we will see the guard towers soon, above the rocks'.

Rhosgoch looks just the same as when we first came almost a month ago. The thatched rooves have gained some snow with the turn of the wind since then. Nevertheless markedly less snow lies on the ground here than did in Northanhymbra or Mierca. To our left clouds laden with rain are almost thrown across the hills from the west by strong winds.

It was said by the Erse king Brian Boru, that the warring Gael giants blew the Danish outlanders onto Aenglish and Wealsh shores. These giants hurled Sigtrygg 'Silkeskegg' onto the lee-shore of Northanhymbra. Sigtrygg was beaten again here, this time by King Aethelstan at Brunanburh. He could not fight his wyrd.

The creaking gates make some of the horses skittish as they are drawn open for us. The riders, unused to their mounts need help from Bleddyn's men to master them and happily dismount after their back-breaking long ride over the mountains from Offa's Dyke to the north-east.

Braenda is taken from me by a grinning Wealshman who winks before taking the reins of Harding's mare. I stare after him as he leads both our horses, and wonder if this is to do with the tale of my bedding my fiery spay-wife.

Harding has been talking, thinking I was with him. When he sees me standing rapt, held captive by my thoughts, he elbows me,

'Time to eat, *then* you can dream. I know you bedded your russet-haired spay-wife after I speared Aethelhun. With some luck perhaps *I* might find a woman here. First and foremost, however, we must seek out Osgod'.

'Thegn Osgod went with Lord Bleddyn', he is told by Ifor, who has come up behind us. 'I hear Aldo betrayed you'.

'How wrong can you can be about these Brothers?' I answer, nodding sagely, then add, 'How is Theodolf?'

'Your friend Theodolf is on the mend, getting his strength back with the help of the Seaxan lady Sigrid'.

'*I am filled with envy!*' I quip, laughing. Deep down I feel gutted. I felt drawn to the Lady Sigrid, not having seen Braenda for too long.

'Aye, Ivar. They are *both* with child!' Ifor shakes, unable to hold his mirth.

'Theodolf is to be a father – *twice* over?' I *am* stricken! Over the years since coming to these islands I have met many a woman I would gladly have settled with. Yet none of them bore me offspring. Now here is Theodolf, having left Dunstan's widow Gerda at Saewardstan to come with us, and he is to be a father, *twice over!* I feel sorry for Brihtwin that Theodolf turned from him. The little lad may have no-one to look to in his youth, a feeling I share in losing my own father when I was still young. Having been fostered by a good man and his wife set me on the right path, I feel.

Nevertheless there is no blood tie with the lad. His own flesh and blood would matter more to him, but I do not think he will be about for them when he is needed. His own roots have been pulled too early, and will find putting down new ones hard.

'The midwife thinks the Lady Sigrid is having *twins!*' Ifor chatters on like an old fishwife, but I am no longer listening. I had hopes of bedding her myself, or at least her maid Aelfflaed, but it was plainly not to be.

Aye, I am sickened at my lot. I am told I have Braenda, but can she have *offspring?* She once told me she had a son by me but has so far neither shown me to him, nor told me his name. What am I to believe? I am a warrior in later middle years, with no land, no wife or children to keep me company. Is it too late to make a start now? Besides, who will give *me* land, *King Willelm?*

Ifor sees I have fallen silent and stops his chattering. He fiddles with a small knife, aimlessly whittling away at a piece of branch. He looks up at me again, offers a weak smile and walks slowly away as Osgod nears.

'*Ivar*, you are *back!*' he hugs me, rests an arm on my shoulder and walks me to the hall, into the warmth. 'Tell me about how Copsig met his end'.

'Harding told you he is dead?'

'He told me to ask *you*', Osgod lets his arm drop and turns to look at me. 'He *did* tell me that Earl Osulf threatened your life - and that Earl Gospatric had to hold him back, not that *he* was your best friend either'.

'That much is true', I have to grin. 'Harding told me on the way there that Osulf hated Danes, and that much *was* true. He may or may not have been cured of his hatred of us, but he no longer wishes to see me spit-roast'.

Osgod laughs loudly, fit to burst. Some of the Wealshmen look up from their talking, startled as we enter the great hall through the end doors.

'Rhiwallon wishes to see you', Osgod tells me when he can talk again.

'And Bleddyn, where is he?' I ask in turn, looking up and down the yard, 'I have seen nothing of him yet either'.

'He will be back with us before we set out for Hereford', Eadric comes up from behind, rests a hand each on our shoulders and pulls on my shoulder to turn me and steers me outside again. 'You have missed much, Ivar'

'I have heard that Theodolf is to be a father, *twice over!*' I try to hide the feeling that life has overlooked me on one or two counts, but he will have none of it.

'Smelly children screaming in the night, feeding babes that spew everything over your best clothes when you pat them on their backs – to burp them, so the saying goes, *eeugh!*' Eadric draws phlegm and spits it out onto one of the chickens.

He looks about, sees no-one was watching and pushes me back through the half-open doorway into the choking, smoky warmth of the hall to sit with Osgod on one of the benches.

'*Ale-wife*, give me three cups of your best brew!' Eadric calls out with a ready laugh as we seat ourselves near the hearth. An old crone looks up from her knitting, puts it down on the bench beside her and struggles to her feet. Before she can rise to her feet Theodolf scoops the three cups into the vat furthest away from us, and limps to our table.

'I was told you are on the mend, Theodolf. I should hate to see what they meant by 'at death's door'!' I bid him sit by me.

'Drink up, Ivar. Waste no time talking about my wounds. This ale is too good to spend idle chatter over!' he stands over me, pointing to the brimming cup.

'You are to be a father, Theodolf'. I look up at him, hovering behind me, a broad grin spreading from ear-to-ear.

'You have been told even before I knew you were here again! What do you think?' he laughs. 'One day they were tending to my wounds, the next they were in bed with me – *not* at the same time, mark, but little time passed before I made sure of seeing to them both'.

'What about Gerda, and Brihtwin?' I ask.

The grin vanishes quickly. He stares glumly into the fire and glares down at me.

'What *of* them?' he spits. '*She* betrayed me with Eadmund, and the little lad is Dunstan's, *not mine!* Gerda should have thought of him before she took that stuck-up son of King Harold to bed!'

'Then why did you marry her?' I demand an answer, Osgod and Eadric sitting awkwardly close by.

'I thought –'Theodolf begins, and stops to put words to his thoughts.

'You thought you would go through with marrying her to keep her from Eadmund's clutches, and to spite her, *or yourself.* When you came with me you still thought you were punishing her – am I right?' I take a mouthful of ale and swill it around inside my mouth before bringing him to an answer, '*Well?*'

'Does it matter?' Theodolf answers lamely. I hoped to hear something better from him, but then he did try to wrench his father from Aethel, to no better end than his leaving Gerda.

'One day, soon, we will swoop down on the foe at the Northman stronghold of Hereford and you will be smitten by guilt, unable to think straight. You will do the wrong thing by your comrades and leave them open to attack, getting them killed or captured'.

I let him think over my words whilst I down more of the sweet ale he brought me. When I hear nothing from him, I add,

'*That* is why it matters. Now you think you have done something wonderful, but it will dawn on you before the summer what you have done to Gerda, Sigrid and Aelfflaed, and your thoughts will be elsewhere, when you should be thinking about spreading your arrows amongst Willelm fitzOsbern's guards'.

'Gerda means *nothing* to me now!' he yells into my right ear, his mouth so close that I feel his breath hot on my right cheek. With my right hand I reach quickly to his left ear and draw him down to the plain wooden boards of the table in front of me, upsetting my ale cup, splashing the nectar across the table at Harding.

'Be careful that *you* still mean anything to *me!*' I hiss into his ear and throw him down to the earthen floor behind my bench. 'I could forget you were *ever* a friend!'

'Ivar, have a care, *he is wounded!*' Saeward pleads with me, staring open-eyed at my treatment of Theodolf.

'He should think about that!' I stand and climb over the bench on my way to the door without looking down at him. Men almost twice my height step back in awe at the speed with which I took Theodolf to task.

'Ivar, I would not ask you to leave', Eadric joins me at the doorway. He stands, awkwardly punching his hands together, awaiting an answer of some kind. When I say nothing he adds, 'Theodolf is well-liked here amongst us. He may be trying to make amends for what he has done to this Gerda, but do not shame him like that again before his peers, or else I shall have to set *you* on your road. Mark my words, I shall be sorry to see you go. Your name as a warrior has spread far and wide; Theodolf is still trying to make his. Let him live *his* life, friend. He must live with his ghosts. Take care, one day *you* may be one of them – *so may I*. Let him think fondly of you in the days ahead'. He rests a hand on my back, pats me and turns to walk back into the hall, telling me as he passes below glowing torches, 'Rhiwallon will see you soon'.

With these parting words he makes me aware of why I am here at all. A sudden sleet squall chases me into the hall after him, to warm myself near the hearth – if there are any benches there that have not been earmarked for Rhiwallon's own men.

My thoughts go back to Theodolf. I should have taken him to task about leaving Gerda long ago, when we met near Oxnaford. For that I am at fault, I understand. I may have to ask his forgiveness before the week is out. Helping others master their fighting skills should close the gulf between us to ease our path back to friendship.

However that will take time, and until then we must learn to live cooped up so close together in this stronghold of Rhosgoch for the sake of everyone else here, and for Hrothulf.

We are seated below the table where Rhiwallon, Eadric, Osgod and Harding are talking earnestly. Rhiwallon is taller than most Wealshmen I have seen, his golden mane more like that of a Seaxan lord, but then I hear his mother is Seaxan. He gnaws at a small bone as he listens, stopping from time to time to break into the talk that goes on between Osgod and Harding. Harding chews hurriedly, wagging a leg of some game fowl in the air at Osgod, and looking my way from time to time, trying to browbeat his fellow thegn with some boast. There is much head-shaking and finger-wagging from Harding before the Wealsh aetheling looks up

'Ivar - *Croeso i Cwmry!* That means welcome in my tongue. Harding tells me you and he wished to take Earl Willelm and his young friend Ricard as hostages. Was that not over-bold; when you think there were only two of you to keep in check the two of them?'

Plainly Harding told him the bare bones of the tale, leaving out the part about him not being able to withstand Earl Willelm's dare to fight him. What else has he not said?

'You are right, my Lord', I bow my head on answering.

'I would say we *were* over-reaching ourselves, having lost one man, Oslac, and being made to leave another behind in Scrobbeshire to tend to a third man, Theodolf. We should by rights have bound them and left them for the wolves and bears'.

The Wealshman grins at me, knowing full well that I will not put any blame on Harding for our mishap as I try to switch his thoughts onto other matters,

'Theodolf looks to be on the mend now, although Oslac's skills with the bow will be keenly missed. They were a good pair, their skills well matched. We lost another friend in Centland, fighting Earl Odo's garrison at Hrofesceaster. Well, we lost many a friend, but young Sigegar was as gifted a bowman as was his friend Oslac -'

'*He* says', Rhiwallon breaks in, smiling and nodding at Harding. '*He* says', Rhiwallon goes on, smiling, waving at me to listen, 'that he took a dare from Earl Willelm to fight, to show the Northman how they fight man-to-man in Deira. Is this true?'

Before answering I look up along the table at Harding. He looks bleakly at me, knowing that he may have landed himself in hot water. A slow nod from him lets me know I can answer truthfully.

Rhiwallon looks from me to Harding and back again, his smile freezing. Harding coughs and assures me,

'You *can* answer'.

'You would be well counselled to answer', Eadric tells me before taking a draught of ale from a silver-adorned horn.

I try to answer without giving anything away,

'Aye, my Lord, he took the dare'.

'You can tell me no more than *that?*' Plainly Rhiwallon is annoyed by the lack of depth in the words I use to answer. 'You can take loyalty too far, you know. Harding has said you may answer more fully, Ivar. Tell me, did you try to talk him out of taking fitzOsbern's dare, or did you merely let him do what he wished?'

'I told him he was a fool, my Lord', is the answer he wanted to hear. His laugh is long and loud, a sound more like a barking dog than an aetheling.

His men laugh with him – or are they laughing *at* him? Osgod shakes, his head buried in his hands as though sobbing fitfully. When he lowers his hands to hold his sides, tears of mirth streak his cheeks.

Even Harding laughs, although his laughter is not as much at my words as at his own foolishness.

'Indeed you did. Well spoken, Dane', Rhiwallon claps his hands in a show of thanks for my honesty.

'Friends, raise your cups to Ivar, my friends, and hope you have a friend as true as he'.

'Thegn Harding, have you once shown thanks to this fellow for his friendship?'Bleddyn asks him.

Harding's offering brings more laughter.

'I warned him that he might be killed by Earl Osulf'.

Jeering and clapping follows, but this dies down under Rhiwallon's cold stare.

'You warned him he *might* be killed? What manner of heathens are they in Northanhymbra that they would kill a man bringing word of a foe to come amongst them? I would have *rewarded* him, and *well*. Tell me, *was* his life ever threatened?'

'It was, Lord Rhiwallon', Harding nods, answering glibly, regretting having to say *anything* that might get back to Gospatric.

'Lord Gospatric would not allow Osulf to follow through his threat however, and in the end he and Ivar parted friends'.

'I *am* happy to hear that'. Rhiwallon beams and then turns to Osgod to ask him, 'What of your master, Morkere – would *he* have killed Ivar?'

Osgod coughs and clears his throat to answer,

'Morkere has no love for the Godwinson clan either, my Lord. I think he would as easily have had Ivar done away with, however, rather than do the killing himself'. He smiles winningly at me.

'As it is Morkere is in Northmandige with the king, out of harm's way with his brother, Eadwin', Osgod answers truthfully.'However, the aetheling Eadgar is friendly toward Ivar. We all fought side by side against the Northmen at Lunden Brycg after King Harold was killed'.

Rhiwallon senses that all is not well amongst us,

'What of Earl Waltheof – is *he* friendly toward Ivar?'

'I think you would have to ask Ivar, Lord', Osgod answers, bringing me under scrutiny again.

'Are you friendly with Waltheof?' Rhiwallon asks me, riveting me with his steel-grey eyes.

'I have always thought highly of him', I answer, keen to steer clear of talk of Waltheof since seeing him ride away from Caldbec Beorg in order 'to look for his men', as he put it to Harold.

'I asked if you and he were *friends*', Rhiwallon growls. 'How come you Danes cannot answer a straight question? *Are* you friends? If you cannot stand the sight of one another, the outlook is bleak for us as allies against this greed-driven king of yours'.

'We *are* friends, my Lord', I lie, smiling, and Rhiwallon grunts, unhappy that my short answer tells him little.

He would sooner hear me tell him that Waltheof and I are as close as earl and huscarl can be, and that I would lay down my life for the young earl. Unable to fathom the truth, he can only shrug. I will deal with Waltheof in my own way one day, should I be able to speak to him before he slips away again. Perhaps he may tell me why he left King Harold's side – even before Willelm showed – and how he squares this with killing several Northmen for Eadgar, when it was my kinsman who gave him his earldom.

Ansgar may have been wondering about Waltheof, but he did not raise the matter with either the aetheling or the earl before the fight in Suthgeweorce. Now, for the time being, having sworn loyalty to the king Ansgar is Willelm's shire reeve and will not openly go back on his oath. Whether Willelm *trusts* him is another matter altogether. Should the king's trust in him be strained, Waltheof could threaten Ansgar's standing by pointing out the shire reeve's fealty to Harold.

'You are deep in thought?' Rhiwallon asks me when he turns to me again later the same evening when tongues stop wagging for a short time.

'Aye, my Lord. I have much to think of', I answer simply.

'Drink, my good fellow, be of good cheer! Bleddyn is here tomorrow with his men and there will be feasting aplenty'.

He nudges me to add that there will be jugglers from Bretland, Erse singers to praise us all and a wise woman will tell us what wyrd awaits us in the summer ahead. Rhiwallon laughs and draws long on his mead before adding, with a look that tells me something is afoot,

'I hear your woman Braenda has been seen about'.

My eyes tell him what he may have been thinking all along. He falls silent and lifts his cup again, then sets it down and asks me,

'You had not meant to be here this early in the year?'

'I would have come with Harold's sons, Godwin, Eadmund and Magnus. We had–'I begin to answer.

Rhiwallon's eyes bore into me as he cuts in,

'I know now. There was a killing, so Theodolf told me. One of young Godwin's huscarls killed his woman because he thought he saw her go into your room. Aenglishmen know nothing of shape-shifters these days. Once – long in their past - their kind knew of them, but now they shun their kind. The Church brings odd bedfellows together, Dane and Seaxan, Bretlander and Northman. Many Aenglishmen have forsaken their true king, Eadgar for Willelm... but not you I think'.

'You know of Braenda?' I ask Rhiwallon, side-stepping talk of the *aetheling*.

'Who does not in this land? Before she was housekeeper to Gruffyd's bride Ealdgyth, Braenda had standing here amongst the wise ones for her Druidic skills', Rhiwallon downs his mead and holds the empty cup high to be refilled.

'She was a *Druid?*' I ask, taken aback.

'No, she is *not* a Druid. She has some of the skills, but only a man can be a Druid', he thanks the maid and pats her behind as she leaves with a squeak of delight. Rhiwallon has a woman, but his good looks allow let him have his way with the women here. Bronwen would be foolish to take issue with his roving eye when it is she he beds.

'*You* are her chosen man', he tells me once he has put his cup down again. 'Of the men who ever dreamed of taking her, she gave you her blessing. That old fool Sigurd somehow held her bodily enthralled. I do not know why she could – or would – not leave him'.

He halts as a wench pours mead for him, and slaps her thighs, sending her off with a laugh and a wink. He then tells me as much as he knows,

'It may be punishment was aforethought for his cruel treatment of her mother, or he held her sister elsewhere'.

'She has a sister?'

This is another bolt from the blue. Rhiwallon tells me these things as though they are common knowledge in this part of the world and now sits, mouth agape, eyes wide open, his cup in one hand on the table before him,

'She has never told you this?'

I reach for my own cup and take a long draught, wondering what the answer might be,

'When we are together we make love. She does not spend the time talking about her kith and kin. What of her *father?*'

'Her father - I do not believe ever hearing of him. She may never have known him. Why do you ask?'

'Well, her mother plainly had no powers, if she allowed herself to be badly treated by Sigurd. As for her sister', I take another draught of ale.

'Her mother *was* hwicce, as the Seaxans say, but this Sigurd had a friend who took his own payment when he felt his due was not forthcoming. This friend *may* have been Braenda's father', Rhiwallon empties his cup and stands, beaming broadly. 'I must go to my bed,

Bronwen awaits me. I should not keep her long when she is in the mood...'

He leaves me at the table, wondering whether Sigurd was killed by this shadowy father Braenda never spoke of, when all along we thought it was Copsig - or even Eadwy?

Plainly Braenda did not trust me with the truth, or she may have felt it too much for me to understand. Her skills were passed on to her by her father, whom she fears. Harding's woman Aethelhun may have been one of his tools, a fetch to do his bidding and enter dwellings linked with his daughter to bring her under his thumb.

'Ivar, are you not going to bed?' Saeward claps his hands on my shoulders. 'We have an early start, to teach our skills to these Wealshmen'.

'Do not be taken aback if they teach you theirs. I think we could learn as much from them as they from us', I answer, drain my cup and stretch before rising.

'We shall see', Saeward eyes me warily, not knowing what I mean by that.

'Sleep well', I give him a friendly shove toward the door. 'Where angels tread, so must you follow. The darkness is to rest your eyes, do not fear it'.

'Deep, very deep – what does *that* mean?' Saeward asks, his brow beetling.

On my giving no further answer he shrugs and walks on. A Wealshman, one of Rhiwallon's household, shows us to our beds. One day I will trust Saeward enough to tell him what I have heard from our host about my woman.

Eadric passes, followed closely by Osgod, their wishes for a good night's sleep ringing in the night air. Harding comes past hard on their heels and belches,

'Forgive me!' he hides his mouth with one hand. With the other he leads a young woman.

I call after him, casting my eyes over his new bed-mate,

'You took no time in finding someone to share your bed'.

She is good-looking, dark-haired with flashing green eyes, and she trips after him, giggling drunkenly.

'Ah, my lad, such is life! Aethelhun is gone but not forgotten!'

'She *will* be hard to forget, that one!' Eirik passes, leading a well-rounded, fair-haired young woman I would gladly share my bed with either of them to forget what has happened of late.

'You will have to find a woman of your own!' Saeward sees me staring after Eirik's new-found friend.

'And you, what do *you* do by yourself?' I ask him in turn.

He rests one hand on my shoulder and slaps it, twice,

'I sleep well enough, deeply - *like a babe-in-arms!* This is my room. I share it with Ifor, who I am told snores loudly!'

'I have heard you shake the rafters yourself, Saeward. You know I envy you', I grip his hand to see him off for the night and let him go. '*I* should sleep that well'.

'Braenda may come tonight', he tells me through the closed door, laughs out loud, coughs roughly and is told 'to stuff something in his fat mouth' by an unseen Aenglishman who wishes to sleep.

'Good night, *friend!*' Saeward calls out loudly and I walk on to my door. I hope sleep takes me as well as he says it does him.

I do not know if I am dreaming, nor even if I have fallen asleep, but I stand ringed by a sharp, painfully bright ring of white light. There are no shapes, but I feel there is something astir around me, like a great bird that will not let me see it for fear of being known. Do I know - *have* I ever known anything like this? This is something new to me, yet I do not feel threatened.

Something takes shape in the brightness. I see eyes, a woman's eyes, pale blue, not staring but gazing at me as though I were a child.

'Ivar, my angel, stand for me', she holds out her hands as if to catch me should I fall.

Somehow my legs cannot hold me up. I sag to my knees and wail. I try to say something. 'Lift me up' springs to mind, but nor can I speak. Small children, young enough to be rocked, are *unable* to speak.

Strong hands reach out to me. A man's hands lift me off my knees to hold me steady. On looking upward into his eyes I see Ulf's fatherly gaze – my father's eyes meet mine and I am speechless, *dumbstruck!* Jarl Ulf is looking at me and I can think of nothing to say to him. Who is the woman – my mother, *Gunnlaug?*

Only God in his heaven can think of taunting me in this wanton manner! What does it *mean*, this dream I am having – if that is what it is that is happening to me? Who is it playing these tricks on me, to render me helpless and wreck me?

'Ivar wake up, you are flailing like a seal in a fisherman's net!' Saeward stands back out of the way of my right fist before I can render *him* helpless.

'What in *Hel's* name is happening to *me?*' I lie still, sweating in the cot bed that I have been thrashing about in, for all I know waking everyone here. *Everything* is bathed in my sweat.

'I could ask *you* that!'

Saeward hands me a water flask and casts his eyes upward when I snatch it from him without a word of thanks. He looks long and hard at me before adding,

'You may be lucky and be ribbed for this in the morning – or you will be heartlessly mocked for waking your neighbours. What were you dreaming of, not Braenda again?'

When I tell him about my dream he looks taken aback, as if when flailing wildly I *had* hit him,

'I wish *my* mother would come to me in a dream! For that matter, I cannot even *think* what my father looked like! Think yourself lucky, Ivar Ulfsson. I would say *many* a man here would be hard-pushed to know what his father looked like!'

'Meaning we are all *bastards?* Go on - *say* it, Seaxan, so I can knock your wool-filled head off your shoulders!' Ifor glowers, a tightly-bunched fist close to Saeward's right ear. 'I for one would like to know who – or *what* - the Dane had with him in bed that he felt we should all share in his frenzy!'

A muffled roar can be heard from the other end of our sleeping quarters. Someone tells him off for shouting.

In answer he is told to shut up,

'Go to sleep, fool! We have to rise *early!*'

'*See* what you have done?' Saeward chides and feels his way in the pitch blackness back to his rest.

Ifor having grumpily gone back to his bed-closet swears into his head bolster in his own tongue before finally dozing off and I am left alone in the darkness again.

'I hear you caused a stir in the night', Osgod sits beside me on the long bench and slaps down a thick stick of bread and cup of ale onto the long boards in front of him.

Harding thumps *his* heavy frame down on my other side and peers sideways at me, bleary-eyed before settling into his porridge. He blows hard on the steaming hot, cake-like oat mass that floats on a sea of sheep's milk and off-handedly asks,

'That Braenda woman was not with you, was she?' On seeing me shake my head he shrugs and goes back to his porridge. Before he takes a mouthful he tells me, 'I blame the cheeses. *I* had a bad dream, but nowhere near as bad as yours must have been. I learned of your nightmare this morning'.

'I wish to God she *had* been here!' I curse my luck. The tale will be all over this stronghold before the day is out! I think of everyone talking about me, telling one another about my hwicce woman putting curses on me for looking elsewhere.

Knowing how stories alter in the telling, I shall hear something altogether different coming back to me by Eastertide and no-one will say anything about the cheeses!

'Swearing is not welcome here on the day of the Lord!' I hear Rhiwallon tell me as he passes on his way to the high seat.

'How can it already be the Lord's day when yesterday was the first of the week?' Saeward barks angrily at the aetheling, unaware of everyone staring open-mouthed at him.

'At least *one* of us is awake!' Eadric looks sharply down at me as he passes behind to join the Wealsh aetheling and asks, 'Who was it you were asking to be lifted up by?'

'It was nothing', I answer abashed, hoping no-one sees me redden.

'Odd things happen in these parts in winter, before the fore-year comes upon us', Rhiwallon winks at me and raises a cheer from the ranks of seated men.

One of Rhiwallon's men snorts in open mockery,

'Odder still what happens when our lovers come upon us'.

'It may be the madness of the hare's mating dance upon him', another snorts, raising rowdy laughter from each and every man in the hall.

Having left his spoon buried in the mass of porridge, Harding stands suddenly, almost knocking back the bench we are seated on. He calls out with a hand on my back,

'Let each man to his own sport!'

'Here, here!' Osgod claps and bids me stand.

'Take a bow, Ivar. Show everyone here how thankful you are that we all worry about you and let us get on with our morning meal!'

To everyone's delight I do as I am bidden. Cups, knives and spoons are hammered on the long table as I bow from the waist as if I had sung for them. Their loud laughter is drowned by the din of serving maids dishing up food and men eating with mouths open.

Before we know it, Eastertide is upon us and we are readying for another festival. The Wealsh are eager Christians. Theodolf has regained his strength to show off his bow skills. Rhiwallon's men have shown him some of their tricks and everyone has gained.

At table he has told of bringing down a number of Willelm's heavily armed Northman horsemen at Lunden Brycg to gaping, raw newcomers. Older comrades wink knowingly at them, to show they think he is spinning yarns again.

'It is true', Saeward tells them but I would not wish to put him right in front of them. He has been showing the Wealshmen his knack with throwing axes, almost skewering Harding once when he walked across the green in front of them. The thegn had backed away, a shade greyer than when he had come that morning.

Eadric and I have been working hard teaching the men – newcomers *and* seasoned warriors - about the shieldwall, to use it against fitzOsbern's horsemen. We have been maddened with their outlook that, *'on the day, if you come away with your life, why should it matter how you stand?* On being told it is the way to beat off mounted Northmen on horseback whilst keeping down our own losses, the answer is a shrug and raised eyebrows. Then, having mastered the shieldwall, they leave gaps wide enough to let in a waggon!

'Give them *time*', Bleddyn told us. His men would sooner rush in and away again, having done our bidding. Rhiwallon is no better, and when I point out that from Eastertide to the summer is only a matter of weeks he grins mischievously like a youth wooing a maiden.

'What do you want *me* to do?' he asks, round-eyed, and Eadric sucks in his cheeks, scratching his beard.

'There is a lot to be said for the way they fight', Osgod says under his breath, 'We merely add new skills to what they know already'.

'Aye, we have to let them fight in their own sweet way', Harding agrees, adding, 'after all, how *else* did Aelfgar make such great inroads into West Seaxe all those years ago? They led us on a merry jig around Hereford shire, my father would tell you'.

'Fire is the key', Bleddyn sinks his longsword into the still snow-covered earth. 'Winter is late leaving this year, even here. But come summer the strongholds that Earl Willelm and his young friend Ricard have built will go up like wicker men! Even if the wood is still damp, pitch will help it burn! Think on where you are, my friend Eadric'.

'He has something there', I agree, tapping on Eadric's broad shoulder.

'You are right, Ivar. I had thought about that, but you know how the teaching of war crafts runs in our kingdom. We must look to the Wealshmen like blocks of wooden pegs when we fight. King Willelm would otherwise not have won his fight against Harold', Eadric tells everyone, sheathes his sword, dusts his hands.

Before he can add anything I break in,

'King Harold lost at Caldbec Beorg because Duke Willelm had brought the fighting forward. Many of our Suth Seaxan fyrdmen were untried and hopelessly drawn by the Northmen seeming to withdraw, panic-stricken'.

'They *were at first*', Theodolf reminds me he was there too, 'when the Bretlanders first fled the hill!'

'You are right insofar as the Bretlanders *were* running, but Willelm saw how he might weaken our shieldwall. Otherwise, my friend, we could have held them there until dark, and there were men coming all the time through the woods from the Hoar Apple Tree'.

Stopping there before I make Theodolf look a liar I smile at him to let him know I mean no ill will. If we are to fight side-by-side again, I want him *with* me. Having seen him turn before, I would not want Eadric's hopes dashed by bad feelings arising between Theodolf and me when we should be cutting down Northmen.

Nevertheless Theodolf wants them to know he is right,

'It was also our lack of bowmen that let our king down'.

'There is that, too', I nod, raising a smile from an otherwise earnest young comrade. 'The Suth Seaxans neglected that much in their war-craft learning, to our cost'.

'And their crossbows did not help, either', Saeward puts in, not wanting to be left out. Hearing talk from Theorvard, Burhred and Theodolf and myself, and seeing how deadly they were at Hrofesceaster, Saeward rightly signals that the Northmen have a weapon the Wealsh will never have seen yet.

Bleddyn pricks up his ears and grasps Rhiwallon's right shoulder. He stares at me, taken aback at talk of crossbows and asks,

'*Crossbows* you say – what are *they?*'

'A crossbow is a bow with a shaft to lay a bolt along it, a sharpened iron rod. The bolt is loosed off by strong cord with a stronger throw than one of our war-bows because it has a thicker cord across a shorter arm. One of its drawbacks is that its reach is not as great as the Wealsh bow if it has to be loosed off uphill', I tell a rapt Bleddyn. 'The Northmen and their Flemish neighbours had to come closer uphill with their crossbows before they could make inroads on our shieldwall'.

'What is the *other* drawback?' Rhiwallon's eyes narrow, thinking I was holding back useful knowledge.

'The *other*', I look from Rhiwallon back to Bleddyn, and then to Eadric, 'is that the cord cannot be unhooked. If damp, the crossbow is useless as a weapon, even closer to'.

Bleddyn chews his upper lip, his eyes twinkle mischievously. With a chortle at my last answer he says out aloud for everyone to hear,

'Hopefully it will be wet but not raining when we attack their stronghold at Hereford. If it rains too much, we cannot set it on fire without first dipping our arrows in hot pitch!' He looks under his bushy eyebrows at Rhiwallon standing next to him, 'We do not want to set ourselves on fire, *eh*, brother?'

To gales of laughter Eirik asks,

'If we set ourselves on fire, might we make a rush at their gates and burn them down?'

'*Be my guest*, Bryn', Rhiwallon claps his hands at the last man's ready wit, 'as long as your wife does not coming chasing after me for blood money!'

'You should fear her chasing you *to be* her husband. Have you *seen* his wife?' Bleddyn guffaws

Saeward cannot help himself. Spluttering with laughter, he nurses his stomach and begs me to slap his back.

Theodolf smiles coolly and winks at me before telling Saeward,

'What are you laughing about, Saeward have you seen the looks she gives *you* when you are near her?'

'I would *gladly* set myself on fire to be rid of her', Bryn hoots. As we make our way to the hall for our main meal Bleddyn cackles on, 'Your young friend shows a ready wit, Dane. I should like him to stay longer with us here at Rhosgoch – after we have dealt that Earl Willelm a bloody nose'.

Theodolf gives me a sideways glance, telling Bryn,

'I should *like* to stay longer'.

'You can stay as long as you wish, Theodolf. You are your own man', I rest a hand on his shoulder. As an afterthought I ask, 'What would you like me to tell Gerda?'

'Tell *her* nothing!' he snaps, then seeming to undergo deep thought he yields. 'No, tell her I will be back to take her on to Aethel's home. Brihtwin will be happy ringed by the elves I grew up with'.

'Did I hear this right, you grew up with *elves*?' Rhiwallon plays with his beard, staring at Theodolf and at me, unsure whether his ears are playing tricks on him.

'He is touched surely', Bleddyn quietly taps his own forehead. 'Touched, and a wit – *and damned good with a bow!* It matters not to me if he sees fairies *or* elves, as long as he teaches my men his tricks! You Aenglish are *odd*, do you know? This is new to me'.

Theodolf is abashed. He had not meant to be overheard, but talk carries far on this crisp mountain air. He falls silent.

'Oh, *what does it matter?*' Rhiwallon walks beside my young friend and leans toward him on our way through the open door. 'I used to see all manner of weird things at your age, Theodolf. Even Bleddyn thought me worthy of his wit'.

A fire roars in the hearth and the smell of food lingers as the kitchen door is opened to let the maids see we are back. Platters of meat are brought to us as we seat ourselves. Shouts for ale echo in the hall as laughter and boastful talk drown out all other talk. We will rest happy this night, our bellies full with ale, meat and food from the fields.

17

Saeward's snoring wakes me in the dead of night and I turn in my bed, pull the head bolster over my ears and try to find my way back to sleep, dreaming of elves, Aethel and...

'If you turn your back on me, perhaps I should seek out Rhiwallon?' Braenda chides, pursing her lips.

I turn hastily. She stands naked, outlined against the dancing light of a sputtering candle.

'*Braenda* -' I begin.

'Who but', she smiles as she caresses my chin. 'You should have your beard trimmed. My skin will be red raw in the morning!'

'You mean to stay that long?' I ask, drawing her to me.

'*Shh* – perhaps, if you pull off your *own* breeks instead of waiting for me to do it for you', she smilingly tells me. 'Better not awaken Saeward or there will be hell to pay!'

'We cannot let ourselves be carried away', I plant a kiss on her neck and she presses against me.

'Do that *again!*' she whispers, and I willingly do as I am bidden. She hisses into my ear, 'Scruffy fellow that you are, you still bring me out in goose pimples when you do that to me!'

As quietly as we can, for fear of waking Saeward, we couple again and again until we can no more. On our backs, close together on a cot bed that is only a little wider than I am, my right arm cradling her head, I begin to unfold my feelings for her.

'*Hush!*' Braenda tells me under her breath, nibbles and kisses my ear and falls asleep.

She is gone again by first light. I fleetingly recall being kissed softly on the mouth, although I could not swear to it. Sleep still had me in its grip and I awoke thinking of her coming to me like that, in the way of folk from the world of shadows – *and elves.*

Saeward snorts like a hog, waking suddenly,

'Did you have your woman with you?' he asks.

'Why do you ask?' I answer. How would he *know* that?

'There is a smell of lavender on the air', he smiles wistfully, pushes his blanket back and stands, his manhood hanging stiffly. '*God*, what is happening to me?'

'That is unlike you', I laugh. 'Pull your breeks on and have a cold wash!'

'That might make it worse!' he hurriedly pulls on his breeks and makes his way outside, into the yard.

There is a shriek outside and the clatter of wooden soles as one of the young women hastens back across the yard to the kitchens. A roar of laughter follows from the guards, and as suddenly as it happened a hush comes over us all again.

There will be a buzz around the stronghold today. Light hearted banter will lead as ever to soul searching, I feel it in my bones. Saeward will bury his head in his hands for shame and thoughts will turn as surely as men's thoughts do to women. What was he doing that frightened the maid?

'*Fool*, his breeks split when he bent to splash his body with cold water!' Eadric tells me, laughing, spooning his porridge.

'Luckily Ifor is the same build as he, but his breeks will be a little baggier around there'. The thegn points to Saeward's front. Saeward reddens deeply at the thought of his tackle being seen by the young women, and even more because Ifor's breeks were meant for a stallion of a man. That will raise more banter and make the East Seaxan's life even harder to bear for days.

'We shall spend all day teaching Bleddyn's men how to fight men on horseback. By the time we are done, it will not matter about how big your manhood is', I thump my fist down on the table to stop myself from bursting into laughter.

'I know a fellow who was very small down there, but he had the women lining up outside his bed closet', Eirik breaks bread to dunk in his broth and winks at Saeward.

'*You* might believe that –'I begin, only to be stopped by a rider stamping along behind us on his way to Rhiwallon's table.

'*My Lord Rhiwallon*, I have word from Ewyas!'

'*Tell*, friend!' the Wealsh aetheling answers, and washes down his food with a mouthful of ale.

'The Northman earl fitzOsbern has been seen with hundreds of men riding our way!' the rider bawls even though he is only feet away from the man he has been sent to pass on a scout's words. 'He has been seen on the road to Clyro!'

'Not so loud, friend I can *hear* you', Rhiwallon signals with his hands for him to lower his tone.

'I have finished, my Lord', he is told.

'Go, eat then and ride back with word from me that I will send men to watch what is happening up there', Bleddyn sends the rider away and enters into a heated row with his kinsman, none of which we can hear from where we are until Bleddyn shouts, 'Have it your own way then! Why you need me here I just do not know!'

He strides from Rhiwallon's side toward the door without looking back at his brother, followed by the jibe,

'Why I need *you* here is something you have never rightly let me know! Eadric take a score of our men to Hay and see what all the fuss is about. Take Ivar and his friends. Do you wish to go with them, Osgod?'

'Aye, my Lord, I will take Harding with me', Osgod rises.

Although he has hardly sat down to eat, he wants to be seen as eager. If we are thrown out of King Willelm's realm, we could come here as Rhiwallon's men. Sooner than leave these islands for somewhere overseas, I think many a man here could see himself looking into his homeland from the outside. Having once already seen the east and Miklagard, I may yet be watching Robert *Guiscard's* Northmen from the emperor's ranks.

'Think only of *watching* the Northmen', Rhiwallon tells Eadric. 'Do not draw them, even if they set foot on Cymru's soil. Should they ride on toward Rhosgoch, send a rider and stay back on the western bank of the River Wye. Is that understood?'

'I understand, my Lord. We must lull them into thinking that there is nothing here worth worrying about. When the time comes, *we will fall on them as hawks on lambs!*'

'Indeed, *well put* my friend! I look forward to hearing from you that Earl Willelm has ridden back to Hereford', Rhiwallon raises his ale cup, slurps a mouthful and looks up with froth on his beard.

Pennons flutter wildly in a stiffening breeze as Earl Willelm's men hold their double file over the bridge out of Hay. Over the river and up the first hill, FitzOsbern and Ricard fitzScrob cut a dash in their hauberks and finery, side by side at the head of at least two score riders.

No others can be seen, whichever way I look.

The earls may be trying to lure us into the open. A trap *may* have been set for us. Should we show ourselves, there would be other mounted men waiting, hidden by the tree line ahead of their masters. The two earls with their escort would be whooping, thrilled when they saw what fish they had caught in their net! A signal from fitzOsbern's scouts would be enough to bring them down on us from behind.

Nevertheless we have been told to keep them in sight, and no more than that. They may not know we are here, but no doubt they have scouts who fanned out from the main body of men. These scouts will have seen what Rhiwallon wanted them to see. There are men below us in the deep dale, who were told to build a fire and keep it burning until word reached them to douse it. Rhiwallon's bid to draw the Northmen seems to have worked.

'We are being watched', Theodolf lets me know without looking my way. 'Shall I see him off?'

'Do you mean to frighten him away, or kill him?' I ask, watching the Northmen below us as they come to a halt.

'If we frighten him away he comes back with more', Eirik notes. So much is plain. The man must be killed.

'Can you get to him without him seeing that you know he is there?' Eadric asks Theodolf.

'Aye, my Lord', Theodolf is distracted by Saeward who is himself making a show of watching the Northmen below. He has something aforethought, I would guess, when he asks Eadric,

'If Saeward and Thegn Harding ride up between Ivar and me, they can hide my leaving', Theodolf tells Eadric and pats the bow resting on the front of his saddle.

'Thegn Harding, Saeward, come forward toward Ivar so that Theodolf can duck away through the trees –', Eadric looks over one shoulder at him.

Theodolf has dismounted by the time the Hereford thegn turns back to him. He strides through the bushes behind us to go around the Northman scout, leaving him watching us as if nothing untoward were happening.

He is still blissfully unaware of his wyrd when the arrow hisses through the air to catch him full in the gullet. He lets go the reins and slides silently from the saddle on the other side of his mount. Willelm fitzOsbern has lost one pair of eyes. Where the others are will soon be made known to us. Osgod closes on us, putting himself between Harding and me, and asks me the whereabouts of Theodolf.

'Did someone say something about me? My ears were burning'.

My young friend comes out of the bushes, shoves the bow back into his saddle pack and winks at me, as an older man would to the younger. It is much like the one he first gave me when he told about Braenda having been at Aethel's steading. I had wondered aloud about whether I had shared my cot bed with a woman, and he calmly told about seeing the woman I later learned to be Braenda.

Is she here now, guiding Theodolf, looking after me again? Now is not the time to think about Aethel's steading. Eadric stretches an arm into the air and we are on our way at last. Earl Willelm must have been told of the camp with its brightly burning fire. He will be making his way there and we follow on, watching out for his 'eyes'. Before he reaches the camp Rhiwallon's men will have gone, either drawing him deeper or warning against coming further into his lands.

We could follow him all day should we need to, or he may see that his is a fool's errand and he will tell his men to double back. Better to look the fool than to lose men!

After a whole day of riding, shadowing the Northmen through the wilderness around Clyro, Earl Willelm leads us back to Hay and Hereford shire. To some it may have been a wasted day, but it was worth knowing he chose watchfulness over bluster. To know your foe is half the fight won.

'It makes the ale taste sweeter when you have seen your lord and master tire his men and mounts for no gain', Eadric laughs and downs his cupful with one swallow when we are finally seated again in Rhosgoch's hall in the evening.

'His friend, Ricard fitzScrob will not be as forbearing toward his overlord after being led on a wild goose chase. He will have wanted to see fighting, no doubt even have our homes burning to draw our warriors from hiding', Bleddyn knows the young fellow well, 'so that his men could ride us down as they did yours'.

He is looking at Eadric now, but he means me – us, those who outlived Harold. The Wealsh aethelings have learned the fate my kinsman, his brothers and fighting men met with. They may not have learned of what happened at Suthgeweorce, but they do not wish to suffer the fate Gruffyd's men dealt him to be rid of Harold.

These men of the hills like to see some sort of gain for their troubles, as they did when they raided with Aelfgar and Gruffyd. A drawn-out war with the Northmen would not suit their ways. Their manner of fighting is much like that of our northern Norse neighbours, who like to stalk their prey and withdraw when they have what they want. Harald Sigurdsson's drive to take Deira was too drawn-out for their liking, and they came off worse against men who spent weeks getting ready for just such a call on their well-honed skills.

Good leadership, and good luck, are needed to bring the best out of your men. That Morkere and Eadwin could not withstand the Norse king at Gata Fulford merely showed up their lack of years in the field, not to their men being less able than their attackers.

Rhiwallon and Bleddyn will have to talk their men into seeing our fight with the Northmen as theirs, because if the Aenglish fail to throw back King Willelm he would see their lands as fit to be overrun next.

'You will not be ridden down as long as you do what you have always done. Strike while the iron is hot, vanish into the hills where they dare not follow you', Eadric assures Bleddyn.

Rhiwallon agrees, jerking his head up and down fit for it to roll off his shoulders,

'Brother we must stay together', he reaches to Bleddyn and grips one shoulder tightly. 'We fight the Northmen our own way or we will be downtrodden in the way their Northman king would wish to trample over our rights. The Aenglish must learn new ways of fighting from us, Bleddyn. Let us show this Earl Willelm we must be reckoned with! It is a shame the Bretlander lord Alan Fergant has thrown in his lot with your foe, Eadric. He would have much more in common with us'.

Bleddyn nods grudgingly, swallowing a draught of mead.

'For now we wait for the summer sun to dry the timbers of their strongholds and stockades'. He finishes his mead before adding, 'Burn them out of the border lands and show them what fate awaits them should they look to Cymru to stretch their carrion wings'.

Knives and fists are thumped on the table to show all are as one in the hall.

'We are not always as friendly as this toward our Aenglish guests when they show on our doorsteps, but for once their foes are likely to be ours before too long. Drive the Northman king from these islands and let us fight one another the way we always have before!' Rhiwallon laughs and raises his cup to us.

'*Hear, hear!*' Eadric stands and answers the toast, 'Never a truer word has been spoken! I look forward to the day when we can lock horns in our usual friendly, neighbourly manner without outsiders stumbling into our paths!'

'Who said anything about being *friendly?*' Bleddyn grins hugely and grapples Eadric in a bear hug. 'Only joking, Eadric, *although... to be honest –*'

Laughter fills the hall when Bleddyn roars with glee at his own wit. He is well-loved by his men. Rhiwallon is less forthcoming in sharing the spoils of raiding with his men, but he is younger and will learn in time.

'Are we ready, my friends?' Bleddyn asks one morning soon after we have risen.

At last the time has come for driving out our foe. Early summer rains have dampened the earth enough to warrant the use of pitch after all. The good side, as I told the Wealsh aethelings some time since, is that the bolts from their crossbows will drop short when they try to drill our men from the stronghold walls.

'We are ready!' Eadric, Harding, Osgod, Eirik and I chorus. Hundreds of spears, swords, bows and axes are raised heavenward in acknowledgement and a roar tells the Wealsh aetheling what he has wanted to hear all winter and fore-year. More men have flocked to his standards in the last weeks than we could have hoped for.

Rhiwallon smiles wearily. He has been feasting all night, bragging about the numbers of Willelm fitzOsbern's underlings he will send to their makers. Now he looks hung over, as though he would sooner his brother sent him back to his bed. Bleddyn has other things he has to think on, but he winks at Eadric to show he has seen how much worse for wear Rhiwallon is this morning after drinking half a vat of mead on his own.

'At least he had Bronwen last night', Eadric tells me.

Rhiwallon has been chasing a young serving woman since Yuletide and she has at last weakened. Having shared some of his mead each time she passed on her way back to the kitchen last night, she would be as drunk as he. If the good folk of Rhosgoch see a copper-haired child next year tottering about in the yard, testing his young legs next year, they will know who his father is. Morwenna will not be happy. She is his woman, thought barren by some but she has offspring elsewhere. That is as much as he is willing to let us know.

'See – down there', Eadric points through the trees. We have been riding for some hours along boulder-strewn tracks. Thankful for the likelihood of a short halt I keenly try to follow his finger, only to be baffled by a thick screen of trees. We have been riding for some hours and come to a halt near the crest of a hill on the way to Hereford.

Rhiwallon enlightens me,

'The tower you can see between the stunted oaks on your left is what Willelm fitzOsbern thinks will stop us reaching Hereford'.

He sniffs and grins happily, telling those of us who will listen,

'He has pulled down Harold's hunting lodge and built a garth with a tall tower to watch the land around'. He sniffs again and guffaws.

'Whoever is in there will see everything to the east, but on this side his men have forgotten to chop down the tree screen. The fools will be hauled across the coals if they are ever taken to task by their lord! We will make our way around them behind these trees'.

Many of Rhiwallon's men have bypassed Ewyas, using mountain roads we followed westward in the winter, together with Bleddyn and his men. With us are Eadric's and Osgod's men, and perhaps a hundred of Rhiwallon's.

Saeward is fearful for Theodolf, worried his wounds will open up again when he begins to rain arrows on the Northmen. My young friend has sworn – to ease Saeward's fears – that he will merely oversee the bowmen he has helped teach their craft. We know him better. He will want to show off his skills to our Wealsh friends and Saeward will be unable to stop him. It could be Theodolf's undoing, but we cannot live his life for him.

His wyrd will show itself soon, whatever has been cast for him.

Some of the men are on foot behind us and we rein in from time to time, waiting on our way east downhill even though they are loping two abreast between the last horsemen. If any of Earl Willelm's scouts came upon us when we pass Ewyas, they would be unseen, shielded by the horsemen. Should we be parted after burning the Northmen's stronghold at Hereford, they have been told by Bleddyn to find their way uphill back to Rhosgoch by another, hidden track.

We have to follow the lie of the land in the lower hills, taking care to use woodland where we can, hoping Rhiwallon's scouts find the Northmen before they can take word to their lord. Eadric has taken care to set outriders on our flanks. Told not to show themselves if they see any of Earl Willelm's scouts, they are to warn us. Few of us have mounts that could outrun theirs. The less the earls know about what is heading for them, the more likely we are to wreak heavy losses on them. We would be given no quarter if they heard of our coming. Their huge catapults would be brought about to bear, throwing rocks over the walls at us, their mounted men with their long lances would cut us down and their bowmen are likely to be armed with crossbows. There is little leeway for error!

No words are spoken. All that can be heard is the steady dull thump of hooves on the rain-softened earth under us.

When we are on our way back for our feast there will be time for laughing and chattering, so we have been told. Talk is never high in your thoughts when you are on your way to a fight. You must always be ready for *wyrd* to draw a line under your life. There is something sobering about that thought that will haunt you, even when you have a cup of ale in your hand to mark winning and living another day.

'*Wait!*' Rhiwallon rasps, stretching a hand sideways, palm downward.

Soundlessly we halt and wait. The men on foot stop between us, looking up at their lord for a sign to pass onward. Someone below us is talking. There are Bretlanders with these Northmen and Rhiwallon is eavesdropping on them!

He grins, but stays silent and presses a finger to his mouth when someone at his side makes to say something. Before long the Bretlander scouts click their tongues and we hear the hooves of bigger horses than ours hitting stones in the road. When he is sure they have gone far enough, he tells me with a smile that they were grumbling about their pay – *or lack of it!*

'We will have fun with these Bretlanders of the earl's. If we can outsmart them, send them riding the wrong way they will never be back at Hereford in time to warn him', Rhiwallon cheers me.

Having told me this, he beckons some of his men to him and gives them their marching orders in his own tongue. When they leave he turns back to me and winks. Something is afoot.

'Earl Willelm's Bretlanders speak a tongue like ours. What I have told my men is that they should try to tell them that we are on our way to Scrobbesbyrig. That is where Earl Ricard is. He will warn Willelm and we could be at Hereford burning the hides off the Northmen whilst their Celtic bees will be buzzing around fitzScrob's hive, thinking someone has done them a good turn!'

There is laughter when they are told the Bretlanders are being sent on a fool's errand.

'I think Alan Fergant has chosen the wrong friend in that Northman king of yours, so we will play with them for a while and send them scurrying in search of shadows!' Rhiwallon tells us. He spurs his horse and we set off behind him to Hereford, making sure the Celts have left first with tidings for Earl Willelm.

Keeping the earl's scouts in sight we ride within the tree-line, but the Bretlanders are soon gone into the next dale as Rhiwallon's warriors struggle to keep in step with our trotting mounts.

'It is enough to know we will come upon Hereford with many fewer guards in their stronghold than there should be', Eadric laughs when Rhiwallon tells him what is afoot.

He looks at me with a mischievous glint in his eye,

'You said something about your kinsmen coming in the fore-year, Ivar. You meant this one coming?'

The matter had slipped from my thoughts since we came here late in the winter. I need time to think of an answer.

'They may have found other things to do', Rhiwallon winks at Eadric', 'I should think'.

'There are some good-looking women where they are?' Eirik asks me, tongue-in-cheek.

'Godwin has lands in Sumorsaetan', I begin an answer as one of Bleddyn's scouts shows to our left. He is shown to Rhiwallon and tells him in his own tongue whatever words he has been told him to pass on.

Rhiwallon beckons me closer. Plainly he thinks I should hear from him first, before he lets others know what it is Bleddyn has let him know,

'My brother has seen Aenglishmen closing on the Northmen from the east. They seem well armed and look ready for a fight'.

'How far away are they?' I ask. 'Who are they?'

'He has never set eyes on their leader. His warriors are strung out too thinly to be of use to him'.

Rhiwallon leaves the worst to the last,

'They seem unaware of the Northmen *behind*'.

'Who are these fools who leave themselves open to a flank attack?' Eadric snorts and nudges my elbow. '*God no*, they are not your kinsmen, *surely! Who* has been teaching them?'

'Is there a way of reaching them before the Northmen close on them?' I ask him, and on looking on beyond him see that Harding is trying to catch my eye, pointing downward through the screen of trees below us. He has seen something.

'Who *is* this, do *you* know?' Rhiwallon asks me again, annoyed at more Aenglishmen hamstringing him and his brother before they can fulfil their aims.

All I can see are shapes among the trunks, leafy branches on the trees. I have to shake my head but keep looking lest I see someone or something I should know. The shapes seem to be heading toward the rearmost Northmen behind Earl Willelm.

'I think there are men trying to outflank the foe', I counsel.

'Whose men *are* they? Surely they would not attack before they know who it is they are preying on', Rhiwallon is hoarse, taken aback by an ally's carelessness.

Turning Braenda I offer to warn my kinsmen.

A track leads downhill to where I saw the shapes, and I feel I should draw Godwin away from a pitched fight with the Northmen,

'I should ride and warn them not to tangle with the Northmen'.

Unable to stop me, Eadric warns,

'You would need to be swift! They could lock horns with Earl Willelm's scouts before they meet the earl's men. We do not want the earl forewarned of something untoward happening in this part of the shire'.

'Fear not, my horse is fleet of foot, a good hillside mount', I assure them.

Rhiwallon nods, staring ahead, and waves me on,

'I know - *ride her well!*'

Bidden farewell, I press Braenda downhill to catch up with whoever is down there, who threatens to upset the Wealsh aethelings. The track is uneven, strewn with boulders, and even when I reach even ground I have some way to catch up with Godwin.

I see the backs of men through the trees on the floor of the dale, but they could just as well be Willelm's men as the unknown Aenglishmen I have come to warn off attacking them. Should I skirt through the scrub and tall bushes I should come alongside them.

'Who have we here, trying to creep up on us?' I hear someone call out, cackling.

'Magnus laughs,

'Where did *you* come from, kinsman?'

'*Hush*, you will give us all away!' Eadmund cannot see me but looks ahead, to see where the earl's men are.

'Aye, *quiet* there!' I rasp, trying to calm Magnus. Just then Eadmund turns and gapes at me.

'*You*, how did you come here?' he rasps. Magnus stares at me, unable to fathom what I am doing there, with them.

'Where is Godwin?' I ask, unaware whether or not they know of their brother's whereabouts. 'I must find him and tell him to hold back!'

'Hold *back – why?* I thought we were here to take on Willelm fitzOsbern', Eadmund shakes his head at me, unwilling to do as I bid.

I have to tell him,

'Rhiwallon and Eadric are behind you, up on the hillside, watching the Northmen ride eastward to Scrobbesbyrig. Thegn Eadric and his Wealsh friends are making ready first to burn down Willelm's wooden stronghold at Hereford, before going on to attack elsewhere.

'As far as I know, Godwin is on from their left flank', Eadmund smiles, while Magnus sits gaping childishly at me.

'Shut your mouth, Magnus. You will catch flies!' Eadmund berates his younger brother with a laugh.

'I am still taken aback that you are here with us', the gaping Magnus smiles lazily and reaches out his right hand. 'Welcome again amongst us'.

'Aye, welcome', Eadmund is about to reach out his hand when a rider breaks in.

'My Lord Eadmund, your brother asks that you close in to your left!'

'Tell him *no*', I answer the rider for Eadmund. 'Thegn Eadric and the Wealsh aetheling Rhiwallon are watching from the hilltop. They wish to allow the Northmen east to Scrobbesbyrig whilst we go on to Hereford and fire their stronghold'.

The rider stares uneasily at me, looks to Eadmund, who nods his blessing, and turns his horse to gallop away again.

'Tell my brother Ivar sends his greetings', Eadmund calls after him.

The fellow spurs his horse on into the woodland he came from and vanishes between the trees.

Eadmund enlightens me as to why the rider would not take my word,

'Aeldwulf has not long been with us, you understand. Your name has not been foremost amongst us since you left. Father Cutha would not hear it, saying you were best forgotten with your heathen ways!'

He and Magnus share a wry smile. Eadmund becoming earnest again, asks,

'What do we do, if we are not to attack them?'

'Wait. Rhiwallon will send a rider to ask whether I found you. He will pass on word from me that I have', I can say no more.

'We just *wait?*' Magnus gapes and throws his hands up, looking heavenward, cursing Eadric for holding him back from ridding the kingdom of a few Northmen.

'We let them through before coming together under the banners of Bleddyn and Rhiwallon', I tell him again.

'Everything has been thought out already. Are we merely *tools* for the Wealsh aethelings?' Magnus sounds put out that the bloodletting will not go ahead.

'What had Godwin aforethought for when you were done here?' I ask Eadmund.

The brothers must have talked through what they meant to do once Hereford had fallen. By the shrug and the dull stare he gives me, Godwin has not looked that far ahead.

'He has land in the west, in Sumorsaete', Magnus offers, 'and he may have thought of riding on from here after we have dealt Earl Willelm a bloody nose'.

'What would he do there?' I ask again, unsure that would be of any use, aside from looking in on his thegns. He may be best counselled to steer clear of his holdings if the thegns have given their oath to our new king to uphold his laws.

'I would say he wishes to speak to his thegns, to raise men for the struggle against the Northmen', Eadmund bears out my own thoughts.

'He has had word from Thegn Gudmund near Glastunbyrig that Eadnoth the stallari, shire reeve of Sumorsaete has been joined by a Bretlander earl, Brian. He swears to put down any uprising by Seaxans loyal to father', Eadmund adds, 'a threat to be taken in earnest'.

'Our winning at Hereford may bring a change of heart', I try to cheer him.

'I hope you are right, Ivar. Word will reach them in Sumorsaete that our strength will be something to be reckoned with', Magnus nods slowly and looks up when Godwin's rider shows again.

'My Lord Godwin wishes you to know he will send word to Eadric through your kinsman, Ivar. He will bring our number to him without attacking Earl Willelm's men', the rider catches his breath. 'He offers to meet the Wealsh aethelings and Thegn Eadric on the road to Hereford'.

'Very well, thank you', Eadmund sends the rider away. 'You heard, Ivar? We will meet again soon'.

My climb to the hilltop is harder than coming down. Braenda picks her way carefully, but more than once I have to leave the track to make any headway. Only when I hear Rhiwallon arguing with Eadric do I know I am close.

An arrow thuds into the back of my saddle. Has one of Earl Willelm's scouts been following me? Thankfully his aim was too short and Braenda can climb a short way further before he has another arrow ready. She has just scrambled around a last rocky outcrop to set foot on the hilltop when a second arrow whistles past my right ear and lands harmlessly before the front hooves of Eadric's mount.

'Ivar is back - *with a friend!*' Eadric tells Rhiwallon. 'When we know his friend, we can give him a fitting welcome'.

A few of the Wealshmen fan out over the hilltop with Theodolf, who dismounts and strides with his bow to the rim of the hill.

I draw level with him on my way to join Eadric. He steps back as another arrow narrowly misses Rhiwallon and embeds itself harmlessly in the earth beside one of the aetheling's horsemen. Once Rhiwallon has calmed his frightened mount he calls out something to his men, bringing a score of them to his side as Theodolf takes the others downhill with him to outflank and hunt down our unknown guest.

Using the trees and undergrowth they make their way on foot, running low, ducking behind bushes and hiding behind fallen tree trunks. Not knowing where they will find their prey, they broaden their line as they press forward.

One of the Wealshmen treads on a dry branch, drawing another arrow from the bowman that skewers his right shoulder. He shouts a warning to his friends and takes cover behind one of the trees, pressing himself for safety against the trunk. Theodolf spins around, finds he was about to be knifed by Willelm fitzOsbern's scout, thrusts out his left forearm and sends the fellow flying backward.

We have all been watching, taken aback by the speed at which our foe was dealt with. Rhiwallon is first to come to his senses and beckons his men to him, with the abashed scout shambling uphill between them. When they near him he dismounts to stand eye to eye with the outlander.

'What are you doing here?' Rhiwallon asks.

He asks again, quickly seizing the fellow's jaw, pressing his cheeks together with one hand to make him aware that he wishes an answer. We hear the man mumble something and Rhiwallon takes his hand away. He speaks slowly in his own tongue and they talk for some time. Eadric coughs to let the aetheling know we are waiting. Rhiwallon nods to let him know he has heard, but carries on talking.

'Would you believe, my friend?' Rhiwallon looks up at Eadric and says again, 'Would you believe I have been told everything I need to know from this Bretlander about the earls' aims? It seems they *were* heading for Scrobbesbyrig, but that Willelm had second thoughts'.

The aetheling gives the now fearful, hapless scout a dark look, to ensure he *has* been given the knowledge he seeks, and goes on,

'He has sent men back to warn the castellan at Hereford that the hills are alive with his foes and to keep a keen look-out. We have been warned. As we are unlikely to hear anything better, this fellow has outlived his usefulness', Rhiwallon casts a fleeting look sideways. The Bretlander gives him a look that shows he is unaware of what is being said. 'Put him back on his horse, take him back downhill a short way, make as if to talk to him and put a knife through his ribs'.

Eadric leans over to one of his mounted Seaxans and asks,

'*Will* you do that for me, Gudmund?'

The man dismounts from his shaggy-coated grey pony and towers over Eadric. As tall as the thegn is, he is still half a head shorter than Gudmund.

'Aye, Lord, *gladly*', Gudmund nods and strides toward the Bretlander, beckoning to him. The man looks up at Rhiwallon, who has mounted again.

'Where is his horse?' Gudmund asks, shrugging. He doffs his battered old helm to the Wealshman, showing a shock of short corn-sheaf hair.

Rhiwallon asks the Celt, nods gravely and smiles.

'He says he hobbled his mount somewhere lower down on the hillside when he saw Ivar. He plainly did not know he would have to walk all that way back again. Very well, walk him back downhill. You will know best what to do'. The aetheling winks knowingly at the Seaxan, ensuring that Bretlander does not see him.

Gudmund puts an arm around the Bretlander's shoulders and, smiling down at the young fellow, leads him to the hillside track. He looks much like the stocky Celt's older brother, or even his father.

'Come, friend, let us find your mount'.

On their way, Gudmund talks to keep the fellow calm, one wit calls out after him,

'Tell him about the soggy oatcakes your wife makes'.

'I am telling him how good your woman is in bed', Gudmund shouts back without turning, raising laughter from everyone. Even the Bretlander laughs.

'Plainly he *understands* what has been said', Rhiwallon notes once the pair are out of sight.

Eadric takes the hint, nods briefly and turns to me. The look he gives me needs no words. I dismount and follow in the footsteps of Gudmund and his new-found friend, striding firmly. As they are no longer in sight, having turned a bend in the track, I hurry to catch them before Gudmund is knifed. However, before I have gone too far Gudmund shows from the undergrowth on his way uphill.

'What are *you* doing here?' he asks, brushing past me, picking his way over loose stones. Looking back at me over one shoulder he asks with a hollow laugh, 'Did Eadric send you to see me safe?'

'Not in so many words. He merely gave me a look that told me everything', I have to own up when I am abreast of him.

Gudmund grins and shakes his head,

'You read his *thoughts*, eh? So, what *other* wonders will you show us?'

He cackles drily, turns and begins to climb again, telling me as he strides on upward back to join Eadric,

'Your time with the spay wife has not been wasted! I had best look to my laurels before Eadric trades me for you!' He is still laughing when we draw level with Eadric.

'What is so funny?' the thegn raises an eyebrow when we reach him at the head of the root-crossed track.

'You are, for sending the old man here to help me with that wretch! When I need a whet nurse, Eadric, think on this. I shall be well past riding with you', Gudmund mounts, laughing hoarsely.

'That old man has sent more Northmen to their maker than you are likely to see', Saeward breaks in on my behalf.

Gudmund stares at him in disbelief, not knowing whether or not to laugh. He laughs out aloud at Saeward's outburst, and is still laughing when Rhiwallon waves us on to Hereford. He will learn.

18

Spread out ahead of us on the north bank of the Wye is the burh of Hereford, with the river bending toward us as it snakes past the burh.

'That tower, up there on the hill is what they call a keep', Eadric tells us. Bleddyn and Rhiwallon nod wisely, not caring about what the Northmen call the parts of their stronghold.

'It is a lot like the one Odo had built at Hrofesceaster', I add, letting them know I have tackled the Northmen once before on their own ground.

'You know about how these strongholds are put together?' Rhiwallon asks.

'It seems to me he *does*', Bleddyn smirks. 'Having attacked one of the outlanders' strongholds, he will be of greater use to us. Do they build them in the same way everywhere?'

'They are as much alike as peas in a pod', I joke.

'All is well in God's green acre, then', Bleddyn beams and hands me a stick. He points to the damp earth at our feet and tells me, 'Show me'.

Before I begin I point the stick at the stronghold. Their eyes follow mine,

'There is a ditch, fed by river water around an outer wall, built long and wide around a hill. An inner wall follows the hill closely, with a tall tower – the keep, as Eadric says - on the hill itself. On the far side of the stronghold the ditch will be bridged'.

'Stables, a smithy and sheds to store food and weapons are ranged within the outer wall', I draw lines in the mud whilst they stand in a half-ring around me. 'Their rooves will be of turf or straw, the palisaded walls and bridge of timber covered in pitch. If your arrows are dipped into pitch there will be no stronghold!'

Rhiwallon straightens, folds his arms and purses his lips,

'This all sounds too easy. What about when we come close enough to loose off our blazing arrows'.

'Take *heart*, brother. There *will* be a way. There is *always* a way! How did you enter their stronghold in Centland, Ivar?' Bleddyn shakes the younger brother from his wretchedness with a thump on his wide back and grins at me, 'Pay no heed to him. He is young yet'.

'We were clothed as ceorls. Saeward wore a habit, a cross and rosary, like a priest, to say the last rites for our friends on the scaffold. Some of us with Oslac and his young friend Sigegar were outside the stronghold, with fire arrows. When Odo and his henchmen sat astride their mounts awaiting the hangings, one of us gave a signal and the arrows were loosed off'.

'What signal was this?' Rhiwallon presses.

Bleddyn scoffs, yet still looks askance at, listening,

'The wording Saeward used to give his blessing was the signal', I answer.

'It could be *no more* straightforward!' Bleddyn laughs and claps me on my back. 'Even *you* could have thought of that, brother!'

The younger aetheling answers with a scowl. Eadric picks up on how easy this all sounds,

'What would we use as a ruse? There is going to be no hanging, and Earl Willelm is at Scrobbesbyrig. *How* do we fool them into letting us in?'

'Theodolf', Saeward asks, 'you still have the war gear you took from the young Northman we stopped in the woods, I take it'.

'We need enough for seven, I think', I add, 'a young noble with six men, trailing men caught trying to steal on of their horses'.

'A young Bretlander noble may be within our reach', Bleddyn tells us, looking slyly at Rhiwallon.

Annoyed, Rhiwallon has to have a dig at his brother,

'A Bretlander noble would need to know the Frankish tongue, surely?'

'I *know* that not all Bretlanders – not even all their nobles – know the Frankish tongue', Bleddyn snorts. 'By the time they grasp that something is wrong, it will be too late for them anyway. We can be in and out again, with their timbers burning, before any of them knows what is happening. Saeward, do you remember what you said for those poor folk on the scaffold?'

'*Whatever* I said would not be understood. By the time they knew what was happening it would be too late for them to withstand us anyway', Saeward answers.

His dry wit raises cackles from the Wealshmen. Shaking with mirth, Bleddyn claps him on the back,

'I wish that were true, Seaxan. As you must know, our Bretland guest gave himself away when he thought he was safe. Be that as it may, you are right insofar as most of them know little or nothing of your tongue. They know some of ours. You have given me food for thought. Earl Willelm may have taken all his Bretlanders with him. One of *our* men should clothe himself in the manner of a priest to give them the last rites in our tongue to a few of my men, hands bound, driven between horsemen into their stronghold. Your men have the gear, Ivar. You can be the Northmen who ride with us between you'.

Eadric, Osgod and Harding sit astride their mounts as if set in stone, looking – no, staring – at me as though I had suddenly become the outlander whose hauberk I still wore. Eirik stares too. Although alike in some ways to those our huscarls wear, the Northmen's hauberks are matchless in that they have a neck guard that can be fastened to lessen the likelihood of an arrow or glancing blow from a sword killing the wearer in the throat. More than that, whereas our sword belts hang loose at our waist, the Northman's hauberk covers his sword belt. A short slit in the hauberk's left side allows the wearer to sheath his sword through it.

Osgod's stare has turned to a smile now. He laughs and slaps his thigh, telling me,

'*You* look every inch the Northman, Ivar. Nevertheless we will be close behind when your *comrades* know you are not who they think you are'.

'Surely, when they see my axe they will know me for what I am', I utter my doubts, 'and Braenda looks nothing like one of their horses'.

'Those of the Northmen who fought against King Harold have been boasting of their new weapons', Bleddyn assures me. 'And they seem to have taken to your horses. They may be fleeter of foot than their own'.

Osgod adds for my sake, reminding me of the trophy hunting allowed by Willelm's nobles,

'Aye - and I would say they have strings of horses they captured from your huscarls' camp at the back of the hill'. He goes on to tell of the countless trophies he saw the Northmen bore when Eadwin, Morkere and the others of the Witan rode to Beorkhamstede to submit to Willelm, 'Some had stripped your men of their mailcoats and wore them because the links on their own had been torn'.

'*I* saw them', Theodolf needs no telling either.

314

Harding looks over his shoulder at my friend and nods slowly before speaking of his own pain,

'At the time Earl Tostig went with his brother Harold to see the Holy Father, I saw the Scots taken at Dunholm. They bore swords taken from my father and brother when they came down with King Maelcolm. My first thoughts were to slay them outright, but Gospatric talked me out of that. He said that the weapons would be taken from them – their own weapons, too – and they would be turned back onto the road north. Before they reached their own land, he told me, the men and women of the land would tear them limb from limb for the pain inflicted by the Scots' on *them*'.

'The settling of scores is my domain, sayeth the Lord', Saeward smirks. 'His ways are baffling, to say the least'.

Someone behind takes him to task,

'You say that as if you do not believe in the Lord'.

'Where was the Lord when our king was killed?' Saeward snaps back. 'This Northman king goes from strength to strength – he even goes home to Northmandige to show off his crown because he thinks his new-found kingdom is safe! Where are the Lord's wonders to be seen?'

'Perhaps not now, my son', an elderly priest presses his mount forward to speak to Saeward. 'Be forbearing, wait-'

'Wait until the Northmen have over-run the whole kingdom?' Saeward groans loudly as if the priest had slain him.

'Father Hywel', Bleddyn speaks up to gain the priest's ear. 'Father Hywel, the Seaxan has seen his homeland trampled underfoot by the Northmen. We should see that ours is not. *Pray* for our souls, but do not preach to the downtrodden-'

'We are not *downtrodden* in East Seaxe! Not yet, at least' Saeward forgets who he is talking to, but Bleddyn overlooks the man's outburst and merely laughs.

'Very well, you are not downtrodden. Fight the Northmen with us and show your skill with the axe!' Bleddyn claps his hands.

'We *have* our priest to fool the Northmen', Rhiwallon stares at Father Hywel. When he sees Father Hywel looking hurt back at him, the aetheling goes on, 'Meanwhile we must find the men who will walk between your horses. They ought to do this of their own free will'.

'They will be unarmed', Bleddyn looks over the heads of those around us, 'and as such could be killed as soon as Earl Willelm's men know they are ours'.

'The horsemen could carry their weapons and hand them down as soon as the fighting begins', I offer.

'Your thinking is sound. I like that', Bleddyn nods furiously and turns to Rhiwallon. 'What do *you* say?'

'It could well work', Rhiwallon's eyebrows rise and fall in the way of waves on the strand. 'Your men hide their bows, swords and axes until the Northmen are within reach around us, otherwise you will all be cut down'.

'*Remember*, they have Crossbows', Eirik warns the Wealsh aethelings. Harding behind him nods sagely.

'Aye, those dastardly crossbows would finish us all off unless their men were amongst us. Wait for their leaders to come close', Saeward nods slowly, staring into nothingness.

'If one of you were to catch one of their leaders, they might give up without a fight'. Saying this, Osgod looks at me. Rhiwallon takes it to mean I should do it.

'Would you do that, Ivar? It would save many lives, not that I am worried about spilling the Northmen's blood. That could never be further from my thoughts. My men look to me as their keeper'.

'I will do it', I answer, eyeing the Wealshman, 'but your men *will* have to shed their own blood before long. If the king offers you silver to stand by, what will you do when his men trample all over Wealas?'

'He will think all he has to do is dangle a full purse and we will melt away', Bleddyn sucks in the cold air.

'Will you deny my friendship for Thegn Eadric?' Rhiwallon gives a warning growl, telling me I have overstepped the mark.

'Would a Wealshman be willing to shed blood for his Aenglish neighbour if there is no real threat to himself?' I ask unblinkingly. 'You could melt away into your mountains and fall on them when they passed across the River Wye. We could be crushed and you would gain land by taking Willelm's pay, think about that'.

'*I* might yet think of doing that if you push me, Dane. What makes you so holy, when you could as easily leave with your kinsmen and sail home', Bleddyn rounds on me.

'I would not need to be asked twice', Rhiwallon adds and Eadric stares coldly at me. I have overstepped the mark with him, too.

'What do you think you are at?' Eadric scolds. 'I *know* these men. They would not take the Northman king's silver!'

'If you are so sure, then I will do as you ask', I turn back to Rhiwallon.

'You were testing me?' he snaps. 'I do not need testing, mark my words!'

'This Northman king will undermine our leadership if we so much as bend his way as the marram grass does in the Gower's strong winds.

316

For now I will make as if I did not hear you. Say it again to – or about – me, and we will hang you out to dry. We will then ask in the Erse kings across the water for help and your men will look elsewhere for leadership', Bleddyn scowls and then grins slyly, aware that I am smarting under that last threat. I can no more hope for my friends to follow me blindly into the fight when his own will be looking for reward before they so much as lift a bow. Rhiwallon signals for us to ready ourselves for this task.

'And where will *your* men be?' Harding looks to Eadric.

The West Seaxan thegn hisses through his teeth,

'Think on *this,* my friend. We have been thrown out of our homes, have *you?*'

I think Eadric too is touchy about what he thinks may be scorn. Harding forgets perhaps that should West Seaxe fall, Mierca and then Deira will soon follow. For my part, Rhiwallon is right insofar as I *could* flee these shores, should I wish to. What he cannot know is that there is nothing for me across the sea. I would be a mere underling to my own, younger half-brothers, should I wish to uproot myself at this time.

We press our mounts forward, down the hillside to gather out of sight in the woods across the river from the Northmen. There we will marshal the men who are to be our hostages, make ourselves look like the foe and await a signal from Bleddyn and Rhiwallon to tell us that they are ranked ready to storm them when we hold one of fitzOsbern's nobles safe in our hands.

The Wealshmen unwillingly hand over their weapons. Rhiwallon coaxes them into trusting us, hiding his own misgivings after our heated talk. Saeward hides a pair of short swords under his cloak. Theodolf does the same with a couple of axes, shoving another man's short sword beneath the straps of his saddle so that it is hidden even from our sight. I take two bows and arrow-bags and hold them against the back of the long shield I freed from one of the Northmen we slew in Centland. Ten men trudge unhappily between us, and three of Osgod's huscarls ride close behind Theodolf.

Before we ride on, Bleddyn asks me,

'Do you know the Frankish tongue, Ivar?' On seeing my blank stare he knows the worst and offers a way out, 'How would you even get through the first gate?'

He beckons one of his men forward, they talk together in their own tongue and Rhiwallon grips me by my arm. Looking into my eyes under the rim of the helm, he counsels,

'Owain knows enough to get by. One of your men should stay with us to let Owain ride in his stead and tell the gatemen to lower the outer bridge, after that the next gate'.

Rhiwallon and his man talk again before the aetheling asks Theodolf to give over his Northman war gear,

'I feel we may be taxing you if you are at the forefront of this fight'.

Theodolf pleads with his eyes. He would like me to talk Rhiwallon out of this, but yields when Bleddyn stares haughtily at him and murmurs so that no-one else can hear,

'The only heroes I know of are dead. You have years ahead of you, Aenglishman. Owain will make good use of your gear'.

Finally we are on our way, Rhiwallon's man at the head of our file, his fellows between the closely paired riders, jostled between the horses as captives would be. Theodolf watches us ride off, wretched. On one of the nearer towers men watch us close on the bridge that has not been raised since a number of ceorls passed through on their way out.

I feel their eyes burning into me. One of the Northmen calls down, to be answered by Rhiwallon's man.

'He asked why we are here', Owain tells me.

'Say we have hostages, sent by his lord', I tell him.

He answers the man in the watch tower and is told something he passes onto me as,

'He said pass friend, and be seen by the castellan'.

'So easily – do you think they know what we are about?' I ask.

'How *can* they? Keep riding, Dane. Will we not look more out of sorts if we stay here bickering?' He beckons to his men and we ride on, six riders in two lines with ten more on foot between us, their hands behind their backs as if bound.

The inner wall behind us, we ride up to what I think is a young noble, who asks something. The Wealshman stares, not knowing what has been said. This Northman speaks his tongue in such a way as our man cannot understand. Is he a Fleming?

One of Osgod's men laughs behind me and mumbles to his nearest comrade,

'Some help he is!' Just then the right-hand gate creaks open. The same fellow yells, 'Get *in* there!'

As the Northmen try frenziedly to pull the gate to, Saeward and I press forward. Our Wealshmen wrench the gate free of the Northmen's grip and break into a run through the opening.

They are followed closely by Osgod's men. With the din we make, our hopes of taking fitzOsbern's men unawares gone and the air is thick with arrows flying all ways.

318

Rhiwallon's Frankish-speaking underling peels away from our file and with his sword waving around his head tries to take on one of the crossbowmen. He is run through his shoulder by a spear thrown by another of the watch. We still have to gain the inner part of their stronghold and we are pinned down by Earl Willelm's bowmen from the walls both ahead and behind us. Before I have ridden far my shield looks like a hedgehog.

The earthworks are still fresh around the bottom of the wall ahead, the timber slightly green. Something tells me fire arrows will not help when Rhiwallon gives his men the order to loose them off. If the timber in the wall is not tarred, their fire arrows will not catch, even if they have been dipped in tar. Arrows rain down from beyond the walls, flaming but not tarred because as they hit the buildings around the outer wall they mostly go out. One does not.

'Get that arrow', I yell at one of Rhiwallon's men on foot, pointing behind him, 'and throw it into the thatch on that stable!'

The fellow turns to look, but before he can bend to it a crossbow bolt hits his shoulder. The next man sees what he was about to do and quickly catches hold of the still-burning arrow.

Ducking beneath one Northman's thrown spear and narrowly missing being skewered by a crossbow bolt, he tosses the flaming arrow upward so that it arcs onto the stable roof. He licks the burn from the flaming arrow along his arm and is brought down by one of the fire arrows. There is no fairness in the world, is there?

As the blaze spreads from the stable roof along the wall men try to flee the flames and belching smoke. Seeing a ladder that offers them a way down, I press Braenda forward and hew at the ladder as two of the Northmen come down together, falling screaming into the flames on the stable thatch. Rhiwallon and Bleddyn burst in through the now loosely-hanging gate where their men have hacked away the hinges to gain entry.

Eadric follows closely behind and shouts to his men. A shieldwall takes shape, behind which the Wealshmen shelter from the Northmen's crossbow bolts, arrows and spears.

'Will you join us, Ivar?' Eadric grins, as if asking me if I wish to share a drink.

Without answering, Saeward and I dismount, holding up our shields against the arrowstorm coming from the inner stronghold. More arrows dipped in pitch are lit and loosed off into their midst, but loosing off arrows upward is harder than it sounds. Arms soon ache, and mistakes can be made.

The Northmen and their Flemish friends learned how hard it was to loose off an arrowstorm uphill at us when we were on Caldbec Beorg. After loosing off a hail of arrows the Wealsh bowmen find the strain hard. Nonetheless fire has taken beyond the inner wall. The young nobles in the main tower atop the mound can only watch as their underlings foolishly try to douse the flames with the stable water, making smoke that swirls and chokes them.

As we push forward, uphill behind our shields at the inner wall their arrowhail lessens. Men behind us use the Northmen's arrows on them, so many there are now on and in the earth around us. Eadric's men hew at the thick binding on the timber wall, shielded from a deadly array of falling weaponry. I beckon Eirik and Saeward to follow me and, whilst Saeward holds up his shield for me I find a part of the wall where the ties are not as tight and begin to hew away at them with my axe.

When the ties look frayed and worn, we lean on the tall posts, pushing them inward, almost falling when they give way. A line of frightened-looking young men looks on as we leap over the posts. Some stand aghast, gaping. Others, their jaws set push forward at us with their spears, axes, longswords and whatever they have at hand, even hayforks.

Pity is short when we cut through the first line of men. The rest, untried youths and older men, cower behind them.

A sharp axe offers a quicker end, when followed through with enough strength to cut through the bone of the skull around the crown. Only the women are left, and the young nobles left by their earl to stop us.

'Do you understand Aenglish?' Eadric asks the first one, ready to strike with his sword. To the young fellow's nod he adds, 'We will let *one* of you live to take word to your earl, Willelm fitzOsbern. Say that his stronghold will be ashes when he finds the heart to show here again. How many of you are there here?'

'There are only three of us', the young Northman tells him, beckoning forward his two understandably unwilling comrades.

'Who among you is the youngest?' Eadric asks.

'I am', the young fellow he spoke to first tells him.

'It is you, then, who takes word to your earl. You know what to tell him?' The youth nods warily at Eadric. 'Go, then. What is your name?'

'I am Rodberht de Warenne'.

How many of that ilk *are* there, I wonder?

'Well Rodberht, understand this. If you bear arms against us again this is what will befall you', Eadric nods to an elderly, one-eyed fellow standing beside a comrade of Rodberht's.

With a nod Eadric's friend raises a two-handed axe to shoulder-height and, without looking again at Eadric, swings the axe around to shear off the Northman's head neatly at the neck. A high-pitched scream shatters my eardrums and a young woman hurtles forward to throw herself onto the dead man's crumpled body.

'Raulf – Raulf!' she sobs, again and again, her arms caressing the dead man's corpse.

The head has come to rest at Rodberht's feet. He staresdown at the dead man's wide-open eyes, pales and tries to hold back from throwing up, both hands over his mouth. But he retches on Eirik's boots, testing him sorely.

'Should your earl try to come to *our* land, Northman, the first noble we capture will be slain outright', Bleddyn stares into the youth's reddened eyes, 'like this'.

He beckons the other young man forward. When he sees a shake of the head from the Northman he nods and one of his men pushes the unlucky fellow forward. Bleddyn, standing head and shoulders over his victim hefts his long sword and brings it down quickly, cleaving the body from the right shoulder to the navel. At this young Rodberht faints after throwing up his latest meal.

'A pail of cold water should wake him', Rhiwallon laughs and strides away, leaving the task to someone else.

The sour smell of Rodberht's bile is blown toward me by a freshening breeze and the corpses are left where they fell. The woman still hugs the first man's corpse. The other had had a weatherproof cloth thrown over it. A pail of water is fetched and upended over the seemingly lifeless Rodberht.

'You *are* the lucky one today!' Eadric rests a hand on the young fellow's right shoulder when he tries to raise himself to his feet. 'Stay there until Lord Bleddyn has left. He may think again on it, and if he sees you hopping onto your horse he may forget he has granted you your life'.

Young Rodberht blenches and looks up at me.

'Fear not. I will not kill you – *not unless I am told to*', I assure him with a crooked grin.

'Aye youngster, unless he is *told* to', Saeward echoes my last words mockingly.

'Mind you that is not to say *I* will not kill you with an arrow', Theodolf has joined us, with Eirik close beside him.

'Aye, his father was killed by a Northman's arrow', Saeward rounds on Rodberht, making him cower. 'How *fast* can you ride, providing you can get to your horse alive?'

'Leave the lad alone!', Eadric shoves Rodberht away.

'Bleddyn has said he can live to take word to his master'.

'Where is your horse?' I ask, in answer to which he points shakily at the burning stable.

'You will have to run then, *all the way* to Scrobbesbyrig', I mock his fear.

'Give him a *horse!*' Eadric points at a horse in the middle of the outer field, the mount that belonged to the Wealshman Rhiwallon sent with us as a go-between to speak to the Northmen on the outer gate, 'What is wrong with you, Ivar? Give him *that* horse. For God's sake, he is a *noble!*'

'Should you have forgotten, my friend, we are fighting these Northmen to *rid* ourselves of them', Osgod berates Eadric light-heartedly.

'I know, Osgod', Eadric answers tiredly, wishing to keep Bleddyn's undertaking, but getting nowhere. When Harding begins to draw his longsword Eadric nods to me. 'If your friend kills the young fellow, then we will fail to put across the meaning of why we have defied them'.

'The best way of putting that across is by sending the earl this fellow's corpse', Rhiwallon puts his standpoint bluntly, staring at Rodberht.

Osgod almost kindly notes the youth's bravery,

'Give him his due, Rhiwallon. He has not batted an eyelid'.

'He would do *more* than bat an eyelid if he understood –'

'I *do* understand', Rodberht puts him straight, a thin smile on his youthful lips. 'I understand only too well, but what am I to do?'

'Pray', Saeward cackles. 'Pray *hard* and cross your fingers. Thegn Harding, Ivar, Theodolf and Rhiwallon wish you dead, Thegn Eadric wishes you to take word to your earl –'

'What do *you* wish?' the Northman stares straight at Saeward. Perhaps he has guessed Saeward's meaning because he looks down again, abashed.

Saeward cackles again, taps the side of his nose with his left forefinger and walks away again, wagging the finger in the air,

'I think you *know,* youngster'.

'Ealdberht, can you bring that horse here?' Eadric asks one of his own men.

Ealdberht loyally strides toward the animal, reaching out for the bridle but before he can catch hold of the reins, Bleddyn stands in the way.

'I too would dearly wish to own this fine horse, Eadric', the aetheling tells his Aenglish friend, 'but she is Rhiwallon's. He might like to have the horse back, as it was one of his men who rode her here. What do you say, brother?'

'Come to think of it, that horse *is* one of mine', Rhiwallon stares, fingering his beard.

'How do I reach Scrobbesbyrig - *on foot?*' Rodberht asks, begging the question. He sounds put out at the likelihood of nursing sore feet after a long walk.

'Scrobbesbyrig is that way', Rhiwallon takes the horse's reins from his brother, pats her nose and jabs a thumb over one shoulder. 'You might be there in a couple of days if you make good headway, start *walking*'.

The young Northman stands, mouth open, staring at Eadric who shrugs.

'You have your life. *Be thankful*', I tell him.

'Were it up to me, I would lop off your head, drop it into a sack and send that with a rider to throw over your earl's wall', Rhiwallon assures Rodberht and shoves him toward the broken gate. 'The rest I would leave for the ravens, foxes and crows, along with all your comrades' remains'.

Some of the Wealshmen and Seaxans are searching the Northmen's corpses for keepsakes. Others comb the scattered bodies for their own kind, careful in turning them over to make out whose kindred they are.

You become able to bear losses such as these when you have borne them often enough. There are also those who will never be able to bear their losses.

As the young Rodberht is jostled on his way to the gate, the only Northman still on his feet, jeering follows him out of the stronghold. An arrow thuds into one gatepost as he passes it. When he turns he blenches as Theodolf draws his bow again to help him on his way. He shows a clean pair of heels.

Theodolf laughs long and loudly after him. Everyone jeers the last outlander with him. Punching the air, I cannot help yelling out aloud,

'They will have a store of good food and drink *somewhere* - find it and feast on it!'

The walls of the stronghold echo with the shouting of men hastening across the open ground, combing the un-burnt outhouses for the Northmen's supplies. Finding little of any use they head for the tower atop the man-made hill. It is not long before some of them break into the storeroom below the kitchens.

'Look what *we* have found!' Men rush out through the door with loosely-bound and opened bundles in their arms.

Saeward, Theodolf, Eirik and I make our way through the throng to find kegs, more bound bundles and meal bags stacked against a wooden arch. A casket sits on one of the benches, hasps still made safe with a chain and lock. Below the keyhole letters can be made out, stamped into the bronze,

'WILLELMVS DVX'

'Saeward, do you see what is cut into the metal on this casket?' I beckon him to my side. 'Do you know what this could be?'

He looks up from his feasting, and comes to see what it is I have in my hands. Some time passes before he answers, time in which the room is filled with drunken laughter as Eadric's and Rhiwallon's men fill their bellies with the earl's drink from kegs and skins of fine wines and the Northmen's apple ale.

'This has to be something to do with the man we now call king', he finally tells me after looking closely at the casket. 'The craftsmanship of the casket surely tells you it belongs to someone who is high-born, but what it would be doing here, in this storeroom, I could not tell you'.

'You have still not told me who it belongs to – have you?' I ask, nonplussed.

He cocks his head, looking at me. A wink tells me this is his kind of wit,

 'It has something to do with the man we now call king'.

Saeward thinks hard, scratches his head and taps a finger on the casket lid, as though doing that will give him a clue,

'It *may* have once belonged to him. These Northman lords are all kindred, I have heard. Could it be the earl is another of his clan?'

'I have met few of his brood, but those I did meet I vowed not to cross paths with again, such as Odo', I tell Saeward, and wait for him to add more to what he has already told me. He has the look of a man who has suddenly been given an insight into the meaning of life.

'The key you found on that fat Frankish priest - what was his name, you know, the one we found on the road in Centland last year after the fight on Lunden Brycg?'

'Earnald, I think his name was. Aye, I still have the key on a length of twine around my neck', almost without thinking I open the throat flap on the Northman's hauberk I am still wearing and begin to fish around for the cord. My forefingers find the key quickly and draw it slowly upward, working the cord around my head, still with the key between my fingers.

When I have it free I offer the key to Saeward in the palm of my right hand.

'*You* open it', he pushes way my hand.

The revellers, who had been drinking and dancing about us, have left the room with their prizes, done with pushing their hands into bags to see what was within. Saeward and I have the room to ourselves. We are alone with the key and a still unopened casket. Their being here is uncanny, as if they had suddenly taken on a life of their own and were eager to join with one another. The finger-long key will not turn, even with brute strength and bends a little. Saeward has a thought. There is pig fat in a bowl near me, ready for cooking with, into which he dips one finger. He smears the fat freely onto the bronze key.

'Try again', he smiles cockily and stands back to let me near again.

This time the key turns with little effort. I have to grin and shake my head at my foolishness. Why could I not have thought of using the fat? Would I have known what to do with it, even if I had seen it? The times I have dealt with locks and keys in my life could be counted on the fingers of one hand. The answer has to be 'no'.

Within are rolled-up scraps of parchment, a rusted spare key and a ring – and there is a layer of dust on everything.

'I could ask Dean Wulfwin the meaning of the words', Saeward offers.

'We will not see him for weeks. What do we do with the casket during that time?' I ask, lifting it with both hands to feel its weight, and letting it drop. 'Why did they need such a big casket for these scraps - a key and a ring? There must have been something else in here with them'.

'Did Earnald take what was in here and leave it somewhere safe?' Theodolf asks from behind me, almost scaring me out of my wits. He walks slowly across the wooden floor toward us. 'Or did someone *else?*'

'What is the earl to the king?' I ask under my breath.

'Dean Wulfwin would know that, too', Saeward proudly heralds. The dean is almost like God to him, all-knowing.His faith in his erstwhile master's learning may stem from being taught how to read and write by him, but it hardly helps us. Is the ring of worth, or the parchment?

'You will not be able to take the casket with you', Theodolf caresses the lid lovingly, 'but the parchment is rolled, and the ring is small enough to carry in your belt purse – the one in which you keep the hammer amulet'.

He grins beguilingly, impishly.

'Take both keys', Saeward counsels. 'By the time the Northmen break into it and find there is nothing in it, we will be a long way from here'.

'Why do that?' I ask.

'You do it from sheer bloody-mindedness!' Saeward empties the casket, thumps the lid down, locks it and hands me both keys. 'There – *now* let them try to make sense of it!'

'You may be a fool, Saeward, but you are my *hero!*' Theodolf hugs him and hands the contents of the casket to me.

As I push the parchment rolls into a pouch on my belt, I stuff the ring into the purse and stride toward the door in time to greet Bleddyn.

'Ah, *Ivar,* I was told you were here. Have you found some gain of your own from this undertaking?'

The Wealsh aetheling rubs the side of his nose with one finger. 'You are not coming to feast with us?

Has he been watching us from the shadows?

'We have been searching for something the earl may have kept hidden from his underlings', I tell him as I walk past him onto the kitchen floor beyond.

'That would not be his silver, by some stroke of luck?'

'I was thinking more of a wine – or drink - he cannot find here. He may have missed the brandwine his monks make at home in some Northmandige'.

'*Did* you find any?' Bleddyn cocks his head and smiles thinly. 'Did you think I would swallow that fool tale? What *else* is in there?'

'There is a heavy, locked casket on one of the benches', Eirik points.

'I shall look closely at it', says a cocky Bleddyn, 'when I have time. We will take it back to Rhosgoch'.

'We found no *key*', I answer baldly, not offering anything further.

'*You* found no key', Bleddyn mouths my words scornfully. 'There must be *some* way of opening it, surely',

He strides further into the store room, stares at the casket, lifts it and throws it down onto the floor in a fit of rage. There is a loud thud, the casket turns onto one side and the lid falls open. A kick at the lid shows that there is nothing within.

'Did *you* take what was inside?' Bleddyn stares at me, holding out a palm. He waggles a finger at me and snarls. 'Keep something from *me*, would you, thieving Dane?'

In hastily pulling out the rolls of parchment from the pouch on my belt the keys fall to the planked floor. Bleddyn's mouth twists cruelly as he bends to pick them up.

'Liar, *thief* – what *else* will we find out about you today, Ivar?'

'We found the first key on a Frankish priest in Centland', I tell Bleddyn, not that I owe him anything, and add, 'the casket *and* the key had letters cut on them'.

He snaps at me, as if I were one of his underlings,

'It is still theft, to take without first showing Thegn Eadric *or* me'.

'It may not be worth anything', Saeward cuts in, and tails off when the Wealshman stares balefully at him.

'Then why bother *taking* it at all?'

'We were going to ask Dean Wulfwin what was meant by the writing on the parchment', Theodolf offers.

'I have a priest here, you know well enough. Ask Father Hywel, I am sure he would be only too eager to let you know what it was you tried to steal from me', Bleddyn smiles thinly, looking up at me from under his bushy brows '*Then* you can leave with your lives, your horses and your weapons, nothing more'.

'Dean Wulfwin is not a priest. He is head of the school at Wealtham, a scholar with rights given to him by King Harold', Saeward avows.

'When I want to know about your dead king, I will ask', Bleddyn tells Saeward without looking at him. 'Show me the parchments'.

'By all means, let your priest see them', I hand them to Bleddyn, who snatches them from me and stares at them without really trying to understand what it is he is looking at.

'He can *read*', he sighs and strides back toward the kitchen, then turns and laughs, 'which is more than I can say for myself. Come, Dane. Let us see what he makes of them. Pray they have no meaning for me'.

'What if *he* cannot understand?' Eirik defies him.

'If he cannot understand, someone will. I have time on my side now', Bleddyn seems to have softened.

We stride up a long flight of wooden steps, taking them two at a time, coming to a great hall on the first floor of the tower. Tables had been decked out for a feast. Now Aenglishmen and Wealshmen drink and stuff themselves on the Northmen's fare.

'Father Hywel', Bleddyn wags a finger at him, beckoning.

'I have something for you to look at'.

The priest sets down a pewter goblet and turns to Rhiwallon to beg his pardon for leaving his side. Rhiwallon stands with him and follows Bleddyn's priest to join his brother, who holds the parchment out for Father Hywel.

'Can you read this?'

Father Hywel takes the rolled up charters, pulls them out and stands pots on the corners, peering closely at the script. He lets the first roll up again and pulls the second open, licking his lips. Staring hard at the parchment gives him no more wisdom and he shakes his head. The third is unrolled and he lets it roll up again quickly,

'Lord Bleddyn, this is *Frankish* script, not Latin. I am sorry I cannot read it'.

'Then what *is* it?' Bleddyn is angered. He stares down at the parchment rolls in Father Hywel's hands and snatches them back again, only to stare at them. He must be drilling holes into them with his eyes, but this does him no good.

He turns back to me and thrusts them back into my hands, 'Much good they will do you, have them back. Take them to this Wulfwin, for whatever they are worth – and do not bother to come back!'

'Aye, much good they will do me –'I begin to answer Bleddyn, using his own words. Saeward cuts in again.

'I am sure Wulfwin will know someone who knows this tongue, should he himself not know'.

With a look of scorn Bleddyn waves us away and turns to speak to his brother. Rhiwallon is not minded to give up so easily and beckons us to him,

'Your friend Saeward plainly thinks his master can tell us more. You must learn to be forbearing, brother', he playfully spans Bleddyn's neck with his right hand, as if strangling him but is pushed away. Bleddyn is not happy, either with us or with Rhiwallon. His priest has been of no help to him, and now he is loth to let us go. Rhiwallon throws his hands into the air and barks with laughter at his brother's childishness.

'Fool! What if knowing what is in those rolls *could* enrich us, do you think you would be so easily let the Dane leave?'

'We send Maredudd and Bryn with them'. Rhiwallon spreads his hands in the manner of a preacher.

'The pair of them ride east with you, Dane. Your other friend stays with *us*. We have the Dane's kinsmen here, watching for Earl Willelm. How can we lose? Godwin is an honest man, after all!'

Bleddyn scowls over his shoulder at me, his younger brother grins sheepishly from behind him. Through the doorway I see Osgod and Eadric standing together, talking, unaware of what has happened. Bleddyn growls,

'If I had an ounce of silver for every so-called honest man I ever met, I could *buy* that Northman king's throne from under him!'

Rhiwallon doubles up with laughter that sounds like the mewling of a falcon and on turning to catch his breath catches Osgod's eye.

'Is there anything wrong?' Osgod hurries to help Rhiwallon, unaware that Bleddyn is already there, arms folded, trying to look as if he were elsewhere.

'Nothing that could not be cured by a swift kick up...!' Bleddyn's loud boasting trails off when he sees Rhiwallon reach for his dagger.

'You could *try!*' The young aetheling grins. '*Only try!*'

'I wish the two of you would stop being oafish children!' Eadric brings them back down to earth. 'What was this about Ivar bring sent with two of your men to Wealtham? Do we not have enough to do without losing four useful sword arms? Ivar must stay with us until his kinsmen summon him to ride south with them; Godwin asked me to spare him and his friends'.

'The Dane's kinsmen are sons of an over-reaching earl, and are not even *thegns!*' Bleddyn howls with dismay at Godwin's nerve. '*I am* what you Aenglishmen call an aetheling – does that count for *nothing?*'

'We are in Hereford shire, not in Wealas', Godwin thumps up the wooden steps of Earl Willelm's tower with Eadmund and Magnus in tow close behind, 'and I need not tell you that you owe your standing to my father. He chased your kinsman Gruffyd into Gwynedd and gave you Gruffyd's lands!'

'He is right, *brother*', Rhiwallon makes Bleddyn mindful of his dues although the way he tells him makes me think this is more tongue-in-cheek than he would own up to.

Godwin overlooks Rhiwallon's mockery and stares at me. When I say nothing he asks, as if I owe him some enlightenment,

'What is this about? Why would Bleddyn want to keep your friend hostage?'

'Ask *him*', Bleddyn scowls, jerking his head toward me.

'I *am* asking him', Godwin smiles coldly at me, awaiting my answer.

19

'I found a key on a dead Frankish priest, Earnald, who spoke on behalf of Eadgar to Willelm before the fight at Suthgeweorce. We did not know what it was for and I kept it. We found a casket here that the kit fit. There were parchment rolls in it that no-one here knows the meaning of and we were going to ask Dean Wulfwin of their meaning', I tell my kinsman. 'Bleddyn thinks I am stealing from him'.

'*It can wait*'. Godwin seethes, looking at Bleddyn as he tells me, 'Keep the rolls for now, Ivar. Let the Wealsh aetheling know what it means when we come this way again'.

Bleddyn stares icily at Godwin, and stares at me, shaking his head in speechless anger.

He is still staring at us both as Rhiwallon steers him away. Eadric puts a golden cup into his right hand and guides both his Wealsh friends to a long table.

'I would like to know the meaning of the writings –'I begin again.

'Be that as it may', Godwin breaks in. 'What is weightier is that I want you with me when we ride for Brycgstoth to take a ship for Dyflin. You were with father when he and Leofric sailed to ask the Erse king Diarmuid for his help against King Eadweard'.

I feel I have to test my kinsman. To be sure he will not go back on his word again and demand I leave his troop if - or when - his priest shows.

'You are sure Father Cutha will have nothing more to say about my dealings with the spay wife, Braenda?'

Godwin offers a hand to give me his word,

'You must ride with us, Ivar. Eadmund and Magnus would like you with us, too. Father Cutha was not well enough for our long ride, you understand. He is a frail old fellow'.

I hold back before reaching out my hand to take his. Inwardly I am happy at this news, but must keep my grin from showing and take pains not to let my glee take hold of me.

He tells me next that Father Cutha misread his hold on the brothers, crowing at my leaving. He goes on to say,

'The men grumbled at losing you to Thegn Eadric so soon. They threatened Father Cutha with leaving him in the wilderness, for the wolves, on their way here. Even Healfdan's friends agreed that banishing you was foolish of me. For one thing, you told better stories at Yuletide than he!'

'There is only so much to say of a man who never left his homeland'. My eyes meet his before I add, 'A man must sail over sea to learn of the world. He must make his way overland and see folk in other lands to understand how the world is put together, do you not agree?'

'True, true...' He blinks and looks down at the straw-laden floor, searching for better words that may show me he agrees without giving way. He stood by Father Cutha against me, his kinsman – would he *still* stand by the priest, were he here?

My holding with Braenda pained him, not wishing to deny her even to make my own life easier. Godwin, like his father, is a man of faith although not wholly bound by its laws – I believe he would slay the men who dared torment his father, not turn the other cheek as Father Cutha might say. Killing will be done, and he would not want to have to suffer as witness to the deed, therefore he pleaded illness.

There are those who say the Christians' faith *saps* their strength, yet there *were* men of the church who strode into the shieldwall on Caldbec Beorg and held fast with sword or axe, dying there in the press when Willelm's thousands gained the hilltop. Aelfwig the abbot of Wintunceaster died in the shieldwall. With him were Leofric the abbot of Burh, Deacon Eadric from East Aengla and abbot Aelfwold of Saint Benet of Holm. And was Willelm's half-brother Odo not at the forefront of the Northmen?

'Ivar, Father Cutha's belief is heartfelt', Godwin sighs.'What do you believe in, if you do not mind me asking?' He takes me off-guard, asking me this and smiles when an answer does not fly from my tongue. I have a name for wordplay, yet this time my thoughts need to be gathered carefully before they can be spoken. 'Come, come, it should not be so hard to think of an answer that might raise a laugh?'

'What is the matter?' Magnus has come up behind me and looks at his older brother, not knowing why he wears a priggish smirk. He looks into my eyes before Godwin answers and seems able to read me too easily. Grinning, he asks, 'Godwin has put you off your stride, Ivar?'

'He has indeed put me off my stride, as you put it, kinsman', I have to allow.

'What *was* it you asked, Godwin?' Magnus laughs, uneasy suddenly, thinking perhaps his brother has offended me.

'He asked me what my beliefs are', I answer for Godwin.

'Why should that be so hard?' Magnus searches earnestly.

'It is not so hard, Magnus', I laugh. 'What with all the fighting of late, I have had no time even as to what my thoughts were, let alone what my beliefs might be. As it happens, they have been hard-tested in the months since Tostig landed in the north with the Hard-Ruler. Braenda has been watching –'

'Braenda has been taking care of you', Godwin nods and looks sideways at a baffled Magnus, who throws up his hands and nudges his mount away to let Eadmund in between us.

'Ivar is talking of his spay-wife again?' Eadmund asks Godwin.

He reads from the raised eyebrows that talk of Braenda has tested him sorely. Saying no more on the matter Eadmund half turns to me and asks his brother,

'He is riding with *us?*'

'Ask *him*', Godwin shrugs and adds, grinning, 'but do not raise the matter of beliefs with him. The strain of months of fighting is beginning to tell'.

'Oh, well, whatever. Each to his own, eh, Ivar?' Eadmund winks and they begin to talk of where we are all going together as if Magnus and I were not here.

'There are men to be found with King Diarmuid', Godwin begins. He thinks back on hear\ing of how his father sailed with Leofwin to Dyflin for help from the Leinster king.

'Like father, we must ask for help to push the outlanders back into the sea. Grandfather went to Flanders with Gyrth and Tostig, but there are Flemings with Willelm. We cannot trust them any longer, even though Aunt Judith is one of them. However, the Dyflin Danes are like us'.

'We are going to Dyflin to raise men to fight Duke -, er, King Willelm?' Magnus is flustered. 'Have we not enough with the Wealsh and Scots?'

'Why do you think King Maelcolm would help *us?*' Eadmund draws hard on his reins to bring his horse to a halt. 'We are after all not his kin'.

332

'Why would he not?' Magnus turns to look under the brim of his brother's helm, fretful suddenly. 'After all, the *aetheling's* mother and sisters are with him'.

Godwin broods over his younger brothers words, his arms crossed over his chest, right hand nursing his chin, and answers,

'We should not hope for help from the *aetheling* Eadgar *or* his blood. Father took the helm of this kingdom because the lad had no-one who knew him enough to fight for him –'Godwin's words are hardly out of his mouth before Saeward stops him.

'King Eadgar was *our* lord until the Witan sold him out for the sake of their land and silver! Ivar fought alongside him and the young earls at Suthgeweorce. Lord Ansgar and your kinsman Hakon were there, too!'

'*Hold your tongue!*' Godwin snaps at Saeward without looking at me first. '*We* are of Earl Godwin's ilk. The line of Cerdic is spent. All their hopes were pinned on a youth whose home he thought was here, but we all know him to be an outlander without a following. He *may* have stood with you at Lunden Brycg, but it was Ansgar who rallied the fyrd and thegns! Remember that, and learn how to speak to your betters'.

My kinsman allows a smile and then turns back to Magnus to finish what he was telling him.

'What was I saying?'

Saeward's outburst has put Godwin off his stride and he is at a loss to think of what he was talking about to his brother.

'You were saying about how the aetheling would not help us take the throne for you', Magnus eyes Godwin levelly.

'I *was* talking about seeking help from King Maelcolm, not Eadgar. After all, the old king sent Earl Siward and his son Osbeorn to help fight the Mormaer Macbeothen with him. Earl Siward lost his son, and that was how this whole thing started with Tostig. Had Siward been able to leave the earldom of Northanhymbra to his elder son, Tostig may have been given father's earldom when he took West Seaxe. *None* of this mess would have overtaken the kingdom!'

'If asked, King Maelcolm would more likely give help to Earl Waltheof, him being Siward's son. Your father had little or nothing to do with putting the Scots' king on his throne. And there was still the childless King Eadward', I have to hark back to the root of our evils. Magnus stares crestfallen back at me. 'True, we would not have had to fight Tostig, but King Harald may still have come with his Norsemen on the winds that held back Duke Willelm'.

'I think Magnus means we would have had Tostig on our side', Eadmund joins in. 'When King Eadward died and father took the crown, even though all these outlanders came we would have had Tostig -'

'Are you forgetting the other Eadward? Eadgar's father might have taken the throne', I stop him in mid-flow.

'If you recall, he died after coming all that way back to Aengla Land', Eadmund tells me.

He was a stripling when Eadward showed at Thorney, still wetting his bed. The old king and his namesake never met before Eadgar's father took ill with the strain of those many miles across the mainland from the east.

'Eadward the Outcast might have lived', I put forward the outside likelihood that another Eadward could have come to the throne, with a son – Eadgar - to follow him. The Cerdicingas could have called on more men to fend off both outsiders, Harald *and* Willelm. Harold Godwinson would still have been earl in West Seaxe, and Tostig in East Aengla. Gyrth and Leofwin would have been at hand in East Seaxe, Centland and Middil Aengla. No-one would have wanted to fight them together!

'Would *that* were only true!' Godwin groans wistfully into the wind.

'Amen to that!' Eadmund laughs. 'But Eadward the Outcast did not live, Eadgar can not come to the throne and Godwin may not without help from Diarmuid'.

'Or from Svein Estrithsson', I add.

'Your half-brother – well, whyever *not* ask him? How would we go about that?' Godwin eyes me warily, one corner of his mouth twisting downward.

He plays with his short beard and laughs openly in disbelief. Yet Svein would not help for no gain at all, I know that also to be true. He would need something more than the knowledge that he has helped rid us of Willelm, but what he might ask would leave many in the kingdom wondering why we wanted the Northmen out.

'He might help with men *and* ships', I stare at my young kinsman, 'but he would not be shy in asking for reward'.

A lesser man might show his feelings had been hurt, yet perhaps my stare gives the same meaning. He shifts awkwardly in his saddle and looks uneasily ahead.

'*What* would he ask for in return for his helping us?' Eadmund reminds me of the self-serving side of my half-brother. 'I would say half the kingdom might not fulfil his hopes. I have heard of what Harald Sigurdsson's nephew King Magnus and King Svein once agreed on, and that was more far-reaching than I could grant, given that some of the earls have no fondness for the Danes. What do you say to *that*, Ivar?'

I would have to say he is right, but I merely nod, saying nothing. We have our farewells to take from the Wealsh aethelings, as well as Eadric and Osgod. Harding is talking to his men and fails to hear Osgod when he calls to him to come forward for our leaving.Godwin turns his horse, his brothers following his lead.

At a nod from me my friends follow. Osgod and those of their men who have lived through the onslaught stand around Eadric, but only Osgod raises an arm in salute when I look back to wave my last farewell. Eirik has thrown in his lot with Osgod and Harding, so he will ride north again with them. He seems to like Northanhymbra, and waves back at me from behind Harding. Will we see one another again?

A cold westerly wind has stirred the clouds above us to empty over Hereford. Godwin orders his banners to be struck, rather than be slowed by their unfurled weight. Our way will take us south to where the Seoferna runs into the sea near Brycgstoth. My young kinsman has lands that abut on the north Sumorsaete foreshore and feels he should show there, before they forget what he looks like. Which way we ride from there rests with how the shire reeve greets him as his lord. There may be a ruck, and a good showing will help Godwin talk the thegns in the Sumorsaete hundreds into following him, not King Willelm.

Overlooking the sea from where we are behind the haven, we can see score of horsemen entering the burh from the east. Whose they are is hard to tell from here, but I would say they have to be Northmen with their long lances and fluttering pennons.

'We must by-pass Brycgstoth', Godwin tells us. 'Although we could easily defeat these, there is no telling how many there are within the burh or even if the thegns here would be on our side if it came to a hard fight. We cannot use the haven, as I wished to for bringing in our Leinster friends –'

'Surely we could *find out* if the thegns are friendly to us!' Magnus butts in, causing his older brother to wince.

'When we have the Dyflin Danes with us, then the thegns here will know we are in earnest. As we are, we could barely hope for them to join in. We are barely four-score', Eadmund sets Magnus right.

'For a pitched fight we would need twice as many as we have to merely hold them off', I add, and turning to Godwin I have to ask him, 'Would your men in Sumorsaete be true to you?'

'Of course they would, Ivar!' Godwin is vexed with me, and stares for a short time until Magnus breaks into his thoughts.

'Let me ride into the burh after dark and ask around, as to whether they would stand with us, or whether the Northmen and their allies have browbeaten them. I may even learn who *they* are', Magnus nods down at the horsemen riding across the causeway through the gates.

'It is hardly worthwhile', Eadmund chides, reaching out to pat Magnus' head, but his younger brother ducks away out of his reach to cackles from Godwin and Eadmund. There is mannered laughter from the men, which fades when Magnus glares at them. It would not do to cross him.

'Very well, Magnus. We will camp in the woods to the south and you can sound out some of the folk within Brycgstoth. Whatever you do, do *not* let the Northmen know you are there'.

'*Fool!* You know he is never far from woe!' Eadmund berates Godwin, but is stared down and holds back when we set off again. 'Can you *believe* this, Ivar? Godwin is going to let Magnus draw us into a fight with the Northmen!'

'Have some faith in your younger brother, Eadmund', I try to calm him. 'He may learn things we could not, without bringing down our foes around our ears'.

He shakes his head and stares dully as Saeward and I pass. When I turn to look over my left shoulder I see him talking with some of his men before nudging his mount to a walk. No more is said until we make camp, the late dusk bringing a thin mist through the woods. Godwin nods to Magnus before turning to Eadmund,

'As Ivar asked, brother, have faith in him. He is *no* fool, give him his due'.

Godwin smiles forbearingly at Eadmund, then turns and calls for kindling to be gathered for fires. That is the end of that - all we can do now is wait until we see Magnus again. He has taken two armed men with him, to help find men who might be true to Godwin. Meanwhile Eadmund hands his brother a skin taken from Hereford when Rhiwallon's men were not looking.

'What is it?' Godwin sips and smacks his lips. He holds back a smile but his brother can read him and grins foolishly.

'We saved it from Rhiwallon's men. It tastes like some sort of apple ale – very strong'. He adds, chiding after Godwin coughs on swallowing a draught, '*And* a bit rough! Take it like a man!'

Laughter fills the air. The mood is a little lighter now, but my thoughts are still with Magnus. He will need his wits about him with two other young men – hopefully not as foolish as he – who might unwittingly fall into a wily foe's hands and mire him.

Drizzle has set in, waking me in time to hear stirrings in the woods behind us. I stretch out my right hand to reach my sword and Eadmund wakes with a start.

'Godwin!' he hisses, 'Godwin someone is coming through the woods from Brycgstoth!'

'What – *who is that?*' Godwin is on his feet, sword in hand.

Saeward has been resting close by and wakes himself snorting like a wild hog.

'*What, who is -?*' he sits and rubs his eyes like a child roused from deep sleep. Godwin holds a hand over Saeward's yawning mouth, lest he say anything to alert a foe who might creep up on us.

There are scuffles as one of Godwin's lookouts wrestles a prowler to the earth.

'*Hey*, what are you *doing?*' a young man yelps like a pup, 'It is me!'

'*Osfrith*, where is Ulfkel?' I hear the man shout, who earlier told us his son and a young kinsman had gone into Brycgstoth with Magnus.

'He is with Lord Magnus, uncle! Why, what is the matter?'

'Is he well – where *are* they both?!' his uncle grabs the lad's jerkin with both hands.

'They *are* both well!' the lad laughs uneasily, unable to understand why his older kinsman is so worried.

He tries to put us all at our ease by letting us know what they saw, seeing the dark looks that Godwin and Eadmund cast his way,

'Lord Magnus sent me ahead to tell Lord Godwin that he has friends in the burh. The Northmen did not see us as we entered by the east gate, well away from their stronghold. My Lord Godwin –'

'Aye, what do you have to say?' Godwin hastens to the lad's side. A deep frown hides his relief at hearing his brother is safe.

'Lord Magnus spoke to thegns in one of the inns, asking how they felt about the Northmen spreading across the kingdom. Two were going to Earl Brian, to give us away when their fellows drew them back and threatened to kill them there and then', the lad tells Godwin breathlessly.

'Slow down Osfrith. Where are they now?' Godwin tries to calm the lad.

'They are on the hillside, my Lord', Osfrith points downward at the dark woods, 'below us'.

'Are they on *foot?*' Eadmund snaps, 'Where is your horse?'

'I left her with the others', Osfrith waves toward where the lookout stopped him, 'finding it easier to climb the hillside on foot. Horses could not come as fast and the track winds so much'.

The lookout growls threateningly and glowers, raising an arm as if to strike at the lad,

'He came with no horse!'

We all look to the woods as one, as if likely to be assailed by hordes of Northmen coming at us. Osfrith's tale of Magnus talking to Brycgstoth's thegns somehow does not ring true.

Another of Godwin's men speaks out,

'No-one brought any mounts back whilst I was over there, my Lord Godwin!'

'Wait here with us until Magnus shows, Osfrith', Godwin fixes the lad with a stare, 'and let us hope he *does*, for your sake. Were there many of the Northmen down there in the burh?'

'My Lord, Brycgstoth was *crawling* with them when we first reached the burh, but they rode up to a wooden stronghold we could see plainly from the gates. Lord Magnus then took us to an alehouse where we sat in a darkened corner, out of the way of anyone who entered'.

'Why so?' Eadmund's brow furrows. 'Why were you not out on the streets?'

Osfrith answers, rushing through his words, not meeting Eadmund's eyes

'Lord Magnus told us he would ask of those who were drinking what we might not learn from tramping the streets and hugging the shadows'.

'He is right, Eadmund', Godwin nods sagely. 'He is right'.

'Again', Eadmund sighs, 'How is that so? These folk might have wondered why they were being asked and told the Northmen about the outsider asking awkward questions. We must surely know from this that Magnus has been cap-'

'You do not trust the folk of Brycgstoth not to betray one of their own?' Magnus has come up stealthily behind his brother and, standing behind him to hear Eadmund's thoughts on the undertaking let him know he was wrong.

Eadmund wheels and stares at his younger brother, who stands grinning up at him. Osfrith wipes his brow, his load lightened by his master's coming.

'Why was Osfrith sent back on foot when you had his horse?' Godwin asks of Magnus.

'The hillside track snaked so much so that Osfrith felt he could run a straighter way to let you know we were safe', Magnus laughs, telling his brother what Osfrith had already told us. 'You thought I was taken, I know. Have you no faith in my skill to stay out of harm's way? Ulfkel has Osfrith's horse'.

'He shows the Godwinson knack for blending with the background!' I laugh, thumping Magnus on his back. 'I do not know how anyone else feels, but I am thirsty. Let us drink to your brothers' growing trust in you as a scout, kinsman. I wish your father had thought of sending someone to seek out Willelm's whereabouts'.

'You mean the Northmen took father unaware?' Eadmund's eyes open wide at the thought that his father, known far and wide for his leadership skills, had lost through an oversight. I wish I could tell him there was more than oversight to blame for his father's downfall.

'It was more like Duke William's ears were wide open to news. He sent out scouts to give him the lie of the land. Your father may have been tired from weeks of riding and fighting. Earls Eadwin and Morkere had fallen down in their duties to the kingdom and allowed themselves to be overawed by a Norse king who did not know the lie of the land, yet was still able to use their own land against them'.

'So... it was Morkere and Eadwin who lost the kingdom for father?' Godwin bares his teeth and thumps one hand into the other.

'You might say that, but there were others who did not help with their deeds', I know this is no answer, but I am tired.

Godwin and his brothers must also rest the night; we still have a long ride.

Their mother Eadgytha and grandmother Gytha are in Exanceaster, as guests of their aunt Eadgytha. The afteryear is closing on us, and many tracks will be unusable, rivers un-crossable. However rich the red and gold of the leaves might look as we ride beneath the canopy, when our horses sink to their withers in flooded rivers our curses will be even richer!

Godwin knows from my answer that I no longer care to be asked about their father's mistakes,

'Sleep overtakes us, Eadmund. Leave be, even my head aches after this full day we have had! I am sure Ivar will tell you more when he has rested'.

Eadmund shrugs glumly. He plainly wishes to know more, but with Godwin telling him to let me sleep he must leave it at that for now. Another day awaits and he will doubtlessly make up for lost time when he can.

A chorus of woodland birds heralds the dawn and we are already saddling our mounts, having had little time to snatch a few mouthfuls of food after Osfrith sighted riders a short way downhill from us.

On being warned first, Godwin had quietly come around the camp and roused each of us from our slumbers with a thump on one shoulder. One day I shall see how he likes to be awakened in the same manner! For now we must stir ourselves, leave here quickly lest the Northmen do find us. Dealing with them here and now may bring more of them down on us in greater numbers when we are least ready for them.

Until we know the folk around here *are* friendly toward us - aside from the odd innkeeper or thegn – we must stay low. Once we are greater in number we can risk being seen, but that will not happen before we have reached Exanceaster. Queen Eadgytha, Godwin's aunt, owns land and buildings there and she opened Wintunceaster to Willelm before he was crowned. She will not be happy to know her nephews are to join them and close the burh to Willelm's earls.

'A few hours' ride south from Brycgstoth will see us safe', Godwin swears, 'and we can follow the hills south-westward through Defna Shire. There will be men there still true to father'.

'Are there Northmen in those parts too, do you know?' Saeward asks out of turn, knowing my kinsman will not easily stand for an underling breaking in even though he and I are on even standing. Godwin, even though is no lord in Willelm's kingdom, still behaves as though he were a nobleman. One day he may be king, but for now he is merely Harold's eldest son.

'I trust not', is all Godwin says, taking in Saeward with a long, cold stare.

'Let us hope not', Eadmund raises an eyebrow at Saeward, more willing to show friendliness toward him than his brother, nevertheless askance at the way Saeward thinks he can butt in at will.

'How else will we reach Dyflin unharmed?' Magnus scowls, his brows knitted. He scratches his growing beard, giving Godwin a sideward glance. 'We do not have enough men to fight the Northmen as we are'.

'*We* did', Saeward tells him, out of turn again.

'You *did?*' Magnus looks riled at my friend and turns to me. '*What* is he talking about?'

'He means when we rode into Centland there were six of us. Now we are only three and one, Theodolf – who I hardly think will last out another year - is still with Eadric. We have lost many friends and much blood between us since we stood on Caldbec Beorg with your father.

340

Our oath was given to the *aetheling* Eadgar that we would be his men and he freed us from that oath, knowing he may never *be* king'.

'What was the aim of riding into Centland and Suth Seaxe, when you might have taken a ship?' Magnus asks, frowning.

'We went to see where the duke's stores and fresh men were coming in to these shores, hoping to be able to cut their lines when the wind came around from the north again', Saeward braves another of Godwin's stares. 'The wind was against us'.

'You were lucky to have come out *alive!*' Godwin snaps. 'One day that luck may run out. *We* cannot trust to luck. There must to be more than luck to taking the kingdom from this outlander king!'

'There *will* be more than luck, brother', Eadmund smiles brightly at Godwin. 'God willing, there will be *men* too – *many* men to swell our number.

'I wish *I* were blessed with your cheer', Godwin climbs into his saddle and turns his mount so that he can see his brother better.

'Have *faith*', Eadmund mounts and slaps Godwin lightly on the back. 'All will be well'.

'Do you not wish you were as cheerful as this brother of mine?' Godwin smirks, unable to believe his ears.

He cannot help but smile broadly as Eadmund chuckles behind one hand, hoping I cannot hear,

'I told you all will be fine. You and Magnus, *both of you*, need your spirits raised. Ivar is also down in the mouth. We should all hope for the better and – who knows – everything *will* be better!'

'I will believe that when it happens', I tell him, letting him know I heard him. His mouth clamps shut and he shrugs, shaking his head.

Godwin grins sidelong at me and prods his knees into his horse's flanks to speed her on, Magnus following close behind. Eadmund lets me ahead and when I look over one shoulder to see if he is following he digs in his heels to spur his own mount. The brothers' 'huscarls' – such as their weapons skills warrant them calling themselves - close on our rear as we ride downhill southward toward Sumorsaetan. They will be sore-tested before too long.

For a few days we follow the coast, passing hills to the east. From time to time numbers of horsemen are seen coming from our left toward Brycgstoth, but we let them pass without being seen ourselves. Godwin wants to take the outlanders off their stride in Defna shire, so we allow them to think they are the masters here.

Word has it there is a Bretland earl around here, but we shall test him at the same time as we test Godwin's huscarls. There is no need to take them on now. Time will tell who has the upper hand.

For now, as the year wears on, we must reach Exanceaster before the bad after-year weather makes the tracks hard to follow over the Sumorsaet and Defna uplands. Deep peat marsh blocks the way between some burhs, and the going could be worsened by wet weather and thick moorland mists.

We have to give a rivermouth in the north of the shire a wide berth, as there are Northman *conrois* everywhere where there are bridges. A ford is hard to find, but after a long ride we come across one on a bend upriver of Aethelney, where once the West Seaxan King Aelfred hid from Guthrum, a fellow Dane.

From here it is easier. We can talk amongst ourselves as we ride. This is nowhere the Northmen would want to be, with thickly wooded Cantuc hills that offer them no shelter. Beyond that the bare uplands are mist-enshrouded already. We need someone who knows the tracks.

'In the next hamlet we must find someone who can take us over the hills over there', Godwin's right hand waves toward the south-west. Thick morning mists glide slowly over the land ahead of a breeze that has come up over the land from the sea to the south. It seems to me he is not talking to any one of us, but Magnus takes it upon himself to do his brother's bidding. He looks first at me before offering,

'I will take three men with me to seek a guide, brother'.

I nod, as does Saeward when he feels the young man's eyes on him, not that Magnus would heed him if he said no. A fourth is Ulfketil, one of his own followers. We ride ahead of the others to where I had seen smoke rising above woodland to the west. Someone there would know the way, I feel.

There is no homestead, no shelter of any sort. The smoke drifts up to the treetops from an untended fire - the woods here are damp, so there is no fear of the fire spreading. Who knows how the fire was started, but some dry kindling no doubt lay to hand nearby.

'We must seek elsewhere', Magnus turns his mount to pass the fire and we are about to follow him when Ulfketil calls out.

'My Lord Magnus, a man lies here'.

We turn back and Saeward dropped down from his saddle. He strides slowly toward where we can see a man lying flat on his belly. Saeward bends over the body and in a flash is himself on the earth, the fellow holding a knife to his throat.

'I fear nothing for myself, outlander!' the woodman is about to draw his blade across Saeward's throat when I yell at him to stop.

'Hey you, *stay that blade!*'

'You are not Aenglish?' he stares at me, one hand gripping Saeward's collar tightly. The blade in the other is now held tightly against Saeward's throat, red marks of scratching already on my friend's neck.

'I am East Seaxan!' Magnus snaps, 'As is my friend on the ground below you. *Stay your hand!* This man to my left is my kinsman'.

He drops to the leaf-strewn woodland floor and walks on.

'I am Magnus Haroldson. My father was king until not long ago. Let the man go or you will taste *my* blade on your *own* throat!'

'*You* look like a Northman', the woodman tells me, and turns to stare at Magnus and stands back to let Saeward up and sidles toward Magnus. 'I would have taken you, too, for one of the outlanders – you look much like one yourself, Lord. I am sorry friend'.

'I shall forget what you have done –'Magnus begins before Saeward breaks in, snarling,

'*I* shall not forget!'

'Saeward *let me finish!* I wish you to show us over the moors there to Exanceaster', Magnus asks the woodman after shouting down Saeward.

My friend glowers at the woodman whilst Magnus awaits his answer. Saeward's dark looks do not frighten him. Instead he lets Magnus know,

'*I* cannot take you, Lord, but I know a man who can. His name is Ingwulf and he has a hovel to the right past that brook', the fellow points to a narrow strip of fast-flowing water. 'Be careful up there, as some of the land is soft underfoot. Your horses will sink in. One of your men should walk there'.

'What is your name? I would sooner this Ingwulf does not do the same to my man as you did just now?' Magnus asks.

'Just that your man tells him Wulfweard sent him, Lord', the woodman winks at the still-scowling Saeward and points at Ulfketil. 'Best send this one. He looks more like one of *us*'.

'Ulfketil, go with Ivar', Magnus is about to tell his man when Ingwulf stops us before we both drop down to the earth.

'I said *one* of you!'

'Do not get *above* yourself, woodman!' Magnus barks, but Ingwulf snarls at me like a wounded wolf.

'Your kinsman looks too much like an outlander, Lord. Go yourself, if you feel you need someone to go with your man. These two', Wulfweard glares, 'will bring his wrath down on you!'

343

Magnus looks at me, shakes his head and stares balefully back at Ingwulf,

'You had best not test my wit, woodman! Ivar and Saeward stay with him. Ulfketil come with *me*. If this fellow Wulfweard is pulling my leg he will pay, *dearly!*'

'I *know* Ingwulf, Lord. You might hold *me,* but do not test *him!*' Wulfweard hunches down on the ground by the still thickly smoking fire. 'He has not been found wanting in his wrath when men have tried to test him before. He is a well-schooled bowman!'

'Stay with him', is all Magnus adds to me before striking out across the brook, almost sinking to his calves in the soft soil before Ulfketil helps him to his feet and they push onward.

It is not long before we hear men talking, coming back toward us from the still mist-clad woods into which Magnus and Ulfketil vanished.

Saeward and I reach for our weapons, ready to take on the outlanders before seeing the three men come toward us from the trees.

'Where is my friend Wulfweard?'

'He is not far', I hear Magnus answer Ingwulf. No more is said until they draw close to the brook.

'This way, Lord', Ingwulf beckons to Magnus. It seems to me he is trying not to laugh as Magnus sinks to his knees again before taking another stride 'That way you could sink out of sight and no-one would be wiser as to your being here'.

'Thank you for telling me', Magnus, looking sheepishly around, holds up his arms for Ingwulf and Ulfketil to help him out.

Trying hard not to sink in with him, Ingwulf pulls him back by hooking a shepherd's crook into his belt, and when he is within reach they lift him by his arms from the mire.

They reach us on our side of the brook by a very roundabout track and Magnus casts a black look at Ingwulf for waiting until he had gone too far before giving him the warning. Saeward has to fight down the yearning to utter a witty aside, but need not have bothered.

'Say it, friend. You have something aforethought that you wish to get off your chest. I am sure the wit will bring gales of laughter', Magnus waits, and when Saeward's thoughts are not forthcoming he shrugs and strides back to his mount. 'Has your spirit left you?'

I climb back onto Braenda and Ulfketil heaves himself back onto his saddle, glad to be back on the right side of the brook.

'Do I have to run all the way between you?' Ingwulf asks crossly.

'We will ride slowly', Magnus allows.

'All the way from here to where your men are', Ingwulf coughs, 'over the hills and far away?'

'What are you trying to say?' Magnus looks down at the fellow, and understands what it is Ingwulf is trying to say.

'Wulfweard, have *you* a mount he can have?'

'I have an ass at my steading', the woodman answers, looking sidelong at his friend, who nods grimly back.

'How far must we go to this steading of yours Wulfweard?' Magnus barely hides his dislike for him, but the woodman is not looking at him.

'Who are *they?*' Wulfweard points behind us.

I am first to see the newcomers,

'They are *not* ours, Magnus!'

My kinsman wheels his horse and draws his sword slowly but there are seven of them, with lances.

'They are on the wrong side of the brook,' Ingwulf laughs. 'Let them learn the hard way - They will not be cocky for much longer!'

'Start your horses cantering', Magnus tells us.

'Aye, make it look as if we are afraid they will catch us', Ulfketil adds, 'or they will smell a rat!'

Wulfweard dashes back to where his fire smoulders and we press our mounts into a canter after Magnus. Ingwulf draws his bow, ready to loose off an arrow. When the first Northmen ready their mounts to jump the brook they find themselves bogged down. Ingwulf lets fly one arrow after another until four riders have fallen dead from their saddles. The others flee leaderless, back across the low hills from where they came.

We must find Wulfweard's steading quickly, for Ingwulf to get mounted on his friend's ass and leave here before the Northmen bring their friends back with them. The will be wiser next time. Once we are back together with Godwin and the others it will be less easy for our foe to overwhelm us.

20

With Ingwulf at our head we climb the upland tracks, past tor and mire, ever south-westward to Exanceaster. We must make headway, hoping not to meet any more of the Northmen.

'Where can they be encamped?' Godwin asks Ingwulf.

'There is nowhere nearby that could offer shelter for any number of men. They may have taken over one of the moorland hamlets. As they came from the north of the dale, they may have been lost. There are no outlanders in Defna, Lord', Ingwulf counsels.

'I almost feel sorry for them, getting lost and coming to grief from your bow', Magnus shakes his head, laughing.

'Be glad men like Ingwulf are about at the right time', Godwin cannot see the funny side, his wit often lacking these days.

'What I liked about that skirmish was that it was Ingwulf's knowledge of the land that led to their downfall', I have to give the man his due.

'And it was he who did all the work', Saeward adds, a wicked smile spreading across his lips as he looks sidelong at young Magnus. My kinsman treats the aside with the scorn it warrants. Under a frown from Godwin, Saeward clears his throat as if he had said nothing, whistles feebly and drills one ear with a leather-gloved finger.

'When we reach Exanceaster you shall name your reward', Godwin turns to the fellow, cold-shouldering my East Seaxan friend. I should not wonder he heard Saeward, but Magnus would one day be given an earldom and Ingwulf would be forgotten.

'When you reach Exanceaster I shall have to be on my way back here', Ingwulf is not worried about reward anyway. The fellow's lack of smugness is heart-warming.

I like him already and I have only known him a day. Godwin and his brothers would warm to him, given time.

By this time next year we shall have forgotten all about him. Saeward, however, will recall him a long time from now. In the manner of a dutiful wife, he will raise the man's name when he thinks I have forgotten.

Sleet drives across the land from the north-west as we struggle past the high tors on the moor high above the River Dart. I have been this way before, long ago with Harold and Leofwin on the hunt for stag. Hunting could not be furthest from Godwin's thoughts right now.

The task he has given himself – and us – is to let their mother and grandmother know he and his brothers are well. There is no better way known to mankind of doing that than by *showing* they are well, hence our overland trial by weather. Why he could not have taken one of Bleddyn's ships, I do not know. Is it because *I* set out overland? Believe me, had I enough men with me for a crew when I left Naesinga, I would have taken a ship.

Hopefully he knows a shipmaster at Exanceaster. These overland rides are taking their toll of me. With the best will in the world – and I wish my horse no ill-will – I would sooner be aboard a ship right now, even given the after-year squalls in the western sea to Dyflin.

But I am not at sea.

Instead we are being buffeted by stiff winds high up here, and we will see nothing of the *burh* of Exanceaster for at least another day. Ingwulf knows his way, nevertheless, and we have to be thankful for that at least. Braenda plods steadily upward over the sodden land amid Godwin's mounts that are best ridden in the East Seaxan lowlands, slipping and sliding on the old half-hidden stone-clad roads.

'Tell that brother of yours, Lord Godwin, that if he keeps riding over there to the right he will come to grief!' Ingwulf points to Eadmund.

'You may tell him, Ingwulf', Godwin answers.

My kinsman licks his lips at the thought of his brother being berated by this moorland hermit.

'Aye, tell him yourself', Magnus smiles cruelly.

'Very well then', Ingwulf cups his hands around his mouth and yells loudly. 'Young fellow – aye you, if hold to that side of the track you and your mount will vanish for all time in the mire!'

Eadmund cocks an ear, to which Ingwulf beckons him over towards mid-track.

'You said -?' Eadmund asks when his horse has picked its way nearer.

'Just stay in the middle of the way', Ingwulf warns.

Gimlet eyes tell everyone what he thinks of my young kinsman. Some of the nearest men chuckle to themselves and hope the wind carries the sound away to the south.

Whether he has heard them or not, Eadmund does not let on and sets his jaw grimly against a now icier wind. Snow blows drily, bone-chillingly across the track. They will know if he has heard them, when he gives them the night watch when we reach Exanceaster.

High, snow-bedecked moorland gives way to woodland as we drop down to the river.

'You must turn downriver, Lord Godwin, when we part', Ingwulf tells him. He coughs drily and Godwin shakes his head.

'Are you well enough to go back right now? That ass of yours would be glad of some fodder, I am sure'.

'My tasks will not do themselves, my Lord, and Wulfweard can not do without her for long. He has hay enough where he is, take my word'.

'Then God speed, Ingwulf. Thank your friend for us', Godwin fishes around in his coin purse, but by the time he finds what he is looking for Ingwulf has melted back into the damp, mist-enshrouded woodland behind us. My young kinsman is not used to proud men such as Ingwulf and sniffs, drops the coin back into the leather bag, and says aloud what Ingwulf told him earlier, 'Downriver'.

'Downriver', Magnus tells his men and we wheel southward together on the eastern bank, to pick our way along the Exe.

Godwin leans in his saddle to tell me,

'I should have liked to show the fellow my thanks'.

'He knew your thanks, kinsman', I smile.

That is that. Hopefully we would hear no more, but Eadmund has other thoughts,

'Someone should ride after him and give him his just reward'.

'*You* find him', Godwin answers, '*if* you can. He will be at the head of the dale by now. At least the wind will be behind him this time'.

'Thankfully, aye', Magnus agrees. No more will be said now, at the risk of angering Godwin.

Being snubbed by Ingwulf has rubbed Godwin up the wrong way, I can tell. He would much sooner forget the fellow. Soon we shall see the walls of Aelfred's westernmost *burh*, and Godwin will be allowed to fuss over his mother and grandmother. *They* at least know how to smoothe his ruffled feathers.

The thunder of our crossing the wood-built bridge into the burh scares some of the horses, their eyes rolling wildly. They shy and strut

348

sideways, their riders trying to hold them with reins pulled taut. Those around them find it hard to keep their mounts straight and oaths fly like birds stirred in the wind. Men and women at the roadside cower, fearful of being trampled, there being nowhere for them to shelter on the bridge-side. A youth flattens himself against the mid-bridge wall and is almost toppled into the icy, swirling waters below by one maddened mount.

'Keep those horses quiet!' a priest flaps his arms, spooking the other horses that have so far behaved well.

'Be still, Father Eadwig!' Godwin roars above the whinnying. 'You are not helping by flailing with your arms!'

'Young Lord Godwin, welcome to our *burh*! God be praised you are safe and well!' the priest acknowledges him.

'Not for much longer, I fear', Godwin answers.

'How so – are you being chased by the outlanders?' Father Eadwig is old and does not understand.

'No, your arm-waving is frightening our mounts!' Godwin bends and, grinning, shakes the old priest by the hand. Eadwig holds onto him with both hands, almost pulling him from the saddle as the horse trots on. How he stays mounted only his *wyrd* knows, no thanks to Eadwig.

We leave the frantic priest on the bridge and wind our way between walls of wood and stone to Queen Eadgytha's hall. Some of her household men and maids come out into the hall garth, the men to take our mounts to stable, the maids to offer drinks or food. Eadmund bends and kisses one of them, earning a slap. The young woman pleads with her eyes to Godwin, who laughingly chides his brother for his forwardness,

'If you wish to come again to your aunt's hall, leave her maids alone! There are women around who would welcome your cheek'.

'Very well, brother. If you wish me pox-ridden, then so be it!' Eadmund less than jokingly answers his brother's wit.

'What makes you think this one is so clean?' Magnus laughs behind his hand at his eldest brother. 'I would bet she has been around the hall-thegns more than once'.

Godwin scowls and jumps down to the ground after me. Saeward takes Braenda's reins and hands the reins of both mounts to a young ceorl before leaping to the greasy, wet cobbles. Where we had been sleeted and snowed on up on the high moors, here they had merely seen drizzle.

We are ushered into the hall to doff our ringing wet cloaks and headwear. My helm drips icy water onto a hall maid's offspring and he writhes at my feet, giggling wildly, to be snatched out of the way by an angered mother. Seeing the child sets me to thinking about Gerda's young son Brihtwin, leading me to wonder how has grown since we last saw him.

'The lad has done no harm', I tell her, my friendly smile met with a scowl. She turns back to him, slaps him on the backs of his legs and leads him away, out of sight somewhere. I can her, still scolding when I next turn to Saeward. He has watched everything without a word, shrugs and takes a cup of ale from a maid who seems to have been eyeing him. I tell him, 'You could be well off there'.

He watches as she makes her way around the brothers, and shrugs when he sees her ogling Eadmund. He has no answer for that, and downs his ale in one draught. The next maid to pass takes his empty cup and hands him another full one.

There is stirring in the poorly lit hall as their mother, Harold's 'widow' Eadgytha, enters the hall next behind her namesake's *discthegn,* Thurswegen. He had been the queen's discthegn and stayed even after the cut of her silver waned. Harold's lands have been awarded by the king to one of his own, after she had cheated him of Harold's corpse with the help of one of his own knights. The Northman – I have yet to learn his name – paid silver to his overlord at Caldbec Beorg, after Willelm had turned down an offer by Gytha, of Harold's weight in gold.

'Ivar', Eadgytha, Harold's swan-necked wife greets me. What had she thought, I wonder, when her man wedded Earl Leofric's daughter Aelfgifu in the old king's abbey church to 'build bridges' with her brothers. Although Eadgytha was wedded to Harold in the eyes of the law, and she had borne him six offspring, Aelfgifu had been his queen and was now in Ceaster, awaiting her first child by him. 'How wonderful to see you!'

She comes to my side and kisses me on my right cheek, adding,

'I have missed you. Where have you been these months?'

'Here and there', I have to answer truthfully, lost for words to soothe her, 'mostly there'.

Where I have been would take too long to go through. At a loss for more to ask me, her sweet smile is turned next on her sons.

'Are our sisters and Ulf with you, mother?' Magnus is the first to speak.

'You say that almost as if you had forgotten your sisters' names, Magnus!' Eadgytha chides with a soft slap on his mouth with her fingertips.

'Very well mother, how are Gunnhild and Gytha – *and* Ulf?'

350

'Your sisters are being taught not far from here how to be young ladies', Eadgytha answers with a wan smile to me. She knows I would have my own thoughts on that. 'One day they will make good brides for fine, upstanding young thegns'.

It was at the behest of her namesake, her sister-in-law that Eadgytha's daughters were being schooled at the nunnery her heirless namesake was sent to by her father Earl Godwin. Then Eadward came back from Northmandige and the earl offered her as his queen.

Their lives are at odds with their new standing in the kingdom and I have been cheated of my own right by the same odds. We must make the best of what we have in the hope that one day the outlanders are thrown back from these shores. Harold will be sorely missed, but there is little any of us can do about that any more. Will Eadgar be crowned king one day?

'There is to be a meeting of the thegns of southern Defna', their grandmother Gytha tells them. 'Talk is afoot of closing Exanceaster to the Northman duke'.

She is still unwilling to speak of Willelm by name or as king, and would dearly love to seem him thrown to the wolves. Had it not been for the Northman noble who asked on her behalf, her son's corpse would have been eaten by the seashore creatures where Willelm wanted him buried, standing up to his neck in the shingle at Haestingas' seaward-most foreshore.

'I should like to meet these fellows, grandmother', Godwin greets her warmly, pressing his lips to her forehead. Godwin was barely out of his crib when the old earl died.

In turn Eadmund and Magnus greet their grandmother fondly. They are close-knit, my Aenglish kindred. As for my father Ulf's younger sister, she has lost the bloom of her youth yet still holds herself well.

But for Wulfnoth, her youngest – still held at Falaise – she thinks all her sons have been lost to her. Does she know Tostig to be alive and well, with Judith and their sons in Flanders? I somehow fail to see how she could. If they were brought together, how would they speak to one another? Could it ever be as if nothing had ever happened? With Tostig by his side, surely Harold would have beaten Willelm?

'You are sad, Ivar?' Gytha sees me at last.

I greet her as warmly as I would have greeted my own mother, had she been alive. My half-brothers know their mother Astrid, but not our father. I would have told them about him but for my banishment from Sjaelland by Knut. By the time he died they no longer wished to know about Ulf Thorgilsson. Although it was their saving, it was still a shame. Harthaknut no more wished to hear of Ulf than did his father.

And so I grew up with my aunt's sons, wishing to believe I was another brother.

'Tiredness, Gytha', I answer, smiling as best I can. She knows the lie of it and feels the sadness, but says no more about it. She will not press against my wishes.

'Have you seen your woman, Braenda of late, kinsman?' Eadmund asks, handing me a cup of ale and he comes by me.

He stops beside me long enough to hear me say I have not, nods and takes another cup to Magnus. Godwin is elsewhere, out of sight, and Saeward has been taken to task by Thurswegen for spitting on the floor.

'I take it you were raised by a swineherd?' the discthegn stares down at the ugly, creamy-white stain on the boards by his feet.

'No more than you were raised by the shepherd, from the way you talk to your guests', Saeward answers back.

'Saeward –'I hiss loudly enough for him to hear. No-one else seems aware of his shame, not even he. 'Saeward, say you are sorry and come here!'

He looks askance at me, back at Thurswegen, and pouts.

'Saeward –' I say again.

'Oh, very well', he sneers, wipes his nose on his sleeve and hisses at the old fellow, '*I am sorry you saw me!*'

Thurswegen looks horror-stricken at him, and withdraws. A little later a maid comes, goes down onto her knees and rubs away at the floor. She stands again, scows at my East Seaxan friend and withdraws from sight.

'Do that again and know you are on your own.' I hiss behind one hand, gulp down my ale and stride away for more.

On being given another cupful by a hall wench I turn in time to see Saeward leave the hall. Should I have warned him? I do not know I should have needed to. Still, being shunned would not go down well with him, but he ought to know he is amongst his betters. I shall see later how he is. Some time on his own to think things over will do him no harm.

Until then I shall seek out Eadmund and Magnus. Their mother is with them, and has already begun talking of better times.

'Do you recall stealing the bishop's apples?' Eadmund asks me when I near them.

'*Would* I?' I grin, looking at the way Eadgytha puts on a look of shock. 'You would see me in fetters over a few under-grown russet pippins?'

'They were amongst the best in the south-west', Magnus licks his lips.

'Then I should hate to see the worst', Eadgytha laughs out loudly, drawing everyone's eyes. She reddens and punches me on my chest, laughing, '*Thief!*'

Gytha stares open-mouthed at her. It is not so much for her laughter, but because she looks to be more friendly toward me than the time would allow.

It is only a year or so since my kinsman, her husband, was killed two hundred miles to the east. She reddens again and talks of the lately gathered apple harvest. Everyone goes back to their drinking and talking, and Gytha heads away toward the smell of cooking meat. Suddenly I am overcome by hunger, not for food but for my woman. I have not seen Braenda since we were at Aethel's steading. I try to steer my thoughts away from either of them, only to begin thinking of Harding's woman Aethelhun. How could he not know she was *hwicce*?

This is not good enough. My thoughts linger on Braenda. My groin aches for her. How can she stay away for so long? My thoughts stray to when she told me there was something darker at hand in Centland than she could deal with. Is there also some spiteful spirit *here*, too strong for her?

My only hope is that I can find a hall wench willing to share my bed, or one of the maids I can lure away from *her* elders and betters - or drink so much I fall into my bed, *witlessly* drunk.

I have been able to talk one of the maids into my bed. Now sound asleep beside me, lying on her front, head turned away, her ample breasts are pressed outward under her arms. Tousled, dark hair spread over the nape of her neck and over the small of her back, candlelight picking out the reddish hues of her crowning glory. Looking at her, my eyes feel heavy and I doze off...

Until something stirs at the foot of the bed - a grey-brown shadow that hurries from the foot of my bed and onto the maid's shoulders awakens her. She turns to look across her shoulder at me, sees the rat sitting at the foot of the bed and shrieks,

'*Where did that rat come from?*' She pulls back the pelt cover, scrabbles around in the half-dark of the early dawn for her clothing, and scurries dumb with fear from my bed-closet.

I turn the head bolsters over, pull back my own bed-cover but see no rat. When I roll onto my right side to sleep someone or some*thing* - shakes me awake again and I hear Braenda chide,

'Is this what happens when I turn my back?!' She tugs me onto my back and straddles me, naked. Pulling my hands onto her waist she demands, 'You should not want other women if you can fill me with your manhood – I want your *child!*

Forgetting myself I foolishly ask,

'Do you not already have one?'

Looking at her again I lose myself in her womanhood, willingly overlooking that I have already had the maid and do Braenda's bidding with a freshened hunger for womanhood.

Morning comes and I wake to the crow of a cockerel nearby. On turning over I find Braenda still sound asleep beside me. How is that? I have *never* before woken to her still being with me.

I raise an arm to shake her. She is already awake, however, and sits bolt upright on the bed. She looks first at me, and at the sunlight that fingers its way through the laths of my bed-closet, and stretches out a hand to me. Her cool fingers toy with my chest hairs, but she is deep in thought.

'If I give you a child, you should give *me* something', she tells me, looking up at into the darkness of the roof above.

'Name it', I feel able to give anything after last night. *Anything* could be a ring for her finger and my name for the child. Many times I have thought over what I might say to a woman who told me she is carrying my offspring. 'Whatever you w-'

'*You*', she answers.

'What do you mean - *me?*' I think I know what she means but I would like her to put her finger on it for me. 'Do you mean you wish to give your hand for a ring?'

'I mean I want you', she stares into my eyes, taking me across the stars. My thoughts wander to somewhere far off, beyond living knowledge. I do not know where I am when I awake, if wakefulness is what I have reached. My eyes are open, I know, but my thoughts are entangled with hers now. Things I could never know run headlong through my head, like a horse in fear.

Not long afterward I wake again. This time I am alone. Braenda is gone, my clothing and mailcoat on the floor around my bed. Have I given her something under her spell that I would have given willingly anyway? Someone rattles the door to my room, and Saeward pokes his head around.

'Has the big rat gone yet?' he asks.

'*Big rat* – what is that about a big rat?' My head is in a whirr and I have this fellow here asking about a rat.

'One of the maids tells me that after you fettled her she was scared out of her wits by a big brown rat', Saeward tells me, standing leaning against the door-post with his arms crossed, forgetting that I am naked in this bed with the door open.

'You might shut the door on me whilst I dress', I ask.

He looks blankly at me before coming to his senses and steps back out of the doorway. Through the closed door he tells me,

'It is most likely her tale has been spread around this burh like wildfire'. There is no comfort in this. Yet all she claims to have seen – or felt – is a big rat. There is no link to me, or to Braenda, so I have no need to worry. Braenda is hopefully far from here by now.

'A woman here says she is yours', I hear Thurswegen outside. 'Is this true?'

'*Whose* woman is this?' I ask.

'*Yours*, my love -', Braenda answers warmly.

I thought she had gone. There is no time to think of an answer now.

'Let her enter', I sigh. This will be around Exanceaster like lightning. Thurswegen will keep it to himself, I feel, faithful as he is to Eadgytha. What I fear are the wagging ears, and then the wagging tongues. I cannot do without Braenda, but Godwin has sent me away to the wilderness once this year for the sake of his beliefs. He will likely do so again.

Braenda enters the bed-closet again, dressed in finery I have seen her in before, wearing a cross around her neck. What tricks is she up to now? What promise did she wring from me that she wears a cross. She has read Godwin well.

'Anyone would think you were unwilling to have me here', Braenda chides, tongue-in-cheek. Thurswegen, thinking everything settled and in order, leaves for the hall to take care of more pressing matters. He has enough to do without being at our beck and call.

'The Northmen are camped around the *burh*', Eadmund tells me a few days later. 'Earl Willelm fitzOsbern must have sent word to his king that we have shut the gates on them'.

'They have been known to act quickly when it suits them', Saeward cuts a slice from an apple and feeds it to a hall hound that seems to have taken to him. His wit is not always lost on my kinsmen, but Eadmund does not see the joke and Saeward sucks air through his teeth. The hound takes this as a whistle of command and sits, ready to be told what to do and Saeward laughs, 'Whoever this hound belongs to is a good teacher'.

Eadmund stares at the hound, glares at Saeward and asks,

'Can we talk?'

'My Lord, if you wish me to leave'. Saeward sniffs and leaves with the hound.

Eadmund waits until he has left for the hall before asking me, disbelief showing in his eyes,

'Is it true your woman is here, the *hwicce* woman?'

'My woman is indeed with me', I answer with a yawn. 'If you had seen what she wears around her neck you would not call her *hwicce*'.

'What she wears around her neck may only be for show', Eadmund is sharper on the uptake than I took him for.

'You should believe in what you see, kinsman', I counsel, then warn, 'as even your mother believes in what she is told. That Braenda is my woman is no longer in question, rather *why* she is here'.

'Why, then, is she here?' Eadmund almost sneers. He needs to be told, perhaps soon - the sooner the better, lest he goes spreading tales of her shape-shifting.

I should answer, but lie. Who knows, I may be telling the truth,

'She is here because she is carrying my son'.

His jaw drops. Whether he is taken aback, overjoyed, or whether he is saddened I cannot tell, but I shall learn soon enough what his thoughts are on my tidings.

'You *trust* her?' Eadmund will need to be taken aside by Godwin. He will upset everyone unless he hears from his own brother that Braenda is to be left alone. For the time being I must choose my words carefully lest I upset him. I must win Godwin over to my side before it is too late.

'Why would I *not*? I might tell her not to bother me with foolish tales, but that brings with it a risk', I scratch my chin, looking into his eyes.

'You are afraid of her?'

'I am afraid I could lose her', I shrug. 'She is closer to me now than my own kindred'.

'What would your half-brothers say?' Eadmund chuckles, 'Svein might look askance at your woman'.

'You have seen her, Eadmund. Does she look *hwicce* to you?'

'To my eyes she is a winsome woman. Even at my age I know a good woman when I see one', Eadmund allows, smiling shyly under her gaze. She has come to stand by my side and gazes up at him, fondling the silver cross she wears on the short chain around her slender neck.

'He looks much like his father'.

Braenda smiles up at him more in the manner of a loving aunt than someone he has met only fleetingly.

'You knew my father?' Eadmund is taken aback. He is still young and my woman's warm, hazel eyes search the blue-grey of his for the key to his soul. She has this uncanny skill of reading a man's deepest thoughts through his eyes. Eadmund has as yet not learned how to hide from a woman's gaze.

'Well –'she lies, and turns to look at me.

'Aye', I nod. 'They crossed paths at the Earlsburh in Jor-*ah*, Eoferwic'.

'You have earned the right to give the burh its Norse name. Father sometimes let it slip. He told me Tostig gave it the Norse name even amongst Aenglish nobles', Eadmund allows, and stops to greet Magnus.

'No wonder, then, that the Northanhymbran nobles wanted rid of him'; Magnus has caught Eadmund's last few words.

'It was his tithes that lost him the earldom', I have to put him right.

'And that he was a half-Dane, and a son of Earl Godwin of the West Seaxans. He made friends with the wrong Gospatric and did not punish King Maelcolm for raiding through Beornica'.

Magnus shows he knows more than most here. Then again, he and his brothers were guests of the Scots' king at the time Willelm landed in the south. Gospatric – having kin in the Lowlands – would also have been with the '*Canmore*'. They would have learned from their uncle, Tostig, of the old scores that festered within the hearts of the Beornican kindred. He fixes my woman with a cold stare and asks off-handedly, 'You have Braenda with you?'

'I *have* Braenda with me', I nod gravely with a sideways look at her to see how she takes his slight. Yet she smiles at him and says nothing, taking the wind from his sail. He cannot think of anything to add and unwillingly allows his brother to tell him my news.

'Ivar says he is to be a father', Eadmund crows to Magnus, who dare not believe his ears. He winces at his brother's over-glad tidings.

Braenda's smile turns into a thoughtful stare and she elbows me behind my sword arm. It is a warning to me to keep to myself anything else she tells me.

'Lord Godwin would like Ivar, Eadmund and Magnus with him', Ulfketil saves us from growing ill will between Braenda and Magnus. 'He has word that the outlanders are within a few miles of us and wishes to talk over what we should do to hold them back'.

'What would you say to *that*, Ivar?' Magnus tests me.

'I would say to hold back from doing anything rash as yet', I answer, winking at Eadmund. The older brother runs his tongue along the inside of his mouth, hoping not to laugh out aloud. Magnus must guard against sounding foolish for his years. Where he gets it from I fail to see.

'Speaking of rashness, Ivar, what gives *you* the right to laugh after risking everyone's lives to watch over Willelm's crowning?' Magnus smirks.

Ohhh! That was below the belt!

Eadmund almost chokes on an apple he has been chewing on. He stuffs a clenched fist into his mouth to stay himself from spraying us with apple flesh. When he can speak again – albeit hoarsely – he slaps Magnus on the back with a few words brotherly fondness,

'I have never seen a sharper arrow make its mark!'

'Ah, Ivar', Godwin greets me gladly. He has come up behind me and takes me off guard. Has *he* at least good news for me? I feel pinched by Magnus' arrowhead.

He strides toward me with one of Exanceaster's thegns close behind. 'Aethelred here has some thoughts as to what we should do to halt Willelm on his way here. Can you tell my kinsman?'

Godwin stands aside to allow the thegn forward and listens closely as the thegn offers his thoughts,

'There are woodlands nearby that would let us put the Northman king off his stride as he nears –'

'How far away is that?' I ask. What he has to offer is brave, but could cost men's lives to no end. If these woods are too far away, the men could be ridden down as they withdraw to the *burh's* gates.

'What do you think?' Godwin looks hopefully at me.

'I think we could lose too many men before the king feels the pain of his own losses. Not being able to reach us now without great effort or loss ought to make him think anew about trying to take Exanceaster. Best not give him something to gloat about'.

'*What then?*' Godwin sounds annoyed.

'Sit tight and make him sweat', I counsel. I can sit my words rankle. He wants to be out there, leading his men to glory, but they would be cut down by Willelm's horsemen with their *lances* before they could make any headway.

The king could then *walk* into the *burh* that wishes to close its gates on him. Can I make him understand that?

'Look at it this way, Godwin', I begin to try.

There is no need to go on. He has read me well and nods briskly, one finger resting on his lower lip, the others of his right hand nursing his chin. His left hand is tucked into his belt and he looks upward as if asking for help from there.

'I know, *I know*. The king's horsemen would cut them to *shreds*', Godwin hisses through his teeth on the last word. 'I have heard you say before. Do we have bowmen enough to keep their heads down?'

'We can summon those within a few miles to the west and south, and they should be here before the day is out, before the *Northmen* reach us, even', Aethelred swears. 'The fyrdmen here are well-taught in their bowmanship skills, and *they* will make the Northmen keep their heads low!'

Godwin smiles like a child at that. As a king he would be well liked, but he would not be the leader his father was. Yet Harold made mistakes, and hastening south was one of them. At least Godwin listens well, that has to be a good omen. He can build on that. Meanwhile we have things to do, and Aethelred puts him to the wise there,

'We need to strengthen the walls', he begins, 'bring in men who not only know how to aim a bow, but how to use a sling'.

Godwin's eyes open wide and he hisses, balling his fists,

'*Slingers* - I should have thought of them myself'.

'You cannot think of everything', Eadmund tries cheering him.

'That is why you have *us*', Magnus adds, tongue-in-cheek, although we all know that the more there are of us who think earnestly about how we can outwit Willelm, the less likely we are of falling prey to his wiles. I know many across the sea have fallen foul of him without even trying. Word-of-mouth brought tales of hardship to us from lands he brought his harsh rule to bear on.

Gytha shows at the door to the garth. Godwin sees her and calls out,

'Grandmother, it is good to see you! How are you today? I was told you were ill when I spoke with mother this morning'.

Gytha walks warily across the rutted earth to us, looking to left and right, and greets me first,

'Ivar, I am *glad* to see you are well. Do you have a wife at last - are you *looking* for one, at least? With the land you have you would have silver enough for the bride-gift, surely?'

'I have *never* had land, Aunt Gytha', I have to tell her. I would have thought she knew, but Harold plainly never saw need to tell her.

Broadly speaking, a *huscarl* would be given land, in the way a *thegn* held land either from the king himself or from the Church. Like *thegns* also, a *huscarl* might be left land from fathers, mothers or kindred, but with me land was not forthcoming. King Eadward saw me as one of Earl Godwin's brood when I was younger, Harold's father who died before I came back to the kingdom from sailing east with my younger half-brother, now *jarl* Osbeorn. When Tostig was made earl of Northanhymbra I went north with him.

Although Tostig would have gladly given me land to go with my rank as *huscarl* in his household, there was none to give. When I came back south again as one of Harold's household my kinsman would also have given me the five hides due to me had there been any to give that was not his own. Instead I was given silver for my upkeep from Harold's chest, but that river dried up on his death. When Willelm was made king it was too late to be granted land or silver.

I know Eadgar would have given me the land, gladly. He did not bear the ill will Eadward had borne against Godwin's ilk, although he had been told of the killing of Eadward's younger brother Aelfred in Godwin's care. That Harold Knutsson, the king known as 'Harefoot', had wished Aelfred's death did not seem to matter to Eadward. Godwin, he felt, was the sinner.

'Ivar - I did not know', Gytha holds a hand against my jaw, running her thumb across my beard.

I rest a hand on hers and we stand there, she looking up at me as she had done when I was in my raw youth. My looking down at her raises a smile from her lips and she adds, looking at Godwin next to me, 'I am sure my grandson will do his utmost to make amends when the time comes'.

'I am sure he will, Aunt Gytha', I smile. She lowers her hand from my jaw and strokes Godwin's cheeks, pinching them as though he were a child still. Godwin reddens as Eadmund and Magnus grin broadly behind their grandmother's back.

'I must see your mother now', Gytha tells Godwin after first hugging her other two grandsons, making them squirm under the eyes of their peers. 'Little Ulf has a mild fever'.

Ulf is almost old enough to bear arms, but to Gytha her youngest grandson will always be 'little', no matter how tall he grows. Her own youngest son Wulfnoth is almost lost to her. The only one she bore Godwin who is still alive is a long way away still, a *hostage* of King Willelm at Falaise.

We stand watching wistfully after her as she makes her way back unsurely, holding her skirts clear of the muddy straw, until she vanishes from sight into the darkness of her elder daughter's hall.

She was a spry young woman when her brother-in-law, my uncle Knut gave her away as a bride to Godwin.

To reward him for his leadership and fighting skills in Knut's Danish wars, Earl Godwin was first given Knut's younger sister Thyra, who died in childbirth. Gytha, my father's younger sister has been a stalwart to Godwin since his early loss but her own grief has weakened her. *Think* - if you are a woman - how *you* might bear losing almost all your sons within such a short time, fourteen years after having to yield your youngest, now held by Willelm in Northmandige.

'...Are you listening, Ivar?' Godwin peers at me. I do not know what he said. but nod all the same. Later I will hear from one of the others what I should know. 'There are things we must learn about the foe, how he will feed himself, what he will use to shelter from the harsh weather in the winter months to come. Where he means to keep his weapons would be worth knowing, as if we can ruin some of them he will be hard-put to press home his attack'.

'That goes without saying', Magnus shrugs, 'but *how* do we learn what we need to know?'

'*We* cannot understand their tongue', I offer, 'but do we have anyone in the burh who does - what about that priest on the bridge the other day?'

'Eadwig, you mean? - I cannot tell whether he knows their tongue. You would have to ask him yourself. *How* would you use him? He would surely be found out', Eadmund stares warily at me.

'Perhaps not', I stretch to my full height, hands clasped tightly behind my head to loosen my limbs. Sometimes I think better this way. 'The Northmen *are* Christian, are they not? They would never think that a priest could spy on them, even a West Seaxan priest. See what he says first.

'Aethelred...?' Godwin turns to the thegn.

'I will ask', Aethelred nods. 'When do you wish to know?'

'Soonest, I would think', Godwin tells him, and seeing me nod says again, 'Aye, soonest'.

21

Eadwig stands before me, between Magnus and Aethelred, eager to learn what it is I want from him. His eyes are bright and he stands panting, much like a hound awaiting a reward but more likely it is because he has climbed to the walkway behind Exanceaster's palisaded walls.

An elderly fellow, Eadwig has given up the flower of hisyouth selflessly to the Church. What he has now is a big belly, most likely from taking food at each home on his rounds around his parish.

'My Lord Ivar', Eadwig puffs, propped against the wall. 'What is it you wish from me?'

'Firstly, do you speak the Northmen's tongue?'

He stares at me, fish-like, with bulging eyes. Does he understand his *own* tongue, I wonder? I ask again and he starts to giggle.

'*You might tell me what you find so funny!*' Magnus snaps. 'My kinsman asks you if you speak the Northmen's tongue and you start to giggle like a foolish maiden'.

'Forgive me, my Lord', Eadwig tries to shake off the giggles. Finally winning the fight, he adds, 'I thought I was brought here to be scolded for shouting at Lord Godwin when you came over the bridge. Aye my Lord, as it happens I know their tongue. Long ago I studied the writings of Saint Denis at Bayeux. With me was a young man named Odo, brother to the young duke, about to be made their bishop. I *do* speak the tongue, aye my Lord'.

At least that is over and done with. Now I must put forward my need to know if he will spy on them,

'Does the duke, our king know you, Eadwig?'

'I hardly think so, my Lord. He would not have seen me, as I was often in the *scriptorium* or the *librairie*. Although he was a keen church-goer, his brother did not bring him anywhere he would have seen me. It was almost as if he were ashamed of those of us in the *cathedral* he studied with'.

'So then you would not fear him, even if he stopped you in his camp?' I ask.

'You want me to *spy* on the king?' He shivers, whether from fear or because he feels the chill I cannot say. He stares, as if boring into my skull.

'You understand what I am asking of you?'

I should not have to ask, but there is no telling. He might misunderstand why I am asking. Eadwig shivers again. Great risk missing from his daily life may make him dread what I ask of him. I will soon know.

'I *will* do it!' He seems to leap at the task, still bright-eyed. We have another Saeward here. I need not have worried about him turning it down, although many would.

'I will let you know what I want from you, Eadwig', I smile and pat him on the back. Aethelred has been asked by Magnus to take him back down. 'I will let you know soon enough'.

The priest is not given to keeping fit, I see, as he lumbers downward on the log-built steps, almost tripping over the long cord around his waist. Hopefully he will be up to the task I set him.

'Is he able?' Magnus asks, half aloud.

'*Able?* He says he speaks their tongue. All we need him to do is make his way around their camp', Eadmund chortles.

'He only has to listen to what they say, answering or giving blessings if or when asked'. Eadmund takes in the priest standing before us and beams brightly at him. Whether he believes Eadwig *can* do what we ask is for him to know. He keeps *that* to himself.

'Time will tell', I say and Saeward nods sagely.

He has said little of late. On looking sidelong at him I see nothing troubles him – at least he gives nothing away. He has been *deepening* these last months, withdrawing into himself from time to time. I worry he is ailing. Having lost too many friends this past year, I do not wish to lose another. Theodolf could be next, the way he over-stretches himself, although the Lady Sigrid may make him slow down. Talk around Rhosgoch was that she was not so much nursing him any more as fulfilling his need for a woman since he left Gerda behind at Saewardstan.

Oslac will be sorely missed. Taking the crossbow bolt meant for me was his greatest show of friendship toward me.

Wulfmaer, still in Saewardstan and Cyneweard in Rhosgoch will both be missed, for their company if nothing else. But at least they are both still alive – I hope.

'Eadmund, what became of Guthfrith, Hemming and the others sent by Ansgar to teach Godwin's men their weapon skills - what became of them?'

I am suddenly aware they were not with Godwin when we met before the attack on Hereford. Why I failed to be aware earlier that they were not with him I do not know - half asleep, like as not.

'There was a parting of the ways after you left. Healfdan was kept fettered at Naesinga and Guthfrith felt it a waste'.

'Even though he knew Healfdan had killed Ingigerd?' I wonder at the fellow's lack of feeling. Was it that she never wielded a sword, or that she spurned him?

'Healfdan was to bring Godwin's men west', Magnus breaks in. 'Ansgar called his men back to Eanefelde. He had been bidden by Earl Willelm fitzOsbern to raise men for the king in Northmandige.

'They could even be *with* Willelm on his way here, to fight us. Our wyrd mocks us, I would say', Eadmund snorts, trying to hold back laughter.

'If indeed they are with him', I bury my head in my hands, fretting about what has become of this world. Friends may be made to fight one another at the behest of this soulless king of ours. We may yet see Aenglishmen fight one another to safeguard his kingdom.

'Would Eadwig put his head into the lion's mouth on his own?' Eadmund asks, suddenly aware of the hazards the priest could meet in doing Godwin's bidding. I wonder whether the priest is likely to lose his head if met by Willelm himself, on his way around his men's camp.

Understanding the Northmen and moving amongst them is one thing, knowing what to do should he be taken to task by no less than the king himself could turn him. He could let them know – without even wishing to – how to enter the burh. After all, if he could leave without them seeing him why not use his way out as a way in? The thought makes me shudder.

'Someone has walked over your grave, Ivar?' Eadmund has seen me shiver. I have to tell him of the likelihood of a lone Eadwig coming to grief for our sakes.

'Tell me, Ivar', Eadmund rests a hand on my sword arm, 'since when have you had pangs of guilt about the welfare of others?'

'I would not leave *any* man in the lurch, kinsman – not even you!'

Unable to think of fitting wit by way of an answer, he quickly takes his hand from my arm. I have put my kinsman on the back foot. Godwin saves him by asking me if Eadwig will be on his own.

'My thought, too', I have to agree and nod hastily. 'I think I will have to go with him'.

'*You* – go with Eadwig? You give me nightmares sometimes... Have you heard the tale of Daniel?'

'He must know what you look like, surely?' Magnus shakes his head at me, arms folded across his chest.

'We cannot let you, for our own sakes if not yours. All the king has to do is have you shackled, and both grandmother and Godwin –', Eadmund starts again, but his brother butts in.

'Leave *me* out of this, Eadmund! If Ivar wants to put his head in a noose then let him –'

He in turn is not allowed to finish. Magnus comes in anew,

'I think Eadmund means grandmother would make you *yield* the burh to save Ivar, brother'.

'Then I would have to put her right. As it is, I do not think she would wish to be seen at odds with me', Godwin is against me risking my neck, but he would do nothing to save me.

I know where I stand – it has to be said I might have thought so – but he has not heard me out,

'When I went to the West Mynster I was dressed as a Benedictine Brother. I would not make myself known to Willelm'.

'Then how do you think you will go out there with the priest?' Godwin would sooner be elsewhere, but he does not want to be seen talking me down. He sees me as a black sheep, I know, but I can show his flock the way ahead.

'Hear me out, Godwin'.

He shuffles, at a loss, and looks heavenward for a blessing,

'God give me strength!'

'He will indeed!' I agree. 'This time I shall make myself look like a dirty swine-ceorl. These Northmen will come nowhere near me when they smell me. Saeward can tell me how far I should go to make myself look right'.

'I can do more than that', Saeward speaks up. 'I can go with you as the priest's helper. I know what to do, when to do it and how. You could be a lay brother'.

'Would I need to shave off my beard again?' I ask. I see myself with hair missing at the back of my head.

'Not as a learner', he laughs.

'A *learner* – what do I do as a learner?' I have to ask, knowing little of the Church and its ways.

'Men enter the order at all ages, you know that. You recall that priest in Centland, where we buried Theorvard?'

'I do, indeed, very well! I was taken aback at seeing one of the old king's huscarls as a priest in a church'.

'Well, then. And you could be *dumb* – unable to speak. We would speak *to* you, but you would have to make noises like a poor dumb creature', Saeward is at home doing this.

Eadwig is back. He smiles now he thinks he has two helpers, but turns our thoughts to another likelihood,

'What if, *God forbid*, the Northmen find you out? Will you not carry arms?'

'If we are searched, how do you think that will look?' I shake my head hard, almost to rattling my skull.

'Brothers have knives, to sharpen their quills when writing, and for cutting up food when they are out, away from their abbey. Carry a knife by all means, friends. I have some that would not look amiss on a man of the cloth – *sharp*, too!'

'*How can we fail?*' I slap Eadwig on the back and he coughs hard. Reddened, he looks up at me beseechingly.

Before I can put a hand on his back he shrinks away. All I can say is,

'I am sorry, father'.

'How would you think to come amongst these Northmen?' Eadmund tugs my mailcoat sleeve and jabs downward with a bony finger. 'There are no side gates we could let you out through'.

I stare into nothingness, thinking hard. Someone taps me on my sword arm,

'A rope chair, perhaps?' Saeward offers and grins broadly when I look his way.

'You said -?' I want to hear him tell me again.

'We could be lowered in a rope chair', he says brightly.

'Then you are *not* afraid to go beyond these walls?' Godwin pales. He cannot baulk at our errand now, surely?

'Why *should* we be?' I ask in turn. 'With Eadwig and Saeward, how should any harm come to me? Saeward has a taste for Northman blood nowadays, so he would have no second thoughts about sinking his knife into any of them who asked too much. No, kinsman, I shall be safe with these two. I wish we had known Eadwig when we went into Suth Seaxe instead of the fat, rank-smelling Frankish turd!'

'Earnald, - ?' Saeward grins hugely, relishing my anger.

'Aye, Saeward – *Earnald!* I could cheerfully have throttled him but his maker was faster than I'.

'Who *was* Earnald?' Magnus looks at me, scratches his chin and turns to Saeward when he answers before me.

'Earnald spoke with Duke Willelm on behalf of the young king Eadgar before the fighting began in earnest at the bridge'. Saeward looks fleetingly at me before adding, 'Then we saw them off!'

'You beat them', Magnus knows the tale already.Nevertheless he is ready to listen, if Saeward wants to add to it. However, Saeward has finished for now. He merely smiles and Magnus looks to me to finish the telling.

'That is all there is to it', I shrug and look back at Saeward for more on how we can be lowered from the walls. 'Now, as to the matter in hand, I think you should tell us how we put this rope chair together. You have seen one before, I take it?'

'With the Wealtham *fyrd* –'he begins.

'With the Wealtham *fyrd* –'Eadmund echoes. 'How come *I* have never seen this wonder?'

Saeward stares icily at Eadmund, sizing up this son of Harold's.

Like his father only in his looks, Eadmund has led a sheltered life. I hope he awakens before the Northmen do it for him – or Saeward. Godwin hisses at his brother to be quiet before asking Saeward to tell us more,

'*Go on*'.

Saeward looks uneasily at Eadmund, and goes on when bidden by Godwin. He draws on the mud beneath our feet and begins,

'Simply, a length of thick rope, twice as long as these walls are high, looped with a slip knot for the chair itself so that whoever goes down has something to hold onto', he shows us with long strokes of his sword. 'It needs only one strong fellow up here to lower the chair and raise it for the next man, two could make light work of the task. Even in this light, unless you saw the walls from the end, you would not see the rope being raised if anyone was to pass below'.

'In the dark no-one could see... It is *wonderfully* easy!' Godwin's brows rise to show wonder.

'How soon could it be made?' Magnus asks, and nods hastily when he sees Saeward shrug and look heavenward.

'When can you have it ready?' Godwin asks, eager for us to be amongst the Northmen, forgetting that no so long ago he was fretful about my safety, worrying that Willelm might see me.

Should I be caught, he would be at a loss as to what he should do, as the king would use me for a way in into the burh. I cannot see me being handed back alive. That much I know. Rest assured, Godwin and his brothers would be kept under lock and key, like Wulfnoth, somewhere in Northmandige as surety against further rebellions until Willelm thought they would be forgotten. How wrong would he be in thinking them foremost amongst Aenglishmen! In his dukedom he was first among his peers, and he may think Harold's kin to be so in this kingdom.

'We can be ready for nightfall. What do you say, Eadwig?' I look his way and see him take a step back lest I slap him on his back again.

'I already *am* ready', Eadwig answers weakly.

'You will need a cassock, father', Saeward warns. 'The night will be long and chill. Best be guarded against it, or your shivering may be taken for fear'.

'You may indeed be right', Eadwig edges away and hails one of Godwin's men to light his way down the steps further away than he need. He is wary of me and dare not take the nearest stairway, behind me.

Eadmund snorts, holding in his laughter, watching Eadwig vanish into the gloom below.

'What about the pair of *you?*' Godwin asks. 'Do you not think you should go after him to find suitable wear? Should the Northmen catch you, they will see your mailcoats and boots. Go, find sandals and take off your mail. Be back here soon. Some of my men will try out their rope skills on Saeward's rope chair so that by the time you come back here I want them ready'.

I touch my forelock and follow Saeward after Eadwig.

'You will need your hair trimmed, too', Eadmund adds.

Saeward looks upward at me when he reaches the yard and nods,

'Aye, Ivar. He is right. Brothers have their hair shaved back over their foreheads. Eadwig might have something to do that with'.

'Do I need the back of my head shaved as well?' I ask, grinning lopsidedly at him.

'Best have that done', Saeward winks.

'Really – you think so?' I hope not, although it would grow back within weeks.

'To be safe, aye', he nods sagely, leading the way to Eadwig's priest house.

'And you?' I ask, hoping the same will be done to him.

'I shall be the priest's helper, you are a Brother – a dumb one, remember', Saeward smiles wryly. He knows what a priest does, and I do not. Being their dogsbody is my *wyrd*, therefore. I shall be glad when this is all over and done with!

We weave our way between the walls of homes in the darkness, Eadwig, Saeward and I. Our way is lit by a small number of rush lights on the walls. I feel odd. As Saeward warned, my hair has been shaved from my forehead, and from the crown of my head. I stumble in the dark over the hem of the oversized cassock I have been given. The man who wore this before me had to be a much longer-legged ceorl! 'Roll it up under the belt', Saeward had offered. The belt is still loose even when tightened several times along the way.

'I must look a fool!' I groan.

'A *dumb* fool, do not forget!' Saeward hisses through clenched teeth. This is crushing. In the light of Saeward's rush-torch I see Eadwig smiling over one shoulder. Hopefully he knows what he is with us for. His look of glee will die with him if we are caught!

We pass along behind the wall from the top of the wooden stairs, fire lights winking through the trees and tall bushes below. Godwin and Magnus await us where they think it safe for us to be lowered. Eadmund is nowhere to be seen.

'He had things to see to', Magnus tells me when he sees us. He knows I am looking for his older brother and grins broadly, knowing I am keeping my mouth shut in the manner of a dumb Brother. 'Very much in the spirit, eh – I like it!'

He laughs at his own wit, but gives a start when I stare back at him. Godwin sighs and snaps at me,

'Ivar, get a hold on yourself! Think, keep your eyes to the ground when tested or your strop will be your end!' Although he is only half my age he is right. I have to keep part of the deal, after all. We will have to be in amongst them for Eadwig to learn something, and I am only there to look after him – as is Saeward. We must both do his bidding.

Saeward peers closely at the rope-work and nods. He likes what he sees.

'Who made this?'

'Raedwald made it. He looked at the marks in the mud, nodded and tried it out with one of my huscarls', Godwin answers.

'Sigemund was happy to sit in the chair, as you called it, up and down on the inside of the wall'.

'*Raedwald* made it?' Saeward's eyes open wide. 'He is a better learner than I took him to be when I taught him how to fight with an axe! Let us away, then.'

I nod, saying nothing and Eadwig stands back whilst Saeward tests the chair first,

'Lower away', he looks over his left shoulder.

The fellow lowers him, arm over arm, whilst Magnus looks down over the wall. I look down beside him and can barely make out the ground below in the moonless night. Before Eadwig is lowered away we look around, down at the waiting Saeward and along the wall.

Eadwig is out of sight in the gloom as a cloud passes over. Saeward hisses for the chair to be raised again and it is my turn to be lowered. I clamber over the wall, struggle into the rope seat, clutch the knot and nod at Sigemund, then I too am on my way down. Before I reach the ground I hear rustling amongst the bushes and freeze. Saeward looks over one shoulder and Eadwig vanishes into the undergrowth. The chair stops and I am left hanging at least the height of two men above the ground.

'*Jump down!*' Saeward hisses up at me.

Should I? If whoever is in the bushes hears me crashing to the ground he will know something is afoot and raise the alarm. *Then* our goose will be cooked! Well, mine will be, as Eadwig will be able to bluff his way to safety and Saeward could vanish with him.

'*Ivar, I said jump!*' he hisses, plainly not relishing my hanging the height of two men above the ground.

Working myself loose from the rope, I drop onto soft earth and roll noisily into the undergrowth – out of sight of the wall. Hopefully Sigemund hauled the rope back up again.

I kneel on one knee for a while in the pitch blackness, breathless. Saeward nudges me to stir myself,

'All is safe, Ivar. There must have been a deer in the trees. Eadwig awaits us close by, come'.

Crouched beside me, he looks around in the pitch darkness as another cloud passes overhead. I say nothing, which brings forth a smile from my friend. He rests a hand on my sword arm, pats it and stands again,

'Let us be away to collect Eadwig. *You* were the one who thought of this, if you recall'.

There is no need to tell me. I have my misgivings, but we must follow this through now. It is too late for second thoughts now.

With Eadwig a few steps ahead we walk slowly on along the bottom of Exanceaster's heavy, thick, pointed stave walls. Eadwig carries a senser at his side, ready for Saeward to light when we think there are Northmen coming. Being this close to the foe is no longer new to us, Saeward and I, but we were more and better-armed then.

'*Bon soir, mes Amis*', someone says to our right.

Eadwig makes a half turn to greet the fellow, a Brother who has left a nearby tent. He stammers his answer, but the fellow does not take it amiss. They talk as we stand two steps behind the priest, and then part company.

The Brother turns to his right and vanishes amongst the tents, whilst we follow the line of the wall. Saeward waits until we are out of hearing of the nearest tent dwellers, and then asks,

'What was that about, Father?'

'He said his name was Aistulf. He is a Frankish Brother of the Order of Benedict, and wondered why he had not seen you before – you *and* Ivar. I told him we had only come during the afternoon, and had not had time before readying our tent dwelling to look around. He said we should meet him again after we have done'.

'Not if I have anything to do with it!' Saeward tells me under his breath. 'We keep going until you learn something useful, Father Eadwig. Did you give him your name?'

'Even if I had given him my name, there are many Seaxans in Frankish or Northman abbeys or churches. Men of the cloth do not take sides in worldly matters', Eadwig sighs.

Saeward does not answer. We know that is untrue. Odo of Bayeux is a man of the cloth, and he knows full well on whose side he is. He has been given great swathes of land south of the Temese. We press on, between the tents... praying we are not found out.

HERE BEGINS A NEW TALE.

Lightning Source UK Ltd.
Milton Keynes UK
UKOW03f1924071014

239772UK00001B/2/P